THE ENEMY OF THE GOOD

Praise for *The Enemy of the Good*

'An engaging exploration of contemporary manners that is tragic and comic: a mild and forgiving book about the damage that vehement religious ideas do to ordinary lives' Ruth Scurr, *Daily Telegraph*

'Arditti's writing has such a deliciously Victorian scope and power... *The Enemy of the Good* is a big, serious novel about big, serious things that are almost impossible to put into words' Kate Saunders, *Literary Review*

[The] 'discussions about religion and whether faith can help us to navigate the modern world are fascinating and intense... A lovely vein of humour runs through the book... This absorbing and intelligent novel' Naomi Alderman, *Financial Times*

'A fascinating read that raises hard issues and gives no easy answers' Clare Colvin, *Daily Mail*

'Surprising, enthralling and never less than very clever' Alexander Lucie-Smith, *Church Times*

'Arditti, like Trollope, writes fiction filled with wit and acute social observation, all placed in a religious setting... He also deftly highlights the absurdities of rigid belief without any trace of a sneer' Catherine Pepinster, *Independent*

'A wonderful observer and storyteller' Peter Stanford, *The Tablet*

MICHAEL ARDITTI was born in Cheshire and lives in London. He is the author of eight highly acclaimed novels, *The Celibate, Pagan and Her Parents, Easter, Unity, A Sea Change, The Enemy of the Good, Jubilate* and *The Breath of Night*, and a collection of short stories, *Good Clean Fun*.

THE ENEMY OF THE GOOD

Michael Arditti

ARCADIA BOOKS

Arcadia Books Ltd
139 Highlever Road
London W10 6PH

www.arcadiabooks.co.uk

First published by Arcadia Books 2009
This B format edition published 2010
Reprinted 2013 (fourth impression)

Copyright © Michael Arditti 2009

A catalogue record for this book is available from the British Library.

ISBN 978-1-906413-62-0

Typeset in Garamond by MacGuru Ltd
Printed and bound by CPI Group (UK) Ltd, Croydon CR0 4YY

Arcadia Books supports English PEN www.englishpen.org and
The Book Trade Charity *http://booktradecharity.wordpress.com*

Arcadia Books distributors are as follows:

in the UK and elsewhere in Europe:
Macmillan Distribution Ltd
Brunel Road
Houndmills
Basingstoke
Hants RG21 6XS

in the USA and Canada:
Dufour Editions
PO Box 7
Chester Springs
PA 19425

in Australia/New Zealand:
NewSouth Books
University of New South Wales
Sydney NSW 2052

For the Lemonia Three:
Amanda Craig, Liz Jensen and Marika Cobbold

'The best is the enemy of the good.'
Voltaire

'Everyone wants to change humanity, but no one wants to change himself.'
Leo Tolstoy

'Men never do evil so completely and cheerfully as when they do it from religious conviction.'
Pascal

'De t'ings dat yo' li'ble
To read in de Bible –
It ain't necessarily so.'
Ira Gershwin

1

CLEMENT

1

Clement wondered whether, as a Muslim, Rafik would object to removing his pants. His willingness to work in a bar proved that he was not devout, but nudity might be a taboo too far.

'I have no shame for my body,' Rafik said. 'When Mike speaks to me for your painting, I know what I have to expect.' The reply, while solving the immediate problem, roused Clement's suspicions of his boyfriend, who did not usually take such interest in his models, especially when they were sitting for the figure of Christ. No sooner had he announced that he was looking for someone new, however, than Mike had suggested Rafik. At first he had been dubious. His best models were actors or dancers who were trained to submit to a stranger's gaze. He knew in the instant one entered the studio whether he or she would inspire him: whether they possessed that indispensable quality, not beauty so much as poise, stillness, a way of carrying themselves. Which, in Rafik's case, was straight from the doorway on to his pad.

He liked to work from life, preferring the stimulus of a model to a photograph or his own creative memory. Unlike his former teacher who had described his subject as the celebration of the female form, he painted both male and female nudes. He was reluctant to idealise the object of his desires. His concern was with the transcendent, the art behind the artist. At the heart of his creed was the word made flesh; at the heart of his credo was the word made flesh made colour; and, although wary of the presumption, he thought of it as a sacramental act.

'I hope you won't be cold. I've turned up the heating.'

'There is winter in Algeria too.'

'Well then... if you'd like to take off your clothes behind the screen.' Clement, for whom nudity was an artistic statement but stripping an erotic routine, was eager to show Rafik that he recognised the distinction. Rafik gave him a blank look, on to which he projected all his own inhibitions, as he stood in the centre of the room and shrugged off his shirt.

Clement explained that he wanted to do a few sketches to assess his suitability. He made very specific demands of his models. Should Rafik fail to meet them, it would be no reflection on his body but simply that its proportions were wrong for the picture. Rafik smiled faintly and stepped out of his pants.

Unnerved, Clement described his intentions, considering it both courteous and prudent to keep his models informed. His *May Day Crucifixion*, a radical reinterpretation of the traditional image, had been compromised by a model whose grin looked more like a rush of masochistic pleasure than a smile of solidarity with a suffering world. The new work was to be a Harrowing of Hell, the apocryphal story of Christ's rescue of Adam, a theme which, while popular in Orthodox art, was relatively rare in the West. He had been invited by the Dean and Chapter of Roxborough Cathedral to submit a design for the great East window. It was set above a dull sixteenth-century altarpiece of the Crucifixion, which it would need at once to complement and transform. The obvious subject would have been a Resurrection, but he had opted for a Harrowing of Hell: not the Hell that the Church taught so much as the Hell that it had created. To which end, it was to be overseen by three clerics: an Anglican bishop; a Catholic cardinal and a Presbyterian minister. He had yet to discuss them in detail with the Dean.

Gazing at the taut perfection of Rafik's body, the slight frame, satiny olive skin with the thin line of hair running from the cleft of his chest to his pubis, and the disturbing trace of a bruise on his upper thigh, he knew that he had found his model. He picked up his pencil and began to sketch. The question, as ever, was how to put God in the picture. He envied Buddhists, who could express their faith in the abstract and call it *Meditation*. His was a harder task. As a Christian, he lived in a material world which was also a world of spirit and symbol. As an artist, it was his constant endeavour to recreate the reality that would allow the spirit and symbol to breathe. He had begun to feel, however, that the attempt was doomed. How could people who knew only the bare bones of the Christian story respond to his iconography: the juxtaposition of a clothed Adam, whose body filled him with shame, and a naked Christ, who was literally shameless; let alone his use of the same model for both? Holman Hunt's *The Scapegoat* had baffled a public unable to make the link between Christ and a barnyard animal. The confusion would be all the greater in an age when *The Light of the World* was nothing but waves and particles and the *Agnus Dei* no more than the Sunday roast.

'Am I right in thinking that Adam is a prophet in Islam?'

'He is the first prophet.'

'Was he created out of mud?'

'The Quran says to us that Allah makes Adam out of dust from many lands. This is why the children from Adam are so different as many lands: white, red, black and yellow.'

'That's very beautiful.'

'In the story, yes.'

'All religions are beautiful in the story, as you say. It's when they're put practice that they grow ugly.' Clement felt a pang at the thought of his fa who had come to the opposite conclusion.

'It also says to us that Allah makes woman out of bone from man.'

'That's the same for us.'

'The Prophet says that man must be gentle with woman because this bone is very easy to break. But I do not see this to happen today. A friend of me is taking bus in Annaba when she is meeting some holy men. They see that she is wearing paint on lips. "What is this?" they ask friend. "It is nothing," she say. She puts tongue very fast on lips. "Look, it is gone now." "You must take it off with this," they say and they give her cloth.' He grabbed a rag from the bench. 'Like this. "It is gone," she say, but they are angry. When she will not hold cloth, they hold it themselves. Inside is blade from razor and they cut off her lips... Sorry, sorry. You do not wish for your Adam to cry.'

'It's Christ,' Clement said, feeling his own eyelids sting. 'He's the naked one. And I do wish it. And He'd cry too.'

After drawing for an hour, he asked Rafik to dress. He confirmed that he wanted to work with him, explaining that he had to present the finished sketches to the Dean and Chapter in early March. So he would need him for occasional sessions over the next six weeks, and then, provided that the design was accepted, every morning for a month. Rafik assured him that he could meet the schedule.

'I must not be at bar until afternoon. In my land I work to become guide for tour people. Rich people who give Rafik big thanks. Here I must wash up dirty glasses. But I am not dead. This is good, no?'

'This is very good, Rafik.'

'When I think of my home and my mother and sisters and I have tears, I think Rafik is in England and I am not dead. This is good.' Clement was struck that he mentioned only female relatives. 'Now we have meeting today and this is good too, no?'

Rafik stepped forward and Clement thought that he was about to kiss him. A tingle of excitement vied with alarm at the breach of his professional code, and he drew sharply away. Rafik seemed not to notice, prowling around the cluttered studio, exuding a proprietorial air which Clement found strangely endearing, examining CDs and journals, picking up paint-smattered pots and flicking brushes over the down on his arm.

'Is there a number where I can reach you?' Clement asked. 'In case I need to rearrange sessions.' Or add more, he thought, on seeing the model so in his element.

'It is best you must ring me in the bar. They are very good persons. They

everything. I live with this man, Desmond. He is kind man. He loves
... very much. He loves Rafik too much. You understand, yes?'

'I think so,' Clement said in increasing bafflement.

'If he knows that I come here – even with my clothes – he kills me. I do not lie. And I think he kills you too.'

'Really?'

'Oh yes. He is very strong man.' Rafik's smile was so sunny that Clement attributed the threat to linguistic confusion. Any attempt to find out more was forestalled by Rafik's unlicensed rummaging through a stack of near-finished canvases.

'Why must these be here?'

'I still have some work to do on them.'

'So many? It takes how long to make a painting?'

'It all depends. I've been working on that one for four years.'

'Four years?' Clement caught the mixture of envy and awe in the voice of a man who was paid by the hour.

'I know I only have five more minutes work to do on it. The trouble is I'm not sure which five.'

Fearing that Rafik would regard him as a dilettante, he prised the picture gently from him and placed it back against the wall.

'Each painting you make comes from the Bible, yes?'

'Not each, but a lot of them.'

'But Mike, he say you are his lover. This can never be so in my religion.'

'It's not always easy in mine. I never planned to specialise. It just came about.' Lazy journalists liked to suggest that, as a bishop's son, he had entered the family business. Nothing could have been further from the truth. His father had never sought to influence any of his children. It was pure coincidence that the son of the Anglican Church's most notorious recent iconoclast was one of its foremost iconographers. At first, he had played down his faith. Art schools might encourage their students to find their own paths, but those leading to Canterbury or Rome were deemed to be off limits. So strict was the prohibition that, years later, when a friend recalled his struggle to come out as gay, Clement swore that it was nothing to coming out as a Christian at the Slade.

True to tradition, he had been liberated by Paris, where he spent three years after graduation. In his case, however, he was inspired less by the *vie de bohème*, in which he had already dipped a toe in mid-eighties London, than by encounters with the Gothic, above all the medieval painting and sculpture in the Musée Cluny. He filled sketchbooks with transcriptions of his favourite pieces, insisting that he was simply studying their techniques in the way that Delacroix and Picasso had studied the Old Masters. His tutor, however, had known otherwise. Aware of his weekly attendance at Mass as well as his passion for Kierkegaard and Dostoyevsky, he claimed that there was a vital element missing from Clement's work and that he would never fulfil his promise until he acknowledged it. Clement was furious, accusing him of wanting to banish him to an artistic backwater. He returned to England, intent on critical acceptance and convinced that he had the perfect subject matter in his sexuality.

Depictions of carnal excess, whether on paper or in mixed media, brought him no more satisfaction than the activities themselves. Then a family friend introduced him to her aunt, who planned to publish her own translation of the Book of Ruth and was looking for an illustrator. Although initially nonplussed, since the friend had failed to warn him that her aunt was a paraplegic who spoke through a voice synthesizer, he came to find her a great inspiration, as uncompromising in her art as in her person. He spent three months making forty lithographs, of which she rejected twenty, and then a further year painting a series of oils based on the prints. The subsequent show in the cloisters of St Mary Abbots changed his life. Not only was it enthusiastically reviewed and sold out within days of opening, but he was taken on by the Albemarle Gallery which had represented him ever since. While he continued to paint both portraits and landscapes, it was his religious work for which he remained best known and of which he was most proud.

He gave Rafik twenty pounds, overruling his protests that 'I come here for nothing. This is to see if we are good, no?', and arranged for him to return the following morning. After showing him out, he made a desultory attempt to clear up, leaving the half-full mugs to fester in the sink with a nonchalance that he would never have shown at home. He double-locked the studio and walked down the corridor, lingering at the doorways of the various painters, potters, sculptors, jewellers and woodcarvers with whom he shared the restored Victorian complex. He longed for someone to come out and chat but respected their work far too much to disturb them. He made his way outside and, wincing at the nip in the winter air, went to unlock his bicycle, from which, for the second time in as many weeks, thieves had removed the lights. He gazed at the denuded frame in silent fury. What was worse, he knew better than to hope for sympathy from Mike who, after the previous theft, had claimed that leaving an expensive bike on the street in Kilburn was asking for trouble.

A brush with the north London school run increased his frustration. Belsize Road was icy and he wove a tentative path through the line of hatchbacks, frenziedly pinging his bell as a distracted mother pulled out in front of him without indicating. He felt doubly vulnerable, knowing that a cyclist occupied as small a place in her mind as in her mirror. With a sigh of relief he turned off the main road and entered the park, which brought a measure of protection. Yet, no matter how stressful the journey, he had long dismissed any thought of working at home. He had no desire to convert the conservatory into a studio and so taint his art with domesticity. Travelling to work put him on an equal footing with Mike and his daily struggle to educate the young. He had known from the start that his best strategy with a boyfriend whose puritan conscience was the sole remnant of a nonconformist childhood was to treat his vocation as a job.

The exigencies of the school timetable meant that he cooked during term-time while Mike took charge in the holidays and at weekends. For all his grumbles about vegetarian cuisine, he was happy to abandon the easel for the gentler demands of the Aga. This evening, he was keen to prepare something special, both to thank Mike for introducing him to Rafik and to atone for his rashness over the bike. So, discarding the overripe avocado, he set about making a broccoli and stilton soup. He was so preoccupied that his first hint of Mike's arrival was a gentle warmth on the nape of his neck. His body flooded with happiness and he swung round to return the kiss. He felt Mike's grip tighten in a bid for reassurance more urgent than the usual six o'clock confirmation that there was life after school. He squeezed his waist and waited for him to speak.

'Do we have any wine left over from yesterday?'

'There's half a bottle of the Sauvignon in the fridge.'

Mike poured two glasses, downing the first and handing the second to Clement, who took the rush for a refill as his cue.

'Rough day?'

'No more than normal. But there's a limit to what flesh and blood can stand. Snotty-nosed youths sticking out their scraggy chests, waggling their pimply bums and shouting "I bet you'd like some of this, sir." Why? "Because you're a pouf, a fudge-packer, an arse-bandit." I only wish the rest of their vocabulary was as rich.'

With the soup simmering, the flan baking and the salad waiting to be dressed, Clement led Mike up to the sitting room. Knocking a pile of papers off an armchair, he told him to lean back while he bent over him, rubbing his temples and kneading his neck.

'I could get used to this.'

'Be my guest. But, seriously, can't you teach them to value diversity?'

'For the moment I can't teach them anything not on the curriculum.'

'That doesn't sound like you.'

'Some of my Year Nines were making fun of "poufs getting married", explained that I regard marriage as a reactionary and oppressive institution but that gay people have as much right to be miserable in it as anyone else.' Clement was glad that Mike could not see his grin. His own view, born of respect for Church liturgy rather than its doctrine, was that the marriage service was unique to a bride and groom and that same-sex couples should be given a service of blessing but, when he had put it to Mike that on balance he would rather be blessed than married, he had been surprised by his violent rejection of any hint of settling for second best. 'A couple of the Muslim girls told their parents. The parents complained to Derek that I was preaching immorality.'

'Don't tell me! Six of the best in the Headmaster's study?'

'Something like that. Derek's running scared. After the business in the Jewish cemetery last autumn, his one concern is that no one should rock the boat. He warned me that I'm not their head of year and I don't teach RE and insisted that from now on I stick to history. So I asked him to define what he meant by *education*. He said much the same as I meant by *marriage*. Equal rights to the misery at the end.'

Mike's spirits revived during dinner and Clement looked forward to a quiet evening at home, reading or watching a DVD. Their tastes, in many respects at variance, converged in a love of *film noir*. Mike, however, reminded him that he was going out for a drink with Jonty Hargreaves. Clement tried hard not to feel aggrieved. Of all their separate friends, Jonty was the one he was happiest not to appropriate. A fifty-three-year-old music journalist, he was among four Manchester University graduates with whom Mike had founded a commune in the late seventies. Although it lasted a mere eight years and comprised no more than ten members overall, it had achieved legendary status, not least for its bed rota which, in a bid to remove any taint of monogamy, set out the sleeping arrangements for the week ahead. Even desire was to be collective.

The bed rota collapsed long before the commune although, much to Clement's chagrin, he was to find that it had left an indelible mark on Mike who, on the pretext of being progressive, divorced his emotional from his sexual needs with the skill of a Victorian magnate.

'You can't teach an old dog new tricks,' he said, with an apology for the cliché rather than the conduct.

'No, but you can put him in a muzzle,' Clement replied.

Mike insisted that Clement's longing for exclusive bonds was simply a hang-up from childhood and that he had a right, indeed he sometimes made it sound like an obligation, to enjoy a similar freedom. Clement resented Mike's need to sleep with other men and blamed himself for his lack of libido, even if

9

ascribed much of it to his medication. As he watched Mike put on a leather jacket that was far too young for him, he reflected that perfect coupledom was to be found only in the womb.

'Are you going somewhere special?'

'It's up to Jonty. Just a club. A few beers and we'll see.'

'So you may not be coming home?'

'If not, I promise I'll give you a ring.'

Then, with a kiss so tender that it might have been a prelude to their making love, Mike went out. All at once Clement was overwhelmed by lassitude. Unable to decide if it were the result of Mike's departure, the stress of a new commission or toxicity in his bloodstream, he abandoned his book, went up to the bedroom and counted out his pills.

2

Clement kissed Carla warmly on both cheeks and led her into the sitting room. Her wan look was a particular worry in view of their prospective collaboration. Ever since his first stained-glass window for the lady chapel in St George's, Chichester, she had been his fabricator. Although the purist in him believed that he should effect every aspect of the design in person, the realist knew that, even had he possessed the skill, he lacked the patience. He was heartened by the fact that Matisse and Chagall had left the making of their windows to others. Besides he felt responsible for Carla, whose abilities were undervalued. He used to joke that, if he took the Bible literally, he would be duty-bound to marry his dead brother's wife. As it was, he just gave her work.

'I've left Peter,' she exclaimed as soon as she sat down.

'What?'

'You never liked him.'

'I wasn't living with him.'

'You warned me against him.' It was true that he had mistrusted Peter ever since learning that he wrote his name in all his books the weekend before Carla moved in, but then he would not have welcomed anyone whom she had chosen to replace Mark.

'I suppose there was a touch of brother's keeper. Don't get me wrong. I didn't want you to become the Widow at Windsor. You were so young when he died.'

'So was he.'

They paused to reflect on the man whose death had been the defining tragedy of both their lives. It was Clement who had brought Carla into the family. He had met her at the Slade and been entranced by her gentleness, her grace, her humour and her talent. She was exactly the sort of woman he would have fallen for had he been Mark, as was confirmed by their instant rapport when he introduced them. Even so he was taken aback by their whirlwind romance and fearful of his own exclusion. In the event, their growing attachment both cemented his friendship with Carla and deepened his bond with Mark.

For all that Mark, who posed as a philistine, claimed to find their artistic alliance a threat, he was grateful for it the following year when he went off to India, entrusting his new wife to Clement's care. 'I know about all you arty types. I don't want some long-haired minimalist sneaking round the moment my back's turned to borrow a bowl of turps.'

Mark was one of a team of agronomists working for the Indian government in a project to produce high-yield wheat. They thought they had found the holy grail, a grain that would enable the country to be not only self-sufficient but to export a surplus. What they failed to take into account was how the irrigation needs of the new crop would foster inequalities between farmers in the valleys with access to water and those on the hillsides whose land was arid. The traditional structure of village life was destroyed in a single generation. Families who had collaborated happily for years turned to sabotage and murder. Mark was caught in the middle of one such feud and died after drinking water from a contaminated well. Although the inquest concluded that his death was accidental, Clement was convinced of a cover-up. While he inveighed against God and man, Carla was more resigned, taking comfort from the Buddhist teachings which had sustained her ever since.

'I'm not young now though,' she said, breaking the silence.

'Come on. You were forty last year.'

'Not if I want to have children.'

'I see.'

'It may sound trite but, ever since my birthday, I've been deafened by a non-stop ticking.'

'What does Peter say? Oh, I suppose you've already answered that question.'

'I've barely begun. You know of course that Mark and I had planned to start a family?'

'I presumed so, yes. Though he never said anything. I suppose he was afraid of tempting fate.'

'For years I felt that, if I couldn't have children with Mark, then I didn't want them at all. I think the fact that Peter had two of his own was a part... a large part of the attraction. I'd have a family, and an easily manageable one, without betraying Mark.'

'But it wasn't enough?'

'Nowhere near. Every time I took the pill, I used to think what if just for tonight I forgot. Of course I never did. But when I finally acknowledged what was missing from my life and talked it over with Peter, he said it was impossible. He'd had a vasectomy.'

'Without telling you?'

'Without trusting me.'

Suddenly, his pettiness over the books paled into insignificance. Clement pressed Carla's hand in support, letting it drop when she pulled him so close that their noses brushed.

'I was out of my mind. With grief, with rage, with everything. I've left him, but that only solves half the problem. And then I realised that the solution was here all along. It's you, Clement. Don't you see? I want to have a child with you.' He recoiled as, for one ghastly moment, he thought that she wanted him to lead her straight up to the bedroom. Then he realised his mistake and began to laugh. A whole new world was opening up before him. Every nerve in his body thrilled as if he were deep at work on a painting. He felt dizzy and grabbed at a chair, sitting on the arm in a bid to look casual. 'I know it's a shock,' she said, 'but it makes perfect sense. This way I won't be betraying Mark but honouring him. My baby will have his genes just as if he'd fathered him himself.'

'So what does that make me? The father or the uncle?'

'Maybe a bit of both?'

The more he thought, the more intrigued he was by her proposal, which felt at once perverse and rich in possibilities.

'It's true that when we were kids, no one could tell us apart. If we'd had less indulgent parents, we'd have had the perfect opportunity for revenge. At prep school we played practical jokes to amuse our friends. Then in our teens something changed. I don't just mean that he broke his nose – the kink was barely perceptible – or cut off his fringe. The difference in our desires affected everything about us, from the way we moved to the way we talked, making it impossible for anyone ever to confuse us again.'

'I used to wonder why I wasn't attracted to you. You were so brilliant and kind and obviously good-looking and already a part of my world. I supposed it was just that you and Mark had a different energy. Yin and yang.'

'Two sides of the same coin.'

Even after eighteen years he felt Mark's death like a gnawing pain. He had never been as close to anyone as he had to him, his other self in both flesh and spirit. For all his resistance to Freud, he held it to be the key to his personality. While other men might seek to re-establish the primal relationship with their mother, he sought to do so with his twin, yearning to return to the embryonic embrace.

As a boy, his favourite reading had been stories of twins. He was horrified by the bloody dissension of Romulus and Remus but inspired by the mutual devotion of Castor and Pollux. Later, when he came to study Shakespeare, he felt a special affinity for *The Comedy of Errors* and *Twelfth Night*. One of his happiest memories of school was of an all-male production of *Twelfth Night* in which he played Viola and a diffident Mark, Sebastian. So whenever anyone suggested that their relationship must have been tricky, he would instantly set them straight. 'Everyone should be a twin,' he insisted, 'it keeps you from becoming self-obsessed and drives you to define your own identity.'

Even so, he could not help wondering if the need to measure himself against Mark had hampered him. Consciously or not, they had defined themselves by their differences: straight, gay; scientist, artist; Buddhist, Christian. Now he had an opportunity to blur the boundaries, to live something of Mark's life without giving up any of his own. He would be a father, a role for which he had long since ruled himself out. Yet it was as absurd to think that his sexuality denied him the chance of children as for men of past generations to think that it denied them the chance of love. Nevertheless, it was impossible to ignore the implications of Carla's request. If, in effect, he was interchangeable with his brother, a mere source of genetic material, what did that say about his essential nature? Was he a purposeful being with a soul breathed into him by God or just a random combination of proteins and cells?

The weight of both his religious belief and artistic practice had led him to proclaim his autonomy. He was as perturbed by the thought that behaviour might be determined by genes as a Victorian cleric by the claim that humans were descended from monkeys. Yet what if the distinctions between Mark and himself had been superficial, or even illusory? What if the desire to prove their uniqueness had blinded them to their uniformity? For the greater part of human history, people believed that their fates were shaped by inexorable forces, first by many gods and then by one. It was only for a few brief centuries that, whether god-fearing or not, they supposed that they had free will. Current thinking simply redressed the anomaly. People once again believed that they were powerless, controlled by their own DNA.

'You look so solemn, Clem. You're making me tense.'

'I'm sorry. There's just so much to think about.'

'I know I'm in no position to make demands, but please don't take too long.'

'I hear you: the ticking.'

'Talk to Mike. It concerns him too. You'll have to decide how big a part you – both of you – want to play in the child's life.'

'Are you planning on just the one or...?'

'Let's take it a step at a time, shall we? You never know; I might have twins.'

'Really?'

'Aren't they're supposed to run in families?'

'Twins would be good.'

Mike's arrival prevented further discussion. He flung his arms around Carla, with whom he had always felt more at ease than with any of Clement's blood relatives. Seizing his chance, Clement escaped to the bathroom where he doused his face in cold water, but it failed to provide the necessary clarity. He resolved to dismiss the matter from his mind until Carla went home and he could talk it over with Mike. There were so many people to consider, not just the living but the dead. He gazed intently at the mirror in the hope of seeing past himself to Mark but, try as he might, he was unable to bridge the gap between his forty-two-year-old reflection and his twenty-four-year-old twin. Certain features remained constant: the deep brown eyes, high cheekbones and full lips that they inherited from their mother. It was impossible, however, to picture Mark in spectacles, let alone wearing his hair swept back behind his ears and down to his shoulders. As if to punish himself for the betrayal, he twisted a hank around his fingers and tugged.

He composed himself and went back downstairs, where they ate a subdued dinner.

'Are you and Carla up to something?' Mike asked after her early departure. 'She was giving you pregnant looks all through the meal.' Clement laughed nervously. 'I'm sorry. Is it a private joke or can anyone join in?'

Steering him away from the sink, Clement relayed the gist of Carla's request.

'Yes, I can see it must have been awkward. So how did you get out of it?'

'I didn't. That is, I'm not sure I want to. I want to discuss it with you.'

'What's to discuss? Tell her you're sorry. End of story.'

'What's stopping me having a child?'

'A little thing called HIV?'

'You've always said it shouldn't keep me from living a normal life.'

'Come on, Clem, don't be obtuse.'

'You must have heard of sperm-washing.'

'Yes, for men in committed relationships, not sperm donors. No, don't interrupt! That's what you'd be. Plus, it's not a hundred per cent safe. Think of all the women who abort Down's syndrome babies, when you might be bringing one into the world with HIV!'

'Perhaps we should let Carla weigh up the risks?'

'So why didn't you?'

Clement said nothing. He sat despondent at the collapse of a dream of which a few hours earlier he had been unaware but which now felt like the one thing in the world that he wanted. He hadn't told Carla of his diagnosis for the same reason that he hadn't told any of his family. Before the prospect of treatment, he had been determined not to scare them. Now, thanks to his cocktail of drugs, the revelation was superfluous. He kept in excellent health, although he lived in terror of the side effects: the hollow cheeks and bloated belly that would label him as clearly as the lesions of the previous decade. He knew that his silence was an affront to Mike who, for all his talk of the right to privacy, demanded total candour from anyone remotely in the public eye. But, even if Mike were right in saying that the disclosure would not harm his livelihood, he was less sanguine about the impact on his parents. Mike accused him of arrogance in assuming that they would be so distressed by the news that they would rather be kept in ignorance, but he, never forgetting that they had lost one son, refused to leave them in dread of losing the other.

He feared that Mike's mission to demystify the virus had led him to underestimate its impact. He spoke of being infected and affected by HIV as though they were the one and the same. He even professed to love Clement more for being positive, citing all the work he had done on himself since his diagnosis. To Clement, however, the virus was the embodiment of his negativity, the death wish that had haunted him ever since losing Mark. And, for all that he dismissed the idea of HIV as a punishment, there was a part of him, however small, however secret, that contrasted his having been infected by one callous lover with Mike's having remained immune despite an army of partners. Carla's request had given him a chance to restore the balance. Now that too had been taken away.

Mike subscribed to an ideal of brotherhood rather than fatherhood. It was this that had first brought them together when, in an attempt to recover from Oliver's betrayal, Clement went on an HIV retreat in the Scottish highlands where Mike was a voluntary facilitator. The moment he entered the house, a run-down Victorian pile owned by a hippy collective, whose every bedroom was named after a type of bean, he had longed to return to London. He was unused to the rigours of a support group and, while his companions listened to each tortuous confession as intently as to a string quartet, he found himself counting the minutes to the break. His one intervention having met with an affronted cry of 'This is my shit!', he was doubly amazed when Mike detained him at the end of the session and offered him a massage.

Although his recent split had left him so wary of physical contact that he had even shunned the circle dance, he accepted at once, arranging to meet Mike after dinner in the Aduki Room, and spent the rest of the day in a frenzy of anticipation that was hard to reconcile with the knowledge that Mike had trained in shiatsu expressly to help out on the retreats. To his combined relief and regret, the massage was legitimate. He disgraced himself only once when, with Mike manipulating the base of his spine, he confirmed the claim that it was the seat of suppressed emotion by bursting into tears. He was glad of the chance to turn over, at least until a gentle pressure on his nipples threatened to provoke a more humiliating release. By a supreme effort of will, he was able to contain the stirring under his towel so that it expressed a healthy vigour rather than a blatant need.

That need was satisfied the following night when Mike invited him to leave Lentil for a tent in the glen. Clement had not slept under canvas since he and Mark camped out in Wells on their eleventh birthday, zipping together their sleeping bags in all innocence. With Mike he discovered a new kind of innocence, one that was knowing but not calculated, where passion wiped out the past and rekindled lost pleasures. He had never felt so free from the confines of his body. His consciousness grew so vast and his senses so heightened that he speculated on the nature of the mushrooms in the evening's soup. But the only magic ingredient was Mike. Their lovemaking was imbued with such meaning that he began to contemplate a future beyond art. Which made his disillusion all the more acute when, after waking him the next morning with a kiss and a bowl of muesli, Mike went rowing on the loch with friends. He told himself that it showed strength – even nobility – of character for Mike to honour his existing commitments, a view he revised when he was abandoned again after dinner. For all Mike's friendliness over the rest of the week, he was unable to banish the suspicion of having been the dreaded 'mercy fuck'.

Back home he responded by turning the retreat into a dinner-party anecdote, accentuating the absurdity of the rooms which now became Baked, Broad and Butter, of the heterosexual woman so desperate to identify with the victims that she had had affairs with two haemophiliacs, and of the mountainous lesbian cook who had sworn never again to be a sex object for men. The tactic worked until he received a phone call from Mike who, as facilitator, had access not only to his address, date of birth and next of kin, but also to his hopes for the week. He presumed that a stray glance at 'to restore my faith in my fellow man after a bitter break-up' must have pricked his conscience, since he invited him to dinner in Brixton on any Thursday before Christmas. The memory of their night under the stars was potent enough to dispel his doubts. Displaying a dignified reserve, he accepted for a date three weeks later. When the time came, he was so anxious to remain in control that he masturbated an hour before he left the house.

His pre-emptive strike failed, however, when they rounded off the surprisingly tasty shepherdess's pie and brown rice pudding by going up to Mike's room for some green tea. After slumping on a beanbag, he agreed that he would be more comfortable on the bed. He sat on edge, on the edge, as determined to keep his feet on the floor as a thirties film star, but no sooner had Mike placed his hand on his thigh than he advanced the action by several decades. As tongues darted, fingers stroked and bodies deliquesced, he realised that their rapport in the tent had been no accident. Finally, their passion sated with a frequency he had hitherto ascribed to barroom myth, he laid his head on Mike's slick chest and challenged him to defend his capriciousness on the retreat. Mike demurred, insisting that he was a free agent and that Clement must take responsibility for his own emotions. Although stung by his defiance, Clement was soothed by his tone, detecting a conflict between words and feelings. Over time, he found that Mike was content to put his feelings first.

He, in turn, was completely besotted. He loved Mike's looks: the rugged, open face and square jaw; the sea-green eyes and brilliant smile; the pepper-and-salt hair – cayenne pepper in line with his Celtic roots. He loved his powerful frame, solid without an ounce of fat, that put all the pumped-up musclemen to shame, and the riot of freckles on his arms, chest and back which, with uncharacteristic coyness, he refused to let Clement paint. He loved his passion for teaching, which he sustained in the face of interfering politicians and a politicking headmaster, of obstructive parents and destructive pupils, even the one who, high on his grandmother's anti-Alzheimer's pills, had plunged a knife into his thigh, leaving a jagged scar. He loved his social commitment and his willingness to make fun of it, as when he hung a *Meat is Murder* poster alongside one urging *Eat the Rich*.

'Does that include me?' Clement asked.

'You're the dish of the day,' Mike said, before taking a bite out of what, in deference to Clement's father, he described as the parson's son's nose.

For three years they commuted between Regent's Park and Brixton. Clement longed for Mike to move in, but he was loath to force the issue since he knew that what was for him the clearing of a few shelves and the emptying of the odd cupboard was for Mike a seismic shift. Events conspired in his favour when the Brixton household plunged into schism and Mike was voted out. Clement repeated his offer, presenting it as a practical solution to the problem. Mike was not fooled, but he agreed to a six-month trial, which had so far been extended by eight years. Clement had never been happier and yet, faced with the reality of his infection, he wondered if happiness was just another word for self-delusion.

'You're right,' he said. 'It's madness even to think of it. Me, a father! But for a moment it seemed to be something I could do: for Carla; for my parents; for Mark.'

'Haven't you done enough for him already?'

'What's that supposed to mean?'

'I don't need to spell it out.'

'Please do. I can be very slow.'

'You shouldn't spend the rest of your life feeling guilty. Mark died. It was a tragedy. You lived. That's the way things are.'

The flaw in Mike's argument, which Clement was quick to point out, was that he had felt the need to prove himself – to justify his existence – even when Mark was alive. He admitted, however, that the need had grown more urgent since his death. He had been determined to convince everyone, starting with himself, that it was not the better twin who had died. Mark had been so decent and frank, so healthy in every respect, engaging fully with the world rather than keeping it behind a shield of canvas. For all his parents' even-handedness, they must have realised that, had Mark been the one to survive, they would have had grandchildren. All he could give them were pictures which, however much they brightened their walls, would never touch their hearts.

3

The journey to Oxford was as ever tinged with melancholy. The carriage was cramped and airless but, for Clement, the real discomfort lay not in his seat but in his head. Whichever route he took, he couldn't hope to recapture the idyllic childhood he had shared with Mark and their younger sister Susannah in the charge of the most benign of parents. On paper it was hard to imagine a more mismatched pair than his father, an Anglican bishop of county stock, and his mother, a Polish Jewish anthropologist, whose *The Eden People*, a seminal study of a Stone Age tribe, had been credited with inspiring many of the protest movements of the sixties and seventies. But, for all their differences of background and belief, he regarded them as the perfect couple, at times too perfect for one eager to demonstrate the strength of his own partnership. He remained in awe of the love that had been at once the bedrock of their careers and an inspiration to their family and friends.

They were the lodestone of his life, the fixed point from which he determined his identity, and yet of late he had had a disturbing sense that the balance of dependency was shifting. This was his first trip home for two months and his guilt at his absence was compounded by a more corrosive guilt at its underlying cause. He couldn't bear to picture his parents changing. He could accept their growing old – not even the most dewy-eyed sentimentalist would expect them to hold back the clock – but not their losing what was, in every sense, their distinction. He remembered his unease about a boy at school who was younger than his nephew and feared the far greater anomaly of a father who grew younger than his son.

He was met at the station by Mr Shepherd, the gardener and handyman who, with his wife, had lived at Beckley since his grandparents' time. The one short and wiry, the other tall and stout, they might have walked straight off an old-fashioned seaside postcard, but the physical incongruity belied what, at their recent golden wedding, Mr Shepherd had shyly described as 'fifty years of congenital bliss'. Both now in their seventies they showed no sign of retiring, although their duties had been so reduced that their wages doubled as pensions. Mrs Shepherd had Susan and Jilly from the village to help her in the house and Mr Shepherd had young Charlie Heapstone in the garden, whose fondness for working shirtless in all weathers was one of the strongest incentives on Mike to visit. Mr Shepherd rarely drove any more, but he insisted on making an exception for Clement, who soon began to wish that his sense of loyalty were less acute. As they hurtled down narrow lanes, the sharp bends fraught with peril in the gathering dusk, he was forced to feign exhaustion to keep his driver's mind on the road.

'Safely home, Mr Clement,' Mr Shepherd said, as they shuddered over the cattle grid and swerved down the drive, whose length bore witness to his fore-bears' desire for seclusion. He felt his customary rush of admiration for the park which their founding father had landscaped with complete confidence in the family's future, dotting it with classical statuary in a bid to obscure the novelty of his wealth. Clumps of crocuses and snowdrops were early heralds of spring, while the yellow trumpets of winter jasmine cascaded over the kitchen-garden wall. The Queen Anne house loomed benignly before them, its façade unmarred by accretions, its perfect proportions attesting to the builder's faith in his own rectitude. Looking back from an age in which impermanence was the common condition of life and doubt the orthodox viewpoint, he longed to trade places with people who believed in order, both human and divine, and who even expressed their dissent in exquisitely measured prose.

Entering the hall, he tried to recapture the emotion it had inspired in him on boyhood visits to his grandparents, but he was crushed by the weight of expectation. Not even Bonnard could have used a palette as bright as his memory. The house itself had scarcely changed, but the child's enchantment had given way to the adult's reserve. He was greeted first by Ajax, his parent's collie, who jumped up to nuzzle his chest, and then by Mrs Shepherd, who met his kiss with her usual diffidence.

'The Bishop gave us the magazine article about your *Harvest Festival* picture in New York. They did you proud.'

'Did you like it? Collages never photograph well.'

'It was grand. Quite what a Harvest Festival should be. I remember when it was all about offering the fruits of the earth to the Lord. Now it's "no perisha-bles, just tins that can be sent to Comic Relief."' She snorted and smoothed her apron. 'I stuck it next to the *Two Marys* in the album.'

Feeling a pang at this latest sign of her devotion, he promised to call on her for a proper chat in the morning. Then he hurried into the drawing room where he found his mother, father and sister nursing drinks in anticipation of his arrival. His mother rushed towards him, exuding such vitality that he was ready to discount all his fears. As he prolonged their hug, she gazed at him with a quizzical air.

'How's Mike?' she asked.

'Well,' he replied. 'Busy. He sends his love.'

He moved to his father, who was sitting by the fireside in the wingback chair that had served as a fortress for Mark and himself at a time when anything over four foot high was an adventure. He leant down and kissed his cheek, grateful that no misplaced reticence had forced them to resort to handshakes. He turned to Susannah, whose butt-filled ashtray betrayed her own unease at returning to the bosom of the family. In appearance, she resembled their father. They had the same blue-grey eyes, long nose and dimpled chin (his father claimed that they had the same russet hair, although it had been years since he could produce any evidence), whereas, in both colouring and features, he and Mark took after their mother. Susannah looked drained and he suspected that, for all her success, she remained unfulfilled. He longed to draw her out but knew that the competitive, at times even combative, air which from early childhood she had adopted towards both her brothers would prevent her admitting to any disappointment.

'Hiya sis,' he said, 'how's life among the A-list?'

'I've just won the contract for the new Weston tea campaign,' she replied tersely, as he pressed his cheek to her lips.

'That's brilliant,' he said, mortified that his attempt to show interest in an alien world had sounded like a snub.

'She's a very clever girl,' his mother said.

'Thanks, Ma,' she said dryly, as if refusing to credit her mother's praise for any intelligence that was not academic. Clement felt a surge of sympathy towards her. The indulgence she might have expected as the youngest child had been forfeited by having twins for her older brothers. She had always felt undervalued and, despite having built up a thriving PR business, claimed that no one in the family took her seriously. In private, Clement acknowledged the charge. Despising the relatively tame publicity campaigns he was forced to undertake for his own work, he found it hard to summon enthusiasm for her promotion of an airbrushed film star or pop group, and his parents were even more confused.

'Why do they call themselves Hiroshige?' his father had asked of one of her New Rave bands.

'It's just a name, Pa,' Susannah replied.

'Are they Japanese?'

'It's just a name.'

Clement poured himself a glass of whisky and sat down, listening while his parents and sister resumed their discussion of Leon Marks, the RAF officer who had brought his mother to England after the war and whose funeral in Banbury the next morning was the reason for the family gathering.

Karen Mullins' arrival offered a distraction. 'Da dum,' she trumpeted, standing in the doorway and slowly pulling off her scarf to reveal the acid green tips to her dark brown hair.

'What on earth…?' Susannah said.

'It's very colourful,' his mother said.

'You're twenty-three years old!' Susannah said.

'Don't worry. We'll soon get used to it,' his father said.

'You look like an after-dinner mint,' Susannah said.

Karen's lower lip quivered and, while Clement might have wished that his sister had chosen her words with more care, he knew that they sprang from genuine concern for the girl to whom she had become a second mother after she moved in with the loathsome Chris.

For years Susannah had bullied their parents into inviting Chris, now officially designated as 'the biggest mistake of my life', and his children, Karen and Bill, to Beckley, claiming quite unjustly that their doubts about his character sprang from prejudice against his class. By the time that those doubts were confirmed – and more conclusively than they could ever have supposed – she had long since walked out. Even so, she had felt responsible for the children, whose mother had committed suicide when Bill was born and who had looked set to be taken into care. So she had appealed to her parents who became their legal guardians, sending them to Linden Hall, a progressive boarding school run by a family friend. Leaving with no formal qualifications, Bill joined the army, straining his guardians' liberalism to its limit, and Karen moved into an estate cottage, where she dabbled with a series of ill-fated schemes, from making goat's milk soap to writing romantic fiction, and dallied with a string of unsuitable men. Nevertheless Susannah was eager for her to stay, leading Clement to wonder if she shared his guilt at having failed as a source of grandchildren and saw Karen as the next best thing.

Karen's self-serving chatter over dinner soon exhausted his goodwill. 'I've become a pagan. You don't mind, do you?' she asked his father. 'It's not all that different from being a Christian except we worship the Goddess instead of God.'

'Of course, I don't, my dear. You know that the Church took over many pagan practices, including the Eucharist.'

'Who are these pagans?' Susannah asked dubiously. 'More deadbeats?'

'Susannah darling, that's not kind,' his mother interjected.

'It's not her fault, Aunt Marta,' Karen said in a buttery voice. 'People have too many preconceptions about pagans. They think it's just about drinking chicken's blood and sacrificing virgins. They're frightened of us because we worship the earth, dance naked and don't hate our bodies.'

'Do you do that here?' Clement asked anxiously.

'Of course. Beckley's a very ancient and sacred place. Frank and I are starting a coven.'

'Frank?'

'My boyfriend.'

'That's all we need,' Susannah said. 'The *Sun* will have a field day. I can
cture the headline already: *Batty Bishop In Wicca Worship.*'

'You shouldn't always think in headlines, darling,' his mother said, 'even
t is your job. But take care, Karen, or you'll find yourself calling up forces
yond your control. I've seen it in Africa.'

'Frank and I are going to Sicily in the summer,' she said defiantly. 'On a
pilgrimage to Aleister Crowley's Abbey.'

'You'd be better off on the beach,' Susannah said.

Mrs Shepherd brought in the beef, glowing as she was showered with
compliments. As he watched his father carve, his steady hand a further
proof against senescence, Clement was grateful for the chance to indulge a
taste denied to him at home. Although Mike had never asked him to stop
cooking meat, he had chosen to do so, partly because separate meals struck
him as almost as sad as separate beds, but mainly because he hoped that Mike
would treat his beliefs with a similar respect and accompany him one Sunday
to church. That hope had yet to be fulfilled.

Between bites, he outlined his latest commission. He knew that his father
would be intrigued by a selection process which offered fresh evidence, if any
were needed, that the inner workings of the Church of England rivalled the
machinations of MI5. He had received no formal invitation but been advised
by Canon George Dickinson, the *éminence grise* of Anglican art, that the
Dean of Roxborough was looking to install a new window. 'He urged me to
investigate, so I did. The curtains in the cathedral close must have been twitching! There I was in the apse, studying the churchmanship and chewing over
possible designs, when I felt a tap on my shoulder. It was the Dean. Straight
out, he asked if I had any ideas. I mentioned the Harrowing of Hell, which
seemed to thrill him. I thought he was going to kiss me.'

'Urgh!' Karen said. 'Oh, sorry, Clem!'

'No, you were right first time. Urgh! He arranged for me to put it to the
Chapter, insisting that we had it in the bag. No such luck! From the word go,
I was bombarded with questions – some borderline insults – from one of the
lay canons, a retired army officer – major I think – by the name of Deedes.
After giving him his head, the Dean played his trump card, saying he'd been
promised cash by both the county council and the Normington Trust. The
cathedral would not only not be out of pocket but get loads of free publicity.'
He tried to catch Susannah's eye but she was toying with her food. 'In the end
the Chapter deferred its decision while agreeing to fund my sketches.'

'Brilliant!' Susannah said, without looking up.

'I'm proud of you, my boy,' his father said. 'But watch out, Harvey Harvey can be a tricky customer.'

'Harvey Harvey?' Karen asked with a giggle and a burp.

'The Dean,' Clement said.

'How cruel of his parents!' his mother said. 'Another parsnip?' she asked, holding out the dish to Susannah, who patted her stomach and shook her head.

'On the contrary, it's been his calling card since Cuddesdon,' his father interjected. 'That said, he must be due for retirement.'

'Next year. He wants to go out with a splash.'

'Thank God for self-important clerics! Or else the C of E would never have any new art at all.'

'How much will they pay you? Or is it a rude question?' Susannah asked, with a hint of mockery which Clement chose to ignore.

'I've no idea. I leave all that to the gallery. Of course, the Dean is playing the usual trick of acting unworldly as if it were the same as being spiritual but, take if from me, he's as sharp as a knife. He'll try to get away with less than the going rate on the grounds that it's a large-scale piece and will create a stir.'

'Which is no doubt true,' his father said.

'But still no excuse for exploitation.'

'That Deedes fellow: I've a feeling he's one of the ones who had a go at me after *Spirit of the Age*.'

'Perhaps that's why he was so hostile?'

'I'm pretty sure he's a six-dayer. The sort of chap who gives religion a bad name.' Clement knew that this was a serious charge from one who placed his faith in the Church rather than in God. 'Yes, I'm convinced of it. Not quite the "God put fossils there to fool us," but "there's no fossil evidence to support evolution" brigade.'

'And this is a man who was high up in the army?' his mother said. 'Has he never heard of myth?'

'Even as myth,' Clement said, 'Genesis leaves a lot to be desired. By placing mankind at the pinnacle of creation, it enables us to justify the harm we do to the planet.'

'The Goddess is groaning,' Karen said.

'She's not the only one,' Susannah said.

'We laugh at the fundamentalists with their literal readings, but are the symbolic ones so much better? They make the world seem nothing more than a scientific experiment, with God as, at best, a Newton and, at worst, a Mengele. To my mind, we can't divorce the creator from creation. He is architect and blueprint and material. The earth and the earthworm, the sky and the skylark, the sea and the sea breeze and the sea lion are all part of His being.'

'Are you talking literally or symbolically?' his father asked.

'Both. God is subject and object, word and meaning. The experiment, if it can be described as such, is on Himself.'

'You'll none of you be surprised to learn,' his mother said, 'that the most profound creation myth I know comes from the Hadza. Put simply – which it is anyway – it states that, in the beginning, the Hadza were all baboons. One day, God – who in their language is both male and female – asked them to go down to the river and bring back some water. They took so long that God went to look for them and found that, instead of doing what they'd been told, they were playing games. God was furious and put a curse on them, condemning half to become human while the rest remained baboons, leaving the two groups at war with each other till the end of time. So there you have it, the story of creation, evolution and the origins of human behaviour in a few short sentences.'

Clement flashed a glance at Susannah, who returned it with a smile that harked back to the nursery. There were, indeed, few matters on which his mother would not cite the superiority of the Hadza, the remote East African tribe she had studied for her doctorate and to which she had paid repeated visits over fifty years. Although as children they had hated the very mention of the name, afraid that it heralded another trip to the Serengeti when she would leave them in the care of a nanny who, however kind, could not hope to fill a mother's place, the more they learnt of her life in Occupied Poland, the more they came to appreciate her need, in his father's words, to 'exchange the so-called civilised world for one where the horrors that wiped out her family and friends are unknown.'

'Good try, Ma,' Susannah said. 'Maybe you should write the Hadza bible?'

'I thought she already had,' Clement said. 'A little thing called *The Eden People*?'

'Mock all you like. I only hope that when you have children... Oh I'm ready to drop!'

'You and me both, Ma,' Susannah said lightly. 'And we've a busy day tomorrow. So, if you'll all excuse me...'

Susannah's departure was swiftly followed by Karen's. Considering her wine intake, Clement wondered if he should walk her back to her cottage, but weariness drowned out both gallantry and concern. Instead, he accompanied his parents to the drawing room, where his mother served coffee: the one instance when she allowed his father to ignore medical advice. After making Clement promise not to keep him up late, she went upstairs.

'Dean Harvey asked me to tell you how sorry he was that you were no longer a regular on the airwaves.'

'I'm eighty-one! Besides, I felt enough of a fraud sounding off when I was a bishop. At least then I could claim the authority of my office. Now I'd see it as a double deception. Since I no longer regard the Christian cosmology as true, I can hardly claim a special mandate.'

'I admire your integrity.'

'You're on your own. Most people would say that it showed a distinct lack of integrity to remain in the Church after abandoning my faith. And I'm not sure I wouldn't agree. But I was able to justify it to myself because, although I couldn't believe in an actual God: a real presence: a creator, I could – and do – believe in the idea of God. I believe in God not because He made man in His own image but because man made God in his. What's more, I believe the ideal of goodness we invest in God is itself a good. The very fact that we can conceive of an ultimate good means that somewhere in the infinity of the universe it must exist. The concept of God is God.'

Clement grappled with an argument which he had heard in various forms over the years as his father sought to explain a stance that appeared untenable to many both inside and outside the Church. Critics had scoffed that he was too wedded to the privileges of office, but his friends knew that it took far more courage for him to stay at his post than to resign. Moreover, by remaining in the Church after renouncing its doctrines, he had shown a belief in humanity far greater than any humanist's, since he had credited it with the creation of God.

'Do you remember when I was a kid and I'd fall and graze my elbow or knee? You'd tell me to grab hold of your hand and let the pain pass to you. I wish I could return the favour. Only not with pain. With faith. There's nothing worse than to lose it.'

'But I haven't lost it... just redirected it a little. As a boy, I had a Gentle Jesus Meek and Mild faith. Then, as an adolescent full of self-disgust and self-doubt, I had a Crown of Thorns for us Sinners faith. After that, I went through various forms of Anglican observance. Now my faith's been turned inside out. If the Church is the body of Christ, I believe in the body and not the soul.'

'For most of us, it's the other way round. We believe in God in spite of the Church.'

'Oh, I'm not talking about the Creed. I was loath to affirm my faith in one God even when I had a faith to affirm. Nobody who's studied comparative religion can do that with much conviction.'

'Was it Mark?'

'What?'

'I've always wanted to ask but I've been too afraid of the answer.'

'And you're not now?'

'No, it's not that. But I think I'm more afraid of being left without an answer when... if...'

'I'm eighty-one years old. There's no need to be coy.' He laughed. 'So was it Mark what?'

'Was it his death that destroyed your belief in a benevolent God?'

'Omnipotent and omniscient?'

'That too.'

'No, Clem, don't worry. It wasn't Mark. Of course losing him didn't help. It didn't help anything. But there've been too many disasters, too much suffering, too long a history of non-intervention. You can only take the free will argument so far. The question isn't why I stopped believing but why I carried on doing so for so long. I wanted... I wanted desperately to believe in that all-in-all God. I was ready to defy science, history, logic and my own experience into the bargain. But it was spiritually and intellectually dishonest. The time came when I had to face the truth.'

'So where does that leave me, a man whose religion is not only the heart of his life but of his art?'

'I was serious when I said I believed in the Church. Just as religion expresses the best in man, religious art expresses the best in religion.'

'I doubt your views would find favour in orthodox circles. Wasn't it St Augustine who held that it was a grave sin to respond to the singing in church rather than to its message?'

'I can live with his disapproval. On the other hand, I'm not so sure I can live with your mother's. I'd better go upstairs. Good night, my boy. We can continue this discussion whenever.'

Clement saw his father into the hall and returned to the drawing room. He sprawled on the sofa, rapt in reflection. An artist, someone had said, was a man who was true to his contradictions. Such contradictions would always be at their starkest in those whose subject was faith. For them, the struggle wasn't simply to make their canvases worthy of their ideas but to make their lives worthy of their canvases. From Fra Angelico to Eric Gill, there was a long line of those who fell short. He would take heed from their example. The conflict between spirit and flesh would be resolved in paint.

4

Clement examined his watch for the third time in less than a minute. There were only five days before he was due to present his designs to the Fabric Advisory Committee and Rafik was one hour and sixteen... no, seventeen minutes late. It was his own fault. He should have stuck with an actor or a dancer who respected the artistic process, rather than gambling on an amateur.

A glance at his sketchbook served to increase his frustration. For all his unreliability, it was clear that Rafik was an inspired choice, his soulful beauty lending weight to the imprisoned Adam and lustre to the liberating Christ. Refusing to work with a lesser model, he called the gallery and asked Gil to negotiate an extension of his contract. He slipped on his coat, desperate to escape the enforced indolence, but, just as he reached the door, the telephone rang. The relief of hearing Rafik's voice faded on hearing his news.

'I am in prison.'

'What?'

'Police prison. They put me in arrest.'

Clement struggled to make sense of a story which was made more confusing by loud and disturbing background noise. The one ineluctable fact was that Desmond had stabbed a man and, in the course of the investigation, Rafik had been charged with entering the UK illegally and served with notice of removal. Clement shuddered at the thought of his return to a country where rough justice was dealt out with razor blades on a bus. He was anxious to help, but his knowledge of police procedure stopped short at hazy memories of *Inspector Morse*.

'Is it just one phone call you're allowed, do you know?'

'Who else must I call? I wish to say to you I am sorry. So sorry. You wait for me and I am not there.'

'Don't even think about it,' Clement said, disgusted that he should be thinking about it himself. He turned the sketchbook face down to prevent its making any further claims on his consciousness, 'The first thing we must do is find you a lawyer.'

'What for? The thing that they say is true.'

'Well don't say it! Don't say anything, except "I reserve the right to stay silent." Did you get that? Meanwhile, I'll call my solicitor and ask her to send someone round. Don't worry,' he said, with more confidence than he felt. 'We'll soon have you out.'

Fired with indignation, he rang Gillian Wrenshaw, who explained that, while it was outside her own field of expertise, she knew a first-rate immigration lawyer and would contact him at once. Ten minutes later, James Shortt called to introduce himself and, after a few words with Clement, undertook to go straight to the police station.

Clement remained at the studio waiting for news. To keep from brooding, he opened the copy of the Quran which he had dusted down after his first conversation with Rafik. He had made little headway with it in the past, finding its confused and apocalyptic tone closer to the Book of Mormon than to the Bible, but Rafik's account of the creation of Adam had inspired him to read it again. Even perched uncomfortably on a studio stool, he was surprised by how much he warmed to the new perspective on the familiar story. Not only was it free from misogyny, since it was Adam rather than Eve whom Satan tricked into eating the apple, but Adam himself was less of a sinner than a dupe. His expulsion from paradise was an integral part of God's plan to 'make a vice-regent on earth'. So while the Genesis Adam was condemned to a life of toil and shame, the Quran Adam was hailed as the first prophet. This welcome corrective to Original Sin chimed with his own belief that what was known as the Fall would be better described as the Stumble, and that Christ came not to save mankind but to share in the suffering that was the inevitable result of our existence in time.

His reflections were punctured by the phone, which he rushed to answer, knocking over a jar of charcoal. To his relief, the call was from Shortt, who explained that he had made a claim for asylum on Rafik's behalf, persuading the immigration officers to grant him Temporary Admission. Promising to ring again on his return to the office, he handed his phone to Rafik.

'You are why I come to England,' Rafik said.

'I beg your pardon?' Clement replied, more bewildered than ever by Rafik's English.

'You are so kind when you know me so little. I carry nothing but trouble. Your window...'

'We'll have plenty of opportunity for that. The important thing is that you're free. Go home and ring me as soon as you've rested.'

'That is now. I am well. I am strong. I can be standing for two hours... three. I can come to you in next minute. You can make drawing of me in afternoon.'

'Really, it's not necessary. Tomorrow – '

'Now, please. I wish it.'

Having put up a show of resistance, Clement was delighted when Rafik chose to ignore it. He told him to waste no time but to borrow the cash from Shortt and take a taxi. Then, calculating that Mike would be on his lunch break, he rang him with the news. Far from expressing surprise, Mike declared that, apart from a few powerful families with contacts at the British consulate, it was well nigh impossible for Algerians to obtain visas.

'So you're saying you knew about Rafik all along and didn't tell me? How bloody irresponsible! What if I've committed a crime?'

'I didn't say I knew; I said I suspected. I've only spoken to him a few times in the Elliot. You're the one who's cooped up with him for hours on end. I thought you liked your models to talk.'

'But he's reserved. It's one of the first things that struck me. There's a gravity to him... a weight – in spite of his slight physique. Which is precisely the image I want for Christ.'

'And no doubt you think it's something innate, breathed into him by God, and not the result of everything he's been through?'

'Don't you have marking to do?' Clement asked sharply.

'Touché!'

Mike offered to drive round after school and talk to Rafik himself, adding that it would give him a chance to look at the sketches. Clement put down the phone and pottered about the studio, suppressing the urge to rush out for a bottle of champagne. Temporary Admission was a small victory in what promised to be a long and bloody campaign. The buzzer sounded and he let in Rafik, who was wearing a T-shirt that was far too thin for early March even without the disconcerting rip in the sleeve.

Rafik made straight for him and kissed his hand, which Clement, feeling more English than he would ever have expected, trusted was a traditional Arab custom.

'You are saving my life.'

'I'm only glad I could help.'

'If is not for you, they are pushing me on the plane to Algeria where they must kill me.'

'I promise you it won't come to that. Mr Shortt said he was filing a claim for asylum. Which I'm sure will be just a formality.' A hundred tabloid head-lines rose up to mock him. 'And I've spoken to Mike, who said you also have the right to claim residence under the Human Rights Act.'

'Yes, I hear this thing from Mr Shortt. He says that Desmond and I can say to government we are lovers together.'

'Which is brilliant!'

'No, is not so much brilliant. Not for Rafik. Because I am come to this land with bad card, they do not permit me to say this here. First I must go back to Algeria and make claim. But when plane stop, they push me quickly inside prison or army. So I never have chance.'

'Then applying for asylum's the only choice.' Clement baulked at the Lewis Carroll logic.

'You are kind man... you are very kind man to pay money for Mr Shortt. But I pay you again. You must believe me! I work in bar. I work in two bars. This way I pay you again.'

'That's not an issue. There are far more serious things for you to worry... to think about.'

'You won't want Rafik now. Not for Jesus. But I clean. I wash dirty brushes. I brush floor, yes?'

'Of course I want you for Jesus. I can't think of anyone more fitting. He was condemned as a criminal. He was executed by a brutal occupying force... no, I mustn't push the parallels too far.' His mind, however, was spinning with possibilities. 'If you're sure you're up to it, I'd like to do some sketching. While I do, maybe you'll tell me how you came to end up here?'

'Rafik speak and spoil your picture, no?'

'Not unless I'm drawing your mouth.'

Under the circumstances, Clement decided to work on the clothed Adam rather than the naked Christ. He watched while Rafik settled into position and then moved to adjust both his arms and the light. He picked up a pencil and made a few quick lines on the paper, filling them out as Rafik filled in his story.

'I am come from north-east side of Algeria. Not good place for now. Many religious men with guns. The Groupe Islamique Armée. You hear of them?'

'No. And, by the sound of it, I've not missed much.'

'I have friend, good friend, who is teacher. Kind man. Old man. Like you.' Clement felt the epithet like a punch in the guts. 'My friend is in trouble from boy. He say if friend give him no money, he tell everything they do together. He make everything they do with smile sound bad. My friend afraid so he run away. My brothers, they hear I know him. They say Rafik do bad things too. They say they kill me if I speak to friend ever more. And they do; I know this to be true. So I take money from father and I sail on ship to France. I am safe in France but cold with much hunger. Then I meet man. Englishman. Justin. He tell me to come to this land with him. I say: "Yes, thank you very much, sir, I come. First, we go to English government. We say things very bad at home for Rafik." But Justin, he say there is no chance. Persons there, they laugh at Rafik. They call him dirty man. So he buy for me card. French card.'

'An identity card?'

'Yes. With picture of Rafik. This person make it in Marseilles. Just like real.'

'Which is how you entered the country?'

'It is how, yes. I go with Justin to his house. 32 Rensfield Avenue, Bournemouth. But he not good to me. I wish to leave. I ask for card. But he hide it.

I look all places through house, but I find nothing. So I run away. This is my mistake.'

'Not if he treated you cruelly.'

'I am safe there. I have tears but I am safe. I come to London. I must sleep on street. I ask persons if they give me money.'

'I'm so sorry.'

'Some persons, they do not see you. Other persons, they laugh. They spit. They do many bad things. You know what is milkshake?'

'The drink?'

'The drink, yes,' Rafik said with perplexing eagerness. 'I sit on street when four men come near to me. Young men with big coats. Warm. Much money. "Do you like milkshakes?" one man ask me. "Yes sir," I say to this man. I am not good understanding, but he has kind smile so I say yes. Then he pull box of milk from bag and he shake it like this.' Rafik frenziedly waved his arms in the air. 'He shake it all on me. Then four men, they laugh. They see Rafik all white and wet and they laugh.'

Clement detected a new expression in Rafik's eyes, no longer sadness but righteous fury. This was not the Christ of *Turn the other cheek* and the Beatitudes; this was the Christ who cursed the fig tree and purged the Temple. 'But you managed to get away from the streets.'

'This man... man from good family like you, he say to me how to find job in kitchen, washing dishes. Then he say to me how to find bed in hostel. I speak to man in kitchen of my story. He take me with him one night-time to club. Gay club. It is like dream. I say to him: "This cannot be real. All these men who take off shirt and kiss each other. It is dream."'

'I remember the feeling.'

'It is here I meet Desmond. He is big man. He does not take off shirt. I like this... I like him. I like him very much. I think of him and I make tears. I meet him one time more, in café not club. We go to bed and we like us very much. It is so good. You understand Rafik, yes?'

'Oh yes, I understand Rafik.'

'Desmond, he ask me to live with him in Willesden. He has one small room in house. He is sad for this. He speak of it often. But I do not care; I like him so much. What I do not like is his jealous... very jealous. When I talk with man,... any man, he say I want to go to bed with this man. He make world where small things are big. Rafik is young and good to look at. You think Rafik is good to look at, I know.' He smiled for the first time in the afternoon but Clement refused to let it colour his image.

'I think Rafik is good to draw,' he replied sternly. 'But I hope he won't become big-headed.'

'You think my head is too big for picture?' Rafik asked in a worried tone.

'Not at all, no. It's just an expression. Please carry on. I'm sorry I distracted you.'

'Desmond, he think Rafik is good to look at it,' Rafik said tentatively. 'He think everyone is wishing to look at Rafik and no one is wishing to look at Desmond. He say I have no love for him. I stay with him because I have fear of streets. But in little time I show him how I love him. I show him in ways you cannot trick. And he is happy. And Rafik is happy. Every one of us is happy. And then Steve moves inside house.'

'Steve?' Clement had switched his concentration from the sketch to the story. Even so, he wondered if he had missed a vital link.

'Steve is man who work in bar. He like woman but he has not one now. He say he can find Rafik work in bar. Desmond does not wish it, but I say "yes". I do not like work in kitchen. Too many Nigerians. It is there I meet Mike. He remember me of my teacher friend at home.' Clement trusted that the resemblance was purely professional. 'He come with friends at end of school. One special woman.'

'Red hair? Deep voice? Chain smoker?'

'This is she.'

'Anita.'

'I think at first they marry.'

'No. Mike says they like each other far too much for that.'

'This is English joke, yes?'

'Well, it's Mike's.'

'Mike is very kind person. Rafik is happy he meet him. But when I speak of him to Desmond, he is not happy. He remember me I come to England with bad card. He say Mike is maybe policeman.'

'Some chance! He still thinks he's the student rebel of thirty years ago.'

'Desmond wish that I leave bar. He say he make enough money on site. I say no. And he hit me. Not hard. Not like Justin. Not because he wish to see me with blood. But because he is hurt too. So I am understanding of him. But he is not understanding of me. He say I go to bed with Steve. I swear to him on Holy Quran this is not true. But he listen only to himself, not Rafik. This is why I never tell him I am coming here. He must kill me.'

'Yes, you said so before.' Clement felt nervous now that the threat was so much more real.

'So I tell him I work more hours in bar. And I give him more money. Which make him happy. Then last afternoon he go to bar and find no Rafik. He think to himself I am with Steve. He is very quiet until it is evening and we eat. He tell me I go to bed with Steve all day when he is on site. He hit me when I tell him "no". Then he pick up knife from table and walk into next room and he push knife in Steve's chest. Like this.' Clement was chilled by a gesture as poised as a fencer's thrust. 'There is too much blood. Everywhere. It fall on me and I am by door. I shout and persons from house they come and call hospital. I know then my time in this land is finished. I think to myself I must run away. But there is too much blood and I must not leave Steve.'

'Be sure to say that to Mr Shortt. It'll count in your favour.'

'The police come and they take away me and Desmond. They ask questions... so many questions. They find out soon I must not be here. And their faces change. And their voices change. It is like I am man with knife. This is when I make call to you. Now you know story of Rafik's life.'

Clement knew that it was an outline rather than the story, nevertheless he found it both poignant and enlightening. He returned to the sketch while Rafik lapsed into silence. At four thirty, having waited as long as he could to see Mike, Rafik left for his shift. Clement dismissed his offer to remain, assuring him that Mike and his friends would call in for a drink very soon. 'Try keeping them away,' he said brightly. After confirming the next day's session, he showed him out. He decided against ringing Mike who was sure to have been caught in traffic, hoping that Rafik's presence in the drawings would make up for his absence in the flesh.

Even after eleven years he remained uncertain of Mike's opinion of his work. Friends related his pride in commissions and prizes, but that spoke of love for the artist rather than the art and, unlike Clement, he was able to divorce the two. He played the devoted consort at dinners with collectors and curators but showed little curiosity about the creative life, viewing Clement's ten-foot mosaic of *Jacob and the Angel* as if it were a Victorian lady's languid pastels. Clement never complained, since he knew that Mike spent his days among children who would as soon burn down a gallery as step inside one. Nevertheless, he could not shake off the suspicion that his reluctance to engage with his work owed less to his self-professed ignorance than to a distaste for Clement's themes. Magritte-style jokes or Matisse-style decorations would have been fine, but God was beyond the palette.

Mike arrived and, as ever, Clement found that the studio seemed to shrink in his presence. He passed on Rafik's regrets, to which Mike responded with a tirade against redundant roadworks. Stifling a cyclist's smug smile, Clement asked if he wanted some tea, adding that they could pop to the community café across the road, but Mike preferred to take full advantage of his 'private view'. Clement busied himself at the sink, surprised by his keenness to defer the verdict.

'You are aware how much you give away in these?' Mike asked, leafing through the sketches of Rafik.

'How much of what?'

'I think the polite term is *ardour*.'

'Nonsense,' Clement said, trying to wrest them from him, unsure whether to feel insulted or relieved by Mike's amusement.

'Don't knock it. At least it's something real.'

'He's sitting for Christ.'

'Oh well then, ardour's out! I remember your story about the Renaissance painters who used women models for Christ because they were afraid to show his masculinity.'

'I said that that was the practice, not the reason.'

'I've never understood why Christians are so scared of the body.'

'Says who? I'm perfectly happy with my body. But, unlike some – ' he glared at Mike who continued to hold the sketchbook out of reach, 'I maintain that a person is bigger than his body. Just as a painting is more than a set of pigments, so a person is more than a set of cells.'

'If I were to choose an official symbol for Christianity – '

'Dream on!'

'I'd ditch the cross for a pillar.'

'Why?' Clement asked, intrigued in spite of himself.

'Not Christ suffering to save the world but St Simeon Styletes running away from it. Stuck on top of that giant erection for God knows how many years!'

'You may have turned your back on the Brethren – '

'As I recall, I didn't have a great deal of choice. "I wish you were dead" – no, I tell a lie: "I wish you'd never been born" – is fairly unambiguous. So much for the Prodigal Son! But then, of course, he didn't send a few mildly racy loveletters to a seventeen-year-old classmate.'

'Your parents were mad. Believe me, I'd never defend them – '

'I'm very glad to hear it.'

'But you must still know to respect other peoples' faith.'

'Why? We don't respect any other delusion. We lock up people who believe they're Christ, yet we're supposed to humour those who believe in him.'

'By definition, faith is irrational: a belief you hold against the normal rules of evidence.'

'In which case I believe in Jedi.'

'There's no point discussing it. You're just out to make me look loopy.'

'That's because there's no one I'd rather see sane.'

'I'm sorry to disappoint you.'

'You don't. You excite me. You intrigue me. You delight me.'

'Don't change the subject!'

'But for such an intelligent man you have this extraordinary blind spot. Religion is the triumph of tradition over truth.' Clement feigned a yawn as Mike mounted his hobby-horse. 'The relic of an age when superstition was enough to explain the universe. We're living two centuries after the Enlightenment.'

'It's a miracle, all things considered, not just that we're still together but that we haven't murdered each other. Oh I forgot; you don't believe in miracles.'

'Says who? I just look for them in different places. Take these wonderful sketches –'

'You like them?'

'I don't know which is the greater miracle: the beauty of the model or the drawing.'

'Thank you.' Clement savoured a compliment which showed that, however much they disagreed about God, they shared a deep and abiding faith in humanity. 'Shall I lock up and meet you at home? We can both use the journey to cool down.'

'I'm afraid you're stuck with me a little longer. If you ask very nicely, I might give you a lift.' Clement looked at him in bemusement. 'I passed your bike on the way in. Somebody's nicked the saddle.'

5

'*Noli me tangere* doesn't apply to painters,' Clement said with a forced grin. The Dean and his allies laughed, while Major Deedes and Sir Brian MacDermott sat with faces as stony as the cathedral bosses. Clement shifted in his seat and thought of all the indignities heaped on artists since the first cave painter had seen his antelope mistaken for a bison.

He was in a fusty Roxborough consistory room to present his sketches to the Dean and Chapter. The Dean had described it as a mere formality, but so far the formality had been shown in their treatment of him rather than their endorsement of his work. The committee consisted of two lay canons and three clergy and their degree of support for the project reflected the professional divide. The first stumbling block was the fee, which the Dean assured them would not come out of cathedral funds. Nevertheless Sir Brian, a local poultry tycoon, was appalled by the figure of £75,000. 'For one window?' he asked, glowering at Clement as if he had caught him stealing lead from the roof. Struggling to stay calm, Clement cited the expense of his fabricator and materials. 'We're in the wrong business, eh?' Sir Brian said to a neighbouring canon, who looked outraged at the thought of being in business at all. The Dean took it as a grudging acceptance and moved on to discuss the design.

It was now Major Deedes' turn to take the offensive with his claim to be deeply disturbed by the juxtaposition of the clothed Adam and the naked Christ. It reminded him of a painting, whose title he failed to recall but which, from the self-revealing description, Clement identified as Manet's *Déjeuner sur l'herbe*. He had anticipated such objections and outlined the thinking behind the image, explaining that he did not accept the existence of Hell, either physical or metaphysical. Just as his father believed that the concept of God was God (a statement that sent the Major into a fit of coughing), so he believed that the concept of Hell was Hell. Human beings were condemned to eternal suffering in a doctrine of their own making. They could be freed from it by their faith in Christ, not the traditional Christ who came laden with two thousand years of baggage, but the essential Christ, unvarnished and free.

'And this Christ will be – how shall I put it? – in a state of nature?' the Major asked.

'Absolutely. Although I'd prefer "a state of grace".' Clement thought he heard the Dean suppress a snicker. 'What's more, it avoids setting him in any particular period. Or would you prefer him in biblical robes?'

'And why not?' the Major asked.

'Because it immediately restricts his meaning. It makes him remote to ordinary visitors who may not possess your grasp of history.' Clement bit his tongue. 'Adam wears a suit because he's our contemporary, but Christ will be clothed in nothing but light.'

'Yes, let's not forget, Major,' the Dean added in voice at once unctuous and steely, 'that we're talking about a window. I might take a very different view if it were an altarpiece or a statue, but this will be as insubstantial as air.' Clement smiled, grateful for the backing if not the analogy.

'That's all very well. But how do we know that it won't attract the wrong sort of people?'

'Like who?' Clement asked disingenuously. 'You might as well ban Van Gogh's *Boots* on the grounds that it would attract shoe fetishists.'

'Well I think that about wraps it up,' the Dean interjected quickly. 'Thank you all for a most interesting exchange of views. I really don't think that we need take up any more of Mr Granville's time. I'm sure he's eager to return to London.' He cited the capital with the wistful air of one who had felt his talents wither in the provinces. After shaking the committee's hands, by turn limp, fleshy, clammy, cold and calloused, Clement took his leave of the Dean, who promised to ring him as soon as he had a result.

Clement returned to London in an overheated train opposite a sulky ten-year-old who sucked her plaits. He had barely begun making dinner when the Dean called with the news that the majority view had prevailed and the design been accepted. Shrewd as ever, he insisted that unanimity would have been a sure sign that the image was bland. After restating his belief that the window would be a splendid addition to the cathedral, which Clement, anticipating future guidebooks, read as a splendid monument to the Dean himself, he sounded a note of caution. 'We still have to gain approval from the Fabric Advisory Committee over which I have no – I repeat, no – control. But I trust that that won't deter you from celebrating.'

'As soon as he saw my face, my boyfriend brought out a bottle of champagne,' Clement said, emphasising the relationship.

'Quite right. Water into wine, as I always remind the Methodists,' the Dean replied, leaving it unclear if he were diplomatic or deaf.

Although the imminence of the meal forced them to open the champagne before it was chilled, Clement professed not to notice. Mike proposed a toast to the window, which he insisted on interpreting as an allegory of a repressed man being liberated by his bolder self and calling *Coming Out*.

'It's *The Second Adam*,' Clement retorted.

'Oh sure! And St Teresa never had an orgasm.'

Mike's marking and his own self-restraint meant that they drank only half the bottle, so he took the rest in his saddlebag when he made his way to Dartmouth Park the following morning. He was having lunch with Carla, ostensibly to discuss the window, but he knew that she was preoccupied with thoughts of the child. He was anxious not to leave her in suspense and reckoned that, while a full bottle might raise her hopes, a half-full or, rather, half-empty one would let them down gently. In the event he miscalculated for, as soon as he opened his bag, her face lit up.

'Oh Clement, thank you.'

'Please, wait a second! It's only what's left over from last night.'

'I think it's great news. Really great,' she said, in a voice so flat that he was eager to fill it with bubbles.

'I thought we could have it at lunch. But if you'd like a glass right now.'

'No, lunch is good.' She led him to the spacious workshop which, without his qualms about working at home and with no Crown Estate Commissioners to object, she had built in the garden. A faint odour of linseed oil hung in the air. 'Sit anywhere,' she said, switching on the heater. 'I've laid out some samples.'

'You look stressed. I'm sorry. Shall we leave the window and discuss the other matter first?'

'If you think it's appropriate.'

'I think it's essential.' Carla paced the room, as if anticipating the worst. 'First I want to say how touched I am – and flattered – that you should ask.'

'Oh God!'

'I'd do anything... anything within my power to help. But I wouldn't be bringing you life but death.'

'I don't understand.'

'I'm HIV positive.'

'What?'

'And I have been for twelve years.'

As Carla burst into tears, Clement knew that his instinct for secrecy had been sound. Even so, he felt an immense relief at having finally opened his heart to a member of his family. 'There's nothing to cry about. Truly! I'm in excellent health. God and the drug companies willing, I'll live out my biblical span.'

Her initial shock gave way to hurt, tempered with resentment that he had kept the truth hidden for so long. 'And all this time you've said nothing? Do you trust me so little?'

'Believe me, it's not you I don't trust but myself. Knowing I'd never manage to tailor different stories to different people, I decided that the best thing would be to tell no one.'

'Not even your parents?'

'Them least of all. You, more than anyone, know what they've suffered. I can't put them through hell every time I catch a cold.'

'Yes, of course. I'm sorry. It's very brave of you.'

'Mike thinks it's cowardly.'

'Then he's wrong!' she said with unexpected vehemence. 'I've always known you were a compassionate man, Clem. I never realised how much.'

'You'll make me blush!'

He explained that keeping well was a routine matter of taking his pills and managing the modest side effects. The real problem lay in his mind. The sense of playing host to a deadly virus not only alienated him from his own body but threatened his intimacy with Mike. He found it increasingly hard to respond to his lovemaking, let alone take the initiative. Mike had little patience with his fears. For him, the safer sex guidelines were protection enough but, for Clement, the comparative contained a warning. So, night after night, he lay beside the love of his life, longing to give himself without restraint, tortured by thoughts of ulcerated gums and split condoms.

'I think I'd like that champagne now,' Carla said. She led the way to the kitchen, the gleaming white cabinets looking even more sterile in the aftermath of Peter's departure. While she heated the soup, he tentatively broached the subject of using an anonymous donor.

'Never!' She shuddered.

'Not even a Nobel Prize-winner?'

'I want to raise a child, not breed a racehorse.'

Fearing he had wounded her, he was doubly grateful for her keenness to return to the workshop and restore their relationship to its former footing. He showed her the sketches and ran through the budget hammered out between Gil and the Dean. He suggested that they mix different kinds of glass, something opaque, either antique or semi-antique, for the figures, and hand-blown, even streaky, for the surround.

'What's behind it? Are there any buildings we need to blot out?'

'None at all. One advantage of such a backwater is that the close is completely unspoilt.'

'I suppose you'll want the figures painted?' He nodded, knowing that she thought it old-fashioned but also that he had to carry the conservatives on the FAC.

'Unless there are serious financial implications.'

'It's much of a muchness. What you save by not using flash glass, you lose by spending longer on the painting and cooking.'

Their wariness with each other made it easier than usual to agree on a scheme, although he was aware that it left scope for future conflict. He set out a provisional timetable. He was to present a scale design to the FAC at the beginning of April. Then, provided that the glazier was prompt with the template, he hoped to have a cartoon ready for her to start work within six weeks. She in turn confirmed that, other than repairing a large art deco panel for an exiled sheik in Godalming, she was totally free. 'After all, I shan't have any reason to take things easy.' Feeling as though he had been kicked in the teeth, he kissed her and cycled home.

He spent the next two weeks in the studio. Despite having finished the drawings for *The Second Adam*, he asked Rafik to sit every morning. As he filled his pad with sketches of a man whose every pose was as natural as sleeping, he knew that he had found not just a model but a muse. Besides, it was clear that Rafik needed distraction as well as cash. The manager of the bar had sacked him the moment he learnt of his status, leaving him far too much time to brood, especially after his interview at the Asylum Screening Unit in Croydon. 'If they wish to make me feel bad to stay here, they have success. Persons are as cold and hard as building.' Then, on the eve of the FAC meeting he arrived, wrapped in gloom, and without uttering a word held out a letter. A quick glance confirmed Clement's worst fears; the Home Office had rejected the appeal. He longed to take him in his arms but was afraid to offend him. So, with his sunniest smile, he pointed out that it was exactly what Shortt had predicted and that the real test would come in court.

'I ask who they will put in court first: Rafik or Desmond?' Rafik said, presenting Clement with a quandary that was painfully remote from his own experience. Beyond registering the irony that Desmond's morbid fear of losing Rafik had been self-fulfilling, he had trained himself not to think of him. He could no more conceive of the horror of being held on remand in Belmarsh than of being sent back to a country overrun by homicidal Islamists. He was forty-two years old, but the bitter reality of countless lives was merely a TV-lit flicker in his brain.

Thinking that a trip out of London would lift his spirits, Clement invited Rafik to accompany him to Roxborough. 'It is kind, but I am saying no. Rafik bring only bad luck.' So the following morning he took the train alone. His anxiety about delays ensured that he arrived two hours early. Braving the drizzle, he strolled through the market square with its quaint rows of family-owned shops, their ornate signs proudly proclaiming the dates of their establishment, and at the centre a monumental allegory to monarchy over a drinking fountain that had run dry.

With the drizzle turning to rain, he made his way to the cathedral office of works where, after a dispiriting wait, he was ushered into an oak-panelled room to find his six inquisitors sitting at one end of a walnut table that had been designed for twenty. The FAC was younger and more varied than the Chapter and he presumed that the additional layer of bureaucracy, along with its exclusively lay constitution, was intended to reflect the cathedral's new role as a heritage site rather than a mere place of worship. The chairman, a surveyor, introduced his five fellows by profession as well as by name: archaeologist; architect; artist; accountant; and builder, which Clement construed as a pledge of their expertise. He noted wryly that the artist and builder wore charcoal grey suits and ties and the accountant a maroon rugby shirt. Past acquaintance with such bodies had taught him that, having volunteered their services, they believed themselves both obliged to speak and bound to be heard. He swapped glances with the Dean who, as though to underline his role as an observer, sat at an angle to the table with an empty chair between himself and the rest.

The chairman dispensed the usual pleasantries, after which Clement presented his design. He began by discussing his choice of subject and its relation to the building and then unwrapped the painting, sending the Dean, who had hitherto seen only pencil sketches, into a paroxysm of delight. He sat down to a chorus of approval, which experience had taught him to distrust. Moments later the dissenting voices broke out although, unlike those in the Chapter, they were concerned less with the orthodoxy of his naked Christ (he wondered slyly whether they had failed to identify the olive tone as flesh) than with the formal qualities of the image. True to type, it was the local artist who spearheaded the attack, his trifling objections making it clear that he had earmarked the commission for himself.

'It's very bright,' he said.

'That's because it's two foot rather than twenty,' Clement replied, struggling to sustain his smile. 'It would have been very dull if I'd painted it any other way.'

'I'm not sure about the blue. There's so much blue in the building already. I prefer purple.'

Clement stretched the silence to breaking-point. 'Oh, I'm sorry. Was that a question?'

The artist retired hurt and the accountant took his place. 'Any idea how it'll reproduce on a postcard?'

'No, nor on a tea towel either.'

The Dean, unable to stomach any further attacks on his monument, rose to his feet. 'Gentlemen... and lady –' He bowed his head to the archaeologist, an afterthought which Clement feared might cost him dear – 'Mr Granville is one of the most distinguished... some would say *the* most distinguished artist working in the field today. We're extremely fortunate to have secured his services. It's not for us to question his integrity.' Although Clement was more conscious of the sparseness of the field than of his own eminence within it, the committee appeared to be chastened. The archaeologist, glaring at the Dean, raised the question of biblical authenticity and the architect of the scale of Hell, each of which Clement neatly parried. The chairman then asked him to leave the room while they deliberated. He picked up the painting and went out. The secretary looked nervous as he paced the office, examining first a set of Roxborough landscapes so bland that they might have been jigsaws and then a devotional image of Christ astride a cliff of clouds. Just as he was turning to the ledger-laden shelves, the Dean ran out and pumped his hand.

'We've won!'

6

If Robert Louis Stevenson were alive today, Clement reflected, he wouldn't use a drug to effect Dr Jekyll's transformation but simply stick him in a traffic jam on the A4.

'What the fuck is this?' Mike asked. 'A car park?'

'Don't worry. It won't stretch far.'

'Thank you for that, Pollyanna! Do you have X-ray vision as well?'

'I'm only trying to help.'

'Well you're not,' Mike said, venting his frustration on the horn.

They were spending the bank holiday on a retreat in the wilds of Wales. It was an offshoot of the one on which they had met, although over the years much had changed. Medical advances had reduced the participation of gay men, who preferred to take their pills and spend the weekend clubbing, and increased that of African women, who lacked peer acceptance to offset the stigma of the virus. Mike had felt honour-bound to remain as facilitator, but Clement suspected that, despite his maxim that HIV did not discriminate, there was a part of him that pined for the long-lost camaraderie of a community under siege.

'If this goes on much longer, we'll miss dinner,' Mike said.

'I've got some biscuits in the back.'

'I'm not hungry!' Mike snapped, and Clement knew better than to comment. Gazing out of the window, he feigned an interest in the featureless landscape, refusing to counsel the patience that would be dismissed as the easy virtue of a non-driver. He felt both cramped and useless. With a five-mile tailback and a well-signposted road, he wasn't even called on to read the map.

The traffic began to move and Clement was relieved to be spared a further outburst before reaching the retreat, where his praise for having made up so much time was met with a grudging grunt. They unloaded their bags and entered the hostel, whose spartan decor made him yearn for the quirks of the Scottish 'bean' rooms. In the hall they were greeted by Mike's two co-facilitators, Blossom, a plump Nigerian social worker with hidden prickles, and Brian, a rebirthing practitioner with designs on Clement since he had yet to work with a twin. Bedrooms were shared and, while Brian and Blossom lamented the drop in numbers which showed how HIV had 'slipped off the radar', Clement was grateful that he and Mike had a room to themselves.

At seven o'clock, they went down to a dining room which reeked of Jeyes

Fluid. Having assured a nervous newcomer that any resemblance to the first day at school was deceptive, Clement was appalled to find his words belied by the food: toad in the hole, with a vegetarian option of macaroni cheese (and an apple and crisps for the solitary vegan), brusquely doled out at a hatch by two blistery cooks. After the dispiriting meal, the nineteen-strong group gathered for an introductory session in a drab lounge dominated by a poster of the solar system and a relief map of Wales. They arranged the chairs in a circle, and Blossom played several choruses of *Kumbaya* on a tinny upright, urging the company to sing along with the fervour of a pantomime dame. Brian then asked them to take turns stating their names, where they lived and, in one sentence, what they were hoping to gain from the retreat: a process Clement dreaded, less for the profusion of Proustian sentences than his dire memory for names.

He was glad to recognise three faces – and recall two names – from the previous retreat: Dembe, a forty-year-old Ugandan grandmother, with her twenty-five-year-old husband, Augustus; and Bill or Ben or Bob, a middle-aged solicitor from Liverpool, whose bittersweet fate was to have outlived all his friends. Among the fresh faces, his eye was caught by two men whose clothes (leather jacket and jeans for the one sprawled in the chair; denim jeans, black mesh T-shirt and studded collar for the one squatting at his feet) would, he felt sure, be the subject of heated debate between Mike and Blossom at the facilitators' meeting. Two chairs away, but seeming to hail from another world, was a dumpy woman in a dun-coloured suit who looked as if she would find the Jam and Jerusalem of a W.I. meeting racy. Most unnerving of all was a man with an eerie resemblance to his former boyfriend, Oliver, even allowing for the twelve-year interval. In a voice that compounded the mystery, he gave his name as Newsom, his home as Bethnal Green, and his hope from the retreat as peace of mind.

Newsom's position straight opposite him provided the perfect cover for Clement's scrutiny, while making it impossible to work out if his smile was aimed at him or just at his place in the circle. The confusion was resolved when, after Mike and Brian had outlined the structure of the retreat and Blossom had listed the three cardinal sins (aggressive behaviour; sexist, racist or homophobic language; and smoking), the session broke up. As Clement stood in line at the hot-water urn, Newsom moved to join him.

'I've often wondered if I'd bump into you again.'

'So it is you!'

'Who else?' Clement gazed at him numbly. 'Don't I get a kiss?'

He struggled to find an appropriate response. This was the man he had met on his return from Paris, the first love that tainted all later ones by its loss.

This was the man with whom he had lived for five years, only to find, while painting their anniversary portrait, that he should have been painting a group. This was the man he was convinced had infected him when they gave up using condoms as a token of trust. He was lashed by waves of violent emotion, as anger, bitterness, curiosity and excitement surged through his head, along with a reflex sexual tingle in his groin.

'Do you hate me?'

'What? No, of course not.'

'Well then?' He held out his arms. 'Kiss and make up?'

Wary of his easy charm and needing greater proof of transformation than a name, Clement compromised with a hug. The familiar contours of Oliver's body confused him and he felt faint.

'I need to sit down.'

'It must be my fatal charisma.' The epithet revived all Clement's suspicions. 'Would you like some air?'

'I'll be fine, thank you.'

Oliver opened the door. 'It's a beautiful night. Let's take a walk. Don't worry, I'm quite harmless.'

'I doubt that, but I'm strong.'

'You always were.'

'No. Then I was just single-minded. Still, I could do with stretching my legs. I've been sitting all day.'

'Do you mind if I tag along? I'd like to talk.'

'You can't expect me to welcome you with open arms, Oliver.'

'Newsom... But there's no call to keep me at arm's length either. It's been twelve years.'

'I can count.' Clement was shocked to find the memory of his betrayal so raw. Resentment of Oliver vied with anger at his own vulnerability. He was determined to rise above both. With Blossom's equation of disease and dis-ease fresh in his mind, he refused to let Oliver compromise his health a second time.

'Come if you like. I'll just tell Mike.'

'Do we have to ask our leaders' permission?'

Clement smiled as the misapprehension empowered him. Seeing no sign of Mike, whom he took to be conferring with his fellow facilitators, he joined Oliver for a walk through the grounds. Stinging branches hung above stony paths and, although his eyes grew accustomed to the dark, he was reluctant to venture far.

'So when did you change your name?' he asked, as they stood gazing into a shadowy paddock.

47

'I've been Newsom for six years.'

'Why? Were you wanted by the police or were several ex-lovers after your blood. That is if the blood weren't...' Clement could not bring himself to finish the sentence.

'I never had you down as a vindictive man.'

'I wasn't... I'm not.'

'I went to see a numerologist. I wanted to change my life.'

'Is it that easy? Jacob becomes Israel. Ba-boom!'

'No, but it's a start. Oliver has a three vibration, which was fine when I was young. It's a warm name that allowed me to harness my sexual and spiritual energy, but it left me in danger of spreading myself too thin. I needed a new vibration for the next stage of my journey. Newsom's a seven – a mystical number – which helps me on my chosen path.'

Clement recalled Oliver's lifelong quest for an inner child that had never seemed so close to the surface. 'What about boyfriends?'

'One or two. No one permanent. I have a dog.'

'I'd like one but Mike's phobic. He broke into the Acropolis as a student and an Alsatian bit his leg.'

'Mike?'

'The facilitator. We're an item.'

'Of course! Camden and Regent's Park. I thought they were two different places.'

'Just two different states of mind.'

'Congratulations! He's a hunk.' Clement frowned. 'You're lucky to have found someone.'

'What? You mean now that I'm damaged goods? Don't think just because Mike volunteers for this that his whole life is a charity!'

'I wasn't thinking that at all.'

His genuine bewilderment forced Clement to acknowledge that the only one who had such thoughts was him. 'I trusted you. Stupid, sure! Naïve, sure! But I felt what we had was good. I never supposed you were grabbing every opportunity to screw around.'

'Screwing up, more like.'

'That's easy to say.'

'Do you think I haven't looked back... wanted to make contact?'

'Don't tell me you were scared!'

'Yes I was, of hurting you... of bringing back too many memories.'

'So why come here now?'

'It's not a private view, Clem! Your name wasn't on the leaflet. Whatever you...' Oliver's voice was lost in a hacking cough.

'Is there anything I can do?' Clement asked, resentment replaced by alarm.

Oliver shook his head until a few words broke through the wheezes. 'I'm fine... no... used to it... go back.'

Guiding him along the path, Clement was shocked by the erosion of his once muscular biceps. Any qualms about touching him vanished, and his one thought was to see him safely inside. Progress was slow, but they finally made it to the lounge where, with a quick nod to Dembe and Augustus, sole survivors of the general exodus, he helped Oliver up the stairs to his room.

'Are you sure you'll be all right? Do you want me to help you undress?'

'Funny. I've often pictured you saying that again. Just not like this.'

Clement felt a disconcerting rush of tenderness. 'I'm in Room 12 if you need me.'

'I'm fine now, Clem. Just go.'

'You asked for a kiss,' Clement said, unwilling to leave him alone.

'What was it you said about charity? Just go. Please!'

'Of course.'

Clement walked down a corridor lined with grainy prints of Victorian miners and entered his room. Finding Mike in his underpants at the washbasin, he made straight for him and stroked the warmth of his back.

'Is that a tall, fair and handsome man?' Mike asked without turning.

'That's for you to tell me.' He wrapped his arms around Mike's chest.

'I'm sorry for being so cunty in the car. I had the day from hell.' Clement smiled as he wondered what Blossom would make of the language. 'Forgiven?'

'Don't be silly!' He relished Mike's toothpaste-tinged kiss. 'Oddly enough, that's the second time tonight I've been asked the question.'

'Really?'

'I've just been talking to Oliver... Oliver, my ex.'

'There's no Oliver on the list.'

'He's changed his name to Newsom. He swears he's changed everything else. Funny but there are some things I wouldn't want him to change. I didn't realise until I saw him there.'

'Are you OK, Clem?'

'Sure. Fine. Just a little taken aback, that's all. Believe me, that chapter of my life is well and truly closed.'

Mike, who knew the story too well to feel threatened, clasped him in his arms and stroked his hair. Clement basked in the restorative touch until a sense of weightlessness heralded the approach of sleep. So he gently extricated himself and, after a token wash, walked over to the clinical beds.

'Would it be against regulations to push them together?' he asked.

'I've a better idea. Let's make do with one.'

'It'll be a squeeze.'

'I certainly hope so.'

With a gusto that prompted Mike to suggest that they come to the country more often, Clement pulled off his underpants and jumped into bed. He snuggled up close to Mike, drinking in the warm sandy smell of his skin. All the confusions of Oliver's return were resolved when they slowly began making love. Fears and inhibitions melted away as he lost himself in Mike's embrace.

He paid the price the next morning when he yawned through Blossom's seminar on anger, although he was cheered to see that 'I can get by on four hours a night' Mike was equally bleary-eyed. After a lunch in which the toad in the hole and macaroni were replaced by burgers and cauliflower cheese (with a banana and crisps for the vegan), the group split into three for a workshop on living with the virus. Against best practice Clement found himself with Mike, and against his better judgement with Newsom, now fully recovered from the night before. Their fellow members were Douglas, the nervous newcomer, whose casual attitude to his infection ('at least I no longer need to worry about catching it') put Mike's non-judgemental ethos to the test, and two Botswanan women, Tembi and Linda, who were so softly spoken that Clement missed large chunks of their stories, although the theme of errant husbands and credulous wives was familiar enough for him to fill in the gaps. After three years of life-saving treatment, they faced the threat of its removal, having been refused asylum in a country for which *Commonwealth* was merely a metaphor.

Their final member was Christine, who had exchanged her suit for a more relaxed grey woollen skirt and cardigan, but whose face and body remained rigid. With a voice that gained in confidence as her story progressed, she explained that her father was an evangelical vicar who, at the start of the AIDS crisis twenty years earlier, had claimed to be on a God-given mission to cure homosexuals. 'Daddy gathered half a dozen young men... confused and damaged young men, gave them a home – my home – and set them on the path to righteousness. To start with he had some success... one or two girlfriends, even an engagement. Then, little by little, the Devil – what Daddy called *the Devil* – began to assert himself. The men began to break away. And not quietly. There were stories in the papers. Even a report on *Points West*. Daddy was worried that the publicity would threaten the funding. In the end there was only one man left, Luke. The most confused and damaged of them all. Daddy asked me to marry him.'

'You're kidding!' Douglas blurted out, breaking all the rules.

'I wish I were,' she replied. 'I expect you all despise me for agreeing.'

'No one's judging you, Christine,' Mike said gently.

'I'm judging myself!' she cried, before recovering her composure. 'But if Daddy could have such a powerful hold on strangers, imagine what it was like for us, his family. He persuaded me that the marriage was God's will. I pictured a husband's love as little more than the love of a younger father. Luke was thrilled... or at any rate flattered. He jumped at the chance to show that he was the number one disciple, my father's right-hand man. And I like to think that he felt something – if not love, then a kind of affection – for me. So we married and in some ways we were happy... I don't have to talk about bed, do I?'

'You don't have to talk about anything you don't want,' Mike assured her.

'Good. It's just that, as you can imagine, that side of things left a lot to be desired. Well, desire for a start.' She giggled. 'I'm sorry. But the one thing I learnt from my mother was patience. Daddy felt vindicated. Luke was his success story. He trusted him so much that he sent him out to spread the word in bars... homosexual bars.'

'Shit!' Douglas said.

'Yes, you're right. Shit and fuck and bugger.' She looked shocked. 'I can't believe I said that! Even now I expect someone – God or Daddy, it doesn't matter which – to strike me down. At first I was pleased when Luke went out. It'll sound selfish, but the only nights he ever tried to make love to me were when he came back from the bars. I thought he was giving thanks for what he had. But I see now that he was trying to cleanse himself for what he'd done... cleanse himself and, in the process, infect me. Although I didn't find out about that until much later, two years after he left. He wrote a letter saying we were living a lie and he'd fallen in love with a man. Only he didn't send it to me but to my father. I think I can forgive him everything else but that. After three years he still wrote to my father!' She broke down, making full use of both Newsom's handkerchief and Mike's encouragement to take her time. 'There's nothing more to say. I went back to live at home and work part-time as a doctor's receptionist. I find it helps to be around people who are sick. Meanwhile Daddy carries on with his mission, blaming every setback on Satan. He won't hear a word about my HIV. It would be like admitting he'd failed.'

The clapping as she drew to a close was long and heartfelt. Clement felt that for once the sharpest anticlerical gibe would be justified, but Mike held back and called on Newsom to speak. He began by confessing that the retreat had stirred up painful emotions in him since he had met an old boyfriend whom he had treated badly. Clement baulked, but to his relief Newsom made no attempt to identify him. He wondered at whom the remarks were aimed, since Mike was unmoved and the rest of the group perplexed. His question was answered when Newsom described how, over the past six years, he had instituted huge changes in his life, giving up his job as a picture researcher in order to travel to Japan and study ceramics. On his return he had begun making pots. Even so he was racked by the thought of unfinished business. He had lived with the virus for at least twelve years and his T-cell count was plummeting. He had been through four different drug combinations and the doctors were running out of options. The uncertain future made him all the more anxious to settle outstanding accounts.

Clement echoed the ovation at the end of the speech, but his hands felt numb. Twelve years confirmed his worst suspicions. He failed to see why, if he were so keen to make amends, Newsom had made no attempt to contact him. Even one who believed in 'leaving everything to the universe' could have picked up a phone. Nonetheless he refused to brood and focused his attention on Mike, whose turn it was to speak. He opened with a graceful allusion to the accident of his not having contracted the virus and to his gratitude for everything he had learnt from his positive friends (this time Clement longed to be singled out, even though he knew that it would breach all Mike's official boundaries). Trusting that no one would take offence, he asked for a moment to acknowledge the upside of HIV, not just the individual acts of courage, but the maturing of a community that had done so much to care for the sick, educate the vulnerable, and ensure access to drugs. He feared that a lot of what had been achieved was being lost, as the success of new treatments led to an erosion of responsibility. Short memories resulted in shortened lives.

After joining in the applause for Mike, Clement embarked on his story. On previous retreats, he had chosen to disclose as little as possible, but this new combination of people and circumstance induced him to voice thoughts he had barely articulated. Averting his eyes from Mike and Newsom, he described how his despair at his brother's death had driven him to explore his dark side. Rather than abandon God, he had defied Him to do His worst, while doing everything in his power to help Him. It had been a miracle (a word he chose in direct response to Mike's *accident*) that he had survived. On emerging from the darkness, he had attempted to disown the experience but, inevitably, he had failed. There was a part of him, however painful it was to admit it, that remained wedded to death. So, while he had always ascribed his infection to another's betrayal, he had to acknowledge his own share of the responsibility. To bear a grudge would be to deny all that had happened, both good and bad, since his diagnosis. He was rewarded with the statutory round of applause and the respective tears and smiles of his past and present lovers.

The day sped by and, after a dinner in which the hostel fare was boosted by the cold meats and salads that Brian, sensing mutiny, had brought back from Neath, the group assembled in the lounge. Filled with newfound confidence,

Clement made for the two leather-clad men who were sitting alone by the fire.

'Mind if I join you?' he asked.

'Go ahead,' Phil replied, pointing to a spare armchair.

'You're not using it?' he asked Tim, who was crouching on the floor.

'Permission to speak, sir?' Tim asked Phil, giving Clement such a chilling insight into their relationship that he longed to escape to Dembe and Augustus.

'Granted,' Phil replied, whereupon Tim explained that he had no right to sit at the same level as Phil. It was only as a concession to the other retreatants that he was allowed to eat off a plate rather than from his dog bowl.

'That strikes you as sane?' Clement asked, realising for the first time that the sexual code was as hierarchic as the religious.

'I live to serve my master,' Tim replied, kissing Phil's boot.

As they continued to talk, Clement was amazed to find that not only was Tim the more articulate of the two but, unlike Phil, he was HIV negative.

'Why should that surprise you?' Tim asked.

'I'm sorry. It's none of my business,' Clement replied, hoping that his flushed face would be attributed to the heat. His discomfort was relieved by Mike, who announced that the fire ritual was about to start in the paddock. Clement flashed him a sympathetic smile, aware of his unease at the more aggressively New Age trappings of the retreat, which were Brian's province. For himself, he enjoyed the spectacle, while remaining dubious that his negative traits would be destroyed simply by writing them on a scrap of paper and tossing it into the flames. Making his way through the grounds, he ran into Christine.

'Are you all right?' he asked. 'I looked for you after the group but you'd disappeared.'

'I'm sorry. If I'd known...'

'Don't worry, I was just checking.'

'I needed some time to myself. It was quite a lot for me to take in. You know, that's the first time since my diagnosis I've discussed it with anyone except the doctor. Even now Daddy thinks I'm spending the weekend with an old friend from school.'

'But that's dreadful! You must feel so isolated. When we go back inside, I'll give you my number. Feel free to ring me at any time – and I mean *any* time – you want to chat.' Having stifled the impulse to invite her to stay, he was doubly embarrassed when she started to cry.

'I'm sorry. You see, I'm a great fan of your *Pier Palace Christ*. Luke and I went down to London when it was in the Park.'

'I'm flattered.'

'I still have my photograph at home. My father said it was blasphemous.'

'He wasn't alone. We had to move it inside the gallery to protect it from vandals. Still, the publicity attracted the crowds.' He took her hand, less to guide her over the crumbling path than to express support. They reached the bonfire, which Brian and the hostel staff had built during the afternoon. Its ferocious blaze – wood crackling and sparks flying – filled Clement with a sense of both annihilation and new life. Spotting Newsom on his own, Clement excused himself to Christine and walked over to him.

'Are you thinking what I'm thinking?' Newsom asked.

'Bonfire nights at Beckley?'

'Right! We had some good times, didn't we?'

'Too many to count.'

'Thank you for what you said this afternoon.'

'I meant it.'

'I'd like to think we could see each other in London. Once in a blue moon,' he added quickly.

'You mean we shouldn't leave it another twelve years?' Clement asked, to his immediate regret.

'No,' Newsom said softly. 'We shouldn't do that.'

Mike came up to join them and, a moment later, Brian asked everyone to hold hands and form a ring around the fire, leaving Clement with a gratifying sense of bringing his own life full circle. He stood between Mike and Newsom as Brian led them in a chant of 'I surrender to love'. Mike's palpable discomfort made it hard to surrender to anything, but as he gazed across the fire, first at Tim and then at Christine, both of whom had taken the injunction literally, Clement appreciated the virtue of detachment. Brian invited them all to throw an object on the fire that symbolised the behaviour patterns they wished to change. Clement moved forward and, with the flames snapping dangerously close to his skin, threw on a blurred photograph of himself and Mark 'so I can see more clearly.' He was followed by Mike, who threw a handful of husks 'so the seed can fertilise more freely,' and by Newsom, who threw a broken pot, 'to release space for ones that are whole.'

With an ear-splitting bang on his drum, Brian faced each point of the compass in turn and enjoined the group to invoke the fire spirit. 'Connect to the spirit of fire in your heart. Let your consciousness expand and imagine you become the fire. Feel the warmth of its flames radiate through you. Be aware that you are loved. Love is everywhere around you and inside you. You are in harmony with the spirit and you know that you are infinite, immortal and universal.'

'You are my fire spirit; my energy, my light,' Clement whispered to Mike, who returned his gaze with tears in his eyes.

'May the fire that flows through you bring blessings to you all and to this place,' Brian entreated.

'Amen,' Clement instinctively replied.

7

The taxi drew up outside Taylor House and Rafik indicated James Shortt, waiting for them on the pavement. Clement was struck by the discrepancy between his orotund voice and angular features. After a strained greeting, they made their way into the building and up to the second floor, where they found themselves in a vast semi-circular vestibule. Men and women in their Sunday best milled around like an evangelical congregation without a pastor. Children sat sombrely in the play area, as if forewarned of their fate. Leaving Shortt to scan the noticeboard, Clement and Rafik headed for the lavatory, standing self-consciously at opposite ends of the stalls. A stark notice about controlling germs hinted at a greater contagion. Clement duly scrubbed his hands, while Rafik displayed a touching faith in the virtue of neatly combed hair. They rejoined Shortt who, announcing that the case was to be heard in Court 23, led the way down a winding passage clustered with anxious people. Even the lawyers were black, and Clement allowed himself a guilty hope that Shortt's white skin would work in Rafik's favour.

'I suppose prayer must be a comfort,' he said to Shortt, as they passed the chapel for *people of all faiths*.

'I prefer a glass of claret.'

They entered the court, where Shortt chatted to his opposite number and Clement and Rafik sat quietly at the back, until an Asian clerk summoned Rafik forward with a smile that Clement read by turn as sympathetic, smug and indifferent. However inscrutable her expression, there was no mistaking the fact of her race. Shortt and the Home Office lawyer moved to their designated tables as Appellant and Respondent and Rafik to that of Witness. The judge entered discreetly and took his seat on a small dais in front of Rafik, ignoring his deep bow. After busying himself with his papers, he turned to Shortt to ask 'Does he speak English?', a question that set the tone for proceedings in which Rafik's position was peripheral to legal niceties. During the long intervals when the judge read the documents, Clement allowed his attention to drift around the room. With its low ceiling, whitewood furniture and boldly patterned carpet all designed to create an air of informality, he hankered for the archaic splendour of the Old Bailey. The majesty of the law instilled hope as well as terror, whereas the judge's complacent remarks and ill-concealed boredom felt less as if he were ruling on Rafik's freedom than vetting his application to a golf club.

The relentless trade of formal argument at least served to reduce the tension. The Home Office lawyer made much of Rafik's entry to the country on a forged identity card and his failure to claim immediate asylum, declaring that ignorance was not only no excuse but not an option. Shortt in turn outlined Rafik's sustained efforts to find work, explaining that he was now employed as a studio assistant to the painter Clement Granville, who was present in court. Clement smiled sweetly at the judge, trusting that he would respond to the picture of middle-class respectability (always granting artistic license for the hair), only to feel snubbed when, after a cursory glance in his direction, the judge sniffed and turned back to his papers.

Shortt addressed the key issue of Rafik's safety should he be repatriated, citing a recent Amnesty International report to the effect that, while homosexuality in Algeria carried an official jail sentence of three years, the reality was far harsher. Thousands of men had been murdered by either the government or the Islamist militias. Rafik, with no influential friends and having been disowned by his family, could expect a similar fate. Having fled military service, he would be arrested as a deserter and thrown into prison, where he would be systematically raped by both officers and inmates, the very Islamists whose threats had forced him to flee.

Having listened to the statement and flicked through the report, the judge asked Shortt whether he had any evidence to back up his claim.

'What more evidence do you need?' Shortt asked.

'It is not for you to ask questions of me,' the judge replied with an affronted dignity worthy of the Woolsack. Shortt apologised so abjectly that Clement suspected him of mockery, although the judge appeared to accept it as his due. Announcing that he would publish his decision within two weeks, he adjourned the case. As he left the court, Rafik was once again the only one to stand.

Clement, who had made Rafik's body his particular study, discerned the anguish in the curve of his neck and the strain in the stretch of his shoulders. Shortt, more professionally detached, shook his client's hand before exchanging pleasantries with his opposite number, which Clement was thankful he was too far away to catch. He was not naïve. He no more expected lawyers to sustain their hostilities at the end of a hearing than actors at the end of a play, but this was less a matter of Richard II and Bolingbroke joining hands at the curtain call than of their declaring a ceasefire halfway through Act Three. The kindest explanation was that their love of the law outweighed their concern for justice, the way that his father's love of the Church overrode his doubts about God. Stifling the diffidence intrinsic to a courtroom, he walked up to Rafik who stood stock-still, staring at the judge's chair. They were joined by

Shortt, who inexplicably claimed that proceedings had gone as well as could be expected.

'So you think he must let Rafik stay?' Rafik asked eagerly.

'It could go either way,' Shortt replied. 'But don't worry, if we lose this one, there's still the Reconsideration.' Then he patted Rafik's arm, shook Clement's hand, and ambled out.

'Always one thing else,' Rafik said. 'When they push me on to plane, he will say: "Don't worry, there is still chance it must crash."'

They left the court, passing two middle-aged Chinese men with the earnest faces of exiles from Tiananmen Square. Once on the street, Clement extracted Rafik's promise to eat something, insisting – only half in jest – that he would have no use for a skinny Saint Sebastian, before flagging a taxi to take him to Dartmouth Park. He had a three o'clock appointment with the Dean who, deaf to all requests that he wait another week, was coming to inspect their progress. Aware that a committed client was the key to a successful commission, Clement had nevertheless been reluctant to sanction the visit, arguing that the work was at a highly delicate stage, with the panes cut out and painted but not yet assembled. The Dean, however, had forced his hand with the news that, far from admitting defeat, Major Deedes had stepped up his campaign against the window and that he would be in a much stronger position to fight back once he had seen it for himself.

With no time for lunch, Carla led Clement straight out to the workshop where the top portion of the window was propped up on an easel. Even though he had warned the Dean to expect no more than a crude impression, he had often found that it was before the fragments of colour had been framed in black that a window was at its purest. He walked round the easel, examining every aspect, before leaning against the wall to gauge the full effect. He nodded to Carla, who carefully removed the lightly glued panel and replaced it with the next one. They repeated the process down to the base, at which point he professed himself delighted, not least with her use of fused glass for the bishop's cope. He told her to go ahead with the leading which, for all his scruples, was one task he was glad to be spared. The soldering iron and horse-shoe nails might have changed little since the Middle Ages, but the romance soon palled in the face of work that was tedious, tiring, and messy.

A prolonged ring on the doorbell punctured their euphoria, but the deflation was only temporary for, having studied the window section by section, the Dean showered it with praise. 'Splendid. Quite splendid. It will make a real contribution to the life and worship of the cathedral. There's just one point. It's so niggling I hesitate to raise it. Nevertheless, these three figures who are guarding Adam in Hell: did I see them on the original designs?'

'Yes, although remember they were sketches. Impossible to include every detail.'

'Quite. However, the detail may be significant. A bishop, a cardinal and some kind of nonconformist. I'm all for ecumenism, but in Hell...?'

'It's a Hell of their own creation, to which they've confined Adam and, by extension, everyone else.'

'A fascinating argument but not without flaws. True, the Bible makes little mention of Hell, but then the Bible makes little mention of much that is central to the Church's teaching. And I worry about handing another weapon to the dreaded Deedes.'

'Don't forget, you're standing on top of the glass,' Carla interjected. 'The figures won't be so clear from a distance.'

While grateful for Carla's support, Clement bridled at any suggestion that the window would be little more than local colour. Like his medieval counterparts, he was aiming to make a theological as well as an artistic statement, which he proceeded to explain to the Dean. 'I find the very idea of Hell anathema, even though in many churches I'd be anathematised for saying so. No loving God could condemn us to an eternity without Him; no loving God could condemn Himself to an eternity without us. For, in abandoning the least one of us, He is diminished: His love is diminished.' The Dean, who had shown more concern for posterity than for eternity, looked anxious, but Clement was determined not to be deterred. 'The concept of Hell was devised by men to excuse their cruelty. "We're burning your body to save your soul." No, you're burning my body to preserve your power. The greater the punishments they could ascribe to God, the greater the justification they could find for their own. And it worked. Even I, who grew up in the most liberal of church households, feel uneasy about tackling the subject. The most significant human invention may be the wheel, but the most enduring one has been Hell.'

'That is why we should trust in Christ,' the Dean replied. 'Our sins may be great, but His love is greater. And why we should trust in the Church, which is the living body of Christ.' Clement recalled that, for all his worldliness, the Dean was a priest and intent on asserting his authority. 'Your window is a timely reminder that Christ burst open the gates of Hell – on whatever level you wish to take the metaphor – and set us free. Wouldn't you agree, Ms...?'

'I don't have any opinion. I'm a Buddhist.'

'Really? May I ask why?'

'You might just as well ask "why not?"'

'I'm sorry. I assume – perhaps wrongly – that you weren't born one.'

'No, you're right. My husband introduced me to the Dharma when we first met. It's what kept me together when he died. And it has done ever since. It's the faith, religion, value system (call it what you will) that suits me best.'

'Isn't it for you to suit your faith, rather than the other way round?'

'That's a little strong,' Clement said, impelled to stand up for Carla, despite his sympathies lying with the Dean. Ever since Mark's first retreat, he had regarded Buddhism as a soft option; even the names of its saints and sites and practices ended in vowels, in contrast to the consonant-constrained West. The surer he grew that there were many different roads to God and that Christianity was simply the one on which by culture and circumstance he had found himself, the weaker he considered the argument for turning off and turning East.

'Forgive me,' the Dean said to Carla. 'I'm not casting doubt on your sincerity. But, having seen so many Westerners turn to Eastern religion, I've begun to wonder if they look faraway because it's easier than looking into themselves.'

'I meditate twice a day precisely in order to look into myself. Though, of course, the paradox is that I'm aiming to reach a deeper consciousness where I'll see that the self is an illusion.'

'I am an illusion?' the Dean asked incredulously.

'The consciousness that divides you from the rest of the universe is an illusion. We have to learn that all things are one.'

'I'm indebted to you. You've given me a feast for the eyes.' The Dean gestured graciously to the glass. 'And food for thought.' Then, with a smile honed on generations of pew-polishers and flower-arrangers, he apologised for the inconvenience and asked to have a private word with Clement. Looking piqued, Carla returned to the house. Clement, who was expecting a mention of money or transport or some other matter which the Dean deemed to be unsuitable for mixed company, was astounded to hear that Deedes' latest move had been to make a formal complaint about the window to the Cathedral Council, another group of local worthies for whom the Dean had little time. The Council, unable to reach a decision, had referred the matter to the Bishop in his capacity as Cathedral Visitor, and he in turn had referred it to his Chancellor sitting in the consistory court.

'You have to admire the man's tactics,' the Dean conceded. 'He knows better than to complain about the installation of the window, since the FAC's approval means it falls outside the Chancellor's jurisdiction. So instead he accuses me – along with the Chapter – of Conduct Unbecoming for accepting a design that contravenes Anglican doctrine.'

'Might he have a case?' Clement asked, feeling nauseous.

'Oh, don't worry,' the Dean said blithely. 'It's remarkably hard to prove that anything contravenes Anglican doctrine when Anglican doctrine is itself so nebulous.'

'I wish I shared your confidence.'

'My fear is more that he might try to mobilise public opinion. He's very well-connected.'

'Even so, it'll be a nine days' wonder. I've been there before with both my *Two Marys* and my *Pier Palace Christ*.' Clement sought to reassure the Dean, whose desire to create a stir stopped short of causing a scandal.

'There is another matter. I should stress that it's of no concern to me personally, none whatsoever. But it's incumbent on me to speak...' Clement wondered what could be so disturbing that it was causing the Dean to twist both his syntax and his handkerchief. 'He alleges you have AIDS.' Clement was aghast. He felt as if a red light were flashing above his head. His immediate instinct was to deny it, as in all conscience he could, but, scorning to be saved by a technicality, he explained that what he had was HIV and asked how the Major had discovered something he had kept secret from his closest friends.

'I'm not certain, but I understand it's from a woman you met... in Wales, was it? Her mother's some connection of the Major's wife.'

'Christine... it can't be. It must be.'

'Small world.'

'No, just small-minded.'

'We'll fight and we'll win. Of that I have no doubt. But I thought it only fair to warn you.'

The forewarned, forearmed axiom was disproved the following Sunday when Clement was woken by a reporter from the *Daily Mail*, asking him to comment on the revelations in the *News of the World*. While Mike, who picked up – and slammed down – the phone, ran out to buy the paper, Clement sat transfixed by the answer-machine which registered three more such calls. He remembered his father, faced with a media onslaught after *Spirit of the Age*, informing his besieged family that 'in ancient Rome, *editors* were the men in charge of entertainments at the Colosseum. And they're still throwing Christians to the lions!' The memory steeled him to take a call from the *Daily Express* offering £10,000 for sole rights to his story.

'There is no story,' he yelled down the phone, only to find his words refuted when Mike rushed in and flung two copies of the paper on the kitchen table. Clement grabbed one and flicked through it, his confidence growing with every unsullied page, until a glance at the centrespread sent him reeling. Under the headline, *Bishop's Sick Son in Nude Christ Scandal*, was a photograph of himself so grainy that he looked about to expire. Next to it was a report which, while stating the facts with tolerable accuracy, reeked of innuendo, suggesting that he was in league with his parents, aka the Atheist Bishop and Feminist Guru, to destroy everything the nation held dear.

The thought of that pair of unlikely anarchists roused him to action. His painstaking efforts to spare them had backfired. He longed to assure them of both his health and his good faith. Mike offered to drive him to Oxford, but a reluctance to brave the reporters at the gate left him reliant on the phone. As usual, it was his mother who answered. Any hope of breaking the news to her gently was dashed by her announcement that Mrs Shepherd had shown her the paper.

'So she's read it too?'

'She swears that she never takes a single word it says seriously.'

'Let's hope the other three million readers feel the same.'

She tentatively asked him how he felt. Her discreet concern reduced him to tears and he struggled to regain his composure. He promised her that he was fine, quoting the official line that HIV was as manageable as diabetes, but he sensed that she remained unconvinced. After urging him to come down to Beckley and offering to come up to London, both of which he dismissed as impractical, she passed the phone to his father, who was equally defiant but more hurt. As he repeated the questions: 'Are you all right, boy? Are you sure? Are you sure?', irrespective of the replies, Clement wondered if it were his mother's history or simply her gender that made her better equipped to withstand the shock.

He had barely put down the phone when he was rung by Susannah. While her knowledge of HIV made her slower to panic than his parents, her knowledge of the press made her quicker to protest.

'It's outrageous! You must lodge a complaint. Or I will. There's no possible public interest defence.'

'Funny, Mike said the same.'

'It's no time to hold back. Would you like me to come over... talk through some strategies?'

'That's very kind, but not now. There's an army of reporters outside. I figure the less that happens, the more likely they are to leave.'

'I wouldn't be so sure. You must go on to the attack. If we could only feed them another story. When the *Mirror* was planning an exposé of the Snow Leopards and some teenage fans, I got it spiked in exchange for the low-down on a brothel owned by a TV chef.'

'It's hardly comparable,' he replied with a shudder.

'Why not publish your design? *Let the Readers Decide.* That sort of thing. But I know you, Clem. Promise me you won't get on your high horse. Give Christ a loincloth. You and Carla can easily rustle something up. Show that the offence is all in your opponents' minds.'

He thanked her for her advice and agreed to make a public statement. To that end, he offered an exclusive interview to *The Times* which, as the paper of record, had a duty to set the record straight. Wary of being defined by his decor, he arranged to meet Ben, the interviewer, in his studio. Faced with such a self-confident young man, he was doubly determined to be on his guard.

The introductions effected, tea chosen and tape recorder set up, Ben asked if he could 'plunge right in,' flashing a cheeky grin to make up for the innuendo.

'Be my guest,' Clement replied.

'Are you surprised by the strength of feeling your window has evoked?' Ben asked.

'All change provokes backlash. Many people find it impossible to imagine any improvement in a building they've spent fifty years contemplating, even if it's only contemplating its decline.'

'Surely it's more than that? You stand accused of flouting the basic tenets of the Church.'

'That's utter nonsense! I admit I reject several of the Thirty-nine Articles.' He was grateful that Ben's reliance on a list of prepared questions prevented his having to enumerate. 'But I've found that the Church has always afforded me the space to express my dissent.'

'Should the Church have a policy of employing Christian artists?'

'To my mind, yes. Of course, it's perfectly possible to employ excellent artists with different beliefs – or, indeed, none at all – but it reduces the building to the status of a gallery. Try as you might, there's an element of the ersatz to it. You only have to look at the wealth of stained glass produced in Germany since the war. It's all very cold, very hard-edged and abstract: powerful aesthetic qualities but no soul.'

'Yet it's caused far less offence than your own work.' Clement shrugged, forgetting that it would not translate into copy. 'Don't you care what your critics think?'

'Which critics?'

'Fundamentalists.'

'In a word, no. But then I deny the premise of the question. Fundamentalists don't think: they bray; they parrot.'

'What about their claim that your design is immoral?'

'I regard it as a moral imperative to resist intolerance.'

'One of the canons at Roxborough – ' Clement had no need to ask which – 'has described it as liberalism run wild.'

'If there's one thing on which liberals should be dogmatic, it's championing their own cause. Far from the woolly compromise of popular myth, it's the essence of Christianity: a belief in the sanctity of the individual; a definition of *Love thy Neighbour* that doesn't stop at the people who live next door.'

'Critics – I should stress that these are in religious, not artistic circles –' Ben's grin was yielding diminishing returns – 'claim that your assertion of individuality masks a deep egotism.'

'I can only point to the gospel and suggest they cast the beams out of their own eyes before looking for the mote in mine... Actually, I'd rather you didn't use that. I expressed myself badly.'

'Sure thing,' Ben said, at which Clement knew that he had handed him his opening line.

'Creativity is one of God's greatest gifts to us,' he added quickly, 'and it's through our creativity that we both reflect and honour Him. Next to that, ritual and even prayer strike me as arid.'

'Are you saying that you hope your work will lead people to God?'

'That would be presumptuous. Let's just say that I hope it might be a sign-post along the way. Think of the key events of the gospel story – the Nativity, the Crucifixion, the Last Supper – and I'd like to bet that, nine times out of ten, the first thing that springs to mind is an image. The word of God comes complete with illustrations. In no other area of life is the artist so conscious of working within a tradition.'

'Yet you want to destroy that tradition.'

'Not at all! I want to revitalise it. What's the first thing you see when you enter a church? A broken man on a cross. Most Western churches are even built in the shape of that cross. The Church is literally fashioned on suffering. What does that say about the way we see God?'

Ben clearly resented having his prerogative usurped, but Clement's silence obliged him to answer. 'That He takes no prisoners?'

'Right. I swore never to paint another crucifixion after hearing a little girl in the National Gallery ask her mother whether everyone was crucified when they died. It summed up how the Church down the ages has used imagery to reinforce its power: Christ suffered to relieve our suffering but, if we reject His suffering, then we'll suffer in Hell forever. My own work couldn't be more different. Take the *Pier Palace Christ* – '

'That's the one where people put their heads in a wooden cut-out of Jesus?'

'Yes. The one that's earned me the "controversial" tag in your paper ever since. I was accused of being trivial, offensive and blasphemous, but the piece sprang from a deep conviction that Christ is to be found in us all.'

'Wasn't it vandalised?'

'Twice,' Clement replied impatiently. 'But surely the important thing is that more than 100,000 people engaged with it when it was exhibited outside the Serpentine Gallery, and almost a third of them bought a photograph to take home? Even if they did it as a joke, they made some level of connection.'

'Would it be fair to suggest that your unorthodox views are a way to justify your own very public sexuality?'

'You say "public sexuality" as though I spend my life cruising Clapham Common or Hampstead Heath! My sexuality is only public in response to the people who believe I should lie about it.'

'In that case, why have you deliberately concealed having HIV?'

'It's not always easy to live up to one's principles,' Clement said, suspecting that Ben would sacrifice every principle he had ever had for a regular byline. 'I was eager to protect the people close to me. And I admit there was another, more selfish reason. Much of my work is commissioned by the Church, which has never been as willing to embrace the leper on its doorstep as one that's overseas.'

'Leper?'

'I use the word loosely.'

'Yes, of course.' Ben's grin became all teeth. 'One last question and then I'll leave you in peace: are you really saying that you have no difficulty reconciling your Christian faith with your HIV?'

Clement realised that he had given Ben insufficient credit. For all his youth, he knew enough to keep the crux of the matter to the end. 'I was recently on a retreat where I met a woman whose infection was the direct result of her faith...' He stopped short, determined to preserve the confidentiality that Christine, however unwittingly, had stripped from him. 'No, no difficulty whatsoever. After all, if the Eucharist means anything, it's that no matter what else may be in our veins we all share the same blood.'

8

So many flowers were delivered to the house that Clement ran out of vases. Every shelf in the sitting room and hall was crammed with cards. Old friends from Beckley and Wells, from school and the Slade, wrote letters of support. Some sent more tangible tokens. Newsom brought round a small Native American totem which, out of consideration for Mike and an ill-defined sense of unease, he confined to the shed. Mrs Shepherd, showing her customary faith in the healing power of sugar, baked him a date and walnut cake. Most moving of all was a call from Christine, who confessed through stifled sobs how she had unwittingly betrayed him to Deedes.

'You remember the drawing you did of me on the Retreat?'

'Of course.'

'I was so thrilled, I showed it to my mother. I knew she was friends with Mrs Deedes, but I had no idea of the cathedral connection. I never thought... I feel dreadful.'

'There's really no need.'

'Please don't be nice to me!'

'Believe it or not, you've done me a favour. All that secrecy did me no good... no good at all. Do you remember the Japanese soldier they found hiding out in the jungle forty years after the end of the war?'

'Vaguely.'

'I see now that he was me.'

Not all the messages were well-disposed. The Christian Institute published his phone number on its website, prompting a string of nuisance calls, including one from a man who claimed that reading about the window in the *Daily Express* made him feel so dirty that he wanted to rush out and strangle someone, preferably Clement. Even so, such threats disturbed him less than the blunt demands that he repent his sins and turn to Jesus. One letter warned that 'the millions of decent folk who love Our Saviour will no longer take your insults lying down'. Another wondered whether anyone with children would have produced such an abomination. Several, written in different ink but the same hand, exhorted him to 'think of your father and mother naked next time you heap scorn on the Lord'.

Meanwhile, he started work on a full-scale portrait of St Sebastian, partly to occupy his mind in the run-up to the consistory court hearing and partly to occupy Rafik who was desolate at the dismissal of his appeal. He knew that the choice of subject was ripe for mockery. He had already had to contend with Mike, whose humming of *Bring Me My Arrows of Desire* was off-key in more ways than one. The transparency of the symbolism was precisely why he had chosen it. He was consciously invoking tradition, basing both the composition and setting on Altdorfer's Linz altarpiece. In the foreground Sebastian, leaning languidly against a tree, faced an arc of sinewy soldiers drawing bows; in the background a crowd of upright citizens, cloaking their furtive lusts in religious fervour, gaped at the saint's naked flesh.

He studied the half-finished picture as he paced the studio, waiting for Rafik to arrive. He was more impatient than ever to see his model, who had spent the previous afternoon in court. After Shortt's insistence that only the principal parties should attend, Clement had sat up half the night, aching to know the result. Rafik failed to ring and he was reluctant to call Shortt and risk irritating him further. He told himself that no news was good news, a formula that had failed to satisfy him even as a child, and went on to adapt another nursery adage: that the three heads of the Reconsideration judges were bound to be better, wiser and more compassionate than the single one at the Immigration Tribunal.

He had been disgusted by the Tribunal judge who had ruled that Rafik had nothing to fear from a return to Algeria provided that he practised discretion, treating him as if he were a philandering husband with a bit on the side rather than a young man forced to deny his sexual identity. He had wanted to appeal on the grounds of the judge's inhumanity but Shortt, more soberly, had cited the failure to give due weight to the conclusions of the Amnesty report. As he tried to second-guess the panel's verdict, Clement gazed at the bleeding saint who was emerging on canvas and prayed that the model would not suffer a similar fate.

Rafik finally turned up at eleven thirty, disorientated, as Clement had feared, by his experience in court. Clement made him a cup of tea, which he left untouched, and asked for a full account of the hearing.

'What must I say? There are three judges, but no one of them speaks to Rafik. Mr Shortt says to me it must be like this. They must decide if they wish to send case back to Tribunal. But I am there. Why they speak only to him when I am there?'

'I presume they have strict procedures.'

'One judge asks Mr Shortt to say how I am hurt in Algeria. He says I am not hurt. I have left land so I am not hurt. This judge, he says this is not good enough.'

'I'm sure when he thinks it over...'

'I think he is happy when I am hurt. When I come into court with blood and bandage, he says: "Poor Rafik, you sad man, you can stay in this land."'

'He may still say that. Don't give up hope.'

'I must be like Desmond. If I try to kill person then I stay here for ten years.'

'And even if the worst comes to the worst – I'm not saying it will but it's best to be prepared – nothing'll happen for a very long time. We're constantly told that, because of the backlog, people stay on for years after their applications are refused. By then the political situation in Algeria may have changed.'

Rafik gave him such a pitying look that he felt ashamed. 'Do you still wish me to sit for you?'

'If you feel up to it.'

'What else must I do?' Rafik stared at the canvas. 'You make mistake, my friend. Saint is killed with... how you say this?'

'An arrow. Saint Sebastian was killed with arrows.'

'Yes. For Rafik, you must have saint who is killed with stones.'

'Whatever takes your fancy,' Clement replied, eager to lift the mood. 'Maybe next time we'll try St Stephen?'

'This is how you must paint me. This is how you must remember me. It is what must be.'

'If you go on like this, I won't be able to paint at all.'

'In my head I see all village watch man and woman killed with stones. All persons laugh and make happy. Fathers hold sons in sky so they must see.'

As he spoke, Rafik tore off his shirt to reveal livid bruises on his arms and raw weals across his back. Clement was appalled, assuming that he must have been attacked by racists, until Rafik explained that he had spent the night in a Vauxhall club. He had no idea that his body was so scarred and stood, gazing proudly at it in the mirror, twisting and turning to obtain the best view. Clement struggled to assimilate this new image of his model, wondering if it sprang from deep-rooted desire or recent despair. As though reading his mind, Rafik declared that it was his first visit. 'I have no count of men who fuck me. I am nothing, so I say they must do all these things to me. It is small hurt. Not like big hurt in heart.'

Clement examined Rafik's back, keenly aware that after months of contemplation he was fingering his flesh. The touch of the lacerated skin made him tremble. Some of the welts were inflamed, but Rafik adamantly refused to see a doctor for fear that his records would be passed to the court. So Clement soaked a cloth in antiseptic and dabbed it on the scars, praying that he wasn't profiting from Rafik's pain.

'Please tell me if it's none of my business, but you do know about HIV?' he asked.

'I know,' Rafik replied savagely, 'you think because I do not know English, I must know nothing.'

'Of course not. Besides, your English is very good.'

'I know, but I do not care. I let you poison me with fuck if you wish.'

'I don't wish,' Clement replied, desolate to learn how Rafik thought of him.

'Then I go back to my land and I must poison all men who touch me. I let them fuck me in prison and I must smile.'

Rafik resumed his pose as if defying him to protest. Clement picked up his brush but he was unable to see past the pain in the studiedly vacant expression. The image of Rafik's self-abasement was so strong that he was in danger of colluding in it. So, with an apology to the indifferent model, he broke off after less than an hour and cycled home.

Sweating profusely as he carried his bike into the garden, he was surprised to find Mike. 'You didn't say you'd be early.'

'I didn't know.'

'So what's happened?' he asked, muffling a note of panic.

'I've been suspended.'

'What? Why? Tell me.'

'All in good time. I was just going to get out the deckchairs. Make the most of the sun.'

'The sun can wait.'

'So can the story. No use being idle! Now I'm unemployed, I mean to work on my tan.'

Clement choked back his frustration as he helped Mike carry two heavy wooden armchairs from the shed, before fetching a rag to wipe away two smears of something white.

'So, are you sitting comfortably?' Mike asked once they were finally settled.

'What is this? Some sort of game?'

'I wish it were.' His face suddenly clouded. 'I'm sorry. I wanted to tell you before, but with all the shit you've been through it didn't seem fair.'

'But it is fair for me to dump everything on you?'

'In a sense our problems are the same. The kids have been giving me flak on account of all the stuff in the papers.'

'They read them?'

'They save the cuttings! And the routine insults have got worse. The shirt-lifting, brown-nosing batty boy now has AIDS.'

'What?'

'Stop there! If you say it's your fault, I'm done.' Clement kept silent but his thoughts were deafening. When he'd agreed to Mike's requests to talk to the sixth form and take two school parties round his shows, he had warned him not to be too frank about their relationship. It was evident that his fears had been justified. 'The Muslim kids are the worst. They claim your window proves that British churches are perverted.'

'Don't tell me you were forced to defend the C of E?'

'There are limits! No, I abandoned the Treaty of Versailles and described how, whatever things may be like today, for centuries being gay was an integral part of Islamic culture. The class was in uproar but I stood my ground. I explained – quite coolly, I promise – that the only mention of homosexuality in the Quran comes in the story of Sodom.'

'Now there's a surprise,' Clement said, brushing away a wasp.

'And even if they believe that it was dictated to Mohammed by the Angel Gabriel, they have to acknowledge that language fluctuates. Arabic is very variable. The same word can mean to beat someone and to fuck him.'

Clement pictured Rafik's back and feared that the confusion was universal. 'You told them that?'

'Or words to that effect. Several kids complained to their parents, who in turn complained to Derek. The whole crazy business all over again. But this time it's more serious. Two Muslim families removed their daughters from the class. They mounted a small – but noisy – protest outside the school gates.'

'And you told me nothing?'

'This isn't about you!'

'I'm sorry.'

'No, I am. I'm all keyed up. Derek has launched an inquiry. I know I'm vulnerable after the warning he gave me earlier in the year.'

'What warning?'

'To keep to the curriculum. Don't you remember?'

'Yes, of course. But if he makes trouble, you can move elsewhere. Somewhere they'll value your talents.'

'Somewhere middle-class you mean? Preferably private?'

'You've paid your dues. No one could blame you.'

'How would you like to be told to stop painting all your saints and Jesuses and stick to landscapes or abstracts.'

'Point taken. But I can't bear to see you treated so shabbily.'

'I know. And don't think I don't appreciate it. But I've been in touch with the Union. They'll sort things out.'

'I hope you're right.'

Clement was racked with anxiety. It seemed that everyone around him was on trial. Rafik was waiting for the result of the Reconsideration and Mike for that of the Headmaster's inquiry. Meanwhile, his own fate hung on the verdict of the consistory court.

The hearing was fixed for the seventh of July. Mike drove him to Roxborough, setting off at six to beat the traffic, only to be held up by several emergency stops at roadside bushes. Despite Mike's reminders that he was not in the dock but merely giving evidence, Clement was filled with foreboding, which intensified when they arrived at the cathedral to find the Dean less concerned with the prospect of defeat than the problem of accommodation in the court. Unlike Wells with its consistory room in the bishop's palace, the Roxborough court sat in the vestry. The usual handful of spectators had swollen to over a hundred, most of whom would have to be turned away. The crowd was growing restive. One reporter had accused the Canon Precentor of attempting a cover-up, and another offered the Treasurer £500 for his seat. A newspaper that campaigned noisily for the protection of children had bribed two choirboys to sneak in and take photographs, prompting the Chapter Steward to call the police.

'By removing a chest, we'll fit in another bench and we might sit two to a stall, but it'll be a squeeze.' The Dean's well-padded frame quivered in alarm. 'That wretched man! Hell-bent on making mischief! Aside from everything else, it's costing us a fortune. We've had to call in specialist lawyers from London. Win or lose, the Chapter will be left to foot the bill.'

Mike tried to cheer him with the thought that, whatever the costs, the case had brought so much free publicity that, once installed, the window would attract a flood of visitors. The Dean looked unconvinced and, after further execration of Major Deedes, he hurried off to consult the Steward, leaving Clement to kill time by giving Mike a tour of the cathedral. They lingered by the empty East window until, at a quarter to ten, Mike took his reserved seat in court. Clement made his way to the regimental chapel where, beneath the colours and blazons, he spent the morning waiting with his fellow witnesses, his attempt to lose himself in Balzac thwarted by the hiss from the Canon Theologian's iPod. He met Mike for lunch in the cloister café but, after three reporters accosted him at the salad bar and a blue-rinsed woman told him to cut his hair, they fled for a surreptitious sandwich in the crypt. Safe from prying ears, he pressed for details of the proceedings.

'There's not a lot to tell. It's pretty much like a Crown Court, with the same bowing and scraping, except not to "My Lord" but to "Worshipful Sir".'

'Have there been any big dramas?'

'I wish! Forget about keeping me on the edge of my seat; it's barely kept me awake. First Colonel Blimp – '

'He's only a major.'

'Hey, I'm on your side.'

'A joke, I know. Sorry.'

'I repeat, first Colonel Blimp and then a string of dog-collared worthies were examined about the nature of Church authority. No wonder Perry Mason never took on a case in a consistory court!'

Having assured Mike that the best was yet to come, Clement was given a chance to prove it when he was summoned into court soon after lunch. The room was even smaller than the Taylor House tribunal, but it made up in grandeur for what it lacked in size. The fan-vaulted ceiling was more than thirty foot high and the Gothic windows were surrounded by intricate tracery. Despite the crush of bodies, the air was cool with a hint of damp. The four assessors sat in ancient stalls and the spectators on heavy oak benches, with the Chancellor, a retired judge, resplendent in cassock and preaching bands on an elaborately carved throne which, according to the Dean, doubled as a store for surplus surplices. Unlike the tribunal, the barristers for both promoter and defendant were wigged and gowned.

Clement followed the usher to the witness box and took the oath with a show of confidence. Counsel for the Defence rose and asked him a series of questions about his background, work and previous ecclesiastical commissions, which he presumed were designed to establish his credentials, before turning to *The Second Adam* and, in particular, his conception and depiction of Hell.

'Would you tell the Court on what authority you base your image?'

'The story of the Harrowing of Hell has two main sources: the Gospel of Nicodemus, which is, of course, apocryphal, and the early Church Fathers, who were not. I'm loath to quote scripture in such an august gathering – '

'That is why you're here, Mr Granville,' the Chancellor interjected. 'Try to shed your inhibitions. They don't become you.'

'I'll shed as many as I can, my... Worshipful Sir.' Clement thought he saw the ghost of a smile on the Chancellor's lips. 'There are very few references to Hell in the Old Testament and those that there are come late. It was a concept quite unknown to Abraham or Isaac or Moses or David. As for the New Testament, a glance at a concordance reveals twenty-three mentions and two distinct meanings. The first, Gehenna, is a place of absolute damnation where the ungodly roast in eternal flames; the second, Hades, an interim state that houses sinful souls between death and resurrection. Christ himself favours the latter, seeing it as a place of purification, when he declares in Mark Chapter 9 that "everyone will be salted with fire". If the biblical writers failed to agree on a definition, shouldn't we be permitted similar licence?'

'That is precisely what we are here to determine,' the Chancellor replied. 'Pray continue.'

'The Church's position on Hell has changed – I'd like to say, matured

– over the years. The Victorian theologian, FD Maurice, was sacked from his chair at King's for refusing to teach a belief in eternal damnation. Yet the most recent doctrinal statement of the Church of England declared – and I quote – that "Hell is not eternal torment but it is the final and irrevocable choosing of that which is opposed to God."'

'So are we to understand that in the window you are using the image of Hell metaphysically?' Counsel asked.

'No, I'm using it metaphorically... even paradoxically, by suggesting that a place that doesn't exist is given a reality by the people – the religious authorities – who claim that it does.'

After further questions in a similar vein, Counsel for the Defence sat down to be replaced by Counsel for the Promoter, his thin veil of deference failing to mask his disdain. Commending Clement's photographs of the finished window, he asked about the differences between design and execution, in particular the three clerical figures who confined Adam to Hell.

'Contrary to the reports, I never set out to deceive anyone,' Clement said. 'It's a technical matter and may be difficult for laymen to comprehend – '

'Please try to enlighten us, Mr Granville,' Counsel said.

'The differences between a sketch and a finished work can be huge, especially in the case of stained glass. The sketch is exactly that: a sketch, not a blueprint. Even if it were possible, it would be disastrous to include all the detail and simply scale it up in a mechanical way. Delacroix put it best when he said that the drawing is a rehearsal, the painting a performance.'

After thanking him for his eloquence with a sniff that suggested the opposite, Counsel asked about the portrayal of the naked Christ. 'I've been accused of eroticising Christ. A charge I vehemently deny,' Clement replied. 'On the contrary, I'm offering a corrective to a view that has gained a dangerous stranglehold on the Church. The most misleading description of Christ I know is St Jerome's "a virgin born of a virgin". I'm not interested in whom Jesus may or may not have slept with' – he took pains not to alienate the court – 'but with the implications of Jerome's remark. Jesus was a man, and sex is one of God's greatest gifts to us. To reject it in favour of a bloodless chastity is in a very real sense to reject God.'

'Is that why you've given your Christ – I say *your* because, as has become abundantly clear, the authority for the depiction is nonexistent – such large genitalia?'

'I don't wish to be frivolous – '

'Oh please,' Counsel said smoothly, 'don't stop now.'

'But size is in the eye of the beholder. What to you may be large seems to me to be quite average.' He was pleased to be rewarded with a titter. 'Are we to suppose that Our Lord was under-endowed? Look at Michelangelo's David, so monumental in most respects, so modest in that. I don't intend to make the same mistake in this window.'

'But why – and this, Worshipful Sir, is the key question – does he have to be naked at all?'

'I agree; it is the key question. And I'm delighted to have the chance to address it. You've accused me of lacking authority. So I'd like to turn to my own field and cite the many Renaissance portraits of the Virgin pulling up her baby's robe with a flagrancy that, were she to repeat it today, would earn her a visit not from the Wise Men or the Shepherds but the Social Services. Several revered Old Masters, among them Holbein the Elder, Giovanni Bellini and Correggio, go further and depict the infant Jesus with an erect penis. Of course this is a familiar phenomenon in babies. It may also be a symbol of Jesus' potency. But above all it's intended to contrast with Adam, whose first act after the Fall was to cover himself. Speaking personally, I reject the doctrines of both the Fall and Original Sin. In this window, however, I'm concerned not with my own position but the Church's. It is therefore not only doctrinally correct to portray a naked Christ; it would be incorrect to portray him in any other way. In consequence of Original Sin, our genitals are our pudenda, literally our organs of shame – from the Latin *pudere*: to be ashamed.' He seized the opportunity to goad the classically educated counsel. 'But Christ was born without sin, so he has nothing to be ashamed of. He has no more need of clothes than Adam in Eden.'

Clement concluded his testimony and stood down. He glanced at Mike who gave him the thumbs up, which he trusted was obscured from the assessors. He was the final witness and the Chancellor announced that the Court would adjourn until ten the next day. He felt a distinct sense of anticlimax as the Dean, equilibrium restored, rushed up to congratulate him on the excellence of his answers, followed by the Treasurer and Canon Librarian in tandem, who heaped praise on the window which they had at last had a chance to see 'in its full glory'. Unwilling to point out that 'full glory' was precisely what could not be seen in photographs, he thanked them and escaped to join Mike.

'So, are you ready to hit the bright lights of Roxborough?' Mike asked.

'Are you kidding? This is strictly a forty-watt town. Let's go to the hotel.'

They crossed the close to the Choirman's Arms, where Clement had provisionally booked a room. Repeated bruises from the low-lying beams blinded Mike to its old-world charms, but they both admired the ornate Jacobean four-poster. After a quick meal in a dining room crawling with journalists, they fled back upstairs to enjoy an evening of mindless channel-hopping, fortified by the minibar.

'People have lived and died in this bed,' Clement said as he emerged, spearmint-fresh from the bathroom.

'And a lot else besides,' Mike replied with a smile that set the tone for a night which, whether because of Clement's relief or the romantic setting or, simply, their unusually large intake of whisky, was the most passionate that they had enjoyed in months. Clement realised with delight that he was fulfilling both the Chancellor's wish that he should shed his inhibitions and his own claims for the godliness of sex.

The next morning, the desire for privacy outweighing Mike's scruples, they ordered breakfast in bed before returning to the cathedral, where the crush inside the court was even greater than the day before. Judicious shuffling allowed Clement to perch beside Mike on an already packed bench. The Chancellor declared himself eager to press ahead. With no further witnesses to call, he invited both counsels to make closing speeches before summing up with a discernible bias towards the defence. The assessors – four pillars of the local community, two clerical and two lay – retired to consider their verdict. Clement wished he could share Mike's certainty that it was a foregone conclusion, but he was afraid that the Roxborough laity would prove to be representative of Middle England in ways beyond the map. In the event, the assessors found unanimously for the Dean and Chapter. The Chancellor thanked them for their diligence and dismissed the case.

'I trust,' he concluded, 'that the window will now be installed at the earliest opportunity.'

'I'll say Amen to that,' Clement said, finding to his dismay that he had said it out loud.

The Chancellor withdrew and Mike turned to Clement with a pumpkin-sized grin although, in deference to the court if not the cathedral, he gave him only a playful hug. The Dean's handshake was more emphatic and was swiftly followed by the limp, fleshy, clammy and cold hands that Clement had identified on first meeting the Chapter. There was no sign, however, of the calloused palm of Major Deedes, who had stormed out of the room, destroying all hope of reconciliation. The Dean promised to ring Clement with a revised timetable, before leaving for a press conference. Even before the room had emptied, two cleaners began to replace the vestry furniture as routinely as stagehands changing a set.

He returned to London where, true to his word, the Dean called the next morning to arrange the transportation of the window and to schedule the dedication service for the fourth of September.

'Which is perfect because you'll still be on holiday,' Clement told Mike.

'I may be on permanent holiday by then.'

Clement checked that the rest of his family were free. His mother requested front-row seats, claiming wryly that it was from deafness as much as pride. Susannah assured him that the date was in her diary, adding that he had saved her from a trip to Dover to wave a television gardener off on a Channel swim. Carla announced that, now that her pilgrimage to Nepal had been postponed, it would be the high point of her year.

'It's a good thing you're my brother-in-law.'

'Why? I thought I'd singularly failed in that department.'

'Most artists like me to keep out of sight. Less danger of sharing the glory.'

'It's our baby, sis,' he said, his horror only partially relieved by her laugh.

He issued a special invitation to Rafik, who performed a Berber dance around the studio, displaying a rare pride in his Arab roots. Three days later, he was plunged into gloom by the news that his Reconsideration had been refused. 'Take good look at window. It is all you must see of Rafik.' Clement immediately rang James Shortt who, conceding that they had explored every legal avenue, maintained off the record that Rafik's best hope was to go to ground, since the Home Office investigators would be far too hard-pressed to pursue him. His opinion was endorsed by Mike, for whom such rebellion brought a welcome reminder of his youth. Clement, however, urged Rafik to sign on every week at the Immigration Office.

'There's no way anyone's going to throw you out of the country once you're fixed... enshrined in one of our best-loved cathedrals. They wouldn't only be rejecting Christian principles but Christ!'

Rafik took his advice, although less from conviction than from lethargy. He rejected all encouragement and claimed to be resigned to his fate. Clement continued to employ him at the studio but no longer as a model. He was bleary-eyed, unshaven, scruffy and devoid of all vitality, not Rafik but a Rafik lookalike. Clement gave him the title of studio assistant, largely in order to pay him without wounding his pride, but found that he had as little pride in the studio as in the backroom of a club. He just sat silently, rocking his stool to and fro. Sometimes the smell was the only sign that he was there.

Hoping to inspire him, Clement invited him to Roxborough to see the window installed, but he preferred to wait for the service. So, with Mike spending the week at Anita's cottage in Dorset, he made the journey alone. After a courtesy call on the Dean, he gingerly followed the glazier up the scaffolding, more afraid to lose face than footing. Having confirmed that the saddle bars were aligned, he returned to the Trinity Chapel, where he sat scarcely daring to draw breath while the workmen positioned the glass.

Somehow he managed to laugh when the inevitable joker yelled down: ''Scuse us guv, if we drop this one, can you get us another from Pilkington's?'

It was clear why Carla, whose relationship with the glass was so intimate, couldn't bear to attend. A blast of Bach on the organ brought a brief distraction from the hammers and drills, but even its intricate cadences failed to calm his nerves. Finally the hubbub ceased and, as the men scrambled down the scaffolding, he greeted them with mugs of champagne.

'I reckon I could get a taste for this,' the glazier said, wiping his mouth.

'You deserve it after all your hard work,' Clement replied.

'Don't you believe it!' the joker said, demanding a refill. 'Piece of piss!'

'You haven't half put some noses out of joint,' his mate said. 'Bloke from the *Mirror* offered Harry here a thousand quid for a picture of the window once it was in.'

'But you told him what to do with it?' Clement asked tentatively.

'Dead right I did!'

'Yeah, sure! But only when you couldn't get enough of it in the shot.'

Disturbed by the fresh spectre of tabloid interest, Clement consulted the Dean, who seemed more concerned to laud the loyalty of his staff than to acknowledge the prospect of trouble. When pressed, he admitted to having heard rumours that Deedes was planning to picket the dedication service but assured Clement that there would be a large police presence.

'Large?' he asked. 'How many demonstrators do you expect?'

'No more than a sprinkling,' the Dean replied breezily.

Clement recalled their conversation the following week, when he surveyed the hundred-strong mob waving placards under the gaze of three policemen who would have looked overtaxed at a county show. Some of the slogans, such as the complete set of Ten Commandments, were so arbitrary that they looked recycled. Others, such as the attacks on sodomy, blasphemy and pride, were aimed squarely at him. The Major stood to the fore, clasping a sign declaring that idolaters would burn in hell. Clement longed to reason with him but, conscious of the swarm of photographers, preferred to present a picture of dignified forbearance, as he strolled arm-in-arm with his parents, one step ahead of Carla, Karen and her boyfriend Frank. The group lacked only Susannah, who was meeting them inside the cathedral, and Mike, who was en route from London, having waited till the last minute in the hope that Rafik would turn up. Clement was at a loss to explain his absence. They had confirmed arrangements only the day before. He was to join them straight from the Immigration Office. It was as though, by alienating the one person who truly cared for him, he would be able to justify his despair.

They entered the cathedral by the Galilee Porch, beneath a frieze of faceless apostles. Clement instinctively glanced up at the window which was covered by a blue curtain in readiness for its unveiling. As they made their way down the nave, he had an uneasy sense of people averting their eyes as from the chief mourners at a funeral. They reached the front pew to find Susannah already seated, her burgundy suit and art deco jewellery in sharp contrast to the muted tones in the rows behind. She was clutching a wad of papers which she threw down to give him a strangely perfunctory kiss. He sat beside her, skimming through the Order of Service, when he became aware of the Dean, in full canonicals, looming over him.

'We have a crisis on our hands.'

'What? Why?'

'The Bishop's wife's just rang to say he has food poisoning. He daren't move more than a couple of yards from the lavatory.'

'Since when?'

'She said he'd hung on till the last minute.'

'But then he heard all the ruckus in the close! The man's wasted in the Church of England. He should convert to Orthodoxy and count Pontius Pilate as a saint!'

Clement marvelled at the Dean who, slick as ever, turned to his father and begged him to step into the breach, promising that, since he himself was giving the address, it would amount to no more than reading a short prayer and pulling a string.

'I'd be honoured,' he replied and, assuring Clement that there was no need to worry, followed the Dean to the vestry to robe.

'I do hope he'll be all right,' his mother said, 'he's been looking so tired lately. He doesn't need any extra strain.'

'You saw his face,' Susannah said. 'He couldn't wait to get going. It'll give him a new lease of life.'

Clement was about to echo her words when he was deflected by the sight of Mike squeezing in at the end of the pew. 'No Rafik?' he asked, still hoping that he might be trailing behind.

'No Rafik,' Mike replied sombrely.

Further discussion was prevented by the procession of choir and clergy. Watching his father make his way into the sanctuary, so comfortable in his borrowed cope, Clement knew that there was no one whom he would prefer to perform the dedication. He cleared his head and tried to concentrate on the service, which began with *The Lord is My Shepherd*, a hymn neutral enough to satisfy the most agnostic civic dignitary. As the swell of the organ died down, the sound of chanting from the close set up an unwelcome antiphon to the opening collect. The thunderous strains of *Zadok the Priest* brought a temporary lull but, when the Dean mounted the pulpit, the dissident voices once again made themselves heard. He switched on the microphone with the air of a beleaguered chairman at a stormy shareholders' meeting and began to speak.

'This is a moving and historic occasion. If Christianity is to enjoy its fullest expression in the world, it must harness the talents of artists. What's more, it mustn't confine them to the iconography of the past but, rather, encourage them to find new imagery and new forms. Many of the greatest works of Western art were commissioned by the Church. Yet, today, so much religious art has been reduced to the pretty-prettiness of an Advent calendar, conventionally conceived and executed, designed not to offend the most thin-skinned member of the congregation, as though we weren't witnesses to a profound faith but children in Sunday school.

'Great art is often shocking. It jolts the viewer into a heightened awareness. Christian belief should do the same. After all, what could be more shocking than to learn that God became man and was crucified for our sins? There's a vast chasm, however, between art that shocks for its own sake – one might say, out of devilry – and art that shocks because it challenges us to new and at times uncomfortable ways of thinking. I'm convinced that the window we have the privilege of seeing dedicated today belongs to the latter category. It's a genuinely spiritual work by an artist who has reflected on eternal truths and their place in the contemporary world. It forces us to think about ourselves, our relationship to one another and to God. What's more, it presents us with an original and startling image of Christ.

'A good deal of nonsense has already been written about what I've no doubt in years to come will be known as the Roxborough Christ. There can't be a single person sitting here who is unaware what it is about this image that has caused consternation in some quarters.' As if on cue, the voices in the close grew more clamorous and the Dean's more steely. 'But it's an image that speaks to each and every one of us with a power that is, yes, shocking, but also uplifting. Let those who find fault with it look into their own hearts and see where the fault lies. For it's an image that speaks not of flesh and corruption but of love and innocence. It is an image that does honour to God and, hence, to this great cathedral. I am certain that future generations will claim it as their own. In the name of the Father and of the Son and of the Holy Spirit, Amen.'

The Dean announced that, during the singing of the hymn, *Lead, kindly Light*, he would invite Bishop Edwin Granville, the artist's father, to accompany him to the Trinity Chapel to unveil the window. Clement stood as the Dean led his father out of sight, behind the high altar with its huge Crucifixion triptych. The sun streaming through the lancet windows filled him with hope that, as the curtain fell away, its rays would illuminate the faces of Christ and Adam in a sign of divine approval.

Resuming his seat at the end of the hymn, he heard the Dean's disembodied voice rumble through the loudspeakers. 'Right Reverend Father in Christ, we ask you to dedicate this window which has been designed and given for the honour and glory of God and in thanksgiving for this cathedral church of St Thomas and the blessings here received.'

'I am ready to perform the dedication.' Clement winced as the loudspeaker caught his father's every wheeze, accentuating his frailty. 'In the faith of Jesus Christ and in the honour of His Holy Incarnation, we dedicate this window to the glory of God, in the name of the Father and of the Son and of the Holy Spirit. Amen.'

He drew back the curtain on a sunbeam so dazzling that, to Clement's delight, the window appeared to melt. Gazing at the bleached design, he felt as if Hell had been harrowed not just by Christ but by the light of God itself. The sign was more emphatic than he had dared to hope and was confirmed by a collective gasp. He leant back, relishing the play of colour on ancient marble, when, out of nowhere, a spider-like shadow crossed the glass and a brick or stone shot through and decapitated Adam.

Clement stared in disbelief as his work – and Rafik's portait – lay shattered on the cathedral floor. Steadying himself on the pew, he tried to interpret the welter of sounds: the muffled cheers; the screams; the amplified voice calling for a doctor. By the time he'd identified the voice as the Dean's, he was on his feet and following his mother, Susannah and Mike into the chapel. It wasn't the stone or the hole or even the voice that impelled him but another image forming in his mind, which to his horror took shape on the granite flags, his father lying in a pile of shards, his bald head streaked with blood.

His mother made to kneel, but Mike held her back with a warning about broken glass. Susannah kicked away the stone, which rolled towards the rail where it rested as innocuous as a doorstop. The Dean's appeal was answered by not one but four doctors and even a dentist who offered himself in reserve. The Steward rushed up with the news that an ambulance was on its way. Clement stood aside as two of the doctors examined his father. Having agreed that it posed no threat, they lifted him on to a chair, where he opened his eyes abruptly and announced with a blurry smile: 'I'm just grazed. It's nothing. No fuss.'

Giddy with relief, Clement began to shake. Mike moved up and hugged him. 'Everything can be put right, I promise. Look, half the window's intact.' Clement followed his gaze, but all he could see were the cracks.

He took stock of the activity around him. His mother, as defiant of the broken glass as she was of the doctors, knelt beside his father, whose hopes of avoiding a fuss were dashed when more and more of the congregation left their seats and streamed into the chapel. A photographer sneaked up and snapped pictures of him, a splinter sticking out of his scalp like a sundial, until he was checked by a burly choirman who threatened to kick his arse. The Lord Lieutenant strode up officiously but soon found himself as redundant as everyone else. Two policemen, who had come to assess the damage, postured as ineffectively as they had done in the close.

His father tried to rub his head, despite the doctors' injunctions. They were confident that the wound was superficial but stressed that the glass should be extracted in hospital. Meanwhile Carla bent down and began to gather the fragments, breaking off when a policeman yelled at her that it was evidence. He, in turn, looked shocked when she burst into tears. 'It's all right. She made it,' Susannah explained, moving to raise her up. Clement watched everything but felt nothing, except for the arctic wave coursing through his veins. It was only when he glanced at what was keeping him on his feet that he found it was Mike.

He shared in the general relief when the ambulance crew arrived, recoiling when he realised that the crowd was less concerned with his father's welfare than with watching the drama unfold. To his father's mortification, the men ignored his request to walk and loaded him on to a stretcher. Clement and his family followed it into the cloisters, where it was decided that his mother should ride to the hospital in the ambulance while the others drove in Mike's and Susannah's cars. Emerging into the close, he was grateful to find that the bulk of the demonstrators had dispersed. Only a smattering remained, defiantly brandishing placards, one of which bore the slogan *Vengeance is mine saith the Lord*. He was shocked to discover that, for the first time since his schooldays, he longed for it to be true.

As he headed towards the car, he was waylaid by the Dean. 'I shan't keep you,' he said, 'I know you're in a rush. But you must promise me you won't take any of this to heart. They're just yobs. Vandals. Not even Deedes and his mob could stoop so low. The police'll catch them. And we'll repair the glass. We'll have the Roxborough Christ back up, even if we have to put it behind bars.'

'Rather defeats the purpose of a window,' Clement said, shaking his hand and stepping into the car.

At the hospital he and Susannah sat with his mother in Casualty, while the others waited in the canteen. After an hour, a doctor with a smile that looked to have been ironed on came up to inform them that he had removed three pieces of glass from the patient's scalp, stitched it up, and was sending him down to X-ray.

'To see if there's anything left embedded?' Clement asked.

'Don't worry,' the doctor said, stretching his smile. 'But he's not a young man. Best to check nothing's broken.'

The doctor left. Clement put his arms around his mother, who had started to weep.

'You heard, Ma. The X-ray's just a precaution. He'll outlive us all.'

'No, it's not that. I keep thinking of Mark. I don't know why.'

Clement looked at Susannah who stared at the floor. 'Of course.'

He was filled with remorse. Everything that had happened was the result of his intransigence: his insistence on his absolute right to self-expression; his refusal to admit that his belief in freedom might be just as doctrinaire as his enemies' belief in constraint. His spirits rallied slightly when his father returned from his X-rays, unaided if unsteady, showing no more sign of his ordeal than the two large lint bandages on his head. He told his parents that he and Mike would drive them back to Beckley.

'What about Karen?' his father asked.

'She and Frank can take the train,' his mother replied, brooking no argument.

Clement went up to the canteen to find Mike, who was sitting alone with Carla. He relayed the good news about his father and was surprised by their muted response. Rather than heading straight to Casualty, Mike pulled back a chair and told him to sit down. 'You may as well hear it now as later.'

'Hear what?'

'I picked up our messages to see if there was anything from Rafik.'

'And there was?' For the first time since the attack, he felt a ray of hope.

'No, but there was one from the lawyer.'

'Shortt?'

'That's right. When Rafik signed on this morning, he was detained. Without a word of warning they told him they were deporting him to Algeria tonight.'

'But that's illegal!'

'No, he is. Shortt said it's their new tactic. Snap expulsions. Lower figures and less fuss.'

'It's barbaric!'

'They packed him straight off to Heathrow, with no chance to fetch his clothes or anything. They only allowed him one phone call and since he knew we were here, he phoned Shortt, who said that he'd left a special message for you.'

'What? "Fuck you"?'

'No. "Thank you."'

'Just that?'

'That's what he said.'

'What for? Knowing better than everyone else and telling him to stick within the law? Getting him sent back home to die?'

'Things change,' Carla said. 'He may be lucky.'

'You think so? Well he deserves some luck after meeting me. One of the placards back there read *God is not mocked*. Maybe not. But He certainly has a wicked sense of irony.'

2

SUSANNAH

1

The damp seeping up from the flagstones, the lofty virtuosity of the organist, and the quiescent congregation filled Susannah with a deep nostalgia. As she sat in the front pew of Roxborough, waiting for her family's arrival, she found herself transported back to Wells. She had been three at the time of her father's installation and had measured her childhood as much by the Church calendar as by the school year. Even now, when she confined her visits to high days and holidays like courtesy calls on an elderly aunt, the liturgy was in her blood. Surveying the great cathedral, a monument to almost a thousand years of devotion, she was acutely aware of the void in her own life. For all the attractions of a bulging diary, she longed for the simple faith she had known as a girl.

In a painful irony, it was her father who was most responsible for its loss. As a child, she had been embarrassed by his eminence, envying the daughters of a minor canon. As an adolescent, she had been still more embarrassed when he published *Spirit of the Age*, giving her an early taste of the distinction between celebrity and notoriety, the maintenance of which was now her daily bread. She had been twelve when the book came out but, even so, she could see that for a bishop to deny the existence of God while remaining in the Church was the height of hypocrisy. Mark had weathered the storm with admirable ease but Clement, like her, had been hit hard. She still recalled his elation when, after brooding for months over their father's stance, he had reached some sort of epiphany at an art exhibition in Bath.

'This is it! Can't you see?' he asked, as she stared in consternation at rooms which displayed nothing but empty frames. 'Pa is just like the artist. He's showing us the purpose of the frame... the beauty of the frame... the mystery of the frame, even when there's nothing inside.'

Although at the time she had scorned the pretensions of her two-year-older brother, on looking back she applauded his ingenuity. It was typical, however, that he should have extolled work which the average spectator would have viewed as perverse. The same wilfulness was in evidence nearly thirty years on, when he was so convinced of his own integrity that he refused to accept that his opponents might be equally sincere. The chants of 'Cleanse the cathedral!' and 'No more sick art!' filtering in from the close proved otherwise. If he had only been prepared to add a loincloth, the demonstrators would have been appeased.

'Doesn't an artist have a duty not to cause pain?' she had asked him.

'On the contrary,' he replied, 'his one duty is to speak the truth.'

A murmur in the rows behind alerted her to her family's approach. Instead of slipping in by a side-aisle as discretion demanded, Clement had claimed the mother-of-the-bride privilege of a last-minute entrance down the nave. She stood up to greet him and was struck by how handsome he looked in his charcoal grey herringbone suit. Even his hair, which so often seemed an affectation, matched the medieval setting. His flushed face caused her a surge of panic, until she remembered the welcoming party on the green. She flashed him a supportive smile which faded when, as usual, he presented her with his cheek rather than his lips. She responded with a colder kiss than she would have wished. Then, too late to repair the damage, she wondered whether, far from keeping aloof, he was trying to protect her from even the most notional risk.

She turned with relief to Carla, enveloping her in a hug which was made all the warmer by her compliments for her dress.

'I haven't seen it before. Is it new?'

'Of course. I had to mark the momentous occasion.' She regretted that Clement was too engrossed in the Order of Service to hear.

'You're so lucky you can wear such strong colours. Permanent pastels, that's me!'

'Don't be silly. Powder blue looks great on you.' She cast an appraising glance over Carla, whose ash-blonde pageboy hair and well-scrubbed complexion were as bright and wholesome as ever. She wondered how much her affection for Carla, which could not have been greater for a blood sister, depended on her being no threat. Even during her all too brief marriage, Carla had never tried to come between Mark and his family. Which, in turn, might have sprung from her recognition that, no matter how close she was to him, she could never hope to equal his rapport with Clement, that mystical bond which no one, not even a wife, could break. It was as if, by choosing an artist from the scores of women who pursued him, Mark had sought to reassure Clement that he would not be left out. She banished the thought abruptly, conscious that any slur on Mark's motives was the nearest thing to a taboo that their impeccably liberal family would allow.

She turned swiftly to her father, whose joyful 'Hello Nanna', a remnant of her nursery struggles with her name, made her feel at once warm and foolish. As she kissed his tissue-thin cheeks, she was struck by how much frailer he looked away from home. Eighty-two was no longer old. They were living in an age when medical advances had taken Abraham's late-flowering paternity out of the realm of myth and into that of reality, even if, she acknowledged with a pang, there had yet to be any such grace accorded to Sarah. He should enjoy several more years of active life, provided that he was well looked after. On cue she turned to her mother. Age had done little to diminish her; on the contrary, while a mere five years younger than her husband, she had the vigour of a woman of fifty. One of her pet jokes, a reference to the minuscule frame that set her apart from the rest of the family, was that at her height she needed only half the normal amount of energy to survive.

'You look good enough to drink, darling,' she said, giving her a kiss redolent of lunch.

'You mean "eat", Ma,' she replied, fearful that her mother's hard-won grasp of English was slipping with age.

'No, darling, isn't that dress wine-coloured?'

'Of course.' She gave her mother a hug, while wishing that she would restrict herself to a simple epithet, be it 'happy', 'cross', 'well' or 'tired', that would spare her the debilitating attempt to sift through the layers of meaning. 'You're looking pretty fantastic yourself. I don't know many seventy-seven year olds who could carry off yellow-and-purple crêpe-de-Chine.'

'You don't think it's too much, do you? I wouldn't want all the old hens clucking.'

'Of course not, Ma, you're an inspiration to us all.' *Many a true word*... she thought ruefully. She had long wished that her mother had spent less time inspiring the world at large and more looking after her children, or at least that the disciples who had flocked to her side had acknowledged the primacy of a daughter. Even the joys of living in a palace had been compromised by her determination to share it with striking miners and battered wives. She turned back to Clement, unwilling to risk a return to Wells.

'No Mike?' she asked, too quickly to register her mother's warning.

'He's on his way. He's supposed to be bringing Rafik... my model. But there's been no word. That reminds me; I must switch the mobile to Vibrate.'

'Clement, you perve!' Karen said, leaning forward from the pew behind. 'You're in church!'

'Thank you, Karen,' Susannah said in mild reproof, pecking her on the cheek and wondering whether her sense of responsibility towards her non-stepdaughter would ever end.

She had been twenty-one when she first met Chris. At a stroke, she found the perfect focus for her belated adolescent rebellion. Chris was the ultimate challenge to her parents' values. Unlike her brothers who had asserted themselves by their choice of subject (Clement at the Slade) and setting (Mark at Sussex), she escaped from their cloistered world by refusing to study at all. At eighteen she moved to London, intent on experiencing everything that youth and the capital had to offer, spurning the fig leaf of her mother's 'university of life' by insisting that her sole aim was to have fun. She found a job as an assistant PR in a record company and, in 1989, when one of their groups, The Snow Leopards, got their big break as support for Shakespeare's Sister, she got hers by joining them on tour. It was then that she came to the attention of Chris who, having started out as a roadie for various bands, had set up on his own as a manager.

She was easy prey for his wide-boy charm. Far from offending her by its crudity, his 'When I take you home tonight, will there be a boyfriend in your bed?' disarmed her by its frankness. It set the seal on all that followed. She revelled in his feral energy: his flagrant delight in making money, a far cry from her father's sheepishness about his family wealth; his undisguised scorn of 'oiks', a relief after her mother's academic egalitarianism. Whatever his faults, he was not lacking in self-awareness. 'I know I'm vulgar,' he declared, sprawling on his red leather sofa, 'but I like it.'

She moved in with him after a particularly passionate evening. Her mother warned that she was far too young to make such a commitment, not least because she would be taking on his two small children. It was precisely because she was so young that she saw them as a blessing, picturing herself as Julie Andrews fresh from the convent, bringing sweetness and light to a motherless household. The reality proved to be very different. Five-year-old Karen and four-year-old Bill had been so traumatised by their mother's death that they were more likely to pull the petals off roses and whiskers off kittens than to sing about 'a few of my favourite things'. With a determination that surprised even herself, she set about rebuilding their lives. She stuck it out for seven years, until Chris's drinking spiralled so far out of control that she feared for her safety. She agonised over leaving the children, but Chris, to his credit, allowed her to see them whenever she wished, as long as she never set foot in the house. On his arrest eighteen months later, she took the children to live first with her and then with her parents.

'They're a tribute to you, darling,' her mother had said. 'When I think what they were like when you first brought them here. Swinging on the tapestries. Throwing stones at the swans. It just goes to show; all that children need is the right kind of love.'

'Thanks, Ma,' Susannah replied, forbearing to add that she might have a very different take on the noble savage if, instead of field trips to Africa, she had spent some time in the East End.

For all her efforts, neither child turned out quite as she would have wished. Bill was the first pupil from Linden Hall ever to join the army; but, while commiserating with his teachers, she was secretly relieved that he had found a legitimate channel for impulses which might otherwise have been as dangerous as his father's. Karen meanwhile flitted from man to man and fad to fad, a self-destructive pattern which Susannah blamed on her discovering the truth about Chris. Whatever his faults, he was a devoted father, and Karen had been devastated by the news of his arrest and conviction for an arson attack in upstate New York.

'He didn't do it! He couldn't have! I know him!' she had cried.

'We hired a top-notch attorney.'

'It's all corrupt. Everyone's corrupt.'

'That's what your dad was banking on,' Susannah replied. 'It was his whole philosophy of life.'

It was one which had left him increasingly vulnerable. He narrowly escaped charges after dangling the double-dealing manager of a Manchester nightclub from a fourth-floor window. He was pilloried in the press after Jack-in-the-Box, a decorative but uninspired boy band, complained that supporting Alice's Kitchen on tour meant providing sexual services for a string of middle-aged promoters. By dispensing bribes and trading favours, he was able to stay one step ahead of the law at home, but the Snow Leopards' success in the States proved to be his undoing. Against all advice, he refused to buy off the Mafia, who ousted him after the group went platinum. His public vows of revenge meant that, when the Albany concert hall burnt down on the eve of their first performance, no one believed his professions of innocence. Susannah herself didn't want to believe them. For all her grievances against him, it was intolerable to think of an innocent man being locked up for twenty-five years.

The memory chastened her and she turned round to give Karen a broad smile, happy to see that, with her hair tied back, the green tips might be mistaken for a ribbon.

'You've not said hello to Frank,' Karen said.

'Oh I'm sorry. I didn't know... we've not been introduced.' She gazed at the bloodless, scrawny young man who would have been perfect casting for a Dickensian clerk. 'Hi, I'm Susannah.'

'Ank...' he mumbled, holding out a limp, moist hand. As Susannah shook it with a shudder, she wondered how Karen could bear his touch.

She was jolted out of her reverie by the Dean's news that the Bishop, suffering from an upset stomach, was unable to perform the dedication. Clement, with his taste for the dramatic, muttered something about Pontius Pilate. She stroked his arm protectively while pondering the ghastly prospect that the service might be postponed, requiring them to return another day. The Dean proposed that her father take the Bishop's place. His eager acceptance held the lie to his happy retirement, and he hurried to the vestry to robe.

'I do hope he'll be all right,' her mother said, 'he's been looking so tired lately. He doesn't need any extra strain.'

'You saw his face,' she replied. 'He couldn't wait to get going. It'll give him a new lease of life.' Clement seemed set to agree when he was distracted by the sight of Mike. She suppressed a twinge of envy at their easy intimacy, which felt like a reproach to her own solitary state.

The sight of choir and clergy processing down the nave lifted her spirits. Timelessness was the closest the Church came to eternity and she took heart from the age-old ritual. Her father brought up the rear in his gilded cope. For once she was glad that she had no more than a nominal faith or she might have been offended by the speed with which he had assumed its trappings. The organ thundered to a halt, and the Dean moved forward to welcome the congregation, seemingly oblivious to the chants which showed no signs of dwindling now that the service had begun.

The opening hymn was *The Lord Is My Shepherd*, and she relished its familiar cadences. Her last visit to church had been at Beckley the previous Christmas, when so many of the carols had been in medieval French that she had asked, only half-frivolously, if they were subject to an EU directive. She smiled at the recollection before sitting for the address, feeling a rush of compassion for Clement as he squirmed beneath the Dean's plaudits. During the second hymn, the Dean escorted her father behind the altar, from where their disembodied voices rang out like airport announcements. After offering a prayer of dedication, her father drew back the curtain so discreetly that she longed for the resounding crack of a champagne bottle. She stared at the window, keen to inspect the cause of the controversy, but the sun was so bright that the glass looked molten and the design was obscured.

Subsequent events occurred too fast for her to be sure of the sequence. She heard – or, rather, saw – a smash when a stone shot through the glass.

'Is there a doctor... anyone... a doctor?' The Dean's voice, shocked from its neutrality, filled her with fear for her father. She ran out of the pew, stumbling as her heel caught on a time-worn memorial, and entered the chapel to find him lying covered in splinters like a felled shop-window dummy. Her instant assumption, more reflex than thought, that he must be dead was belied by a faint moan. She stood transfixed as a quartet of doctors hurried to his aid, while a dentist, doing nothing to confound the profession's reputation for perversity, offered himself in reserve.

'The ambulance is on its way,' an official shouted, just as the doctors agreed that it was safe to lift the patient on to a chair. A palpable sense of relief spread through the onlookers, pierced by a loud scream from Karen, whom she calmed with a shake and a hug.

A pack of ghouls descended on the chapel, hovering behind the rail as though distance ensured discretion. A photographer with fewer scruples snapped furiously at her father, who sat like a deposed monarch, a glass splinter the sole relic of his crown. An indignant choirman saw off the photographer but failed to spot the choirboy who was taking pictures on his mobile phone. She was about to object when she was called on to console Carla, whose attempt to rescue the fragments had been thwarted by an overzealous policeman.

The ambulance crew arrived, exuding a welcome air of professionalism. She was relieved by her father's reluctance to lie on the stretcher although, with her own legs threatening to give way, she would have happily taken his place. The Dean led the procession through the cloisters like a party of monks spiriting away an ancient abbot at the Reformation. They reached the close where, to her dismay, they found themselves face to face with a handful of pickets. It beggared belief that any of this ragged bunch, who lowered their voices in deference to the stretcher while keeping their placards defiantly raised, could have thrown the stone. She longed to confront them with the innocent victim of their violence but suspected that, given their loathing of his views, they would regard it as divine providence. Meanwhile, their primary target eluded them, making straight for his car. She followed suit and, stopping only to collect Carla, Karen and Frank, set off for the hospital.

The radio came on along with the engine, bringing a stream of stories about a Hindu riot in Kashmir, a suicide bomb in Baghdad and a victory for the Religious Right in their advocacy of 'intelligent design' in Ohio. It felt as if the attack on the window were part of a wider struggle, although she was unable to determine quite what it was or on which side she stood. Then a lorry pulled out ahead, forcing her to focus on the road.

At the hospital she sat with her mother and Clement while her father was examined. The wait dragged interminably and she was desperate for a cigarette, but the fear of being found wanting kept her rooted to her seat. She attempted conversation, only to find that, having skirted the broken glass in the cathedral, she was treading on more here.

'Don't worry, Ma, he'll be fine. The wound's superficial.'

'Nothing's superficial at eighty-two, darling. Not even shock.'

Silence descended again, although now her apprehension was tinged with guilt, which she sought to deflect on to Clement for his blatant disregard of other peoples' feelings. She longed to make him see that, rightly or wrongly, not everyone thought the same way as he did. He professed to be a liberal but he was just as doctrinaire as any of his critics. Not content with having made religion a seaside sideshow with his cut-out Christ, he had made it a locker-room peepshow with his nude one.

'You don't realise that some people take their faith seriously,' she said, as he tore into the fundamentalists.

'Yes, and I'm one of them,' he replied, 'I just don't take it simplistically.'

After an hour, a junior doctor with a painting-by-numbers smile came to tell them that he had removed all the glass from her father's skull and sent him down for an X-ray. The news that, on his return, they would be able to take him home reduced her mother to tears. Clement moved to hug her, leaving Susannah feeling painfully left out, until her mother's mention of Mark readmitted her to the family circle, albeit a circle of grief. She caught Clement's eye and was comforted to know that they shared the same image: of a brother dying not in the clinical efficiency of a Midlands hospital but the teeming chaos of Mumbai, with no one but a consular official by his side.

Her father's arrival saved her from sinking into depression. His head was as heavily bandaged as for a farce. Her mother echoed the doctor's prescription of rest, insisting on an immediate return to Beckley. While Clement rounded up the canteen contingent, Susannah fussed over her father, extracting his promise to take things easy over the coming weeks. When everyone was assembled, she took her leave of her parents and, feeling that more had been shattered than the window, bustled Carla into the car.

2

However late she had gone to bed, Susannah aimed to be at her desk by eight. It was her private time, when she could make plans and study proposals without having to field calls from clients and questions from staff. This morning, despite the memos and faxes piled in her tray and the email locked in the deceptive blankness of her monitor, she needed a chance to take stock. After the dramas at the cathedral of which she had been a mere onlooker, it was crucial to remind herself that in her own world she was a player. So, doubly grateful for her solitude, she ran her eyes down the rows of posters for past and present projects and the shelves of awards for successful campaigns. She picked up the endearingly misspelt invitation from Precious to spend a weekend at a health farm and, for all that the prospect of stripping off in front of a taut and tattooed rap queen filled her with terror, she relished the token of respect.

The events of the previous day preoccupied her and she was anxious to check up on her father. She began to dial Beckley, before realising that at half-past eight her parents might still be asleep, so instead she called Clement for whom she felt no such qualms. Reaching his machine, she left a message of support with a promise to ring back later. Then, switching on her computer, she scrolled through the stack of email that had accumulated while she was at Roxborough. At the top was one from Wilson Tierney's New York management asking for reviews of his recent UK tour, evidence that her strategy of selective quotes had failed. Wilson, who had split from Alice's Kitchen not long after she left Chris, had been her very first client. He had kept faith with her throughout his glory days and, even though his star had waned, his picture remained in pride of place on her wall.

She searched for his file in growing frustration, regretting that she had ever been persuaded to have the room feng shued. She extended her search to the outer office, where she found no one but Matt, whose files, along with the rest of his life, were electronic. Although she was fond of Matt, she was never wholly at ease with him. Like the rest of the team, he haunted media hotspots, cultivating admen and journalists, but he did it all online. Despite the lip-service she paid to the new technology, she feared that it was leaving her behind.

She strolled to his desk and glanced at his screen, her dread of discovering something unsavoury allayed by evidence of a late-night/early-morning conversation with one of his contacts in LA.

'Anything interesting?'

'He claims to have all the dope on the judges for the Grammies but it's already been leaked to the *Enquirer*. Oh, and you're not a fan of Brendan O'Neal, are you?'

'Do I look like a fourteen year-old schoolgirl?'

'It seems he was rushed in to Cedar Sinai last night for treatment for a gerbil enema.'

'Gross!'

Susannah shuddered and returned to her desk, answering email until she was summoned to the ten a.m. conference. She knew that several of the staff, including Matt, saw it as a whim they were obliged to humour but, schooled in her father's methods – the 'Just call me Edwin,' addressed to the humblest curate – she set great store by such consultation. Stubbing out her cigarette, she took her seat at the table of three women and eight men. Her early defiance of the conventional wisdom that her own sex made the best PRs had long been vindicated. Not only had her gravest crisis – slit wrists and a police inquiry – occurred when a female assistant refused to see that an ageing rock star's 'I love you's' were as routine in his bed as in his lyrics, but her happiest working relationships had been with men. They had repaid her trust and, while she would never have dreamt of abusing theirs, she enjoyed the gossip about 'Susannah and her boys'. She broke into a smile, which was instantly erased by an image of herself twenty years hence as a sharp-tongued, chain-smoking harridan, wearing ever chunkier jewellery, and dyeing her hair some fairground colour in a vain attempt to stop the clock.

'Shall I fetch you a Perrier, Susannah? You've gone red,' Alison, her assistant, asked.

'I'm just hot. And, no, it's not my age, Marcus,' she said, gazing at her newest recruit who, given his youth and inclinations, doubtless regarded any woman over thirty as menopausal.

She turned her attention to Adrian, who announced that he had finished the pitch for the *Reveille* trainers campaign and hoped to run it past her during the morning.

'It sucks that they're making us bid for it,' Matt said. 'They saw what we could do on the Shaughnassy tour.'

'Different worlds,' Adrian replied.

'Are you sure it's worth the hassle?' Davinia asked. 'There'll be no chance of any other trainers for two years, when I know for a fact they're considering us for the new *Nike*.'

'I've sweated blood over this,' Adrian said. 'Ben Dutton swears it's in the bag.'

Susannah expressed faith in both Adrian's work and his relationship with Dutton, before asking Verity for an update on the aftermath of the Diorama launch.

'There's no more talk of a skin graft,' she replied to general relief. 'The company have upped the compensation. Signs are she'll accept.'

'Amen to that!' Susannah said. 'Meanwhile, remember the golden rule. From now on, if anyone asks for a circus theme, make it clowns not fire-eaters. And keep them away from the punch!'

Further damage limitation was required when Robin reported the savage review of the Furry Joists concert in the *Telegraph*, adding that he had already had their irate manager on the phone.

'What did he expect?' Susannah asked. 'I warned him Henty would pan it. He always loathes their stuff. But Jake insisted we invite him. So what exactly does he want us to do?'

'Get the guy sacked,' Robin replied.

'You're not serious?'

'He said he'd call back.'

Seconds later the phone rang, prompting claims that the office was bugged. 'It's Jake,' Alison mouthed to a muffled cheer.

Susannah wound up the meeting and took the call at her desk. After listening to the manager's catalogue of complaints, she offered an equally forthright reply. 'Whether or not you choose to use us again, Jake, is entirely up to you, but I've no intention of taking the matter further. Being two minutes late after the interval is hardly a sackable offence.'

'If you won't do it, I'll find myself a PR who will.'

'Then you'll find yourself a bad PR.'

Extricating herself from Jake, she embarked on the endless round of phone calls that made up her day. Contrary to the popular belief that she flitted from business lunches to champagne launches to opening night parties, she spent more time on the phone than a telesales operator. She did manage, however, to grab a moment between the editor's assistant at *Tatler* and an editorial assistant at *Vogue*, a distinction indicative of Precious's equivocal status, to ring home and ask after her father.

'He insists he's fine,' her mother said. 'He's grumbling because I've made him spend the day in bed.'

'Isn't that a little drastic? I'm not suggesting he go for a five mile hike, but – '

'I'm worried. It's hard to put my finger on what it is exactly, but he's not himself.'

Susannah tried to reassure her mother, angry with herself for noticing the click of her incoming email and even angrier when, more in her clients' world than her parents', she advised her to 'give him his head'.

At five o'clock, she drove Marcus and Davinia to Woking to see the Atlases, a troupe of male strippers for whom they had been invited to pitch. Although at first mildly amused by her passengers' ribaldry, she began to dread the non-stop innuendo, wondering how much mileage they could extract from signs for *concealed entrances* and *heavy loads*. Worse was to come when they reached the theatre to be greeted by Mandy, the company manager, a bosomy twenty-five-year-old with acne scars. Her pretensions were painfully exposed as she led them to the hospitality suite for 'a light repast in line with the evening's entertainment'. Given the conversation in the car, Susannah half-expected coq au vin and spotted dick but, to her relief, found falafel, taramasalata and hummus. 'Atlas,' Mandy helpfully explained, 'was Greek.' Davinia and Marcus fell on the snacks with the relish of those for whom free food was still a novelty. Meanwhile Mandy outlined the Atlases' many attractions, from customised merchandise to obsessive fans.

'What marks them out from the competition,' she said, 'is that they're not heterogeneous.'

'Hetero*geneous*!' Davinia repeated as Marcus looked up from the olives.

'We have a black Atlas and a half-caste... that's a mixed-race one. We even have an Asian Atlas, which is a first. Most of them find it hard to bulk up,' she added confidentially. 'What we want, as I'm sure Gaz and Tel have told you, is to take the group up-market. We have an image problem. In a word *tacky*! The appeal is still mainly to socio-economic groups C and D. The boys deserve better.'

'We do indeed,' Marcus said.

'I meant the Atlases,' Mandy replied with a nervous laugh. 'You and me, Suze – you don't mind if I call you Suze, do you?'

'Be my guest.'

'She has no side, our Suze,' Marcus interjected.

'You and me, if we're bored of an evening, we can read a book or listen to some classical music or... or paint a picture.' Davinia choked on a falafel. 'But these women – the Cs and Ds – what do they have?'

'*Etch-a-sketch*?' Marcus suggested.

'They have us,' Mandy said, her smile wavering. 'Which is all well and good. But we want to broaden our appeal. We want the As and the Bs. That's why we've come to you.'

'I hope we can help,' Susannah said. 'But it's seven thirty. Shouldn't we...?'

'Hark at me: talk the legs off an iron pot, so my mother says. Don't worry, we always go up five minutes late.' Mandy led them back to the foyer, handing them passes to wear round their necks.

'Atlas Security Pass,' Marcus read out. 'Access all areas.'

'That's all areas of the theatre,' Susannah said dryly.

'That's right,' Mandy said, 'you'll need them after the show. I've arranged for you to have a meal with some of the boys, if you have time.'

'We're night owls,' Davinia said.

'I think you'll be impressed. They're not what you might imagine. One's a trainee accountant. Another's a Christian.'

'How does he square it with all this?' Susannah asked, her interest momentarily aroused.

'He says that God doesn't mind so long as he keeps on his G-string.'

As they edged through the teeming foyer, Marcus faltered on finding that he was the only man in the audience.

'I feel like the Pope at a bar mitzvah.'

'Given the way some of these women are eyeing you,' Susannah said wickedly, 'it won't just be the liver that's chopped.'

The show was fast, slick and soulless. The music was so amplified and the audience's yells so deafening that Susannah longed to fulfil Mandy's fantasy of socio-economic group A and lie on a sofa listening to Schubert. She wondered whether the women were aping men, a verb that felt peculiarly appropriate, because they wanted to or because it was expected of them. It was as if the ideal of sexual equality for which her mother and her friends had fought so hard had been for nothing more than the right to shriek 'Gerremoff' as crudely as men. The irony was that the evening's climax was a brutal reassertion of male power. Two bikers appeared astride their Harley Davidsons. After taking off maximum clothing with minimum effort, they called for a volunteer. Far from the usual unease at such requests, the entire audience, apart from Susannah herself and a strangely subdued Marcus, jumped up and held out their hands. Having selected their victim, the men flung her between them like a rag doll before thrusting down on her in a simulated rape. Susannah was appalled, not least to realise that no one else found it disturbing. The theatre resounded with screams of approval which grew even louder when three policemen strode on and, after subduing the bikers in a desultory skirmish, handcuffed them to their machines. They lifted the woman up but, far from helping her, they stripped off their uniforms, twirled their truncheons and took over from the bikers. The routine was greeted with tumultuous applause and, in an attempt to gauge its sincerity, she turned to her neighbours, a grandmother, mother and daughter, who all looked the same indeterminate age.

'Did you enjoy that?' she asked.

'It was great,' the mother said.

'Lucky cow,' her daughter added, while the grandmother was too overcome to speak.

At the end of the show, Mandy led them to a dressing room smelling strongly of patchouli. They were introduced to the four Atlases who were to join them for dinner which, whether because she no longer felt the need to stick to the Hellenic theme or from the lack of a suitable taverna, Mandy had booked at 'the best Indian in Woking'. Stifling her distaste in deference to the anomalous Asian, Susannah made her way to a taxi, where she found herself wedged beside a Yorkshire Atlas with blond dreadlocks and thighs as thick as her waist. She was torn between irritation and arousal at his whispered admission that 'I'm a sucker for older women', toying with the prospect of a toyboy as he rubbed against her leg. His intimacies increased as he led her to the table where, after a brief discussion of the menu, the company split into four. She awarded Mandy full marks for skill, if not subtlety, at the handpicked choice of escorts: the Asian cowboy cracking jokes and popadoms with Davinia; the mountainous biker relaxing his guard with Marcus; the indefatigable Rock ('by name and by nature') paying fulsome tribute to her breasts. '36C,' he judged, with unnerving accuracy. As the meal wore on and his conversational mix of paintball, high-protein diets and kung fu movies proved to be even less appetising than the curry, she realised that the price of a gym body was a gym mind. So when the incongruous cuckoo clock struck twelve, she announced that it was time for the London contingent to depart, to be met with diffidence (Davinia) and brazenness (Marcus) as they offered to make their own way home.

Having reminded herself that they were above the age of consent, even if, in Marcus's case, not always that of responsibility, she reminded them that they were due in the office at nine thirty on the dot. Any vestige of regret at her failure to explore the Rocky landscape vanished when he put his lips to her ear and whispered: 'Are you sure I can't make you change your mind? I'm nine and a half inches,' to which, thanking God and the six penalty points that had ensured her sobriety, she replied, 'Cap or crotch?' The ensuing drive was so dreary that she even began to hanker for one of Marcus's *manholes*. At least she was able to smoke, free of the smug disapproval of people whose organ of abuse was the nose. She arrived home wrapped in misery, which she assured herself was cultural not sexual.

Her spirits sank still further the following morning when she walked into the conference room to find a bright-eyed Davinia and Marcus regaling their colleagues with lurid accounts of their antics the night before. Affecting not to notice the hush that greeted her entrance, she ran through the regular agenda before raising the subject of the Atlases.

'On mature reflection I've decided not to pitch for them.'

'But the contract's in the bag!' Davinia said. 'Mandy as good as promised.'

'That may be,' Susannah replied. 'But I'm not taking on a group of muscle-bound morons who've pulled themselves up by their jockstraps.'

'Someone not impressed by Mr 9½ inches!' Marcus suggested in a whisper as piercing as Rock's the previous night.

'You said it, Marcus! The biggest thing about him is his ego. Listen guys, I'm just being practical,' she said, afraid of being thought priggish. 'What's the point of having the place feng shued if we go for something so sleazy? No matter how hard they try to change their image, they're forever stuck in the nineties. They'll never make the water cooler today.'

Susannah returned to her desk, where her gloom was compounded, first by a postcard from a former colleague who had thrown up her job to 'find' herself in Peru, and then by a phone call from a friend whose tearful account of failed IVF treatment chipped away at the cornerstone of her faith: *That There Is Still Time.*

She spent the morning trying to minimise the fallout from the catalogue to the jade exhibition at the British Museum. The introduction by Sir Peter Lyons, chairman of the principle sponsors, Weston Tea, had been reprinted in Hong Kong and, having ignored her warning that his reference to the Opium Wars would offend the Chinese, Lyons blamed her for the threat of a boycott that had shaken Weston's shares. Although the first rule of her profession held that, when a campaign went well, it was to the credit of the client and, when badly, it was the fault of the PR, she refused to be made a scapegoat, sending him a robust reminder of how he had dismissed her objections as political correctness and enclosing copies of the relevant email. Needless to say, he did not reply.

His rudeness fuelled her disenchantment with the world she had inhabited for more than twenty years: the arrogant editors and venal journalists who considered themselves to be more important than the people they profiled; the celebrities who claimed her as their dearest friend at the start of a campaign and then forgot her name the moment it was over; the rising stars who abused their power and sulked when the media denounced their antics; the fading stars who failed to attract coverage and expected her to bolster their self-esteem; the lovingly nurtured assistants who broke away, eager for 'new opportunities', which invariably meant poaching her clients. On top of which, to the public at large, the work itself was parasitical. No matter how tough the brief or how original the promotion, it fed off other, genuine talents.

Sensing the onset of self-pity, she was especially glad to have arranged a girls' night out with Carla. Unlike Clement whose faith and vocation intimidated her, Carla put her at her ease. Just as she never called herself an artist, preferring the more modest *craftswoman*, so she never called her beliefs a religion. On the contrary, she claimed that the Buddhist 'don't take our word for it, but seek out the truth in your own lives' credo was the antithesis of Christianity. When pressed, she would describe herself as spiritual, quoting a friend's definition that religious people were afraid of going to Hell, whereas spiritual people had been there. The events of the past two days had deepened Susannah's feelings of futility. She longed for a more purposeful existence: to be someone for whom 'having my feet done' meant reflexology rather than a pedicure. She knew better, however, than to confuse escape with discovery. The secret was to find herself in Notting Hill, not Peru.

Having left the choice of restaurant to Carla, she was dismayed to realise that *Ne Goryui*'s authentic Georgian atmosphere extended to personal hygiene. She was determined not to carp and addressed the problem by the judicious application of her napkin and ordering food that was even more pungent than the waiters. They discussed the Roxborough debacle over yoghurt soup, with Carla explaining that the Dean had already consulted her about repairs. Then, while she waited for turkey in walnut sauce and Carla for cheese pie, she described her brush with the Atlases. Carla, who knew of the troupe by repute, said that, for people with no inner life, sexuality had become the all-important measure of authenticity. 'What about people who don't have either?' Susannah asked, feigning a laugh. When Carla failed to pick up on her tone, she described her recent humiliation at a party where, seeing a sad-looking middle-aged man on his own, she went over to talk to him, only to endure a ten-minute eulogy to his girlfriend after which he rushed off to refill his glass, never to return. It was left to her hostess to explain that he was afraid she was chatting him up.

'Who was it said that no good deed went unpunished?'

'Whoever it was, it isn't true,' Carla replied. 'Every good deed adds to the store of merit in the world.'

'I envy you your certainty. You have such resilience... such strength.'

'So do you. As the Buddha teaches us, you just have to look within.'

Susannah had never found Carla's faith more attractive. While she bewailed her single state and the imminence of her fortieth birthday, Carla bore Peter's defection with her usual stoicism. But, however much she longed for peace of mind, Susannah knew that she would never find it in Buddhism. Her one experience of a meditative retreat had been a disaster. She had scarcely quelled her suspicions of a group from whose tongues every abrasive note appeared to have been surgically removed, when she was plunged into incredulity by a plump middle-aged couple, looking like a pair of skittles, who had rhapsodised on the joys of levitation.

'I've tried. Remember the retreat? I've ummed for England... if that's not a contradiction in terms. But it all seems so alien to me. I need a faith, a discipline... call it what you will, that's closer to home.'

'Have you thought of Kabbalah?'

'Oh please!' Susannah laughed. 'I may work in PR, but credit me with some integrity. *PR World* described it as the best networking opportunity in town.'

'I don't mean the Kabbalah Centre. All that Madonna crap! Rachel Gibbon, one of my neighbours – you met her at my summer party – goes to a private class run by a Chassidic rabbi.'

'Thank you very much! They're seriously scary. All those pasty faces and corkscrew curls!' She felt an instant revulsion as much at their appearance as their ideology, before reflecting that that might be part of her problem, which she would need to address if she wanted to engage more profoundly with life. 'Where's it held?' she asked casually, 'Stamford Hill?'

'Don't worry. Hendon.'

'And that's better?'

'You're such a snob! Though I gather they're just as bad. Not so much preaching to the converted as to the chosen. Of course that wouldn't be any obstacle for you, with your mum being Jewish.'

Susannah felt strangely intrigued. The longing to reach beyond her day-to-day existence had never been stronger. Moreover it would be an opportunity to learn about the Judaism that was part of her heritage but had never been part of her life. Her mother had found it hard enough as an atheist married to an Anglican cleric without dwelling on her Jewish background. Clement had an idiosyncratic faith in which Christ was remade in his own image. Mark had rejected all dogma and turned East. She herself had been left with a comfort-blanket Christianity, which was looking increasingly threadbare. What an irony it would be if the side of her she had yet to explore should prove to be her salvation! So, while making no commitment, she asked Carla to contact Rachel for details of the class.

3

Fireworks exploded unnervingly close, lighting up the affluent north London street. Susannah shivered in the early evening chill as she strode down the garden path, striving to keep pace with Rachel. They were greeted at the door by their hostess Layah who, apologising for her floury hands, asked Rachel to show Susannah inside while she finished off in the kitchen.

They walked through the cramped hall past a large leather rhinoceros and into an airy room dissected by a white curtain. 'It's called a *mechitza*,' Rachel whispered, even though they were alone. 'The men sit on one side and we sit on the other. The Rabbi stands there, in the alcove, so he can talk to us all.' Although forewarned of the segregation, Susannah found it disturbing, bracing herself with the image of a TV dating show where only the host knew who lurked behind the curtain, before dismissing it as just the sort of trashy culture she had come here to escape. She was grateful that the women had been placed beside the fireplace, with its impressive display of early Hanukah cards and invitations. While Rachel inspected them, she surveyed the room, peeking through the curtain as though she were back in the school changing rooms. Rachel, a dumpy woman in her early forties who was soberly but smartly dressed, sought to put her at her ease, promising that she would find the Rabbi's words so inspirational that she would soon forget about the partition. Having grown up in the shadow of two older brothers, she remained to be convinced.

She had dithered over taking the class for weeks before finally agreeing to meet Rachel for tea at Carla's. To her surprise, when she thanked her for arranging the visit, Rachel replied that she was the one who should be grateful since Susannah's interest allowed her to perform a *mitzvah* or good deed. 'I've been studying the Kabbalah for eighteen months, ever since my boss dragged me along one evening. He's a Lubavitch – they're a branch of Chassidim who are specially keen to educate other Jews. I expect he thought that Miss Five O-Levels here was the perfect candidate.' Susannah left Carla to dismiss Rachel's self-deprecation, before asking about the exclusive concern with their co-religionists which contrasted sharply with the missionary work of the Church. 'I can't be sure,' Rachel said, 'but I think it's to do with the Tanya, that's the Chassidic Bible – although not officially. Right at the start, it makes a distinction between Jewish and non-Jewish souls. Jews have both a godly and an animal soul, whereas non-Jews only have an animal one.'

'That's me done for then,' Carla said with a grin.

'How do they know?' Susannah asked, at once shocked by the chauvinism and awed by a conviction that was the antithesis of Anglican compromise.

'Lord!' Rachel exclaimed, buying time with a biscuit. 'You've got me there. I think it's to do with the Jews being cleansed when God gave us the Law on Mount Sinai. Only don't quote me on that – especially not to the boss.'

Susannah wondered if she meant the boss at the travel agents, the synagogue or even in the sky. 'So what about me,' she asked, 'with a Jewish mother and a Christian father?'

'That I do know,' Rachel replied. 'The Rabbi says there are no half-measures in Judaism. Any child of a Jewish mother is a Jew.'

Susannah put the exchange from her mind as the far side of the room filled up and she tried to picture the various men from the weight of their footsteps and warmth of their greetings. Their own side remained relatively empty, with the arrival of just two women, one of whom was Layah. They both wore the same long-sleeved, high-necked, calf-length dresses as Rachel, although Layah's was adorned with a large diamond bee.

'It's very good of you to open up your home,' Susannah said as Layah joined her. 'It must be a lot of trouble, what with the curtain and everything.'

'It's an honour,' Layah replied. 'We have a big house, God be thanked. The Rabbi holds several classes here. He's rare – at least in my experience – in mixing men and women. But, as he says himself, God told Moses to teach the women first.'

'Really?' Susannah asked, surprised by the subversion of the usual biblical order.

'Of course the men say it's so we can teach it to our sons, but I say it's because we're a more receptive audience.'

The Rabbi, a portly man with a grizzled beard, bulbous nose and black-rimmed glasses, arrived, greeting the group in Yiddish. Steeling herself for an evening of incomprehension, Susannah was relieved when no sooner had he moved to the alcove than he switched to English. She wondered if it were for her benefit, since so far as she knew she was the only newcomer, that he chose to start with a statement of intent.

'Last week my son, Tali, who's old enough to know better, told me about a pop star who described herself as a student of the Kabbalah. I reminded him as I now do you – just in case anyone remains in the slightest doubt – that the Kabbalah is not the latest New Age craze for people bored with Buddhism, nor is it about putting on a red wristband and studying the Tree of Life… indeed, the tree, although it's mentioned, is of minor importance in classic kabbalistic writing. Rather, it's about exploring the Tanya, the central text of

Chassidic mysticism. The Tanya is both a manual on practical Kabbalah and a guide to the various spiritual problems that you – any one of you – might encounter in the world. Nor is the Kabbalah a philosophy, since a philosophy is the product of human minds and the Kabbalah was given by God.'

Susannah struggled with the novel concepts as the Rabbi discussed the nature of existence and the interplay between the infinite oneness of God, a phrase which despite his disdain for the New Age he repeated like a mantra, and the multiplicity of the world. He explained that the Kabbalah offered two basic models for this. The first was that of the *Sefirot*, the Ten Divine Emanations: wisdom; understanding; knowledge; kindness; severity; mercy; victory; submission; dedication; and kingship; through which, different aspects of God's radiance were reflected like light through stained glass. The second was that in which radiance was reflected through the letters of the Hebrew alphabet. The world was created through words: God's words in the first chapter of Genesis fanning out into all the words of the Hebrew language, containing the essence of everything that ever was.

'The word for something... anything, for instance this cup,' he said, holding up his hostess's Crown Derby, 'is both its formula and its soul. Let me give you an easier example: salt. Just as in English NaCl is no mere convention but the chemical formula for salt, so in Hebrew *melach*, the word for salt, is the true nature of salt, its inner essence. By mastering the word, by changing its letters, you can change the nature of reality. This is verbal alchemy and the core of practical Kabbalah. By studying it, we lay bare the secrets of the universe. By piercing through the finite nature of things, we discover their infinite nature and, ultimately, the nature of God.'

The Rabbi drew to a close, much too soon for Susannah who would have happily listened to him talk all night. Something in both his sonorous delivery and his audience's rapt attention had struck a chord. Beyond that, however, were his words: words he himself had imbued with new authority through his claim that they were the way to reach God. She had grown up in a household where words were held to be, at best, poetry and, at worst, politics, and the way to God – or rather the idea of God – was through ritual and art. It made a welcome change to find someone who upheld his faith without caveats and cavils, standing by the creed to which he had signed up without trying to ignore the small print or rewrite the terms. Even the thought of Clement's attack on Biblical literalists failed to daunt her, since his qualms about mistranslation could not apply to students of the Hebrew. In her elation, she plucked up courage to thank the Rabbi, only to feel cheated when after a fleeting glance towards the fireplace he hurried to join the men. 'Remember Moses,' she whispered to herself as she struggled to commit his ideas to memory.

'So what do you think?' Rachel asked her.

'I can't remember the last time my brain was this stimulated. And not just my brain. I'm buzzing! It's so refreshing to come across someone whose message is simple yet in no sense simplistic, who gives you hope without insulting your intelligence. I've lived among people who...' She broke off, conscious that she no longer wanted to define herself by her past. She had not felt such a wealth of possibilities opening up for her since the agent handed her the keys to her first office.

'Then you'll come again.'

'If they'll have me.'

Susannah's hope that the end of the class would lead to greater integration was dashed by Rachel's request that she join the women in the kitchen. As she edged through the bevy of beards, offended despite herself when several turned away, she joked that even the Iron Curtain had been easier to breach than the deceptively flimsy *mechitza*. Rachel, however, claimed to find the division restful. 'I'm not going to pretend I'm constantly getting hit on. I'm forty-two years old: in other words, invisible.' Susannah grimaced; for all her nascent spirituality, she had no wish to become a nun. 'On the other hand,' Rachel added, 'I've retained enough of my training to feel it's my duty to make myself attractive to men. In the Lubavitch world, of course, I'm a freak. Most of the women my age have been married twenty-five years. With a handful of grandchildren.'

Glimpsing the pain in Rachel's eyes, Susannah began to see the point of matchmakers. Although at eighteen she would been outraged if her parents or any of their friends had tried to find her a husband, her views had changed now that the prospect of a child, let alone a grandchild, was growing more remote by the day. 'But if you're suffering from withdrawal symptoms,' Rachel said, 'I'll introduce you to my boss. I'll lure him out when I take in the pastries. Wait for us in the hall; that's neutral ground.'

Susannah hovered beside the rhinoceros, staring at several portraits of a solemn elderly man whom Rachel had identified as their spiritual leader, the seventh Lubavitch Rebbe. Having anticipated the arrival of the boss, all beard and belly, she was amazed when Rachel introduced her to a disarmingly handsome man called Zvi. As her palms began to sweat, she gave thanks for the taboo on touching. Zvi was indeed bearded, but in every other respect he was a far cry from her imaginings, being tall, broad-shouldered and spruce. He had a reddish tint to his hair (although his beard was darker), pale green eyes, and rugged features. With his meaty chest visible through his heavy suit and his lean waist unconcealed by the fringes under his shirt, he was much more her idea of a god than any pumped-up Atlas. Terrified of gawking like a schoolgirl, she proffered her name. He smiled and she felt a burst of energy between them, which she prayed was a current not a spark.

'Rachel told me she was bringing a friend,' he said in a faint, indeterminate accent. 'What drew you? Idle curiosity or something more?'

'Must curiosity always be idle?' she asked, unwilling to admit that the triggers had been a visit to a cathedral and a strip show.

'I'm sorry. I meant nothing by it. Just a phrase.'

'Of course,' she said quickly, worried that her quibble had offended him. 'Besides we all have to start somewhere.'

'True. I'm a convert myself. Which is why I'm out here talking to you. Not such a stickler for the rules.'

'Is it also why you don't have sidecurls?' she asked, shuddering at her shallowness.

'None of the Lubavitch do, didn't you see?' She shook her head, refusing to trust to speech when 'How could I when I'm barely allowed in the same room as you?' was on the tip of her tongue. 'It's only shaving that's forbidden in the Torah. I know one man who keeps his beard rolled up under his chin, but when you see him in the mikvah he looks like Methuselah. Satisfied?'

The word shot through her, provoking an intense desire to run her fingers through his beard, which to her relief was short, setting off the strength of his chin, rather than disguising it. She glanced at the soft copper hairs on his wrists and pictured his strong arms enfolding her. She forbade her thoughts from straying further, as Mr 9½ inches repeated his smutty innuendo in her ear.

'Well, I'd better go back inside. I hope we'll see you here again.'

'Me too.'

Zvi returned to the men, leaving her gulping for air.

'Are you all right?' Rachel asked, alerting Susannah to her presence.

'Fine. Just a little faint. Don't you find it close in here?'

'I'm quite chilly,' Rachel said, giving her a suspicious look. 'Shall we join the others?'

She followed Rachel to the kitchen where Layah and her friend were stacking plates in one of two large dishwashers. To her surprise, she was starting to warm to a faith that separated milk and meat as strictly as women and men. When they turned down her offer of help, she said her goodbyes and drove Rachel back to Dartmouth Park, plying her with questions about the Lubavitch, the Kabbalah and, with studied nonchalance, Zvi. Rachel answered as best she could, although it soon became apparent that she knew more about life in eighteenth century Lithuania than the domestic affairs of her boss. The one thing of which she was certain was that there was no Mrs

Zvi. Susannah could scarcely conceal her delight. The alarm bells that would normally have rung at the sight of such an eligible forty-year-old were silenced by the setting. No one trying to escape an ex-wife or criminal past, let alone sexual ambivalence, would have chosen such a group. Zvi evidently applied the same rigour to his choice of partner as he did to his beliefs.

Reflecting on the evening's events with increasing urgency over the following week, she was clear that something profound had touched her. What was less clear was whether that something was the Kabbalah or Zvi. Her determination to sign up for the course was tempered by the fear of becoming one of the sad women her father had counselled, whose daily attendance at church owed more to the vicar than to God. In the end she resolved the dilemma by picturing Zvi as the embodiment of the Kabbalah, the righteous student who, in the Rabbi's phrase, would prepare the ground for the Messiah.

Her own concerns were humbler but no less heartfelt when she attended the class on successive Wednesdays, with Rachel as companion rather than guide. On the third visit, after a talk on the Ten Utterances by which God created the world, she had a further chance to speak to Zvi. He was standing in the hall, examining a portrait of the Rebbe as though for the very first time. She was convinced that he was waiting for her and walked towards him, eager to allude to their predicament, but, even in inverted commas, 'We must stop meeting like this,' sounded ill-advised when they were not supposed to be meeting at all. Averting his gaze as though from Medusa, he took the lead, asking about her work, her friends and, bizarrely, if she had any pets. She tried to draw him out but he remained taciturn, leaving her unable to decide if it sprang from a reluctance to talk to a woman or to talk about himself. When after less than five minutes he returned to the living room, his old-world charm began to seem antiquated and she wondered in desperation if the Jewish calendar contained leap years.

Never had she felt Christmas to be such an intrusion. Not only would she miss the class on the twenty-seventh of December but her absence would alert Zvi to her divided loyalties. In the event she delayed her departure until lunchtime on Christmas Eve, having little inclination to return to a world that was so remote from her current interests. On arrival, she found Clement and Mike already installed and showing signs of strain. Mike was ebullient now that, after a term in limbo, he had been officially cleared of any wrongdoing and reinstated in school. Clement, meanwhile, was so subdued that, had she not known of his depression since Roxborough, she would have feared for his general health. She reproached herself for having neglected him. Neither pressure of work nor her commitment to the Kabbalah should come before her responsibility to her brother. She was anxious to make amends but, the moment she tried to discuss anything weightier than the decorations, he turned away.

Her father was on fine form, celebrating a festival whose pagan origins freed him from theological scruples.

'Next year you might be happier going with Karen and Frank to see in the winter solstice on Iona,' she said.

'Don't give him any ideas,' her mother warned.

From time to time he complained of headaches, which her mother, who had been assured by the doctor that his wounds had left no lasting damage, blamed on to too much close reading. She, meanwhile, displayed her usual relish of a holiday which had fascinated her as a girl in Poland and which marriage and children allowed her to observe with the minimum sense of betrayal.

Much to her parents' regret, Susannah returned to London on the morning of the twenty-seventh, claiming that, even though the office was closed, she had an important meeting. She failed to add that it was unrelated to work. Shrugging off any feelings of guilt, she realised that cutting short Christmas to attend the class was the surest proof she could give of her new priorities. In the evening she drove up to Hendon, for the first time without Rachel who, tired of being an armchair travel agent, was spending a week in the Seychelles. She prayed that Zvi was not doing the same and lingered in the car till the last minute in order to catch a glimpse of him as she walked through the room.

She sat alone, feeling at once privileged and exposed, while the Rabbi expounded on kabbalistic concepts of the afterlife or, in his phrase, 'the continuing life'. Against expectations, she found herself closer to Carla's world than to Clement's as he outlined Jewish belief in reincarnation, which was summed up by the lack of a singular form of *Chaim*, the Hebrew word for life. Every human being had a specific mission, a spiritual task assigned by God. Those who failed to achieve it in one lifetime might be sent back in another body. Those who succeeded would go down to Hell, which was a place not of punishment but of refinement, where souls would be cleansed of all the impurities they had accumulated during their earthly existence. Most stayed no more than twelve months, after which they ascended into the Garden of Eden, a spiritual paradise on many levels, through which the soul was constantly rising as it returned to its source in God.

Susannah was far more attracted by this gentle process of ascent than by the vertiginous slopes of her own tradition. Having rejected Carla's brand of reincarnation which, with its emphasis on impermanence and impersonality, offended her strong sense of self, she readily embraced the Rabbi's, in which self and soul were the same. She longed to know more about her spiritual task:

whether it was to work for the Messianic redemption, which the Rabbi had declared to be incumbent on every Jew, or something unique. Meanwhile, she was left wondering whether this was her first lifetime or the latest of many, terrified of joining the ranks of would-be Cleopatras.

She fled from the tangle of her thoughts into the clarity of the kitchen, where Layah, who was in sole charge of the food, asked her to take a tray of sandwiches to the men. Seizing her safe-conduct, she made straight for Zvi, who greeted her with such warmth that she attributed his former reserve to the presence of Rachel.

'I imagine you feel odd on your own,' he said.

'I'm just glad Rachel had a chance to get away.'

'Perk of the job.' He fell so silent that she was obliged to continue on her round, suppressing a desire to fling the tray to the floor and run crying back to the kitchen. Her despair turned to euphoria when, seizing a second sandwich, he asked: 'Would you like to join me for a coffee? There's a café down the road. It's always packed. I doubt we'll get seats.' It was unclear if this oblique recommendation was designed to ease the pain of her refusal or assure her of his honourable intent. Either way, she was thrilled to accept.

'Do we need the car?'

'It really is down the road.'

'I'll grab my coat.'

Careful not to betray her excitement to Layah, she said a quick goodbye and returned to the hall. After a hurried glance in the mirror, she followed Zvi into the street. Once again he fell silent and she concluded that either she had misread the signals or else he didn't know his own mind. On arrival at the café, they found a brightly crayoned notice wishing all their customers a Happy Christmas and a Prosperous New Year and informing them that they would reopen on the third of January. Susannah laughed off her frustration out of concern for Zvi, who looked desolate. 'It's a lovely clear night,' she said, struggling to stop her teeth chattering. 'Why don't we stroll down to the centre? We're bound to find something open there.'

'Only *Starburger*, and that's out.'

'Because it's not kosher?'

'Because it's not you. You're used to the best restaurants. I'm not taking you there. Not on our first...' He stopped himself, but not before Susannah had completed his sentence. Brimming with happiness, she too made an avowal.

'Zvi, with you, I don't care if we go to the greasiest spoon in London. Now, please, let's make a move before we freeze to death.'

They hurried through the deserted streets, past darkened shops which in the past she would have found sinister but which now formed a fitting backdrop to a world that had shrunk to a population of two. They turned into the High Street, where she smiled to see her dreams of starlit romance crudely realised in the gaudy constellation strung overhead. With an apologetic shrug, Zvi opened the door to the café where they were hit by a blast of recycled air. While he waited at the counter, she perched on a stool and studied the scattering of customers. Cramped at a table in the window was a family whose sullen faces suggested that their Christmas spirit had evaporated on their pudding. At the sides sat two solitary women: the first, elegantly dressed, staring at her burger as though unable to contemplate the horror of raising it to her lips; the second, pinched and pallid, wearing a vast cast-off coat and nursing her cup for warmth. At the back, a trio of rowdy teenagers tried to mate Santa and Rudolph on a low-hanging mobile. One of them, catching her glance, returned it with an obscene gesture, which she laughed off, no longer threatened by a youth that she suddenly shared.

Zvi came back with her coffee and his tonic water. He repeated his apologies for the café.

'It's fine. Don't worry.'

'There's no logic to anything this time of year. You can never tell what'll be open and what closed.'

'You should have jetted off to the sun like Rachel.'

'The office may be shut, but I'm on call 24/7.'

'Do you have no family?' she asked, trying to keep her voice neutral.

'In Israel.'

'Yes, of course. You grew up on a kibbutz.' He looked surprised. 'Rachel...' she said by way of explanation.

'I shall have to have words with Miss Gibbon. What other secrets has she been giving away?'

'None. She's discretion itself. It's my fault. I kept pressing,' she said, mindful that, whatever her own relationship with Zvi, he was Rachel's boss.

'I'm flattered to be a topic of conversation. So, is there anything else you want to know?'

'How about everything?'

'I'm not sure I can go that far.' He smiled disarmingly. 'You already know about the kibbutz. Did you know my grandfather was one of its founders?' She shook her head. 'And my father was the very first baby to be born there. They held a town meeting to decide what he should be called.'

'Which was?'

'Chanan.'

'Chanan.' She rolled it on her tongue. 'And your mother?'

'Etta. She emigrated from Estonia after the War. Mauthausen.' She lowered her eyes to show that he had no need to elaborate. 'She lived with an uncle in Haifa before moving to the kibbutz.'

'Where she fell in love with your father?' she asked coyly.

'At first I think she fell in love with an idea – an ideal... at least it was to her. The kibbutz aimed to free women from having to bring up children, what it called their "biological tragedy".'

'Some of us might see it differently.'

'They certainly might. My mother once told me that she nursed another baby at the same time as me because its mother had no milk. All babies the same age were supposed to be the same weight, and breast milk is more nutritious than cow's.'

'It sounds like a science-fiction fantasy. But I'm a bit confused. When we met, you told me you were a convert. Weren't you brought up to be religious?'

'I learnt more about Eskimos than religious Jews! Kibbutz life was unrepentantly secular. We were taught that the Bible was just a book of ancient myths and God was the invention of primitive people who knew nothing of science.'

'In other words, your typical liberal education.'

'No, I tell a lie. We did have a religion on the kibbutz; it was called Marxism. We celebrated May Day and the Russian Revolution, while our fellow Jews were starving to death in Soviet labour camps rather than dirtying themselves with the food. When some elderly parents of the *chaverim* held a service on Yom Kippur, we children stood outside shouting: "There is no God!" May we be forgiven!'

'You were children,' she said, harrowed by his pain.

'It gets worse. Along with the Stalinist ideology came its methods. The entire purpose of our education – I should say, brainwashing – was to perpetuate the movement. They wanted to raise a "human type" – a human type, mind, not a human being... a human type (believe me, it's not a distinction that's lost in translation) that would work on the kibbutz of the future.'

'You're not a type, Zvi,' she replied, confident of having never met anyone like this strong yet vulnerable, private yet passionate man.

'I try my best.'

'Do you ever go back? Do you still have family there?'

'I had a sister.'

'Really?' Susannah wondered if they might one day be friends. 'Younger or older? Has she joined the Lubavitch too?'

'She's dead.'

'Oh. I'm so sorry.'

'Blown up by a bomb in Gaza. Ten years ago. She was in the army. A "legitimate target".'

Susannah shuddered. As moved as she was by his loss, she was awed by the coincidence... the connection. Her fears that the contrast in their background would be a barrier between them vanished with the discovery of what they had in common. She longed to claim kinship but was afraid to intrude on his memories.

'So very sorry.'

'Thank you. But it was ten years ago.' He began to sob. 'Please excuse me. I don't understand. I've told the story so often that I might have read it in the paper. Why should it be any different with you?' He wiped his eyes and stared at her with an intensity which seemed to pierce her soul. 'Where were we?'

'With your sister. And, before that, in the kibbutz.'

'Let's not go back there.'

'Were you also in the army?' She weighed up how much of his attraction lay in a courage and resolve born of active service, so different from the Ban the Bombers of her parents' generation and the Stop the Warrers of her own.

'We all were. It was compulsory. And, in my case, the experience was a revelation. For the first time I came across people from varied backgrounds. People who wanted the best for themselves and not just for the community. They had ambitions as well as beliefs.'

'What did your parents say?'

'"Don't!"' He laughed. '"*Don't!*"' In different ways and over several months. When I told them I was leaving, they claimed that all I needed was a change of scene and suggested I spend some time travelling. They were so certain they'd found the meaning of life that they thought I'd go running back to the kibbutz.' He shook his head. 'They were wrong.'

'That was when you came to settle here?'

'I came, but it was a while before I settled. I got a job working in a travel bookshop. It seemed the perfect chance to mug up on other countries before moving on. But, with more and more customers asking me to recommend quiet hotels and unspoilt spots, I saw a gap in the market and set up on my own.'

Susannah longed to know more, not least about the celebrity clientele whose names even the serially indiscreet Rachel refused to divulge, but she was distracted by the sight of the elegant woman leaving the café and the pallid one scurrying to her table where, oblivious to the teenagers' jeers, she proceeded to cram the abandoned burger down her throat. The graphic display of want encroached on her happiness and, rather than asking about his agency, she raised a more personal subject.

'I don't mean to pry, but what led you to the Lubavitch? Did you go some-where magical and find God?'

'Yes, Brent Cross. No need to look so horrified! I was there one evening, shopping, when I came across a rabbi doing outreach. He asked if I was a Jew. I said "yes". He asked if I could spare ten minutes for God. I told him I was in a rush. So he asked: "How about two?" And God be thanked, I listened. Those two minutes changed my life. I went to the Chabad House. I put on *tefellin*. I learnt about my duty to work for the coming of the Messiah. Now all that remains is to find the right woman to help me.'

Susannah was terrified of misreading his words which, given the rigid modesty laws were tantamount to a proposal, but which, given that it was their first outing (she banished any hint of a *date*), might be simply a statement of fact. She had no idea how to respond. Even a sympathetic smile felt compromising. 'Is that so important?' she asked, trying to sound casual.

'We have a proverb: "A man without a wife is without blessing, joy and goodness".'

'That's a beautiful proverb.'

She gazed at him through a mist of tears and uncertainty. Afraid of trusting to speech, she tentatively placed a hand in the centre of the table. Zvi clenched his cup so tightly that it split. She tapped her fingers and toyed with her spoon before retracting her arm with all the dignity she could muster.

'I wanted to ask...'

'Yes?' Her hopes were revived by his evident confusion.

'I wanted to ask whether you'd like to spend Shabbat in my community.'

'Oh!' She smiled in both relief and alarm. This was 'come up for a coffee', 'see my etchings', and 'meet my parents', all in one.

'Thank you. I'd like that very much.'

4

The office reopened after New Year. Matt had been busy on Broadband, conspiring with fellow dissidents at *IhateChristmas.com*. Marcus had met his perfect man at a Boxing Day disco, enjoyed five days of and on ecstasy, only to be jilted on New Year's Eve, leaving him torn between celibacy and suicide, until his best girlfriend (the intonation left the gender indeterminate), convinced him that there were 'plenty more gorillas in the jungle' and dragged him off to another club. Davinia had spent a week in Plymouth where the Atlases were appearing at a charity gala, her romance with Nirmal having blossomed since Woking in spite of his touring, her qualms and Mandy's disapproval. Susannah knew that the holidays were over when she heard Adrian on the phone to a restaurant – she failed to catch the name but it had to be one of a select group – complaining loudly about his table, insisting that his C-list guest had been an aberration and demanding the same treatment as when he went with Precious or Rickie Day.

She spent the morning offering advice and support to Adrian and Elspeth who were both having trouble with clients. Adrian had discovered the drawback of working for someone as insecure as Ben Dutton, who rang ten times a day to check that he was busy on the campaign, until he finally lost patience and snapped 'Well, I would be if I was given a chance.' He had so far placed stories in two Style sections but he needed something bigger and asked Susannah if she thought she could persuade Precious to wear the trainers on her forthcoming tour. She promised to try but, given the slippers incident at the health farm, she doubted whether the singer would be keen to draw attention to her size eight feet. Elspeth, meanwhile, was being bullied by the London promoter of a Bavarian folk group. He was unhappy with the lacklustre coverage, insisting that he had gone to Granville's for the kind of 'wacky' publicity they had generated for The Pink Elephants, refusing to admit that dancers in dirndls were intrinsically less droll than fat middle-aged comediennes.

After lunch she was waylaid by Matt, who wanted to pitch for a new reality TV show, the first to make full use of the Internet. In a technique pioneered on porn sites, it was the viewers themselves via their computers who would bid to set tasks for contestants. The concept had everything: money; drama; sex. The audience would be global and the potential huge.

'Don't you see?' he urged, 'this is the supreme equality: not just the democratisation of society but the democratisation of dreams. It's a historical inevitability, the ultimate in mass consumption. Think! Up to a hundred years ago, the world had a fixed hierarchy: rich man, castle; poor man, gate. As the market grew more powerful, it demanded greater fluidity. Aristocracy gave way to celebrity. You too could buy your stately pile so long as you sold enough records, scored enough goals or starred in enough films. But even that didn't satisfy the market. The new notability became as distant as the old nobility: gods to revere rather than consumers to copy. Reality TV has gone the extra mile, taken the process to its logical conclusion: the celebrities have become nonentities. It's the final victory of the man in the mall! You don't need birth; you don't need talent; you just need need. Given the right exposure, everyone can be a star.'

Telling Matt that he made her feel old and herself that it was hyperbole, she agreed to study his proposal, but the outline alone plunged her into gloom. Pushing it to one side, she rang Rachel, who was her confidante in all things Zvi. Although she was determined to keep her fledgling feelings hidden – at least until she could be sure of their taking flight – she thought it politic to make an exception of Rachel, whom she suspected of nursing her own hopes of her boss. Much to her relief, Rachel decided that playing cupid to a friend's romance was preferable to pining. She rapidly became its most enthusiastic champion, keeping her as well informed of Zvi's affairs as if she had leafed through his diary. After listening to Rachel rhapsodise about Zvi, with a licence she feared that she might soon have to revoke, Susannah plied her with questions about the Shabbat meal: what to wear; what to take; whether to make any special preparations. Rachel proved to be little help, insisting that her hosts would accept her exactly as she was, whereupon Susannah, realising that she had another point of reference, rang her mother.

'You forget, darling, my parents were communists.'

'But your grandparents were observant.'

'It was all so long ago.'

'Can't you try to remember?'

'They died, darling. That's all I remember. Why do you want to know? Is it for a campaign?'

'Yes. In a way it is.'

She left the office early on Friday evening, prompting speculation that she was jetting off for a weekend of skiing in Gstaad or shopping in New York. Pride as well as policy prevented her from confessing to a night of sexual segregation in Hendon. After a luxurious bath, she tried on a string of outfits before opting for the casual corporate look of a sage green Nicole Farhi suit with a Tiffany topaz brooch and two ivory bangles. Not even the Finchley Road in one of its periodic gridlocks could dampen the soul-stirring blend of religion and romance racing through her. She followed Zvi's directions to the Rabbi's house where, as an unmarried man (how she longed to delete the adjective and possess the noun!), he was a regular Friday night guest. She parked outside a nondescript house, with a pebble-dashed lower storey and a half-timbered top, and walked up the steep drive to the front door. It was opened by a gangly teenage boy with tousled hair, sensuous lips, wan skin and bottle-top glasses, who introduced himself as the Rabbi's son, Tali. Making no move to take her coat (she wondered if it were a boy-thing or a touch-thing), he left her alone in the hall and went to fetch his mother.

She peered surreptitiously into the study, where a crowd of men stood among the overflowing bookcases. One of them was Zvi in animated conversation with the Rabbi, and she seized the chance to gaze at him unobserved. Suddenly he glanced her way, with a smile of such warmth that it took all her self-restraint not to rush in. She edged back into the hall and examined the photographs that filled an entire wall from picture-rail to dado, rows of happy faces in academic hoods, wedding veils and prayer shawls, all with the same thick spectacles and sallow complexions as Tali. Just as she turned to the opposite wall, on which four gilt-framed portraits of the Rebbe hung more formally, the Rabbi's wife climbed up the steps from the kitchen. Introducing herself as Rivka, she welcomed Susannah to the house, took her coat and thanked her for the bunch of snapdragons. Susannah then asked about the picture gallery.

'My family,' Rivka said proudly. 'We have seventeen children and fifty-four grandchildren. Blessed be the Lord God of the Universe!'

'Heavens!' Susannah exclaimed, glancing at her unaccountably trim figure. 'It must make life very expensive at... Hanukah.'

'There are more important gifts than presents,' Rivka said. 'Besides, they're scattered across the globe. New York. Melbourne. Tel Aviv. We only have three still at home.' Although the sleeping arrangements in what must at best have been a four-bedroomed house struck horror in Susannah who in Wells had been given a separate bedroom for her dolls, Rivka's obvious contentment persuaded her that there might also be more important freedoms than space.

'This,' Rivka said, in a reverential voice, 'is our Rebbe.'

'I know. I've seen pictures of him at the Kabbalah class.'

'You'll see them in every Lubavitch house. Many people believe him to be the Messiah.'

'But not you?'

'It's not possible, since he didn't rebuild the Temple. But he remains a vital presence in all our lives.'

Rivka led Susannah down to the kitchen, where she introduced her to four smiling women: Haya, her sister, who was visiting from Chicago; Dina, her married daughter from Wimbledon; Bracha, her youngest daughter, who still lived at home; and Layah from the Kabbalah class, who greeted her with a hug and the heartening affirmation that they were already 'old friends'. The kitchen, with its ramshackle cupboards, mismatched stools and scuffed sinks, was markedly less elegant than Layah's. There was, however, the same abundance of food, with every surface covered in dishes prepared before sundown. No sooner had Susannah taken off her coat than Rivka announced it was time to eat. Mortified at having kept them waiting, she followed Layah into the candlelit dining room which, once her eyes had adjusted to the shadows, she could see was dominated by a mahogany table set for fourteen and a heavy sideboard boasting the kind of ornate silver that her parents had banished to the lumber room on the grounds of both upkeep and taste.

She took her seat beside Rivka at the foot of the table, with Dina opposite and Layah on her right. Rivka sent Bracha to fetch the men, who entered in heated debate. For all that the light was deceptive, Susannah could have sworn that Zvi winked at her as he moved to his place, which she was gratified to see was next to the Rabbi. She was surprised to find the gender divide enforced even at the dinner table, with the Rabbi's two youngest sons, Tali and Yosef, providing the buffer. When everyone was seated, the Rabbi began to chant. The words were mellifluous but impenetrable and she was grateful to Layah who, sensing her bafflement, whispered that, like every other Lubavitch husband on Shabbat, he was reciting a passage from Proverbs with the phrase: 'A woman of valour, who can find? for her price is far above rubies.' As she turned to Rivka, whose eyes were glistening and whose face seemed to have lost its lines, Susannah acknowledged that this must be one of those 'important gifts'.

The Rabbi poured a cup of wine and, after reciting a blessing, raised it to his lips and passed it down the table for everyone to take a sip. He then led the company into the kitchen where they held their hands beneath a tap and recited another blessing. Although piqued that no one thought to explain the ritual, Susannah resolved to see it as a sign that she fitted in. She moved to the sink to wash her hands but was defeated by the blessing. She felt like the Magdalen science scholar who, in her father's story, forgot that it was his turn to say grace in Hall. Knowing no Latin, he panicked until, in a flash, he recalled a household litany: 'Bisto, Sanitas, Domestos, Lux.' She suppressed the image, angry at the note of Oxford flippancy that had crept into her thoughts. It was impossible to tell if the story were true or just a means for her father to distance himself from genuine belief. Either way, it mocked the sincerity of her surroundings. She bowed her head before returning to the table, where the

Rabbi uncovered two plaited loaves, blessed them and broke off chunks for everyone to dip in salt. Disregarding her diet, she followed suit.

She was enchanted by the modest meal of fish balls, chicken soup and roast lamb, and still more so by the women's conversation which centred on Zvi. She wondered whether it marked an acceptance – even endorsement – of their relationship or simply his status as the one unattached man in the room. She had feared that Rivka, with a sixteen year-old daughter on her hands, would see her as a rival. It was clear from her every um and ah that Bracha, although forbidden any thought of romance, was smitten. Rivka, however, was the soul of kindness, gently asking her about her family, eager to establish their all-important ties of faith. In response, Susannah emphasised her Polish side, savouring the irony that her mother's past, once a source of embarrassment, should now be her saving grace. She shuddered to recall how, as a child playing for sympathy, she had made up for the Nazis' failure by transporting her mother to Auschwitz, until a friend exposed the deception by demanding to see her tattoo. At least she had retained the right to boast of her fighter-pilot father. Now, however, it was his background that she played down, describing him merely as a retired theologian, trusting that his notoriety had not penetrated their closed world.

Their conversation was punctuated by snatches of songs from the top end of the table, some wordless, others in Yiddish or Hebrew, which to Susannah's untutored ear lacked both rhyme and reason.

'The men sing when the spirit moves them,' Layah said.

'Does it never move you?'

'Not in mixed company.'

As she eavesdropped on the men, Susannah was amazed to find that their talk turned entirely on religion, which they treated not with the shamefaced air of her father and his colleagues but with passionate commitment. Her initial confusion at hearing them speak of biblical figures as though they were personal friends gave way to admiration that the founders of their faith remained so alive to them. It was not that they lived in the past, but rather that they refused to admit a distinction between past and present. Moses' clash with Aaron, Laban's deception of Jacob, and David's lust for Bathsheba were as immediate as the latest cabinet rift, City scandal or celebrity love triangle. Having been raised on a diet of compromise, she was disturbed when their voices grew strident, but Rivka set her mind at rest: 'We Jews have a long history of disputation – and not just with one another. Remember that Abraham, Moses and Job argued with God.'

Susannah would gladly have sat there all night, rapt by a discussion which showed no sign of flagging, but at half-past twelve she knew that she must make a move. Unlike the other guests, she had to drive home and, besides, she had accepted Rivka's invitation to join her for morning service at the Chabad House. She thanked her for an evening that had been perfect in every respect, adding silently 'apart from not having a moment in private with Zvi'. She should have realised that, in his case, 'Shabbat in my community' meant precisely that, rather than 'Shabbat with me'. Nevertheless, she had felt no strain in their separation. The presence of the others served to validate rather than to blunt her feelings, proof that theirs was a relationship which embraced the world, not a folie à deux.

Anxious not to disrupt the party, she said a discreet goodbye and left the table. At a nod from the Rabbi, Zvi stood to escort her to her car. For the first time they were alone, although she had followed his every word during dinner, as thrilled when he scored a point as when she had used to watch Chris in his Sunday morning league (she angrily dismissed the analogy, which had sprung on her unawares). She felt a knife-edge tension in the air and pictured him taking her in his arms in defiance of all the rules. Yet, while the impulsive part of her longed for the evening to end as it would have done with any other boyfriend, the judicious part gave thanks for the difference. Despite his failure to help her with her coat, even when her arm caught in the sleeve, he had wrapped her in something far warmer. Moreover, he invited her for a walk in the park after the service.

'So long as you don't have to rush away.'

Driving back into central London, Susannah knew that she had come to the moment of truth. In the three months since her introduction to the Lubavitch, her life had been turned inside out. She had joined the Kabbalah class in a bid to find something that would relieve her nagging sense of discontent. In the event, she had found far more than she had dared to hope. These were people whose lives had a coherence that she had never before encountered outside books. They had given up so much of what she had once believed to be indispensable – art, films, fashion, even casual contact between the sexes – but which she now saw to be a distraction. Hard as it was to admit, she had found freedom in a world of constraints. She felt a tremor of unease at the thought of her family's and friends' reactions. She heard Clement's 'You must be mad!' as clearly as the honking of the car behind at the changing lights. It was up to her to show them all that she had never been so sane.

She arrived home and prepared for bed. 'It's like I'm seeing you for the first time,' she said to the face in the mirror. 'This must be how an adopted child feels when she tracks down her mother. I love the people who brought me up. They're decent and honourable and I'll always respect them as my parents.

But I know now that I belong somewhere else. At last my life makes sense. I am a Jew.' Suddenly self-conscious, she thrust her hand over her mouth, picturing what people, not least her clients, would think if they should catch a glimpse of her. Then, with a burst of elation, she realised that she no longer cared.

She had not been at such a peak of anticipation since the sixth form disco. She barely slept and her chief fear was that her eyes, which were accounted her best feature, would be bloodshot and puffy. Unable to risk more than a hint of mascara, she was grateful that Zvi was forbidden to look her full in the face. At ten o'clock, she drove to the Chabad House, following Rivka's directions, which were less thorough than Zvi's. She parked behind a run-down shopping centre, made out the inconspicuous sign and, announcing herself over the intercom, walked in. She climbed a narrow staircase to the first floor, trying to identify the mulchy smell that wafted down from the kitchen. She passed a small cloakroom and stood on the threshold of a drab meeting room with a low polystyrene ceiling. It was unequally divided by a net curtain: the larger, brighter part was filled with men; the smaller, darker part held two old women. She searched for Zvi in the crowd of wide-brimmed hats, long black coats, charcoal suits, white shirts and tasselled prayer-shawls, finally spotting him standing by the window, his face caught in the light that filtered through the slatted blind. She tried to catch his eye, until the awareness of her irreverence forced her into a hasty retreat.

She took a seat close – but not adjacent – to the two women, who welcomed her with a smile and resumed their conversation. She was surprised not to see Rivka, despite the loose 'between eleven and twelve' set for their meeting. She fixed her attention on the lectern, which was perfectly visible through the curtain. She was amazed at the informality of the congregation who, with their prayer shawls over their heads, swayed back and forth, chanting discordantly and bursting into spontaneous song, before striding across the room to talk to friends. Yet, for all that it was incongruous and incomprehensible, she had a strong sense of belonging. Sitting in the austere, inelegant Chabad House, she felt that she had come home. She was connected to a living tradition that stretched back three thousand years, merely skipping two generations of her own family.

Rivka and Bracha arrived in time for the Rabbi's sermon, the one element of the service in English, which, with its review of the Biblical grounds for Greater Israel, jolted her out of her timeless concerns and back to the contemporary world. Then, after the final blessing, the curtain was opened and the women headed for the kitchen to prepare the *kiddush*. To her surprise, Susannah found that, far from resenting her subservient status, she was glad to be given a clearly defined role. She set out the selection of salads and snacks, chicken liver, pickled herring and the aromatic *cholent*, a meat and bean stew that had been slowly simmering overnight. For all that she admired the meal, she was far too nervous to eat, and she was relieved when Zvi asked if she were ready to make a move. Such a public request left no room for confusion, and her pleasure was doubled when, crossing the road, they passed a stream of people walking home from a nearby synagogue whose friendly nods acknowledged them as a couple. They entered the park, walking down a windswept path towards an ornamental pond.

'So did you enjoy our Shabbat meal last night?'

'Tremendously. Although *enjoy* isn't a strong enough word. I was moved and excited and charmed. Oh yes, I enjoyed it.'

'I'm very glad.'

'Everyone made me so welcome. I felt as if I truly belonged... more, as if I'd never known anything else.'

'I'm very glad.'

'The one drawback,' she said, strangely emboldened, 'was sitting so far away from you.'

'Were you? I didn't notice. I felt as if we were as close as we are now.' Susannah thrilled to words which, unless he had developed a sudden flair for flattery, implicitly recognised the bond between them. 'I'm afraid that's the way things are,' he said. 'When I marry, my wife and I must be prepared to spend several days apart each month.' She was surprised to learn that his work took him away so often.

'Your wife will be prepared for anything provided she knows you'll be home.' As he gazed at the brackish water, she remembered his belief in discretion and feared that she might have overstepped the mark.

'It can be hard for an outsider who comes into our community. Especially someone brought up in a different faith.'

'It depends how much she... or he – ' she added quickly – 'wants to be part of it.'

'In your line of work you must meet a lot of men.'

'And women too. Don't forget the women,' she said, eager to acknowledge the achievements of her own sex.

'Really?' he asked, with a look of alarm.

'I mean I come across people of every sort. As do you, I imagine. But if you're asking whether I've had boyfriends, the answer is yes. I can't pretend that I've slept alone for twenty odd years.' As she tossed out the figure without thinking, she prayed that he would see her as an early developer.

'Some women are wedded to their careers.'

'Yes, nuns. But, for the rest of us, it's compensation. I can't disown my past – I wouldn't want to – but I'm not bound by it. That's why I'm here.'

'I'm very glad you are. Very glad indeed.' He was distracted by the spectacle of three rowdy boys feeding the ducks. 'Look over there!'

'I am.' She shuddered.

'It's good to see parents who let their children be themselves, who don't try to squash them.'

'Yes, of course,' Susannah said, choking back the censure on the tip of her tongue. She marvelled at Zvi's unexpected tolerance as the largest boy stuffed a hunk of bread in the smallest boy's mouth.

'You must think that all we do at the Chabad House is worship and study and argue about the Torah, but some of my best times – my very best times – are spent with *Tzivos Hashem*, that's our youth group.'

'I didn't know... Are you very involved?'

'Almost every week. I'm one of the leaders. We run a packed programme. In the summer we take the kids on trips or go camping. We regularly ask in experts to teach them different aspects of Jewish life, anything and everything from making candlesticks to baking challah. It's a joy and a privilege to introduce them to the richness of their tradition.'

Zvi fell silent and Susannah was fascinated to discover another facet to him. As they lingered by the pond, she scarcely even craved a cigarette. She yearned to take their relationship a stage further, but there was no easy way. With anyone else she could show her interest by inviting him for a meal or a film or a drink with friends, with Zvi that was out of the question. Not only was he forbidden to eat in her home or any of her favourite restaurants, but he never went to the cinema and would be offended by her friends. What's more, he would disapprove of her taking the initiative. Although the two men could not have been more different, she would be as dependent on him as she had been on Chris.

Zvi loomed large in her thoughts when she prepared dinner the following week for Clement, Mike and Carla. The superstitious dread of speaking his name had given way to the wish to do so at every opportunity. She planned to use the occasion to inform her family of the changes in her life. In the event she had to wait until they moved to the table, since the aperitifs were taken up with Clement's account of the trial of the Roxborough protestor. All his doubts about the penal system had disappeared and he welcomed the man's eighteen-month sentence, with the rider that the foot-soldier had been punished while the Major escaped scot-free. Carla, meanwhile, announced that she had almost completed the repairs to the window, which would shortly be put back behind sheets of reinforced glass. Rather than celebrating, Clement declared that it would only goad Deedes and his friends into finding fresh ways to vilify him and launched a blanket attack on fundamentalists of all faiths, which alarmed Susannah who knew that, however unjustly, there would be those who applied the term to Zvi.

She waited until the vichyssoise had mellowed his mood before describing how she met Zvi at the Kabbalah class.

'That's fantastic!' Carla said. 'I told you you'd find it enlightening. Of course, I meant spiritually – '

'Believe me, it's that too.'

'So it was your idea?' Clement turned on Carla. 'Brilliant!'

'I just put Susannah in touch with a Lubavitch friend – '

'For which I'll be eternally grateful.'

'The Lubavitch! I might have guessed.'

'Who they?' Mike asked.

'A proselytising Chassidic sect,' Clement said. 'The Jehovah's Witnesses of Judaism.'

'You have your faith, Clem, so does Carla – '

'I'm beginning to feel outnumbered,' Mike said.

'So please don't begrudge me mine. For years I've longed to find something I can believe in – something of my own, not yours or Pa's – and now I have. I know you have issues with them. But if you met them, you'd feel differently.'

'Met them or met him?'

'Zvi is a Lubavitch. You can't separate the two.'

'But suppose for a moment you could... that he hadn't been at the class, would it still have held the same attraction?'

'Do you think I haven't asked myself that? Do you think I'm too besotted to question my motives? But I've realised that in the end it doesn't matter.'

'Oh, really?'

'Yes, really. People come to God in different ways. Some through the head; others through the heart.'

'I just don't want you to be hurt,' Clement said. 'I know these people.'

'Since when?'

'I mean I know their sort. Major Deedes and his friends, wearing yarmulkes and speaking Yiddish.'

Susannah resolved to keep her temper. She understood that he felt threatened. She was worried in turn how Zvi would respond to her brother's sexuality. Her one hope lay in his exclusive focus on his fellow Jews.

'What sort of a name is Zvi?' Mike asked.

'It's Hebrew for deer.'

'Tell us more!' Carla said. 'How old is he? What does he do? Is he gorgeous? What colour are his eyes... his hair? Tell, tell! We want to know everything.'

Susannah was happy to oblige. 'He's thirty-eight,' she said, grateful that no one alluded to her eighteen-month seniority. 'He owns a highly select travel agency. I'm talking new clients by referral only. Although he suggested last week – I'm not sure how seriously – that we should pool our lists: I send him my clients for holidays and he send me his for PR.'

'Cosy,' Clement said.

'He was brought up on a kibbutz. His parents still live in Tel Aviv. He had a sister – Chava – but she was killed in a terrorist attack ten years ago.'

'Shit!' Mike said.

'Yes,' Susannah replied, gazing at Clement and trusting that he made the link.

She longed to say more about Zvi but found herself at a loss. She couldn't cite a love of jazz or windsurfing or vintage cars or any of the thousand and one things thought to be integral to a well-rounded personality. She had fed enough feature writers details of eccentric interests and endearing passions to know what people wanted to hear, but in Zvi's case it was impossible. His life was the Lubavitch. He worked and prayed and studied and spent all his spare time in the community. His faith was who he was.

'He goes to synagogue three times a day,' she said. 'Morning and evening in Hendon and lunchtime near his office in Stepney Green.'

'That's just what this family needs,' Mike said pompously, 'another religious fanatic!'

'Fine. You can all dust off your prejudices before you meet him.'

'I can't wait to meet him,' Carla said. 'You should have invited him here tonight.'

'And put him through this?'

'We're just concerned for you, Nanna,' Clement said, his appeal to their nursery intimacy making her flinch.

'That's very kind of you. But why not try showing me a little less concern and a little more respect? Do you think I'm such a bad judge of character that I'd fall for a man who'd hurt me?'

She bit her tongue as they all fell silent, picturing the black eye and broken rib that led to her leaving Chris.

'It's not that,' Clement said finally. 'But we're your family. We want the best for you.'

'Then you should want Zvi.'

'You're your own woman. Strong-willed. I still bear the scars.' She refused to smile. 'Look at how you've built up the company from scratch. Are you really going to throw it all away for the sake of a man you met five minutes ago?'

'Three and a half months.'

'I stand corrected.'

'And I won't be throwing anything away. You're right that most Lubavitch women work in the home. But it's not compulsory. I can still go to the office. I fully intend to. I just have to make a few adjustments.'

'Such as covering yourself up like a Victorian piano leg!'

'Has it never occurred to you that the Victorians might have found a piano leg arousing? You live in a world where sex comes at you on every street corner –'

'I wish!' Mike interjected.

'But there are still people who value delicacy and restraint, for whom a naked ankle has the power to shock.' Fearing that her vehemence might itself be immodest, she softened her tone. 'It may be hard for you to grasp. Their world is so alien to yours. And to mine too, I admit, until lately. In ours, men and women fall in love, marry, have a couple of children and divorce. In theirs, they marry, then fall in love, have a dozen children and stay together for life.'

'But you do love him?' Carla asked.

'Oh, yes.' She felt tears welling in her eyes. 'Yes, I love him. That's the first time I've said it aloud. And it's wonderful. I know it's strange, Clem, that I can say it to you when I've not yet said it to him, but that's part of the deal. And I've accepted it. OK? I love him with every breath in my body. And my body's never felt so alive.'

'Nanna, please try to see – '

'No, you try to see! For years all I've cared about is myself and my job and staying ahead of the game. I longed for another relationship, but the older and more successful I became, the more conditions I placed on it: the more perfect my perfect man had to be, until I'd talked myself out of it even before the first date. Then the moment I stepped into the Chabad House – '

'The what?' Mike asked.

'The synagogue – I knew that I'd found my roots, my place in the world.'

'Half of you comes from Oxfordshire,' Clement said.

'It was more than a sense of vitality: I can get that at a club. It was more than a sense of fellowship: that's soap opera stuff. It was a sense of being at one with the universe and, yes, with God.'

'That's good, surely?' Carla appealed to Clement and Mike.

'It is to me,' Susannah said. 'Everything's changed. My life's no longer a problem to be solved; it's a pattern to be followed.'

'So there we have it!' Clement said. 'The Susannah we know and love, the girl with the tidiest bedroom in the West Country.'

'Which proves what exactly?'

'My dear little sister, you've always longed for order... for clarity and neatness. Now you finally have them. No more nasty ethical conflicts or moral choices. You can escape them all in a world of "thou shalt nots".'

'Nothing you can say will make me change my mind. I know that what I feel is true. And the greatest proof is that God has brought me Zvi. He's awakened my heart and my spirit and my senses all at the same time. I'm triply blessed.'

5

Susannah opened the glove compartment of the car and took out her well-thumbed copy of *Judaism For Dummies*. Turning to the entry on Purim, she read that it was the first festival of spring, a joyous celebration of the victory of the Jewish Queen Esther and her cousin Mordecai over the Persian Haman, a time for drinking and dressing up and dancing in the streets, as well as offering gifts to the poor and food to friends. Fixing the names in her head, she grabbed the bottle of champagne for Rivka and hurried up to the house.

No sooner had she stepped through the door than Rivka set her to work alongside Bracha and herself preparing Purim baskets. They were taking twelve to the local nursing home, packed with chocolates, biscuits, fruit and *hamantaschen*, a triangular pastry filled with jam, cheese or poppy seeds. While aware that any Lubavitch meal was as much a matter of blessing as cooking, Susannah was surprised to find Rivka blessing not only each ingredient but each separate flavour of jam. Once the pastries were in the oven, she helped to clean the kitchen, gathering a pile of plates, before panicking at the thought that one of them had been used for cheese. She gazed at the sinks, unable to recollect which was for meat and which for milk and even if it were permitted to mix cheese with jam.

Rivka relieved her of both the plates and the problem. 'Remember you're doing it for God and it'll become second nature.'

'That's guaranteed to intimidate me even more.'

'Keeping a kosher kitchen is a *mitzvah*, our way of turning a base human appetite into something spiritual.'

'It's not just the kitchen though, is it, Mama?' Bracha said. 'Wouldn't the same be true of all our laws?'

'Quite right, darling,' Rivka said, beaming at her. 'Not least the different laws for men and women. I know how hard it can be for a stranger coming into the community.'

'Not at all,' Susannah said, fearing that she had betrayed her ignorance.

'Believe me, I think you're doing splendidly. But Jewish life is very different from life elsewhere. It's not about asserting our rights or imposing our wills. It's about honouring the covenant God gave us. It's about sanctifying everything we are and do. Nothing today is more damaging than the illusion that all people are the same and all relationships are valid. "Everything is good as long as it doesn't hurt anyone," is the cry, which begs the question of whether it's hurting God. And don't you find it odd that the people who shout the loudest about respecting our differences ignore the most basic one of all: the difference between men and women? Of course women have an equal place in the world and an equal responsibility to fulfil God's plan. But the Bible teaches that we must set about it in our own way. Women are by nature more compassionate; it's our job to look after the home and bring up the children. Men are more aggressive; it's their job to go out into the world.'

'A few months – even a few weeks – ago I'd have taken issue with you on that. I was brought up to believe that women could do everything as well as men. The rest was just conditioning or, worse, a male conspiracy to keep us down.'

'To some women, everything's been a conspiracy since the Garden of Eden.'

'But since I've come here, I realise that the pressure to compete is the very thing that made me miserable.'

'That's a story I hear time and time again. Feminists claim that they're setting women free when what they've done is to make them slaves to dogma. Everywhere I look, I see unhappy women: women who are unsure of their place in the world; women who are afraid of their own femininity; women who are desperate to measure up to men. Jewish women are exempt from this.'

'You mean Orthodox women?' Susannah asked, picturing two of her most neurotic Jewish friends.

'I mean Jewish women,' Rivka insisted. 'Women who obey the Law. They're assured of their place in the world; they're able to express their femininity; they know that, in God's eyes, they're worth as much as men.'

'I wish I could have this conversation with my mother. I hate to say it, but she's one of the worst offenders. She makes so much of the similarity between the sexes, you'd think we'd never developed beyond the first weeks in the womb.'

'Your mother is clearly an exceptional person. You've a lot to thank her for, not least your birthright. Without it, you'd have had to go through a long and arduous conversion.'

'But if I'm joining the community, I want to be truly part of it. Not some special case.'

'And you will be. The Rabbi's put you in the category of a *tinok shenishbah*, someone who was captured and brought up by heathens. You're regarded as a Jew in every respect. You can even marry a *kohain*.' Susannah looked at her in confusion. 'A descendant of the ancient line of Temple priests.'

'But Zvi isn't a *kohain*,' Bracha interjected.

'You should go and change,' her mother said sharply. 'I'm sorry,' she added, as Bracha left the room.

'Don't worry,' Susannah said, taking heart from Bracha's assumption.

'But when such a good man as Zvi remains unmarried... He's already turned down four fine matches.'

'Four?' Susannah said, at once grateful for his discernment and fearful of becoming number five.

'But I've no need to spell out his virtues to you.'

'No. When I took the Kabbalah class, my interest was purely spiritual. It worried me that my attraction to Zvi – am I allowed to say that? – coloured my feelings for the faith and vice versa. But now I can see that it's both.'

'Zvi is a devout Jew. The two can't be separated.'

'I know. And I'm glad. Everything's such a new experience for me. I feel that I'm learning about him and his beliefs at the same time. At first I thought he was cold... taciturn. But he can be wildly enthusiastic. You should hear him talking about *Tzivos Hashem*... did I pronounce it right?'

'You did, and I have.'

'Of course. I'm sorry.' Rivka shrugged off any offence. 'He's so good with children. He ought to have some himself.'

'I'm sure he will.'

Susannah felt her body crying out, not for Rivka's reassurance but for Zvi's. 'It's so hard. I long for him so much. It's not that I want him to break the rules. I know it would make him less of himself. I just wish that sometimes he'd bend them a little. Is that very wrong of me?'

'I can't wave a magic wand over you both. However much I might like to.'

'I come from a world where you make God in your own image. My brother – a painter – does it literally. It's a seismic shift to a world where you find God in the letter of the Law.'

'I see that it must be hard for you. I only met the Rabbi three times before we were engaged.'

'So it was love at first sight?'

'More like blind terror!' She laughed. 'We were in America. His parents had escaped from Lithuania after the war and settled near the Rebbe – the previous Rebbe – in Brooklyn. My family weren't so lucky. We didn't get out until Khrushchev. It made no sense. The Soviets didn't want the Jews in their country and yet they refused to let us leave. Much of my childhood took place behind closed doors. We lived in a world of backstreet circumcisions, while the West was enduring the blight of backstreet abortions. When we were finally freed, we joined the community in New York. I married the Rabbi, or as he then was the *shaliaich* on a mission to the Lubavitch in Pittsburgh. He returned to Brooklyn to be ordained, after which the Rebbe sent him over here. I was seventeen.'

'No wonder you were terrified!'

'My father thought I was already old. He believed a woman should marry at fourteen.'

'Seriously?'

'That's when our bodies are ready, when we've moved beyond childhood and ought to unite with a man. The longer we wait, the more we find ourselves at odds with the world and our own emotions.'

'All the same, fourteen!'

'I told you that Jewish life was different.' To her amazement, Susannah realised that if she, her daughter and her granddaughter all married at fourteen, she could be on her way to becoming a great-grandmother. No wonder she felt so unfulfilled. 'You know of course,' Rivka added, 'that we categorically reject any form of sex before marriage – '

'Believe me, Zvi and I haven't so much as held hands. Not once.'

'Please don't get me wrong,' Rivka said, taking off her apron. 'I've no doubt whatsoever that you and Zvi have obeyed the laws. What I'm trying to say is that I'm afraid you and Zvi will find it harder to make a life together because of what you already feel for each other.'

'Really? Why's that?' Susannah asked, her faith in Rivka's judgement faltering.

'So many couples today aren't in love; they're in love with the idea of being in love. It gives their lives meaning and excitement. They fool themselves that they can build a lasting relationship on this self-deception. True love – the mixture of commitment, understanding and passion – only comes after marriage. We say that there are three people in a Jewish marriage: the man, the woman and God. Love is what God brings to the equation.'

'Believe me, I shall devote every ounce of my strength to being a good wife to... to my husband.'

'I'm sure of it. And I pray that you'll have your chance very soon.'

Rivka called Bracha, who returned sulkily to the kitchen, ignoring Susannah's supportive smile. Together they removed the *hamantaschen* from the oven, leaving them to cool before putting them in the baskets. Rivka then led Susannah into the dining room, where the table had been extended by two card-tables and set for twenty-four.

'It'll be a squeeze, but I've sat thirty in here before now.'

'Were they all Lubavitch?' Susannah asked.

'We don't invite gentiles to our table. I know there are many worthy ones, but then there are more than enough worthy Jews. People may condemn us for keeping to ourselves – and no one more harshly than the liberal Jews – but I can't conceive of a richer, more satisfying life.'

Susannah walked with Rivka and Bracha to the Chabad House, the wind unseasonably sharp for the spring festival. Masked children preceded them up the stairs, the girls and younger boys sitting in the women's section, the older boys moving self-importantly to the men's. She listened as the Rabbi intoned the *Megillah*, the scroll of the Book of Esther. Although the Hebrew remained unintelligible, the names of the protagonists were clear, the children greeting every mention of Haman with catcalls, whistles and rattles. She was startled by the football-terrace behaviour, but Rivka assured her that it was sanctioned by the Rabbis' claim that 'the sacred noise of children casts out the enemy'. While she might have wished that the sacred noise were quieter or else the references to Haman more sparing, Susannah relished the exuberance of the congregation which, at the end of the service, spilt over into the street. As they joined worshippers from other synagogues, it felt as if New Orleans had come to Hendon. Men linked arms and danced as spontaneously as they had burst into song. Two drivers stopped their cars, stepped into the middle of the road and embraced, one of them whirling the other in the air to a furious cacophony of hoots from the traffic stalled behind them. Susannah laughed to think how, a few weeks earlier, she would have been among the loudest hooters; now, she was leading the applause.

The cars finally began to move, only to face a further hazard when a giant Mickey Mouse and a miniature George Bush leapt from the pavement and flung sacks of flour over their windscreens. Having forced the irate drivers to stop, they solicited donations for charity. Susannah, afraid that they would provoke either an accident or an assault, was astonished by Rivka's composure, not least when she identified the pranksters as Yosef and Tali.

The carnival spirit persisted when they returned to the house, where the Rabbi donned a curly blond wig that transformed him into Harpo Marx. Susannah felt disappointed that, with the exception of a pair of furry ears which made an unlikely bunny girl of the cantor's wife, Dina's pantomime moustache which neatly concealed the traces of her own, and Bracha's pair of plastic lips, the women had yet again opted to observe rather than participate. She gazed into the study past the spindly Frankenstein, overweight Super-man and toothless Tiger to Zvi, who towered above them in a headdress of lit candles and wax fruit. Even a judge less partial than herself would have felt bound to award him the prize.

As the evening progressed, friends and neighbours brought gifts of food at regular intervals. Rivka, meanwhile, sent Yosef and Tali to the nursing home to distribute the Purim baskets. 'At last the old people will have someone they recognise.'

'Do you mean George Bush or Mickey Mouse?' Susannah asked.

'Either. Both.'

Although she had long since learnt that a Lubavitch dinner was no vicarage tea party, Susannah was taken aback by the amount of alcohol consumed. Elderly men downed tumblers of whisky as recklessly as a pop group after its first hit. Snatching a moment alone with her in the hall, Zvi explained that, on Purim, excessive drinking was not just condoned but actively encouraged. The Rabbis held that a man should be so drunk that he could no longer distinguish between the words 'blessed is Mordecai' and 'cursed is Haman'. While marvelling to discover another quirk in the religion to which she was pledged, Susannah prayed that no one – least of all, Zvi – would disgrace himself.

The carousing continued throughout the meal but, though the songs were more raucous than usual and the cantor attempted a headstand after the soup, the atmosphere remained jovial. Spurred on by her conversation with Rivka, Susannah allowed herself to study Zvi more openly, finding something fresh and endearing with every glance. First, there was the way he crumbled his bread with one hand and scattered the improvised croutons on his soup; then, the way he sat ramrod straight to protect the guttering candles as he linked arms with Tali for a toast; then, the way he sent a napkin swan sailing down the table to Bracha. Finally, most enchanting of all, there was the tight-lipped but tender smile that he flashed at her.

Susannah slipped away at midnight, giving what she described as her familiar Cinderella impersonation. As Zvi escorted her to her car, the streetlamps lending his face an ethereal glow, her one regret was that the carnival licence did not extend to matters of the heart.

The long drive to Notting Hill served to accentuate her separation from the community. By the time she reached home, she had made up her mind to rent a room in Hendon within walking distance of the Rabbi's, where she would be able to observe the Sabbath. Rather than ring an estate agent, she scanned the advertisements in the *Jewish Chronicle*, spotting three distinct possibilities, which she set out to investigate the following Sunday afternoon. After rejecting both the elderly widow who identified a 'good listener' and the retired wigmaker whose poodle took an unwholesome interest in her leg, she began to lose hope. Her final call was on a tart middle-aged translator, whose determination to preserve her privacy came as a huge relief. Helen showed no curiosity about her weekly visits, concerned only that she should supply two reliable references and pay three months' rent in advance. After agreeing that, all else being equal, the room would be free from the following Friday, she declared a strict ban on overnight visitors. Susannah assured her that she had nothing to fear.

Although her plans for a weekend retreat had never included a rented room in north London, Susannah could not have been happier had she been handed the keys to a Cotswold cottage. With the Rabbi and Layah offering to act as referees, she set about effecting the other necessary changes to her life. Like Zvi, whose first step to conversion had been to wear *tefillin* under his shirt, she would demonstrate her commitment in her dress. She began by resolving to banish trousers forever. To guard against backsliding, she gave all seven pairs from her wardrobe, plus the two wasp-waisted ones from the loft, to Oxfam. Far from feeling their loss, she was filled with a sense of liberation, her gesture all the more meaningful for being secret. Having never seen her in trousers, the Lubavitch would have no idea how much it had cost her, while her old friends would simply assume that she had put on weight.

The trousers were just a start. On Thursday afternoon, telling Alison that she was meeting a client, she made her way to Peter Jones and Jaeger, modesty not age prompting her to pick stores long associated with her mother. She needed sleeves that would cover her arms and skirts that reached to her calves and, although a reluctance to confide in a friend left her with no one to endorse her choices, she came away with a suitably demure wardrobe. She took a selection with her the following evening when she drove up to Hendon. Helen had gone out without leaving a word of welcome, but she refused to feel aggrieved and put on her new dress with all the excitement of her first mini-skirt. Twenty minutes before sundown, she spread a white cloth on the dressing table and lit two candles, the first to remember the Sabbath, the second to observe it. Then, imitating Rivka, she waved her hands over the flames, covered her eyes and recited a prayer.

'Blessed are you, O Lord our God, king of the universe, who has commanded us to light the Sabbath candles.'

As she repeated the words, time and space dissolved and her heart was filled with God.

6

For all the joys of what she had privately dubbed her 'faith-nest', Susannah was relieved to wake up on Sunday morning in Notting Hill. The widow's garrulousness and wigmaker's dog had acquired a new appeal after three weeks of Helen's ill-concealed hostility. Resentful of the need to let the room, she took pleasure in chipping away at her lodger's convictions. Despite the *mezuzah* on the doorpost, she despised any outward expression of Judaism, saving her strictest censure for the Orthodox women who shaved their heads only to wear luxuriant wigs supplied by destitute Ukrainians. Nothing Susannah said could persuade her that their poverty was precisely why they welcomed the trade, preferring to crop their hair than sell their bodies. She even suspected Helen of deliberately removing the box of tissues from the bathroom, forcing her to tear off loo paper on the Sabbath as reluctantly as she would once have torn ten-pound notes. Nevertheless, she was prepared to face any number of obstacles for the chance to practise her beliefs.

Her reordered calendar had little use for Sundays. She shied away from old friends whom she had yet to admit to her new life, along with films and exhibitions that were reductively secular. Varying her staple diet of newsprint, she studied Lubavitch texts, making up for the forty years of Jewish education she had been denied. Her current reading was a collection of the Rebbe's homilies, chosen by Zvi from the Rabbi's library. She had been deeply moved to see him kiss the book when he took it off the shelf, realising as she rubbed her finger down the spine that it was the closest she had come to his lips. Eager to warrant his confidence, she spent the evening struggling with the knotty prose. Exhausted by the unequal effort, she went to bed at an hour that would once have depressed her, fell into a pill-less and dreamless sleep, waking refreshed to obey the Rebbe's instruction to praise God with the first breath of the day.

Entering the conference room at ten o'clock on Monday morning, she wondered how much longer she could hide the truth of her Friday nights from her staff. Having judged her absences too frequent for pleasure jaunts, they had ascribed them to medical treatment. So far no one had challenged her, but she had heard whispers of both radiation and dialysis. Matt had even replaced his *Barbarella* screensaver and taken to wearing a pink breast cancer ribbon. She checked a guilty smile as she deflected their sympathetic glances and, with a cheerfulness that she knew would be read as courage, hoped that they had all enjoyed their weekends.

In a bid to lighten the atmosphere, she brought forward the announcement that, after extensive appraisal, Granville's had been placed on the PR roster at the Central Office of Information. The whoops of joy that greeted the news bore witness to the achievement. Yet, while the others were thrilled to learn that, in Robin's words, 'they were up there with the big boys,' she remained ambivalent. She had often laughed at the industry joke that the government campaigns for NHS Direct had been spearheaded by a PR with private health insurance, for road safety by a PR who had lost his licence, and for cancer awareness by a PR who popped out in the middle of the launch for a cigarette. It was equally ironic that her pitch for an anti-drugs campaign had succeeded despite the habits of half the people around the table. Nevertheless, she was keen to reward their loyalty, inviting them to a celebration lunch with the proviso that, until then, it was business as usual.

This was a maxim she failed to observe herself. After dismissing out of hand a request for Hiroshige to open a new club in what was to them March but to her Passover, she snapped at Wilson Tierney who rang to protest about a tabloid story which claimed that he spent several hours a day on eBay, monitoring the market in his own memorabilia, intervening should the bids be too low. With uncharacteristic harshness, she suggested that, if he wished to preserve his anonymity, he would do well to use a different credit card.

After a tough day at work, she faced the further strain of throwing a dinner party to introduce Zvi to Clement, Mike and Carla. 'I'm breaking all the rules by coming,' Zvi said. 'You'll land me in hot water with the Rabbi.'

'I'm not going to eat you.'

'Don't worry, I'm kosher.'

She realised with delight that it was the first time he had cracked a joke. Moreover it was a sure sign of his serious intentions towards her that he had agreed not just to meet her family but to visit her flat. Carla had offered to host the meal but she preferred to keep it on home ground, a decision she came to regret when, no sooner had he entered the sitting room than Clement, who professed to deplore television, questioned her about her missing set, maintaining that Lubavitch laws would make it impossible for her to do her job.

Carla, ever the conciliator, stepped in with a breathless account of having fallen for a fellow Buddhist on a retreat. Although piqued at the competition, Susannah welcomed the reprieve, which she trusted would last until Zvi's arrival.

'What's he like?' she asked.

'You'll think him very New Agey. Yesterday he clasped my shoulders and, after gazing into my eyes for a good five minutes, said – promise you won't laugh – "I think you and I are really present together."'

'Who's laughing?' Mike asked with a smirk.

'What does he do?' As Clement made his standard inquiry, Susannah trusted that it would be less exotic than *travel agent to the stars*.

'He's given up long-term goals in order to live in the here and now.'

'In other words, nada,' Mike said.

'On Sunday we went walking on the Heath, past a clump of early bluebells. He heard them saying "Thank you, Curtis, for being the sort of person who doesn't want to pick us."'

'They spoke to him?' Mike asked, accentuating his incredulity.

'On an energetic plane.'

'That explains it.'

'He's such a gentle man, but the one thing calculated to make him see red is the arrogance of thinking that the world has only a physical dimension.'

'Then you'd better keep him away from Mike,' Clement said, cheering Susannah with the thought that Zvi wouldn't be the only outsider.

'When did you meet him?' Mike asked.

'Ten days ago.'

'A whirlwind romance?' Susannah asked.

'Yes and no,' Carla said.

'The plot thickens!' Clement said.

'You'll mock... I know you will,' Carla insisted to the trio of shaking heads. 'He says that we've met many times before over the years.'

'Has he been stalking you?' Mike asked.

'No. Over the centuries. In former lives.'

'I despair,' Mike said.

Susannah longed to champion Carla's cause and atone for her past scepticism, but the doorbell intervened. Deliberately dragging her feet, she cast a final glance over the sitting room, which had been purged of far more than the television. Gone was the ancient Assyrian goddess, whose fecundity had filled one corner of her windowsill. Gone was the Rankin photograph of her sitting among a leap of shirtless Snow Leopards. Gone were any titles from her bookshelves that might cause confusion (*The Naked Chef* and *Vile Bodies* had been sent *The Way of All Flesh*). Only Clement's painting of David and Jonathan had been spared the spare room, as she weighed old loyalties against new.

She greeted Zvi in the hall, which suddenly seemed very cramped. Unsure whether she was allowed to take his hat and too shy to adopt her usual 'Just chuck it in the bedroom' formula, she pointed dumbly to the tabouret. As he handed her a plastic bag containing his food, plates and cutlery, she felt a twinge of disappointment at the lack of flowers. Reminding herself that their relationship rose above such trifles, she led him into the sitting room and introduced him to 'my brother, Clement', 'his partner, Mike', praying that the phrase would satisfy all sensibilities, and 'my sister-in-law, Carla.'

'Please don't take this personally,' Zvi said, retreating from Carla, 'but I can't shake your hand.'

'Don't worry,' she replied. 'I'm not menstruating.'

Forcing a smile, Susannah poured Zvi a whisky while he chatted stiffly about the difficulties of parking to Clement, who didn't drive, and of commuting to Carla, who worked at home. He was more forthcoming about his job, although his blunt rejection of Mike's proposal that he should divulge the whereabouts of his clients so they could tip off the paparazzi and split the proceeds showed that his flawless grasp of English did not extend to irony. Feeling the conversation flag, Susannah sought to establish a link between the kibbutz on which Zvi was brought up and the one on which Mark worked before he went to Sussex.

'He used to say he had the best time,' Carla said, 'swimming in the Sea of Galilee.'

'And hitching to Tiberias to buy dope.'

'Yes,' Zvi said, staring sharply at Clement. 'We also had our share of volunteers bringing hedonism to the *meshek* in their cheesecloth shirts and beaded necklaces. In my experience, all they really wanted was go to bed with one another.'

'And with a lot of the kibbutzniks,' Clement said, 'if my brother was to be believed.'

'What else could we do? We felt nothing for our own girls. They were like sisters. Worse. Ever since the nursery, we'd slept together, showered together, run naked together, even sat next to each other on the toilet. I grew up without any sense of shame.'

'We should all be so lucky!' Mike said.

'That's no way to raise a child.'

'Surely it's the best? Not without guilt, I grant, but without shame.'

'Now you're splitting hairs.'

'Not at all. Take the example I gave to some of my Year Eights.'

'Watch out!' Clement said. 'He's a stickler for discipline.'

Susannah wondered whether Zvi had deciphered the banter.

'If I were to piss myself in front of you, I'd feel ashamed but not guilty. On the other hand, if I were to laugh at the fact that you'd pissed yourself, I'd feel guilty but not ashamed.'

'Do all your examples come from the toilet?'

'Please help yourself to cashews... olives,' Susannah said, appalled that the battle-lines had been drawn up so soon.

'The confusions, as ever, arise with sex,' Mike went on, ignoring the dish that she waved under his nose. 'If I were to leave here and go to the Coleherne… a pub,' he explained.

'A dive,' Clement interjected.

'Whatever. And pick somebody up, I wouldn't feel either guilty or ashamed.'

'Not even at the thought of Clement?' Carla asked.

'I'd only feel guilt if I were betraying the terms of our relationship.' Susannah was sure that she saw her brother flinch. 'And I'd feel no shame of any sort – unless the guy were drop-dead gorgeous and I'd bought into all the media prejudice against my middle-aged body.'

'What if he was cheating on his partner?' Susannah asked, keen to discredit his argument.

'I can't take responsibility for anyone else's behaviour.'

'That's the difference between us,' Zvi said.

'Exactly. And the problem, if I may say so, is the way you go about it. Not by reason or evidence but by claiming to speak on behalf of the ultimate authority figure, by imposing a cruelly repressive code and insisting that we beat ourselves up if we break it. We've only just met, and I don't want to make assumptions, but aren't you in danger of making guilt and shame – the internal and the external – the same thing?'

Susannah was loath to leave them to themselves, but she could no longer delay her retreat to the kitchen. She dismissed Carla's offer of help, issuing her with strict and only half-playful instructions to keep the peace. Rushing through her preparations, she took the roasted fennel out of the oven and heated Zvi's chicken soup in the microwave. In contrast to the 'what the eye doesn't see' principle she had applied to spillages and even sell-by dates in the heat of previous dinner parties, she was meticulous in ensuring that neither Zvi's containers nor his cutlery came into contact with any other food.

Returning to summon her guests to table, she was relieved to find that the men appeared to have settled their differences. No sooner had they sat down, however, than she was disabused.

'I didn't realise it was Bring Your Own,' Clement said as she served Zvi's soup.

'You know very well that Zvi's kosher.'

'But you said we were eating vegetarian.'

'There's still cheese, Clem!' Susannah turned to Zvi. 'I promise you that when you come again – if you can ever bear to come again – the cheese will be kosher.'

'Don't worry. It's a pleasure for me to be with your family. Besides, we use extra-kosher milk. It's harder to find.'

'Extra-kosher?' Clement asked.

'Boiled at a higher temperature.'

'You really do want to sort out the sheep from the goats!'

'No, just the cows.'

Buoyed by how well Zvi was holding his ground, Susannah declared her own resolve to keep kosher. 'What about the kitchen?' Carla asked. 'Don't you have to have two of everything?'

'I'll have it remodelled,' she said, unwilling to discuss her future in the presence of the man on whom it depended. 'For now I'll use separate bowls.'

'Twice as much work,' Clement said. 'No wonder Ma called it a plot to oppress women.'

'But when she grew up, women were oppressed. It was seventy years ago.'

'I think your brother's teasing you,' Zvi said. 'No other religion respects women as much as Judaism.'

'Really?' Clement asked. 'But I understood that your first prayer every morning was to thank God for not making you one.'

'Yes, because it allows us to do the *mitzvahs* that aren't binding on women,' Zvi replied with a composure that Susannah envied. 'They don't have the time to put on *tefillin* or go to prayers when they're busy looking after children.'

'I think that's what's known as a double bind.'

'In any case it's not the first prayer but the second.'

'So what's the first?'

'More fennel anyone?' Susannah asked.

'To thank God for the cock that distinguishes between night and day.'

'Well, I'm with you on that one,' Mike said.

Susannah stifled a scream as Clement and Carla chuckled. Her dream of their all making common cause, despite their differences, lay shattered. She grabbed the empty plates and took them into the kitchen, more inclined to throw them against the wall than to soak them in one of the two brightly coloured bowls she had bought in readiness for her new life. Clement had never taken her seriously. As a child, she had had to make herself the butt of his and Mark's jokes in order to be included in their games. He held her in as much contempt as he had done when she was five. He knew how much Zvi meant to her and yet he had done nothing but goad him from the moment he arrived. Carla and Mike were little better. On a positive note, she need have no fears about divided loyalties. There was no longer any doubt as to where hers lay.

She took Zvi's casserole into the dining room and returned to the kitchen for the fusilli. Her prayer that the conversation would have more in common than the food went unanswered when, after a pause for compliments, Mike resumed the attack.

'Going back to the cock – '

'Must we?' Zvi asked.

'Where do you stand on those of us who give thanks for the human sort?'

'I don't follow.'

'I think you do. For myself I couldn't care less, but I have a lover. Not a partner, Susannah, or a friend or a significant euphemism, but the love of my life. And he believes. And I've watched him tie himself in knots, as he struggles to find a place for himself in texts that were written thousands of years ago, with the deliberate aim of excluding him.'

'Not him, his desires,' Zvi said. 'The Torah tells us clearly that God has a plan for each and every one of us. "Male and female created He them".'

'No room at the inn,' Clement said. 'That is metaphorically.'

'Don't you think I also have to fight my desires?' Zvi asked, filling Susannah with the dread of a revelation that would tear her in two. 'A desire to touch: a desire to kiss: a desire to be close to a woman. But I know they'll be transformed into something infinitely richer when I marry.' At once her fears were assuaged. He had not only spoken of 'touch' and 'kiss' for the first time, but he had done so while holding her gaze, transporting her to an unimagined pinnacle of bliss. The threat of dissension caused her no more concern than the choice of coffee or tisane with which she ended the meal.

She next saw Zvi after the Kabbalah class when they paid their regular visit to the local café. They sat alone in a Formica booth with a leatherette banquette, which in a more fashionable part of town would have been hailed as *retro*. The only other customer was an elderly woman carrying on a voluble conversation with her shopping bag. The proprietor brought their drinks before returning to the counter, which he polished assiduously. Susannah looked at Zvi, who stared deep into his glass.

'Busy day yesterday?' she asked, careful not to reveal her hurt at the lack of a thank you call.

'I heard from your friend Liam Denny. He wants me to arrange for him and his wife to go to the ashram in Rishikesh.'

'Terrific! Play your cards right and you'll have the whole of Alice's Kitchen.'

'It may not be that easy. He's going on to Dharamsala and expects me to set up an audience with the Dalai Lama.'

'Liam? Oh, of course! You remember *Lotus Flower*? It was global!'

'It's his wife's idea. You can tell he's devoted to her.'

So devoted, Susannah recalled, that he had been spotted visiting a prostitute on the night she was in labour. Her efforts to bury the story were not something that she chose to share with Zvi.

'How did you enjoy your trip to darkest Notting Hill?' she asked casually.

'I liked your sister-in-law.'

'Clement wasn't at his best,' she said, angry that she should feel the need to defend him. 'He's been going through a rough patch ever since the business at Roxborough... A window he designed was vandalised.' Zvi's blank look brought home the scale of the Lubavitch seclusion. 'My mother says he's painted nothing since then. And painting's his entire life.'

'It's sad to see a gifted man squandering his talents.'

'It's only been six months. I'm certain he'll soon be back in the studio.'

'I meant more than that. Flying in the face of Nature. Flying in the face of God.'

There was no surer measure of the distance she had travelled in a few short months than that she let his remark pass unchallenged. She refused to allow family feeling to blind her to the truth. She feared, however, that the movement had been all one way. Her commitment to the Lubavitch had yet to be matched by Zvi's commitment to her. Rivka's account of her lightning courtship served to underline his indecision. Afraid of betraying herself, she focused her attention on the café, finding to her amusement that the mad old woman was in fact a devoted dog lover. The sight of the furry brown ears poking up from the shopping bag steeled her resolve to speak.

'Zvi, I know it's against the rules but will you look at me for a moment?' He fixed his soulful green eyes on her and, to her consternation, she was the one who was forced to turn away. 'In five months time I'm going to be forty,' she said hesitantly.

'I see.'

'Is that all you can say? I thought it only fair to tell you.'

'There was no need.'

'Why? Do I look forty?'

'Not at all. You know you don't. You look like someone who doesn't look forty. I'm sorry. I'm not very good at guessing women's ages.'

'Or paying them compliments.' She suddenly warmed to Mr 9½ inches and his statistical precision. 'I wanted to let you know in case you have any plans for... for anything.'

'Plans?' he asked, lost in thought. 'Yes, of course. We should have a party. I'll speak to Rivka.'

'No, not a party.' She stood up. 'I'm sorry. You must have a lot to do. I ought to go.'

'No, it's me who's sorry. Please, sit down. I understand what you're saying. And I'm very grateful. It's just so hard for me to speak of these things.'

'Do you think it's easy for me? Women aren't supposed to take the lead in the everyday world, let alone the Lubavitch. But I had to speak out. I can't pretend it doesn't matter. Not if you want... I want... I want so much. Some men might think twice if they wanted children.'

'I want children. And, if the Lord wills it, I shall have them. But the important thing is to have them with the woman I love.'

His bashful smile was the closest he had come to declaring himself. Seizing the moment, she invited him to spend a weekend at Beckley. Despite the complications of travel and his commitment to the Sunday youth group, he accepted.

Her first task on returning home was to ring her parents. She was sure that her mother must have been given a detailed – if distorted – picture of Zvi by Clement, but she put on a convincing front, greeting the news of the impending visit with joy and surprise in equal measure, even after hearing of the Lubavitch connection. 'My grandmother would have been pleased,' she said cryptically, before handing the phone to her father.

'The man's a duke?' he asked, in dismay.

'No, Pa, a Jew!' she shouted, promising herself to tackle him on his deafness.

Two days later she faxed them a list of requirements as rigorous as those for a royal visit. Zvi would be taking his own food; although, as a concession to her parents' hospitality, he had agreed to a dinner of salmon and fruit salad on their first night. To avoid a clash of crockery, her mother decreed that they would eat off paper plates.

'We'll picnic. It'll be such fun.'

'It's not a game, Ma,' she said anxiously. 'It's his... it's our life.'

Her anxieties were compounded by a bruising few days at the office and a frantic dash to Paddington station on Friday afternoon, where she almost missed Zvi. The packed train ensured that they were well-chaperoned, all the more so when Zvi elected to stand in the buffet rather than risk a nudge from a restless neighbour. They were met at Oxford by Mr Shepherd, who greeted Zvi with the guarded smile of one who had holidayed for the past twenty years on the Norfolk Broads. As they approached the house, rolling through the finely wrought gates and down the sweeping avenue of poplars, she felt the pleasurable tug of her roots, however tangled. She was touched to find her parents waiting for them in the hall. Her mother extended a lacy hand to Zvi.

'I thought it was allowed so long as my flesh was covered,' she said, when he backed away.

'It makes no difference.'

'Even at my advanced age?'

'Not at any age. It's a blanket ban to protect us from the consequences of our desires.'

'You flatter me!'

'No, he doesn't, Ma. He's simply pointing out the law.'

Her mother smiled wryly and led the way into the drawing room. Susannah was moved as Zvi looked around with unconcealed admiration, her Granville self-deprecation having failed to prepare him for either the opulence or the scale. He sat on one of the elegantly shabby Sheraton chairs, between a lapis vase and a Sèvres clock, and studied the Batoni portrait of Benjamin Granville dressed as Cicero on his Grand Tour.

'You have a beautiful house,' he said. 'It's very kind of you to invite me.'

'Not at all. We're delighted. We've heard so much about you.'

'Nonsense, Ma,' Susannah interjected, worried that Zvi would think her indiscreet.

'Susannah tells me you've lived here for three hundred years.'

'Not personally,' her mother said with a laugh. 'Though I have to admit that it sometimes seems so.' She poured the tea and trusting that Zvi wouldn't be shocked, sat cross-legged on the floor, explaining that it was the position in which she felt most comfortable. Susannah feared that she had misjudged her audience and that, if she were waiting for Zvi to applaud her youthful suppleness, she would have to wait a long time. He stared at his knees, clearly unimpressed by conduct more suited to a Hadza encampment than an Oxfordshire drawing room.

Despite concerted effort on both sides, Susannah held out little hope of their forming a meaningful connection. The truth was that, although she was reclaiming her Jewish heritage, her mother had long since rejected hers. Meanwhile, she herself was rejecting the Christian heritage in which she had been brought up. As she gazed at her father, Rivka's phrase about not inviting gentiles to her table rang ominously in her ears. He looked so frail. She was noticing changes in him on her monthly visits which she might have expected on an annual homecoming from the tropics. When her mother suggested that he show Zvi the walled garden, he checked the clock like a child, not so much reading the time as picturing the position of the hands.

Susannah tagged along, anxious to defuse any tension, but they had barely reached the sundial when her father had some sort of dizzy spell and only Zvi's quick reactions kept him from falling flat. 'I've got you. You can lean on me,' he said in a voice of such tenderness that for a moment she forgot that its object was her father. She helped Zvi to lift him on to a nearby bench, squatting by his side and gently rubbing his wrists. He quickly recovered, protesting as always that they were making too much fuss. She made an equally stock promise not to mention his 'silly stumble' to her mother, which she had every intention of breaking the moment they returned indoors.

Ignoring his insistence that he was well enough to continue the walk, she linked arms to lead him back, tingling with illicit pleasure when she inadvertently brushed her hand against Zvi's. Leaving the men in the drawing room to thumb through the family albums, she sought out her mother in the kitchen, where she was trying to soothe the double blow to Mrs Shepherd's pride of the kosher food and the paper plates. Her own suggestion that there would be less to wash up fell on deaf ears, and she followed her mother out, while their housekeeper remained at the sink, plucking the eyes from potatoes with Shakespearian ferocity.

Pausing on the stairs to describe her father's blackout, she was dismayed to learn that it was not an isolated incident.

'I've been so worried, but he refuses to take them seriously. He calls them "senior moments", as if that ridiculous phrase says everything.'

'When does a senior moment become Alzheimer's?' Susannah asked, voicing her gravest fear.

'Not now, darling, please!'

'You must make him see a doctor. Apart from anything else, it's not fair on you.'

'Promise me you won't say a word. You'll only upset him. Trust me, I'm watching him like a hawk.'

Susannah's unease increased when she entered the drawing room to find her father in deep distress. 'Marta, Nanna, come quickly!' he called. 'I'm in a dreadful muddle. I'm trying to show Zvi some pictures of the children, but I can't make out which are Mark and Clement and which are William and Piers.'

'Don't worry, darling,' her mother said, 'there's such a strong family resemblance, you need a magnifying glance to tell them apart.'

Susannah winced. It was one thing for him to confuse Mark and Clement – although, in more orthodox days, he had claimed that his ability to distinguish them even as newborn babies confirmed his belief in the existence of souls – but their cousins were another matter. For the second time in minutes she was put in mind of *King Lear*.

Realising that it would soon be sundown, she hurried into the dining room to light the Sabbath candles, choosing the two plainest from the array of candlesticks that her mother had placed on the sideboard. All her concerns about her father's health and the success of the weekend vanished in the tranquillity of her prayers, and she was filled with a sense of goodwill towards the world which persisted through drinks to dinner. As they took their seats, her father asked Zvi to say grace, which he did, tactfully extending the traditional Sabbath blessing to include 'all our families and friends'.

'Thank you,' her father said, 'that was most generous.'

'*Bon appétit*,' her mother said, staring dolefully at the unadorned melon on her plate.

'Zvi goes to synagogue three times a day,' Susannah boasted to her father.

'Indeed?' he replied. 'Even as a young man, I found prayer to be something of a paradox: asking God to subvert the natural order on behalf of someone who claims to be unworthy.'

'The worth is God's for answering the prayer,' Zvi said, 'not ours for making it.'

'I envy you your conviction. Mine died many years ago. What had once been a blinding truth came to seem an absurdity. Yet I remain convinced that there's a place for religion even in a God-less universe. As I told my son, Clement – I gather you've met him – '

'I certainly have.'

'We create God in the beauty of our depiction of Him.'

'That's like saying a lie is valid if it's elegantly enough phrased,' Susannah said, saddened that all she brought to the table was her discontent.

'Not a lie, my dear, a hypothesis.'

Her mother rang the bell and Mrs Shepherd came in to clear away the melon, her usual deftness thwarted by the sagging plates. 'Are they for recycling or is that forbidden too?'

'Recycling will be fine, Mrs Shepherd,' her mother said, 'thank you so much.'

Snorting her disapproval, Mrs Shepherd went out, returning with the salmon. 'Hospital food. There's sauce for those that want.'

'It looks delicious,' Susannah said brightly.

'I can't answer for the taste.' Her lingering exit left everyone in limbo. Susannah was relieved when her mother moved swiftly to the rescue, serving the fish and exhorting them to eat. She asked Zvi if he wanted his salad 'with or after', but the answer was 'neither', since no sooner had he spooned the rocket on to his plate than he pushed it to one side.

'Is something wrong?' her mother asked. 'It isn't dressed.'

'It's nothing... just. No, nothing. If you'll excuse me... I'm not hungry.'

'What's the matter?' Susannah asked.

'It's nothing really. Just there's a maggot in the leaves.'

'I'm so sorry,' her mother said. 'Mrs Shepherd's eyes aren't what they were.' She turned to Susannah. 'Do you remember, darling, when we found that cork in the Adam and Eve pudding?' Susannah gazed in horror at Zvi, who stood up quivering, a vein protruding on his forehead.

'Oh dear,' her father said. 'Are you phobic?'

'It's only a grub,' her mother said, pulling Zvi's plate towards her. 'Don't worry. I'll ring for Mrs Shepherd. She'll bring you a clean plate.'

'Please stop it!' Susannah cried. 'I'm so sorry, Zvi.'

'I can't believe... I might have eaten it if I hadn't looked.'

'No pesticides, you see,' her father said. 'We grow them ourselves under glass.'

'The Rabbis have said that it's six times more sinful to eat an insect than to eat pork,' Zvi said, struggling to articulate his anguish. 'I'm sorry... I just need... Please excuse me.' He hurried out of the room, leaving Susannah feeling as though there had been a power cut.

'Did I miss something?' her father asked.

'I offered to get him a clean plate,' her mother said.

'You don't understand!' Susannah said. 'This is why he stays within the community. Don't worry. It's not your fault; it's mine. I should never have pressed him to come. Oh why must everything be so hard?'

She sprang up, pushing back her chair, and left the room in search of Zvi. Failing to find him downstairs, she hurried up to his bedroom, knocking furiously at the door. The echoing silence plunged her into a panic and she rushed outside, scouring the shadowy park in a vain attempt to distinguish men from trees. Just as she was giving up hope, she caught sight of him silhouetted against the shimmering blackness of the lake. Regardless of any offence, she approached and apologised for the maggot.

'There's no need,' he said, 'I'm the one who should apologise. You ask me down to this magnificent house, to meet your parents who welcome me so warmly.'

'They're old. They do their best.'

'I know. And I'm very grateful. What must they think of me? Contrary to popular belief, I don't set out to create difficulties. I know how it looks to your parents – and mine too for that matter – but I'm not some cartoon character complaining about the fly in his soup. I live the way I do because it's been ordained by God.'

Susannah had never felt so conscious of the clarity of his faith. Resolving to be more diligent than ever, she kept three steps ahead as they followed the rutted, overgrown paths back to the house. Glimpsing a reddish glow in the copse, she did her best to distract Zvi who, ignoring her claim that it must be one of her father's tenants, marched through the trees to investigate. She trailed behind, only to find her worst fears confirmed by the sight of Karen and Frank dancing naked around a steaming pot as though they were in Eden.

'What the hell are you doing?' Susannah screamed at Frank, who was sporting a pair of giant horns.

'Susannah, hi,' Karen called back. 'Come and join us.'

'You're naked!'

'We're sky-clad.'

'It's the middle of March!'

'We missed the spring equinox to go to the Radiohead concert. So we're making up for it now. Sacrificing rabbits to the Mother Goddess.'

'You're insane!'

'Hiya man, I'm Frank.' He held out his hand to Zvi, who ignored it despite the blatant evidence of Frank's gender.

'And I'm Karen,' she said, moving to Zvi. 'I expect Susannah's told you all about me.'

'No,' Zvi said.

'I'm sorry,' Susannah said miserably. 'Zvi Latsky... Karen Mullins.'

'I don't think this is the moment for introductions,' Zvi said, turning on his heels.

'Zvi, wait!' As he strode off, Susannah vented her frustration on Karen. 'What the hell do you think you're playing at? Put some clothes on at once!'

'This is our religion... our church. In your church men wear dresses. Pagans wear nothing at all.'

'What church? Where's the priest? The congregation? The altar? All I can see are two spaced-out kids who should be old enough to know better! Now put out the fire and go home!'

She hurried after Zvi, catching up with him as he reached the path.

'I'm so sorry. I ought to explain – '

'What's to explain? It's your father's estate. If he's willing to rent it to deviants and dropouts, that's his business.'

'But he's not... they're not. You remember I told you about Chris?'

'The arsonist?'

'Yes.' She blenched. 'Well, Karen's his daughter. She means no harm... Please slow down a little! I'm out of breath.'

'I'm sorry, Susannah; I'm tired. I was at the mikvah at half-past five this morning. If we must talk about this, can't it wait until tomorrow?'

As they trudged back through the park, Susannah upbraided herself for trying to exclude Karen from the visit. When she mentioned Chris to Zvi, she had thought it wise to draw a veil over her continuing contact with his children. The result had been to make everything worse, confirming his prejudices of a house that served dirty food and hosted orgies. Her one hope was to return to London but, short of breaking the Sabbath, they had no choice but to stay until the following evening. Leaving Zvi to go straight up to bed, she made her way to the drawing room where she found her parents nursing brandy balloons, unnerved by the disruption of dinner.

'There you are, darling,' her mother said. 'We were worried. Is Zvi feeling any better?'

'No, worse. We bumped into Karen in the woods.'

'She's under strict instructions to keep away from the house all weekend.'

'What good's that? She's out there dancing with that scraggy man. Naked! He was wearing some kind of devil's horns.'

'Don't exaggerate, darling; they're antlers. I gave them the run of the trophy room. They represent the male godhead.'

'There's nothing godly about it. They were sacrificing rabbits.'

'Not real ones.'

'How do you know?'

'They invited me to join their coven on Midsummer Eve. They melted chocolate bunnies in a fondue pot and danced round it chanting: "We all come from the Goddess." There's an innocence about them that reminds me of the Hadza.'

'How can anyone so intelligent be so naïve?'

'Nanna, don't upset yourself,' her father said.

'I am upset! I'm upset for Zvi. And for Karen. And for you. You wonder why people attack your work, Ma. Well try listening to yourself! You think we just have to learn to love one another like some primitive tribe and everything will be fine. Sorry to disillusion you but it won't! Welcome to the real world, where people aren't sky-clad, they're stark naked. If they don't die of pneumonia, they'll be arrested for offending public decency.'

'It's our land,' her father said. 'Karen has the right to wear what she likes.'

'Strange that you of all people should stick up for privilege!' Seeing his face fall, she relented and moved across to his chair. 'Don't get me wrong,' she said, sitting on the arm and stroking his head. 'I'll always be grateful you took in the children. There was no way I could look after them and run the company. Maybe I made the wrong choice? That's another story. But I don't think you do Karen any favours by indulging her. Oh ignore me! I'm so shattered, I've no idea what I'm saying. I'm off to bed!'

She went up to her room, convinced that the evening's events would have shown Zvi the folly of marrying outside the community, just as they'd shown her the futility of trying to integrate her old life and her new. Opening the curtains at eight the next morning, she had a moment of panic on seeing him set off resolutely down the drive, until she remembered his intention of walking to Oxford. She gave thanks for the nine-mile hike to the Chabad House and the three-hour service that would keep him out of harm's way until four. She spent the morning rummaging through old chests and cupboards, which felt like a final farewell to the world of her childhood, before joining her parents for lunch. With Mrs Shepherd's meat loaf as a palliative, she enlightened them on the Lubavitch way of life.

'If you've found something that works for you, then I'm very happy,' her father said. 'I just wish it were less extreme.'

'It's the truth, Pa. Do you want me to deny it?'

'No, no, of course not. But maybe question it a little. You know my views on such dangerous certitudes.'

'I should do. I grew up on them. "Doubt is the most essential ingredient of faith," isn't that right?'

'I'm not sure I ever used the word *most.*'

'I take it back. But you get the gist. When I first heard it, it sounded so wise... so broadminded. Now it just sounds perverse.'

'That's not kind, darling,' her mother said mildly.

'I'm sorry. The last thing I want is to hurt you. But I can't hide what I believe... what I know. For thousands of years the world has persecuted the Jews – you more than anyone should be aware of that. And why? What was it we had that was such a threat? I can tell you in one word: Truth. If they libelled and slandered us... or, better yet, murdered us, they didn't have to deal with the truth we embodied: the truth God revealed to us. A truth that's to be found in a book. Yes, Pa, a book. Not in our hearts or the beauty of nature. But in the black-and-white beauty of the Torah.'

'Oh dear!' Her father sank his head in his hands.

'What is it? Are you ill?'

'I'm frightened... so frightened. I can tell they're taking you away from us. I'll never see my Nanna again.'

'How can you think that?' she asked, jumping up and wrapping her arms around him. 'They couldn't... they wouldn't try. "Honour thy father and thy mother" stands right at the heart of the faith.'

To her dismay, her words failed to reassure him and, at a nod from her mother, she returned to her seat.

'It's a slap in the face for Clement,' her mother said.

'Funnily enough, it's not about Clem, Ma, it's about me! Your daughter! The girl you taught never to let herself be dictated to by any man.'

Zvi arrived back at half-past four, joining them for tea in the drawing room, making stilted conversation while waiting for sunset to sanction his escape. Any hopes that his spirits would lift on the train were dashed by the desolate face reflected in the window of an otherwise empty compartment. She broke the silence with occasional remarks to which he listened mutely, gazing at his wrist as if transfixed by the pattern of hair. Then, moments before reaching Slough, a town which to her dying day she would hold to be maligned, he looked up and, without ceremony, asked: 'Will you marry me?'

'What?'

'I love you. I want to spend the rest of my life with you. I want you to be my wife. Do you understand?'

'Yes.'

'Yes you do, or yes you will?'

'Yes, I do. I will. Yes, I mean... yes. Yes. Yes, with all my heart.'

'God be thanked!'

At a stroke, all the horrors of the weekend vanished, along with all the frustrations of recent weeks. The tears in her eyes mirrored his as she stretched her arm tentatively across the table. He shook his head, smiling. 'Soon, my dearest, soon. Soon your hand will be mine and my hand will be yours, but we must wait a little longer.'

'I understand,' she said. 'Rivka told me there were three people in a Jewish marriage. We must wait for the third to give us His blessing.'

7

To avert a clash of festivities, they agreed not to announce their engagement until the end of Passover. Even Helen observed the holiday, although her simple substitution of matza for bread paled beside the stringent preparations at the Rabbi's. Rivka and Bracha scrubbed and scoured the kitchen to remove any trace of leaven before covering each surface with foil in case a recalcitrant crumb should slip into a pot. Tali and Yosef brought in a stove from the shed and took down the designated crockery from the loft. The Rabbi, under doctor's orders to avoid exertion, sold all the leavened goods left in the house, notably a full crate of whisky, to a Bangladeshi neighbour who sold them back eight days later at a small profit. To prevent so much as a grain of matza falling into the wine at the Seder table, Rivka gave every guest a paper bag to hold under the chin. Susannah watched Tali and Yosef taking part in the celebrations with none of the cynicism she saw in her friends' children and prayed that it would be a portent.

The Lubavitch disapproval of long engagements came as a relief to Susannah, who would have been happy with a Jewish Gretna Green. Zvi proposed that they plan the wedding for early June, adding that the precise date was a matter for her to fix with Rivka, which she realised from his coyness was a hint at her monthly cycle. Nervous of her friends' reactions, she decided to wait to break the news until she could dazzle them with a diamond, only to find that, so as not to tempt fate, Zvi was forbidden to give her a ring before they were married. Instead, the following Friday night the Rabbi called her into his study and handed her an exquisite rose-gold and ruby *Reverso* watch.

'I'm just the messenger,' he said. 'Zvi can't give it to you himself because, as you know, you're not allowed to meet in private.' His mischievous smile made her blush. 'On the other hand, if there are any witnesses to the gift, it counts as a betrothal and, in the event that it's called off, you won't be able to marry a *kohain*.'

'I couldn't ask for a better envoy,' she said, touched by his solicitude. Then she put on the bracelet, which clipped so snugly on her wrist that she suspected Rivka's intervention.

Rivka and Layah greeted the watch with an enthusiasm she feared would not be echoed elsewhere. Far from impressing people with her fiancé's largesse, she was afraid of confirming their belief in his perversity. With nothing to be gained from showing off the watch, she chose to spare herself the trip to

Beckley and tell her parents of the engagement by phone. With typical generosity, her mother assured her that, for all her reservations about the Lubavitch lifestyle, she had none about the man.

'I liked him. He has character and integrity. What's more he obviously dotes on you.'

'You could tell?' she asked, eager to hear the words out loud.

'Even Mrs Shepherd commented on it.'

'Thank you.' She paused to savour her elation. 'There's a party at the Rabbi's on Saturday night. Please say you'll come. You must. It wouldn't be the same... Pa will be well enough?'

'He's fine. Of course we'll come. But why not at Beckley? It'd be perfect. Your friends can stay.'

'It's not that easy,' she said, trying to conceal her disquiet. 'Since you're not a member of the community, Rivka – the Rabbi's wife – has to act as my sponsor and oversee all the arrangements. It's just a formality.'

'Of course,' her mother said slowly. 'I suppose you'll be married in London?'

Susannah nodded, forgetting for a moment that they were on the phone. Her mother took her silence for confirmation.

'I'd pictured the parish church. Your father performing the ceremony.'

'He always said he'd marry me. Every little girl's dream.'

'And Mark and Clement used to squabble over which of them would give you away.'

'Yes, the sooner the better, as I recall.' Their laughter took her back to her childhood. She wondered if it really had been a gentler world or if memory lent it a glow. 'You'll still have a role to play at the party. Rivka tells me that you and Zvi's mother have to break a plate.'

The next name on her telephone pad was Clement's. They hadn't spoken since the dinner, but it was the perfect chance to build bridges. She rang him several times over the weekend, but he was always out. Refusing to trust her happiness to a machine, she tried again from the office on Monday morning. Finally catching him at home, she trembled as though confessing to adultery rather than announcing an engagement. Any hopes of a reconciliation were shattered by his response.

'You're not serious?'

'Try me.'

'I'm afraid you'll live to regret it.'

'You really know how to make a girl feel good.'

'I'm your brother. I'd be letting you down if I didn't speak out.'

'Well you've spoken. Thanks. Now I'll try to forget that you ever did. Zvi is the man I want to grow old with. I love him.'

'You said that about Chris.'

'I was twenty-one when I met Chris.'

'And now you're forty.'

'Thirty-nine.'

'Call me a liar for four months.'

'Not a liar but a shit.'

'Someone has to say it. Even if you do love Zvi – '

'There's no *if* about it. I've already told you.'

'You'd not just be marrying him but all those beards.'

'You wouldn't say that if he were Amish. No, you'd admire his spirit; you'd praise his authenticity; you'd want to paint him!'

'I spend my life trying to show that religion is a force for the good; now you go and marry a man whose religion is dark and repressive.'

'Tough! But you know something, Clem? This is my life, not yours. And Zvi is a force for good. He makes me feel good. And not just me: everyone around him. I didn't ring to ask for your blessing but your support. To invite you to the *Wort* on Saturday week.'

'*Wort?*'

'Let's get the jokes over with now, shall we? It's the engagement party, for our family and friends to celebrate with us. Fat chance!'

'Of course we'll come. We're always there for you, sis. We were there for Chris and we will be for Zvi.'

'Will you please stop comparing them!'

'And there's the single-sex dancing to look forward to. All the hot young rabbis.'

'No, there's not.'

'You mean the men and women dance together?'

'No, of course not. But I need you and Mike to play down the single-sex-ness.' She winced to think of his face at the other end of the line.

'In what way?'

'Zvi knows the score. He won't make an issue of your sexuality. But some of the others have been more sheltered. It's bad enough that you're a Christian. I'm not asking you to lie; just be discreet.'

'Fine. I'll tell Mike not to wear his *I'm not gay but my boyfriend is* T-shirt and I'll make sure that my pillbox doesn't bleep in the middle of the toasts. Oh, I'm sorry. Perhaps you haven't told them? What is the party line on HIV?'

'It's one evening, Clem. That's all I'm asking.'

'One evening. Then there's the wedding. And the christening – or whatever they have instead. Or aren't we invited?'

'No, not if you don't show some respect to me... to them.'

'I see.'

'See what?'

'You want me to wind the clock back twenty-five years. While you proclaim your relationship, I'm to keep mine hidden. No way!'

'Ma said you were depressed.'

'I am now.'

'I don't want to quarrel with you. Today less than ever. But I won't let you offend the people I mean to spend the rest of my life with.'

'You've made your choice. Fine! That's your right. But I won't deny who I am for you, for Zvi, for anyone. I'm not some tailor's dummy; I have bits. And if you invite me, you get them along with all the rest.'

'No, Clement, I'm sorry. I can't.'

'Then neither can I. I hope with all my heart you'll be happy. Just as I hope that one day you'll understand what you've done.'

Susannah put down the phone in tears. The bridges had not merely swayed but snapped. She and Clement stood on either side of an ideological ravine. At best, they would observe an uneasy truce; at worst, seize every chance to snipe at each other's position.

She immediately rang Zvi but reached Rachel, who told her that he was in meetings all morning. Refusing to disturb him, she sat sunk in misery, only to be caught off guard by Alison.

'Are you OK? You look terrible. Should I call a doctor?'

'What? No, of course not. I'm fine. Never better. I'm going to be married.'

'No?'

Having brought forward her disclosure, she was forced to feign astonishment when Alison too began to sniff, explaining that the whole office had supposed her to be seriously ill. Filled with remorse, Susannah asked her to reschedule her *Reveille* lunch, put some champagne on ice and order food for an impromptu party. At one o'clock she gathered everyone in the conference room and, enjoying Alison's pride as keeper of the secret almost as much as the secret itself, announced that she was engaged to Zvi Latsky, a Chassidic Jew. The kisses and toasts were accompanied by the usual parade of ignorance, headed by Marcus's remark about making love through a hole in the sheet or, as she saw it, the Bed Libel. She sought both to put them right and to assure them that, while in future she might be more selective about clients (there would, for instance, be no repeat of the Atlases), in all other respects they would carry on as before.

The office party offered a faint foretaste of the revelry of the *Wort*. On Friday morning Zvi's parents flew in from Tel Aviv, and the following afternoon she walked anxiously over to meet them. It was her first visit to the house that would soon be her home. She had imagined that, family photographs apart, it would be a replica of the Rabbi's, the tattered rugs and threadbare furniture a mark of contempt for all possessions but books. In the event, the decor of white walls, abstract art and minimalist furniture spoke more of Zvi's finances than his faith. She was equally surprised by Etta and Chanan, whom she found perched on a Philip Stark sofa. Zvi had depicted them as unrepentant ideologues who quit the kibbutz when it abandoned its socialist ethos. They turned out to be warm and welcoming, their joy in their future daughter-in-law seemingly unalloyed by the loss of their daughter ten years before. While wary of the easy attraction of other peoples' mothers, not least in view of the stream of intense young women who had adopted her own, she felt an immediate bond with Etta, which she sought to cement with questions about Zvi.

'I long to hear what he was like as a boy,' she said.

'Then you should ask my nurse,' Zvi interjected. 'I was put in the *kevutza* at five days old.'

'We saw you for an hour each evening and all day on Saturday,' Etta said.

'This is as much as most parents,' Chanan said.

'We wished to build a better world for Zvi, not just a better life.'

'I'm sure,' Susannah said, torn between love and compassion.

'But my son, he chooses to go back to the world of my grandfather.'

'It's the world of God, Father,' Zvi said, cutting him some cheesecake.

At sundown he drove them the few hundred yards to the Rabbi's. Taking Etta to join the women in the sitting room, Susannah strove to ignore the complaints of sexual segregation which, intentionally or not, implied that her own faith was only Zvi-deep. To underline her place within the community, she introduced Etta to Rivka, Bracha, Rachel, Layah and the rest of her friends. Meanwhile she waited for her parents, whose encounter with the Lubavitch would be still more disconcerting. As she gazed around the room, which seemed unusually shabby in the light of their imminent arrival, she dreaded their discretion even more than their disapproval and prayed for a phone call with news of a roadblock or breakdown... but the only ringing was the doorbell and she reluctantly followed Rivka into the hall. She effected introductions, scarcely concealing her surprise when Carla responded by presenting Curtis, a tall lean man in his mid-thirties, who was both better looking and better groomed than his description had led her to expect. He held out his hand to Rivka, who shied away.

'I'm afraid I'm not allowed to shake your hand.'

'That's cool. I was an Untouchable in twelfth-century India.'

Sensing Rivka's confusion, she swiftly pointed the men towards the study, before returning to the sitting room where she introduced her mother and Carla to Etta. As she observed the three women – her mother, Etta and Rivka – she was in no doubt as to which of them was the most contented. Influence and acclaim could never compare with the seventeen children and fifty-four grandchildren whose photographs graced the hall. She calculated how, with four sets of quads, plus the odd set of quins for good measure, she could exceed Rivka's total before the age of forty-five. She was smiling at the prospect when her mother walked up.

'You look happy, darling!'

'I'm ecstatic, Ma. How about you?'

'I like your friend Rivka immensely. Such a bright, powerful woman. What a tragedy she was never given the chance to achieve her potential!'

Saying nothing, Susannah bent over and planted a kiss on her mother's flushed cheek.

She felt a fresh wave of panic when the Rabbi called them into the dining room, where he gave her mother and Etta the ritual plate to smash. As they held it gingerly between them, she feared as feeble an effort as her father's with his eightieth birthday candles, only to be taken aback when it shattered on impact. The room erupted in applause, which the Rabbi cut short by asking for God's blessing on the happy couple. He quoted an ancient Yiddish formula for a successful marriage: 'Give your ear to all, your hand to your friends, and your lips only to your wife,' which he insisted would be no hardship for Zvi. Her joy in the compliment was crowned when Zvi replied by citing the Rebbe's analogy of a Jewish marriage and a human body in which the husband was the head and the wife the heart. Neither ruled over the other. Each was essential to life.

'I feel like an astronaut on a space-walk,' she whispered to Carla. 'I'm seeing the world in a whole new light.'

She met Carla again on Monday evening to choose a dress that would fulfil both the modesty requirements of long sleeves and a high neckline and her girlhood dreams of wafting down the aisle in a cloud of satin and lace. Surfing the Net, they found the perfect design in a sixteenth-century French court gown with a pearl-encrusted cap. Carla put her in touch with a dressmaker friend who promised perfection within a month. Susannah explained, with regret, that she would have to modify the cap. She was forbidden to wear any jewellery to show that Zvi would be marrying her solely for herself.

The wedding was to follow strict Lubavitch principles, although the Rabbi had made one concession by allowing them to hold it in a Docklands hotel rather than Brent Town Hall. They had hired a caterer to kosher the kitchen. 'It's a pity,' Susannah said sourly, 'that we can't kosher some of the guests.'

'I've spoken to Clement,' Carla replied, picking up the allusion. 'I'm afraid he won't relent until you show – his words, not mine – some respect for his sexuality.'

'How about he shows some respect for my religion?'

'One of you has to make the first move.'

'Yes, him,' Susannah said. Then, not wanting to offend her staunchest ally, she questioned her on the state of play with Curtis.

'I wish I knew,' she replied. 'It's hard to sustain a relationship that's already spanned several lifetimes.'

'How can you be so certain?'

'I'm not. He is. He took a course in Neuro Linguistic Programming to investigate his childhood traumas. After a while he started to suffer from a succession of pains for which neither he nor the doctors could find any physical cause and which the NLP therapist insisted weren't linked to any emotional scars. So he started regression therapy and unearthed several past lives: a man who loved women; a woman who loved women; a child who was killed in a ritual sacrifice. In one of the most violent, he was a mercenary captain who was crushed to death by his men. It seems that his current chest pains stem from that.'

'Is there no way to break the pattern?' Susannah asked, struggling to suppress her incredulity.

'Only time,' Carla said. 'Which is ironic when you come to think of it. Meanwhile, he's left with a crippling burden of guilt that isn't linked to his current life but to his mercenary past. All his old friends have lost patience. They claim he's dreamt it up in a bid to make himself more interesting. He says I'm the only one who takes him seriously. Which, to tell the truth, can be a little wearing. But you understand, don't you, from your work on the Kabbalah?'

'I've barely scratched the surface,' she replied evasively.

'According to Curtis, the one thing all these incarnations have in common is a passionate love affair that culminated in the lover's death. He's terrified the same thing's going to happen to me.'

Susannah's outlook on life had changed so profoundly in the past six months that she was reluctant to urge caution on anyone. What Carla needed was someone to guide her through the labyrinth of her emotions: a Buddhist counterpart to Rivka. The thought of her mentor made her long for Tuesday night and the next in their series of preparatory talks on marriage. For once she didn't regret the requirement on Zvi to take a separate course with the Rabbi, since it enabled them to talk with a frankness that would have been impossible in mixed company.

'Marriage,' Rivka said, 'stands at the very heart of Judaism. I can't claim to be an expert but, from what I understand, Christians see it as a sort of consolation prize for those too weak to choose a life of chastity.'

'"Such persons as have not the gift of continency."'

'What?'

'That's the Prayer Book phrase. My brothers and I used to laugh.'

'I'm not surprised. With us, it's the opposite. Marriage is both the source of new life and the way for men and women to transcend their bodies and touch the divine.'

'Quite a tall order.'

'Don't worry, help is at hand. Help is always at hand in the Torah. You know of course about the ritual of Mikvah?'

'I know that Zvi goes every morning.'

'That's different. For men it's a spiritual discipline, a preparation for prayer. A woman goes once a month at the end of her cycle. For the five days she bleeds and a whole week after, she's held to be *niddah*. She's forbidden to have any contact with her husband... and I don't just mean in bed. She mustn't so much as pass him a cup of tea. Then at the end of twelve days she immerses herself in the mikvah and they can resume relations. You look worried? Is there something you don't understand?'

'No, nothing... Just I suppose I'm enough of my mother's daughter to resent any suggestion that menstrual blood is unclean.'

'Believe me, immersion has nothing – nothing whatsoever – to do with hygiene. The woman who enters the mikvah purifies her union with her husband, and her husband too, as much as she does herself.'

On the eve of her wedding, Susannah paid her first visit to the mikvah. As Rivka led her to a door which, the tarnished mezuzah apart, was indistinguishable from its neighbours, she felt a pang of disappointment that such a solemn ritual should take place in such a nondescript setting. They rang the bell, to be admitted to an airy waiting room, furnished with armchairs, a glass table and a smiling portrait of the Rebbe. Miriam, the attendant, greeted them warmly and, after some preliminary paperwork, showed Susannah to a changing room which was so well appointed that she mistook it for the mikvah itself. 'It's an easy mistake,' Miriam said graciously, as she pointed to the various facilities and handed her a checklist to ensure that she cleaned her teeth, trimmed her nails, removed her make-up and combed her hair. 'Spend as long as you like,' she said on leaving. Susannah took her at her word, washing, scrubbing, swabbing, brushing and tweezing, so that there would be no residue of her former life to stand between herself and God.

After putting on the robe and slippers provided and winding a towel around her dripping hair, she rang for Miriam who led her to a small, dimly lit pool, which was surrounded by potted plants. She handed her the robe and towel, took a second shower and slowly descended the steps. Bracing herself for a spurt of cold, she was delighted by the gentle warmth of the water lapping her legs. She crouched until she was completely covered. When she emerged, Miriam placed a piece of cloth on her forehead and asked her to repeat the prayer: 'Blessed Are You, King of the Universe who has made us holy with your commandments and commanded us regarding immersion.' As she stepped back into the water, she thought of the millions of women who had preceded her: the Biblical matriarchs: Sarah; Rebecca; Rachel; Esther; as well as her own ancestors in the shtetls and ghettos of Eastern Europe. She felt reconnected to her history, her family and her soul. She had a new sense of herself as both a woman and a Jew. She longed to stay submerged forever, freed from the temporal world, yet, even as she climbed out and into the robe Miriam held open, she knew that her sense of loss was only temporary for she would be back within less than a month.

Feeling at once empowered and humbled, she returned to the waiting room.

'I see I've no need to ask how it went,' Rivka said.

'I'm so blessed, Rivka. At last I can appreciate what the Rabbi taught us in the Kabbalah class: "We're not human beings having spiritual experiences, but spiritual beings having human experiences."' Without a trace of self-consciousness, she began to sob.

'God be thanked, my dear Susannah.'

'Shoshanna. Do you think you could call me Shoshanna? From now on I'd like to be known by my Hebrew name.'

She stayed the night at the Rabbi's. To her surprise, she slept like a child, waking at seven to spend the morning fasting and reading psalms. At noon Rivka came upstairs to help her dress, her practised calm as mother to six brides guiding her safely through the thicket of petticoats and tangle of lacing. They pinched and pinned and tied until, the transformation complete, she gazed at herself in the cheval glass, swathed in white from beaded cap to embroidered train, and felt both protected and pure.

At two thirty they drove in scorching heat to the hotel, where Rivka escorted her into a vast lounge, partitioned by a wooden screen, and up to a regal white chair festooned with flowers fit for a May Queen. She greeted her guests: her mother and Etta, who were seated respectively on her right and left; Carla; her aunt Helena and cousins Alice and Sophie; Karen, who had dyed her green tips pink in honour of the occasion; Rachel; Layah; Bracha; Dina; and a large contingent from the Hendon congregation. She had decided against asking any of her old friends, afraid to let her happiness be tainted by their scepticism or, worse, their scorn. It was hard enough to see her mother, denied any official role, adopting a professional one, quizzing Rivka about the Lubavitch as though they were an endangered tribe.

The women's chatter was tantalisingly underscored by the bass notes filtering through the partition. Shoshanna's hopes soared as she was sure that she recognised Clement, only to be dashed by the unequivocal sound of Yiddish. She felt a surge of anger, as much at her own folly as his stubbornness. He had resisted all her parents' and Carla's efforts at peacemaking, claiming that she wanted him to deny his identity, when she had simply asked him not to flaunt it. Just when the sense of loss grew overwhelming, Zvi's gravelly voice rang out to rescue her. To judge by the silence that greeted it, he was giving some kind of speech. As he drew to a close, the men broke into a plangent melody which, after fading from earshot, re-emerged when several of them, carrying candles, accompanied Zvi to her door. He headed straight for her, the mixture of joy and resolution on his face making him look more handsome than ever. She caught his gaze and was seized by a sense of such rightness in the world that she feared she would faint. Without saying a word, he took the heavy veil from Rivka, placed it over her head and walked out. To her relief, nobody tried to talk to her and she sat in a dream waiting for the call to the *chupah*.

Ten minutes later she made her way into the garden, finding to her dismay that the *chupah*, a blue velvet canopy with golden fringes and stout wrought-iron poles, had been set up in full view of the Docklands Light Railway. All her misgivings vanished, however, as she walked towards it, escorted by Rivka, her mother and Etta. Zvi, who had exchanged his charcoal grey coat for a plain white *kittel*, was waiting for her with his father and Rabbi Zalman, an old army friend, who had flown in from Sydney to officiate. As the women approached, Zvi stepped into the *chupah* and stood next to the table. Shoshanna, accompanied by her mother, his parents, the Rabbi and Rivka, circled him slowly seven times. After two or three orbits she lost count and relied on the Rabbi to guide her. From the corner of her eye, she glimpsed her father who, as a non-Jew, was not permitted to take part. He looked drawn, and she wondered whether her defection had hurt him more than he cared to admit.

She entered the *chupah* and Rabbi Zalman began the service, his broad vowels in marked contrast to the guttural accents around him. He recited two blessings and handed them a cup of wine, whereupon Rivka moved forward to lift her veil. Zvi placed the ring on her finger and declared in a Hebrew she knew by heart: 'Behold, you are betrothed to me according to the laws of Moses and Israel,' after which Rabbi Zalman read the 2,000-year-old marriage contract in Aramaic. She stood in a trance, unperturbed by her failure to follow a word. The reading over, Rabbi Zalman stepped out of the *chupah* and gave the contract to her father who, startled by his sudden inclusion in the ceremony, held it like the report of a clerical scandal he was anxious to forget. Once again Rabbi Zalman handed her the cup and, as she raised it to her lips, seven men from the Chabad House each spoke a blessing. Zvi then took a glass from the table, placed it on the ground and stamped. The garden resounded with applause and shouts of *Mazel Tov*. She realised with a start that she was married. She had the man she loved by her side and the promise of his children ahead of her. She had a faith to give her life meaning. Her joy was complete.

Their parents, together with the Rabbi and Rivka, led them back inside the hotel to a small room where they could break their fast with a snack of tea and cakes. Confounding her fears, the elders quickly withdrew, granting them their first ever taste of privacy. As she sat beside Zvi, no longer afraid to betray him by an inadvertent touch or herself by an illicit one, she gave thanks for the months of restraint that made the present moment so potent. She smiled at him, but his ardent expression caused her an unaccustomed rush of shyness and she longed for the safety of the veil. All such thoughts – all thoughts of any sort – were swept aside when he leant forward and pressed his lips against hers. She avidly responded and they devoured each other, breathing the air from each other's lungs... the spirit from each other's souls. Even the beard that had filled her with such alarm turned out to be as soft as one of her grandmother's stoles.

He cupped her breasts in his hands, sending a tremor down her spine, and moved to unfasten her bodice, only to be thwarted by the intricate lacing. She wanted to help but he held her so close that she was unable to free her arm.

'Later,' he whispered, as he diverted his attention to her skirt, hitching up her petticoats and sliding his hand up her thigh. Her whole body melted as he slid his fingers into her pants and on to her already moist sex.

'Now,' she whispered, seeking to reciprocate, but her efforts were frustrated by the voluminous *kittel*. For one horrible moment it felt like trying to undo a shroud. Just when she was about to despair, he slipped a finger inside her and her mind went blank.

'Soon, my love,' he said, 'and then forever.'

Dazed by his words, she lifted her hands to his face, stroking his hair and his cheeks and his beard. She ran her tongue down his nose and on to his lips, prising them open until her whole self seemed to be sucked into the kiss. Time expanded and dissolved, making their few minutes grace seem both to last forever and to pass in the twinkling of an eye. A knock on the door brought them back to the outside world, but she felt only a brief pang since she knew that, though separate, they would never again be apart.

Her assurance was put to the test when, after posing for photographs, they were led off to preside at different receptions. They met again at dinner, sitting together at the top table while their guests were divided by a fern *mechitza*. Following the speeches, where she felt a twinge of regret at the Rabbi's assumption of her father's prerogative, a four-piece band of fiddle, cornet, drum and tambourine played traditional Lubavitch melodies to a contemporary beat. Peering through the foliage, she saw a group of men gyrating in frenzy, clapping their hands and stamping their feet while they whirled their partners around, weaving in and out of the wider circle. As Zvi moved to join them, she felt a moment of panic, which she sought to escape by linking arms with a quartet of women who were themselves spinning across the floor. Having danced with Carla and Bracha, she approached her mother, who eagerly accepted. 'It's like being back at Greenham Common,' she said with a smile. As they wheeled round, pushing themselves to the brink of collapse while the onlookers cheered, she had the disturbing sensation of dancing less with her mother than with herself thirty years on.

No sooner had they resumed their seats than the Rabbi edged towards them. 'Forgive me, Mrs Granville, but I thought you should know that the Bishop has passed out.'

'What?'

'He appears to have overindulged a little. No matter. Only to be encouraged at a wedding.'

'Is he all right?'

'Perfectly. He was grinning and gurgling, then, when he tried to stand up, he collapsed.' Shoshanna was moved by the note of concern in his voice.

'Let's leave him to sleep it off, so long as you're sure he's no trouble.'

'None whatsoever.'

'After all he has the right to celebrate his darling daughter's marriage.' Then, taking Shoshanna in her arms, she confirmed the sentiment with a kiss.

3

MARTA

1

Resentment and anxiety were not emotions that Marta had expected to feel at her daughter's wedding. The prospect of Susannah's marrying had grown so remote over the years that she was ready to stomach a great deal in the cause of celebration, but it was hard to endorse a ceremony that seemed more alien than the puberty rituals in a Hadza camp.

As she walked around the *chupah* with Etta and Chanan two painful steps behind the bride, the Rabbi and Rivka, she was determined to keep cheerful. It was bad enough that Clement's obduracy had led him to refuse his invitation, but it was even worse that, as a non-Jew, Edwin should be denied any part in the proceedings. She glimpsed him among the men and flashed him an encouraging smile. Quite apart from its cruelty, such a ban made no sense. Susannah had explained that the *chupah* symbolised Abraham's tent, open on all sides to welcome guests of every nation. How then could they justify shutting him out?

As the presiding rabbi recited the prayers in a thick Australian accent, she was seized by a spirit of irreverence, struggling to blot out the image of him poised on a surfboard, beard streaming in the breeze and paunch encased in rubber, negotiating the breakers on Bondi Beach. Her failure to engage with the service drove her to take the opposite tack, summoning her professional detachment as if she were back in the Serengeti, but, to her dismay, her hitherto steadfast belief in cultural relativity broke down. There was too much at stake, too much of the old Poland she thought she had escaped but which remained buried deep inside her. Her journey from the Warsaw Ghetto to Wells Cathedral had been torturous enough without Susannah's making it in reverse.

'All I want is for you to be happy, darling,' she had said when her daughter announced her engagement. Recent encounters with the Lubavitch had forced her to revise her view. Susannah's alliance with these singular people, so confident of their own creed and so defiant of other peoples', was even more perturbing than her relationship with the unspeakable Chris.

'You're the one I have to thank, Ma,' Susannah had replied. 'If it weren't for you, I could never have become a full member of the community. Now, if I wanted to, I could even marry a *kohain*. Not that I do, of course. But, as I said to Zvi, it's good to know.'

Marta professed satisfaction, but Susannah's words had touched a nerve.

Suddenly she was back in the ghetto, with her parents, grandparents, sister and aunt, when their already cramped room was invaded by a stranger. Her mother claimed that she was an old friend with nowhere else to go, but her father, less protective of her tender sensibilities or more conscious that the Occupation had hardened them, explained that she had been raped. 'By a German?' she asked and her father nodded. It was not, however, the Nazi atrocity that had roused his anger and prompted him to share their meagre resources, but the response of the woman's husband. He was a *kohain* and, under the Law, forbidden to marry a harlot, which, under the same Law, his wife had now become. So he threw her out. Her face, which remained as clear as any around the *chupah* even though her name had been erased from everything but a memorial wall, stood as a haunting indictment of regulatory religion. At the thought, tears formed in her eyes and Etta discreetly passed her a handkerchief. She was grateful for the cloak of maternal happiness which allowed her to keep the horror to herself.

The ceremony over, she followed the bridal party indoors. The Rabbi led the way to a small room where, after a day of fasting, Susannah and Zvi would be able to enjoy a light snack and, more importantly, some moments alone. Marta, appalled to learn that it was the first time they were permitted to touch, trusted that, as in the white weddings of her youth, they had come to some kind of compromise. Not that she herself had resorted to any such subterfuge; on her wedding night it had been the bridegroom who blushed rather than the bride. From the moment she arrived in England as a war-weary sixteen-year-old, she had been determined to taste every freedom her adopted country had to offer. Oxford, with its surplus of men, had passed in a haze of romance. Edwin, meanwhile, true to both his creed and code, had preferred to save himself for the right girl. She smiled at the memory, still vivid after more than half a century, of his rapturous conviction that he had found her.

With similar conviction she took his arm, leaving him looking both comforted and confused. The surge of love she felt for him flowed out to Susannah and she longed to relieve her of a weight of responsibility which could only be increased by the presence of two sets of parents outside the door. Trusting that they would not spend too long on the tea and cakes, she wished them a cheery '*Bon appétit*' and hurried out of the room.

'Are we going home now?' Edwin asked, as they left the Rabbi to stand guard.

'Of course not, darling. We're about to begin the reception.'

'But if Nanna and...'

'Zvi,' she said rapidly for fear of offending Etta and Chanan.

'That's right – have gone to bed.'

'They're just having a quick tea. They've eaten nothing all day. Would you like something?'

'I'm sorry. I'm not much use, I know. I feel as if I have a removal van driving up and down in my head.'

'Why a removal van?' she asked, disturbed by the precision of the image.

'I don't know. That's just how I feel.'

'Maybe the Bishop would like to sit down?' Rivka asked, pointing to a cluster of chrome blocks that looked more like a sculpture than seats. Taking up her offer, Marta was about to remark that he had a name as well as a title, only to recall her own references to 'the Rabbi'. She struggled to check her irritation with a woman who had shown her nothing but kindness. Rivka's adherence to her faith in the face of oppressors who, while less systematic than the Nazis, were equally murderous, had destroyed what little respect Susannah retained for her mother's secularism.

'I used to understand your rejection of God,' she had said, 'but now it seems too easy.'

She reflected on her daughter's newfound beliefs with a growing sense of disquiet. Susannah had always been an obsessive child, keeping everything from the toys in her nursery to the towels in her bathroom in perfect order. No nanny could have organised her charges with greater efficiency than she had her dolls. For years she had longed for a life of fixed boundaries, a formal meal as against the rest of the family's potluck suppers. She only wished that she could have found it some other way.

To keep from brooding, she made small talk with Rivka and Carla.

'It's good to see so many people.'

'We're a tight-knit community,' Rivka replied.

'Susannah tells me they're going to throw a party for her friends in the autumn,' Marta said, determined that the other side of her daughter's life should be acknowledged.

'I met the Bishop's sister,' Rivka said.

'Oh yes?' Marta asked, waiting for a qualifying comment while aware that, were she meeting Helena for the first time, she too would reserve judgement. 'She's here, along with her husband and children. Of course you understand why there's no one from my own family...' To her shame, she felt a need to assert her credentials.

'Of course,' Rivka said, stroking her hand. 'But you know that in our tradition the deceased grandparents of the bride and groom are said to be guests at the wedding.'

'Really?' Marta asked, picturing the joint horror of her parents, who would have shrunk from what they saw as the primitivism of the proceedings, and her parents-in-law, who in their own way had lived in as closed a world as the Lubavitch, their country-house horizons as narrow as any in the shtetl.

She pondered how to extricate herself from Rivka's grasp, while Carla described how Curtis had wanted to gatecrash the women's reception on the grounds that, in former lives, he had been both a geisha and a nun. Marta laughed with added gusto to make up for Rivka's silence. For all that she longed for Carla's happiness, she struggled to warm to Curtis. But she needed to tread carefully. Her mistrust of Peter, however justified, had created a chill between herself and Carla that lingered until his recent defection. She was eager not to fall into a similar trap.

The Rabbi's announcement that it was time to fetch Susannah and Zvi for the receptions enabled Marta finally to disentangle herself from Rivka. A veteran anti-racist, she preferred to reserve the term *apartheid* for its political context, but the all-female reception followed by the segregated dining room caused her to think again. As she studied the confident faces all around her, she saw women with so much sense of who they were and so little of who they could be. Inspired by the Hadza who placed equal weight on women's gathering and men's hunting, she had long opposed any form of separatism. Such divisions were doubly untenable in people who believed that the world was created by God.

Watching the women dance, she was bound to admit that they seemed to be contented. Young and old alike allowed their hair to stream and their faces to glow with a lack of inhibition more familiar from her health club than any previous wedding party. The one exception was Helena, as ever impeccably dressed and coiffed, who looked as though she were trapped with a group of hunt saboteurs. She greeted Marta with a guarded smile. Although the passage of time had reconciled her to her brother's marriage to a Jewish refugee, curbing the need for coded references to the 'ghastly childhood' which made his choice akin to that of sponsoring a Nigerian orphan, she remained reserved, cloaking her distrust of Marta's foreignness in an exaggerated deference to her intellect. Having long since ceased to take offence, Marta found her sister-in-law a source of constant amusement, not least when she contrasted Susannah's wedding with those of Helena's daughters, Alice in St Margaret's Westminster and Sophie in York Minister, the one attended by half the Tory cabinet, the other by minor royalty, and neither with a pearl out of place.

'This must take you back to your youth,' Helena said, pulling up a chair beside her.

'Quite the opposite,' Marta replied. 'My parents deplored what they saw as reactionary superstition. They were committed communists.' She took a wicked pleasure in asserting the connection.

'Well, we can't choose our parents, can we?'

'Not so far,' Marta replied, dreading where the conversation was heading.

'Any more than we can our children,' Helena added with the smugness of one whose daughters could not have been more like her had they been cloned.

'Edwin and I believed in letting the children find their own paths.'

'Oh I know,' Helena said with a grimace. 'That's why I always tried to make allowances.'

'That was very generous of you,' she replied. She knew how strongly Helena and Harry disapproved of her methods and how trying they had found their annual visits to Beckley.

'Where's Clement?' Helena asked, as if reading her mind. 'I know they're fencing us off like livestock, but I couldn't see him in the crowd. Is anything wrong?'

Try as she might, Marta could detect no hidden meaning to the question. She determined to bluff it out. 'No, unfortunately, he wasn't able to come.'

'He's not ill, is he?' This time the meaning was clear.

'No, he's fine. He's just broken his leg.' She took a large gulp of champagne.

'At his age?'

'It's his leg, Helena, not his hip.' She trusted that the ancient antipathy between aunt and nephew would prevent the lie being exposed.

'And his friend?' Helena was the only woman she knew who could give the word such sinister emphasis.

'He's looking after him. I shall give them a detailed report tomorrow.'

'I suppose he can watch the video.' Marta braced herself for the barb, which came perfectly on cue. 'Two photographers! I always thought Jews were frugal... Oh I'm sorry.'

'Don't worry, I understand. You've known me so long, you sometimes forget I am one.' She savoured Helena's unease. 'To be honest, I have the same problem myself.'

'The husband's mother told me he was a travel agent.'

'That's right.'

'So at least they can be sure of an exotic honeymoon.'

'They're not having one.' Marta felt her stomach tighten. 'It's Zvi's busiest time of year,' she said feebly, the pattern of lies now established. For all her wish to escape Helena's scrutiny, she found it painful to admit the truth even to herself. Given the strictness of their upbringing, the vast majority of Lubavitch brides were virgins. The blood on their wedding night was classed as menstrual so, as soon as it was spilt, the wife had to separate from her husband for at least twelve days. Far from its being a time of unbridled passion, many newlyweds slept apart. Such constraints did not apply to Susannah, whose attempt to reinvent herself stopped short of claiming virginity. She and Zvi would have been able to spend the entire honeymoon in bed had she not been so determined to do things by the book that she refused to contemplate 'cheating'. Marta trusted that, in the heat of the moment, she would let her heart rule her head.

Her reflections were interrupted by Susannah herself, who walked up to the table and summoned her to dance. She hurried down, relishing the dual delights of escaping from Helena and taking her daughter's hand.

As she relaxed into the rhythm, she recaptured some of the joy she had known at Mark and Carla's wedding. Banishing her qualms, she called down such blessings on the marriage that against her better judgement she longed for some all-powerful father figure to respond.

Ten minutes on the dance floor brought a sharp reminder of her elder-stateswoman status. Susannah also needed a rest, and they returned to their seats to find Rivka adjusting her wig, which had been dislodged in the crush.

'Forgive me, Mrs Granville, but I thought you should know that the Bishop has passed out.'

'What?' Marta turned to see the Rabbi, the one man licensed to enter their preserve.

'He appears to have overindulged a little. No matter. Only to be encouraged at a wedding.'

'Is he all right?'

'Perfectly. He was grinning and gurgling, then, when he tried to stand up, he collapsed.' She discerned a hint of amusement at Anglican intemperance.

'Let's leave him to sleep it off, so long as you're sure he's no trouble.'

'None whatsoever.'

'After all he has the right to celebrate his darling daughter's marriage.'

Making light of this further evidence of Edwin's frailty, she gave Susannah a kiss and sat for an hour, sipping champagne and chatting to Helena and Alice, whose support for Susannah's new life sprang from her own flirtation with the Alpha course at Holy Trinity Brompton, a source of considerable distress to her mother who looked to the Church of England to contain emotion not to ferment it. Slipping out to the loo, she was accosted by a plump woman who began by telling her to 'call me Dolly Levi,' which she did, only to find that it wasn't her name but a hint at her role as matchmaker. 'If it weren't for me, they'd never have met,' she declared. It seemed only polite to thank her, at which point the woman who identified herself as Rachel began to cry.

Seeing it as a sign, she took leave of her fellow guests and collected Helena who, with characteristic thrift, had asked if she and Harry might share the taxi. She sought out Susannah, explaining that it was time to take her father back to the hotel.

'I hope you'll be very happy, my darling.'

'I already am, Ma. You don't need to hope. Not only do I get to spend the rest of my life with the man I love, but all my sins are forgiven.'

'Just because you've married?' she asked incredulously.

'Yes, isn't it wonderful? The Rabbis say that today God wipes both our slates clean, so we can start again from scratch.'

Marta baulked at the words. Her own secularism, a term she preferred to the negative *atheism*, had been learnt at her father's knee. Nothing in her life, not even marriage to Edwin, had displaced it. On the contrary, she was convinced that it was her distance from her husband's beliefs which had spared her the disillusion common to clergy wives. The irony was that, whereas Edwin had moved towards her way of thinking, their three children had renounced it. Yet, for all the virtues of Mark's meditative spirituality and Clement's prayerful painting, she could find none in Susannah's rigid rules.

The elation of the dance had vanished and she was overcome by gloom. She longed to leave before she infected the rest of the company. Lacking the Rabbi's clerical immunity, she sent word to Edwin via a messenger system as tortuous as the one in his club. She arranged to meet him in the lobby and, ten minutes later, he was led out by two waiters to face the full force of Helena's wrath. It was less his weakness that offended her than its public display. The vehemence with which he rebutted the charge convinced Marta of both his sobriety and his good faith.

'I'm not drunk. And I wasn't asleep. I had the strangest sensation in my head. I knew what was happening but I couldn't respond to it. Like being under the knife without enough anaesthetic.'

'Eddy, really!' Helena said with a shudder, but his subsequent whimpering silenced even her.

'Oh darling, I hope that it wasn't that painful,' Marta said.

'Not painful, no, but frightening. It was so frightening and so odd.'

His exhaustion was evident as he sat with his eyes closed and his head on her shoulder throughout the drive, before slumping in a chair the moment they reached their room. His lack of coordination made the effort of helping him first into his pyjamas and then into bed so arduous that she fell asleep as soon as she lay down. Waking the next morning to hear of his disturbed night, she ascribed his headache to insomnia. Even so, she was loath to take any risks and insisted on calling the hotel doctor who, after a brief examination, agreed with Edwin that he was suffering from a mixture of fatigue and tension aggravated by the heat, and advised that the best remedy would be to spend the day in bed.

With the doctor's backing, Edwin urged her to stick to their plan of visiting Clement.

'I did say I'd give him a post-mortem on the wedding,' she said, instantly regretting the phrase. 'But, if you're feeling the same this afternoon, we'll head straight home.'

'Impossible! There's the Rabbi's party. You know Nanna. She'll be mortally wounded if we don't go.'

'You're not going anywhere if you're not up to it.'

'I just need sleep. I'm so tired I can't see straight. There's a six-foot crevice running through the centre of the room.'

'What do you mean?'

'Talking only makes it worse. Believe me, a few hours rest and I'll be right as rain.'

Taking him at his word, she made her way to Regent's Park. Her heart sank when Clement opened the door, wearing a thick sweater despite the heat, his pallor accentuated by haystack hair and a wispy beard that only a folk-singer would think fashionable. He winced at the light and kissed her listlessly before hurrying back into the muggy drawing room, its star-stencilled walls a testament to more spirited days. Making no attempt to play host, he sprawled in a chair and told her to dump her bags anywhere, indifferent even to the two cakes Mrs Shepherd had baked for him. She perched on the arm of his chair, stroking his cheek, of which he was surprisingly tolerant, while resisting the urge to comb his hair.

'How are you, darling?' she asked tentatively.

'I'm fine. Hunky-dory. I wake up every morning with a head full of soggy tissue-paper, and my legs feel as though they're wrapped in rubber bands, but it's bearable.'

'Have you spoken to your specialist?'

'I said it's bearable. But I'm bored with me. I want to hear about the wedding. Every grizzly detail. Promise to leave nothing out.'

Mindful that his sympathy for Chassidic ritual stopped at Chagall, she passed over the more contentious aspects of the ceremony in favour of the music, which felt as partial as commending the canapés at one of his shows. She was on safer ground poking fun at Helena, playing up her pomposity and endorsing his description of her as 'an old trout out of water'.

'Did she ask after me?'

'Helena?'

'Susannah!'

'Not to me,' she said, wondering at her sudden inability to lie. 'Actually, it's Shoshanna.'

'What?'

'Shoshanna.' She tried to shrug off a change that cut her to the quick. It felt as though Susannah were rejecting not just the name that they had christened her (in Edwin's case, literally) but the love they had heaped on her for forty years. Yet she knew better than to hand any fresh ammunition to Clement. 'From now on she wants to be called by her Hebrew name.'

'Is there no end to it?'

'There are honourable precedents. Think Saul to Paul or Simon to Peter.'

'Sure, but the Bible doesn't say if they kept their old names at home. Maybe Peter's wife and mother-in-law called him Rocky?'

His sardonic laugh dashed any hope that he might be ready to make peace with his sister. The bitterness of their dissension unearthed her deep-rooted guilt. She stood up and moved to the window.

'Would you describe me as a bad mother?' she asked, fixing her gaze on the drive.

'Why? What's Susannah been saying?'

'Shoshanna... and she's said nothing. It's me. I was away such a lot when you were growing up. All those field trips to Africa.'

'Don't flatter yourself,' he said lightly. 'We had Pa and Nanny. Then when you came home it was all the more special.'

'Was it? Even then, how much time did I get to spend with you? I was too busy being Marta Gorski, ubiquitous author of *The Eden People*.'

'Since when?'

'So much easier being a mentor to thousands of ardent young admirers – basking in their clear, uncomplicated devotion – than a mother to my own children!'

'That's nonsense, Ma, and you know it.'

'And what about Susannah... Shoshanna? If we'd been closer, would she still have left home at eighteen? Wouldn't she have gone to university and met someone suitable instead of...'

'Zvi.'

'I meant Chris. But perhaps you're right. Perhaps I'm to blame for both of them.'

'When did I say that?'

'It was obviously the sight of me forever on the move, abandoning the three of you – not to mention your father – that made her go to the other extreme with Chris and Zvi.'

'They couldn't be more different.'

'Maybe not, but they've both asked her to play the same little-wifey role.'

'Come on, Ma, you know very well that people are more complicated than that... and Susannah certainly is! I can remember hysterical scenes when she accused us all – not just you – of somehow suffocating and neglecting her at the same time.' Marta smiled faintly. 'So please, no more talk of bad mothers. You were the best.'

'Thank you, darling. You're very sweet.'

She was doubly grateful for his 'best'. Her own mother had been killed in the war. She herself had survived by dint of a cunning beyond her years. She sometimes feared that, having been forced to grow up so fast, she had lost the ability to relate to her own children, crediting them with a resilience for which, in the gentle English countryside, they had had little call.

Age made her increasingly aware of her vanished childhood. There were no portraits or letters or diaries or objects, let alone people, to fill in the gaps. All that she had were archive pictures to give her a vicarious authenticity. The loss had been compounded by the need to disown her past on coming to England. It was not that people were cruel or that she suffered the prejudice which had blighted survivors in other parts of Europe, but that they had no wish to dwell on the horrors. The most precious reward of peace was peace of mind. It was safer to picture Hitler as a murderous psychopath than as an astute politician who had legitimised a nation's – or, worse, a race's – darkest fears. The truth was particularly painful for Edwin, whose faith had been rocked by the revelation of the camps. She had conspired in the reticence, as tight-lipped on the subject of her life before reaching Dover as the most fervid Little Englander. Yet now when, after more than sixty years, she found herself sharing her solitude with the sights and sounds of the ghetto, she wondered if, the spectre of Edwin's Alzheimer's notwithstanding, the real horror of growing old was not to lose one's mind but to doubt one's memories.

'There were two photographers filming the ceremony,' she said. 'I found them intrusive, but I'm starting to see the point. They make up for the defects of memory.'

'That from the woman who claimed that what we didn't remember was as significant as what we did!'

'Did I say that?'

'I remember it word for word. Ha! You said we remembered what mattered to us and forgot the rest, or else our minds would be as stuffed as a storeroom.' She tried to recall if she had meant it seriously or if it had been a stock formula to comfort a child. 'These days people are so insecure, they're more concerned to record events than to experience them, living not in the here and now but in some imaginary future. It's sick!'

'Darling, it was just a wedding video. Photographs by another name.'

'It goes far deeper than that,' he said, sinking back in his chair and flinging his right leg over the arm in a posture that looked as uncomfortable as it was ungainly. 'Memory lies at the heart of what it is to be human. In fact I'd go further: it's the reason we both need and respond to art. It's the part of our brain that creates and shapes narratives, that filters images, that draws analogies and chucks away inessentials.' Marta rejoiced to see him roused from his torpor. 'What do you think, Ma? Can it be an accident that, at a time when we're trusting less and less to our memories, we're growing less and less discriminating about art? We've lost the power of selectivity and substituted choice. We may have a world of information at our fingertips, but we've got fewer and fewer ways to assess it.'

'Then we'll find more. The human brain is endlessly inventive.'

'Not when it's dumbed down. In any other context, *virtual* means *almost... not entirely*; on the Web, it's become synonymous with truth. We no longer rely on our memories to retain the things that matter but delegate the function to a machine. Even if the motive is pure, the process is corrupt. When everything's recorded, nothing can be valued.'

'Don't you mean evaluated?'

'In this case, it's the same.'

Despite the eloquence of his argument, she yearned for an album of childhood photographs to substantiate her memories. All she had been able to preserve was a single highly charged but painfully equivocal family portrait, so devoid of any frame of reference that she had no way of knowing which of the two little girls in the foreground was her.

'Even an imperfect record is better than a fading memory,' she said. 'I sometimes wonder if my sister existed at all.'

'I didn't think you liked talking about Aunt Agata.'

Her heart soared at the spontaneous gift of the *aunt*. 'The truth is that we weren't very close. I'd find it easier if we'd been more like you and Mark.'

'Easier to talk perhaps. Not to carry on living.'

'You can't imagine how happy it made me to see you together. I remember when you tied yourself to his waist and made out you were Siamese twins.'

'Then you've forgotten how much Mark loathed it. He tried to rip off the cord but only managed to tie himself – and me – in knots. He hated any suggestion that we were freaks – or even curiosities, threatening to beat up anyone who stared at us at school. He longed for nothing more than to be ordinary. He felt better once I'd told him there were twenty million twins in the world.'

'Is that true?'

'Of course, or I wouldn't have said it.'

'I'm sorry,' she said quickly. 'But that's the population of a small country.'

'I know. I spoilt it all when I proposed that we should found one. Twinsylvania.'

He fell silent, and she took advantage of the lull to think of Mark. For all her awe of Clement's artistic talent and respect for Shoshanna's executive skill, she remained proudest of Mark's social conscience. She hesitated to admit it, even to herself, but, with his adolescent schemes for changing the world and adult schemes for feeding it, he had been the child closest to her heart. Life would have been very different had he survived. First and foremost, she would have had grandchildren. It was one of the bitterest ironies of growing old that intellectual triumphs paled beside family ties. Nothing made her feel more inadequate than hearing her friends talk about babysitting. She had even caught herself gazing jealously at photographs of bone-weary Africans caring for grandchildren orphaned by AIDS. So intense was her longing that she barely stopped to wonder if the children themselves were healthy. She was brought back to reality by the sight of her own infected son.

'There's one photograph I don't need to spur my memory,' she said, moving across to his chair and taking his hand. 'I see his face every time I look at yours.'

'What as? An aide-memoire or a memento mori?' Clement asked.

'I didn't mean – '

'Not to worry, Ma, I'm glad to be good for something. What hurts most is not having felt that psychic tremor when he died – that sense of someone walking over my grave times a thousand – which a surviving twin's supposed to feel. I was probably drinking or drugging or sleeping around.'

'Or working,' she countered, refusing to collude in his self-disgust.

'But the sense of loss – as sharp as an amputated limb – I felt that all right. I still do. The better part of myself cut off.'

'You're your own best self.'

'You don't understand! Think of the closeness you feel towards Susannah or me and square it. We were part of each other from the start. Not just the same womb but the same egg!'

Reluctant to risk a reply, she broke away and drifted around the room. As she gazed out of the window, she felt a pressing need for fresh air. With Clement unwilling to accompany her to the park, she suggested a stroll in the garden. She strove to curb her impatience as he searched for his sunglasses, which the gathering clouds were rapidly making redundant, and threw a jacket over his sweater. By the time he was finally ready, the sky was leaden and there was a distinct nip in the air, nevertheless she was determined not to shiver and so give him an excuse to turn back.

The moment she stepped through the door, she saw the reason for his procrastination. Instead of the usual elegant vista, she was facing a wilderness:

the patio unswept and the paths mossy; bindweed choking the pergola and a rambling rose buckling the fence; a few hardy perennials trapped in a tangle of dead heads and withered stalks. Only the lawn showed any sign of recent care.

'That's Mike's domain,' he said, as she challenged him. 'I'm in charge of the bed department.'

'Then I suggest you wake up to your responsibilities,' she said, ignoring the innuendo. 'This is a disgrace.'

'I don't have the energy. No, it's nothing to do with the virus,' he said quickly, as if his physical health were her only cause for concern. 'I used to love coming out here in the evenings. The perfect way to wind down after a day in the studio. Now I've stopped painting, there's no point.'

'There's a simple answer to that.'

'I'm afraid there's more at stake than a few flowers.'

'Such as?'

'Roxborough really changed things for me. Not just what happened to Pa. Though you said yourself he hasn't been the same since.'

'Your father's eighty-three. He wouldn't have been the same anyway.'

'But stirring up all that hatred.'

'Blinkered, twisted people. The hatred's in them. You simply brought it to light.'

'Perhaps. But I can't fight it any more.'

'Then the forces of darkness will win. Don't you remember evil triumphing when good men do nothing? You're a good man, Clement.'

'Your faith in human nature is admirable. It's almost enough to restore my own.'

'I'm glad to hear it.'

'I said *almost*.' He squeezed her hand. 'It's still more extraordinary given everything you were called on to witness.'

'Don't forget that even then there were flickers of hope. I saw people who risked their lives to protect their families, their friends, and sometimes even total strangers. You may think it was a futile gesture, pitting a weak human body against batons and bullets and jackboots. But it wasn't. Quite the reverse. Because in the memory of the survivors – and I'm one of them – not to mention the world memory, that sacrifice remains. Not a Jewish sacrifice to honour God or a Christian sacrifice to redeem man, but a simple sacrifice to the ideal of humanity.'

'What about a Muslim sacrifice?'

'I'm afraid I don't know enough about them to comment.'

'I do. At least about one of them. Rafik, my model.'

'Your Christ?'

'I can't get any news of him. The British authorities bundled him on a plane home and now they've washed their hands of him – a phrase which is horribly apt under the circumstances. I've rung the Embassy in Algiers. I asked them to make inquiries. I explained he was in fear of his life. But no joy! He's a success story, a repatriated asylum seeker. What happens next is none of their concern.'

'Then you must confront them through your painting. When you're blessed with a talent like yours, it's a crime to waste it.'

'You're not consistent, Ma. In *The Eden People*, you described how the Hadza have no art. Your ideal society has no use for Bellini and Caravaggio or Shakespeare and Bach, let alone Granville! Who knows? Maybe discord and dissatisfaction came into the world with the cave painters: the primal ego-tists. Suddenly, there was a new breed of people eager not to do but to document, whether it was the hunt or fertility dances or, as we're now told, erotic fantasies. Yes, that would be fitting, wouldn't it: if I'm the heir to ancient pornographers?'

'True, the Hadza don't need art,' Marta said, brushing aside the hyper-bole, 'but for those of us exiled from Eden there's no greater source of enlightenment.'

'I used to think so. Pa once said that human beings were uniquely poised between Whipsnade Zoo and Chartres Cathedral, but that what tipped the balance towards Chartres was art. Then Mike, who favours the zoo, told me about penguins who not only search for precious stones to decorate their nests but choose their mates on the basis of the decoration. At a stroke, he destroyed any notion of art as a divine spark and equated it with prostitution.'

'I can't speak for penguins,' Marta said, keen to lighten the mood, 'but, with humans, we're talking imagination not greed.'

'After much deliberation, I've concluded that the whole point of art – the reason governments don't just tolerate but sponsor it – is to give people like you and me, the educated but powerless, the fantasy of control. We read books to gain a privileged insight into other peoples' minds; we sit in theatres to watch their lives played out in front of us; we go to exhibitions so that, even though we can't influence the bigger picture, we can weigh up smaller ones.' She flinched as he kicked a pebble into a flower bed. 'You, of all people, should appreciate Auden's despair at the failure of his poetry to save a single Jew from the gas chambers.'

'Like so much despair, it strikes me as self-indulgent,' she said pointedly. 'How can we be sure that there wouldn't have been more Nazis without his poetry? Come to that, do you know how much of it was even translated?'

'I'd go a step further and say that artists actively assisted the Nazi pro-gramme. I don't just mean the Riefenstahls and Furtwänglers and Strausses with their compromised loyalties, but the Mozarts and Beethovens. Listening to the concentration camp orchestras at night gave the guards the peace of mind with which to murder more inmates the next day. They applauded the music while treating the players as lower than the sheep who supplied the strings for the violins.'

'Have you considered that the music might have brought peace of mind to the players as well? To know that, even if they died, it would live on. Art is the part of us that will survive.'

'Art is an illusion, Ma. And the most absurd illusion of all is the illusion of permanence. When the microbes inherit the earth, do you suppose they'll be experts on Titian?'

Weighed down by his misery, Marta sank on to a nearby bench where she soaked up the residual warmth of the cushion. Clement stood beside her, fighting a losing battle with a fly.

'I can't bear to see you like this,' she said. 'Are you doing nothing useful with your life?'

'One evening a week, I volunteer on an immigration helpline, but it's hardly taxing. If only I were more New Agey, I could pretend I was working on myself.'

'And everything's fine with Mike?'

'Oh Ma, even after all these years, you locate every problem in the bedroom!'

'Thank you, Clement!' To her surprise, she felt herself blushing.

'To answer your question: no, it's not. He's such a dynamo. He thinks lassitude is a class thing I inherited along with the house.'

'Depression can damage the immune system.'

'Really? Is that so? Perhaps we can play a game to help me snap out of it?'

'There's no call to be sarcastic, darling. I'm only thinking of you.'

'I'm sorry. It's just that things haven't been easy.'

'I've been reading up on the literature. They say that HIV and AIDS are now no different from diabetes. You can lead a perfectly normal life.'

'Do you remember Oliver?'

'Oliver who?'

'Oliver, my ex.'

'Yes, of course.' It had been so long since he mentioned him that she had supposed him to be as taboo as Shoshanna's Chris.

'Although, actually, it's Newsom. He's changed his name.'

'What for?'

'I don't know. Ask Shoshanna! I think he needed a new vibration or something. He has AIDS. We've been in touch again this past year.'

'Isn't that hard for Mike?'

'On the contrary, he considers it a part of my communal responsibility. Newsom has anal cancer and a blood clot on his lungs that won't respond to treatment. Meanwhile, friends who've been on the drugs for years are suffering heart attacks and strokes. So it's not quite diabetes... not yet.'

'But you told me you were fine,' she said, panicking at the prospect of further revelations.

'Oh yes, the clinic's blue-eyed boy. At least for now. But seeing Newsom so sick has set me thinking. If I should reach a stage where I become more of an illness than a person, then I don't want to linger on.'

'You may change your mind when the time comes... which I'm sure it won't.' She clasped his hand.

'Perhaps. But for the moment I'm not in any doubt. When my own quality of life is destroyed and what's more I'm destroying the people around me, I want to make a dignified exit.'

'What about your faith? How can you take the life God has given you?'

'It's precisely because of my faith that I don't have a problem. I've always thought suicide must be harder for an atheist. I believe God gave me free will, which is to be exercised even *in extremis*. Besides, unlike the priests who hold that I'll rot in Hell for the sin of despair or Carla with her fear of being reborn as a hungry ghost, I know I'll be welcomed into the hereafter.' His face lit up and, for the first time during her visit, she saw traces of the old Clement. 'I've talked it over with Mike. He said that, if the crunch comes, he'd be willing to help me.' She was not surprised that their relationship was under strain if that were the gist of their pillow talk. 'But, if for some reason he wasn't around, would you do it?'

'There's nothing worse than outliving your children. I've been through it once, Clement. I couldn't bear to go through it again.'

'You told me you loved me more than life. I know you meant your own life, but what about mine? That's the 64,000-dollar question. Could you love me more than my life, Ma?'

'It's turned chilly. I'm not wearing as many layers as you. I'm going back indoors.'

2

Reeling from her encounter with Clement, Marta returned to the hotel to find that Edwin had spent the whole day in bed. He refused to recall the doctor, insisting that he had just been catching up on sleep and his headache had all but disappeared. He was so anxious not to upset Shoshanna that she agreed to go to the party alone, in return for a promise that, come what may, they would leave for home in the morning. To cheer herself up and challenge the company, she decided to wear her new red and white polka-dot dress, thrilling to both the coolness of the close-fitting silk and the defiance of her naked arms. She kissed Edwin's forehead as gently as if he were a child, assuring him that she would not be late, and, with a sigh at his innocent 'Enjoy yourself!', made her way down to the lobby, where the doorman hailed a cab to take her to Hendon. She settled back in the lumpy seat, shutting her eyes in anticipation of a wearying evening, only to wake up with a start half an hour later as they rattled through the drably uniform streets of north London.

The Rabbi's door was opened by a surly teenager whose pallid face betrayed a mixture of bad diet, stale rooms and excessive study. He shifted uneasily while she spoke, twiddling the tassels on his shirt and gazing at his feet, as though listening to a chorus of 'thou shalt nots' in his head. Leaving her standing in the hall, he went in search of his mother. She shot an idle glance at the portraits plastered over the wall, torn between envy and dismay at renewing her acquaintance with the Rabbi's seventeen children and fifty-four grandchildren, assembled as for a touring production of *Fiddler on the Roof*. This was a world in which the family reigned supreme and yet, as though conscious of its own deficiencies, it had expanded to the population of a small town.

Spurred on by the sounds of revelry elsewhere in the house, she ventured through the nearest doorway and was instantly confronted with her error. Conversation stopped dead as the roomful of black-clad men stared at her with a hostility she had last met when she led a protest of desperate women into the Oxford Playhouse Gents. The memory bolstered her and she turned to her neighbour with a request for a drink. He mumbled into his beard, casting a panic-stricken look at Zvi who, moving close – but not too close – to his maverick mother-in-law, explained that the women were gathered in the dining room. 'Where else?' she said with a smile and excused herself, at which the talk started up as abruptly as if they had pressed *Resume*. She made her way to the dining room where Rivka greeted her warmly, berating her son for his failure to tell her that she had arrived.

'Boys!' she said in mock despair.

'I know. I had two myself,' Marta replied, before remembering Rivka's ten. She moved to Shoshanna who was deep in discussion with Etta and Rachel. Kissing her daughter, she was aware of a change in her, which she initially attributed to an evening-after glow, only to realise that she was wearing a wig. Although the auburn bob had been carefully matched to her own hair, the difference in texture was plain to the practised eye. She was appalled by the thought that Shoshanna had spent the first day of married life having her hair shorn and longed for reassurance about the wedding night itself. So, with an apology to Etta and Rachel, she drew her daughter aside.

'Well then, how does it feel to be Mrs Latsky?' she asked lightly.

'Bliss. Pure, indescribable bliss. What more can I say? It's like we've been married for years... but in a special way, not predictable. Does that sound odd?'

'Not at all,' Marta replied, striving for conviction. 'And last night...?'

'Admit it, Ma,' Shoshanna said with a grin. 'That's all you really wanted to know. Don't worry! It was perfect. Everything you said about waiting too long and expecting too much... forget it! Your daughter has struck gold.'

As Shoshanna returned to her guests, Marta made her way to the buffet. The food – herring, gefilte fish, pickled cucumber and cheesecake – took her back seventy years to the warmth of her grandmother's kitchen and the traditional dishes that her mother refused to cook. For the first time her hopes of a grandchild were focused on a girl, who would enable her to honour the memory of her own *Bubbe*. Then, wondering whether those hopes might at last be fulfilled, she cast a furtive glance at Shoshanna's stomach.

At a signal from her son, Rivka collected Shoshanna, Etta and Marta and led them across the hall. Marta's longing to break down barriers was thwarted again when, instead of entering the study, they sat on four chairs strategically ranged outside the door. Zvi stood next to them, while remaining firmly in the sanctum, and spoke a Hebrew blessing over a cup of wine.

Marta used the opportunity to assess her new son-in-law. His resonant voice and powerful presence were undeniably attractive, but his earnestness and insularity were hard to bear. Although he did business around the globe, she had yet to hear of his showing an interest in anything beyond his own backyard. She was roused from her reflections by a burst of clapping as Zvi drank from the cup and handed it to Shoshanna, who followed suit to further applause. Zvi then hurried back into the room, leaving the women stranded.

With Rivka announcing that she had to check on the food and Shoshanna that she should go back to her friends, Marta turned to Etta, with whom she felt a rapport that was independent of their children.

'I feel as if I've travelled back in time,' she said.

'You have. We both have,' Etta replied. 'I find it very... what's the word?... disconcerting. Zvi would say that it was the war that made me join the kibbutz: that I wished to live in a world where religion was not of importance, a socialist state that has been given the name Israel.'

'Was he right?'

'In parts. But my loss of religion was much bigger than what I saw in the camp.'

'Which one were you in?' Marta asked gently.

'Mauthausen.'

Marta trembled as the bond was reinforced. She was struck by the possibility that Etta had known her mother, that they had shared the same hut, even the same bunk, crammed in so tightly that they were forced to turn together when the night guards prodded them with their sticks. Suddenly, the remote chance became a certainty, and she yearned to know whether the bunk-mate had ever mentioned a daughter of about Etta's age. But it was too great a burden to place on a new acquaintance. Besides, Etta had a story of her own which she began to relate.

'Both my parents were gassed, then burnt in the crematorium from the camp. One day I was walking in the yard with my little sister when an old woman out of another hut came to us. If this was a fairy tale, she would be a witch... but she was not a witch; she was far too much broken. I clasped on to Sara's hand so tightly. "See that smoke," this old woman said, "it's your mother and father." Her words made no sense in my mind. I remember thinking: I am just a child; I cannot be understanding this well. But she went on. "They're dead. It's their bodies. They're burning them." Then she laughed like in pain and disappeared. Although not in smoke. This came later.' Marta felt the fumes from the chimneys misting her eyes. 'I'm sorry. You're sad. I should not have spoken of it.'

'No, don't worry. It's nothing you said. I have memories of my own.' Etta's confession spurred her to speak. 'My mother and sister were also in Mauthausen. You might have known...'

'Maybe I have. But the years... so many names... this old head. But we must not be sad, no? We are having a party! I once heard my cousin in Haifa speaking to another survivor. They did not cry or make complaints about what has happened. On the contrary, they made jokes about it. Bad jokes... terrible jokes. "What was your hotel like then?" my cousin asked. "Far too crowded," her friend said, "they let everyone in." "And the food?" "No taste, no taste at all. Although they had their own special dishes: grey water; green water." I was angry. All the many dead people and they were laughing at them. Now I understand what they were doing. More, I am full of... what do you say when you do this?' Etta clapped her hands.

'Applause?'

'That is right. I am full of applause for it.'

Conversation was interrupted by Chanan, who had escaped to use the lavatory. 'I have smiled and I have nodded and I have raised my shoulders like this, yes, when people talk to me about things that I do not understand and I do not care. I need you, Etta. I need you to tell me again who I am.'

'And I need some air,' Marta said. 'Do you think anyone would notice if we sneaked outside?'

'Good idea,' Chanan said. 'Fresh air! Oh yes, this is a blessing.'

The three crept through the kitchen and into the garden like truanting children. Their delight in their daring faded in the face of overgrown grass, overrun borders and a ramshackle shed, the only splash of colour coming from a red plastic car seat upended on the wasteland of the lawn. Marta recoiled from a contempt for nature that made Clement's unweeded flower beds look positively Edenic.

'With all those children,' she said, 'you'd have thought one of them could have handled a mower.'

'I think how my father would have hated this,' Chanan said. 'It was because of this reason he left Poland.' Marta pictured a street of slovenly neighbours. 'He had the feeling we had become like jokes of ourselves... you understand?' Marta nodded. 'Everything was narrow. The world we lived in was narrow; the thoughts in our heads were narrow; the jobs we were given were narrow. Even the streets of our houses were narrow!'

'Chanan's father was one of the founding men of our kibbutz,' Etta said, as proudly as if he had sailed on the *Mayflower*. 'Chanan was the first of our childrens to be born there.'

'I grew up living in a dream. Zvi, my son, accuses us with throwing away God. If this is a crime, then yes, I am guilty. But we did it for a reason – '

'We did it because we have reason,' Etta said.

'And because we had trust that children who were born with no God would give all their good faith to man.'

'We believed we were bringing the path not just for the Jews but for the whole human beings,' Etta said, effortlessly picking up Chanan's theme. 'In time – maybe not so soon but in time – all peoples, all countries would be like the kibbutz. Women would not take rules from their husbands. Childrens would not take rules from their fathers. We would not judge who we were by what we could buy... But we were wrong.'

'Say rather "We were not yet right",' Chanan said.

'We were wrong,' Etta insisted. 'We are living in a world with the spirit of a fitted kitchen. And my son, he is not happy with this. Good! But what does he do? He does not look forward, no. He does not try to change how things are working. Instead, he runs back into the Middle Ages.'

Etta's pain was so raw that Marta feared she would burst into tears. As Chanan took her in his arms and rubbed the small of her back, Marta had the disturbing sensation of seeing her parents. Dismissing it as sentimentality, she hurried to resume the conversation.

'It isn't the Lubavitch faith I find so hard to take but their certainty. I've lived among people of faith most of my married life. But they were people who dared to doubt... who declared that doubt made their faith stronger. Not in Edwin's case, it's true...'

'Where is the Bishop?' Chanan asked. 'We have not seen him this whole evening.'

'No, he's resting at the hotel. Yesterday was quite a strain for him. He's not a young man.'

'We are none of us young,' Chanan said. 'Of course I make exceptions for you.'

'You flatter me,' Marta replied, raising her eyebrows.

'And your dress,' Etta said. 'May I?'

'Of course.'

'It's so delicate,' Etta said, fingering the cloth.

'Mousseline,' Marta said. 'I'm afraid that some of our fellow guests have me marked down as a scarlet woman, but I felt an intense desire to assert myself. Besides it's cool.' As if on cue, Chanan took out a handkerchief and mopped his brow. 'But, to return to Edwin: I hope I didn't make him sound glib. For years he struggled to reconcile his faith with the anomalies plain to a man of his intelligence and integrity. I blamed myself. It couldn't have been easy singing *All things bright and beautiful* alongside a wife whose family perished in the camps.'

'He must have loved you very much,' Etta said.

'Too much, I used to think. But not now. Over the years we've grown closer. It's as though our minds have caught up with the rest of us. When I said Edwin had lost his faith, that was only half-true. He lost his faith in God, but not in humanity. And my own remains as strong as when my parents taught me how people – *the people* – would change the world. Of course my critics... my detractors regard it as perverse. They maintain that my sole concern in going to Africa, in "latching on to the Hadza", in their phrase, has been to prove that what happened to me – what happened to us all – under the Nazis was an aberration and so put it behind me. To this end, I picked on a society as remote as possible from the modern world and claimed that they were alone in living authentically. Patronising drivel! Besides, why should I fabricate the evidence when it's everywhere to see? And nowhere more compelling than in Germany itself. It's been called a *miracle* that a country which had been devastated – and not just physically – was rebuilt so soon after the War. But, to my mind, it shows that, however far fascism may have spread, it didn't run deep. The fundamental decency of human nature survived and took the first opportunity to reassert itself.'

'I wish you would have spoken up at the town meetings,' Chanan said. 'Especially when the troubles came. In one minute you would have made ten people change their minds.'

'But for how long would it last?' Etta asked. 'Oh, I do not question your thoughts, Marta. I know how important they are. I too have read *The Eden Peoples* when it is first published.'

'1964. The same year the twins were born.' Marta was warmed by the memory of her *annus mirabilis*.

'No, it must have been after this – when it is first published in Hebrew. It will sound foolish to you, but I felt that you were writing this book directly for me... for us. You were writing about a justice society. We were living in it. Or we were trying. For this we have given up so much. I am not now speaking of shekels. We have given up so many happy things of family life, because we thought we were building for the future.'

'And I'm sure you were,' Marta said. 'I can't speak from personal experience; I only made two brief visits to kibbutzim to lecture. But I spent years, all told, with the Hadza, who bring up their children communally. It allows them to bond with the whole tribe, not just their parents, and to grow up far more securely, free of all the neuroses we've been taught, post-Freud, to view as universal.'

'Maybe you are right,' Etta said. 'But even if these values are still true for the Africans, they have been lost for us. Little by little the hope of the kibbutz, it has vanished. The new kibbutznik, they have new ideas.'

'No, they do not have ideas,' Chanan said, 'they have demands... is this how you call it?' Marta nodded. 'For them the kibbutz is just a place to live; it is not a way of life.'

'It is not a way to change life,' Etta said.

'No, it is most certainly not this,' Chanan said. 'They make quarrels with giving up their children... as if they think it has been easy for us. They make quarrels with the way we run our farm. They make us start new businesses to bring money, and it destroys our dream.'

'And they do it with much cunning,' Etta said. 'They have a revolution of language. What is once individualism is becoming choice.'

'Worse, my Etta, it is *consumer choice*. And we make ours by moving far away.'

'I can see that it must have been heartbreaking,' Marta said.

'We have come to Tel Aviv,' Chanan said. 'Our friends from abroad, they tell us we must leave Israel. They have been watching while this country gives up its dream the same as the kibbutz. But we are too old. We have lost too much blood here. These are our people. This is our home.'

Marta recalled Shoshanna's account of their daughter's death in a bomb blast and marvelled at their equanimity. After securing their promise to visit Beckley on their next trip, she went indoors to say goodbye to Rivka and Shoshanna, who showed no signs of flagging either under the pressure of the present party or the prospect of repeating it in a different house but with the same guests, food and conversation, every night for the next two weeks. She returned to the hotel, where she tiptoed into the room to find Edwin snoring. Fumbling for her nightdress, she changed in the bathroom and slipped into bed.

She lay back on the pillow, but exhaustion failed to induce sleep. Chanan's story of his father's flight from Poland had stirred up memories of her parents' similar disaffection with their native country, although, as disciples of Marx rather than Herzl, they believed it their duty to stay and establish the new order in Europe rather than in Palestine, even after Hitler's aggression had put the entire continent at risk. Their convictions cost them dear when, as Jews, they were herded into the ghetto to share a foetid room with her aunt and, in the cruellest irony, her grandparents who, before the Occupation, had refused to so much as break bread in their non-kosher house. With a skill honed by twenty years in the print union, her father persuaded the guards to allow Marta and her aunt to work in a leather factory outside the ghetto. At twelve she was too young for the job but, overnight, he added three years to her age. Besides she was attractive. If the War taught her one thing, it was that even the most zealous official was prepared to bend the rules for a pretty face.

At the factory, her aunt put her father's escape plan into practice. The Nazis were fanatical about hygiene, a fact which, in later years, Marta suspected had left their victims so vulnerable to the offer of showers. Three times a week they marched the entire workforce from the factory compound to the communal baths. After familiarising herself with both the route and the timetable, which the well-drilled guards never varied, her aunt outlined the initial steps. Once she had washed and dressed, Marta was to hide in the lavatories until her aunt knocked on the door. Then, when the guards turned their backs, they would dash across the courtyard to the laundry, waiting for the main contingent to move away before making their bid for safety.

This was the world of the medieval woodcut, with salvation on one side of a cliff and damnation on the other. The path was steep and craggy but, as her aunt explained, it was all that they had. She urged her niece to be brave, an unnecessary injunction since, at least in retrospect, her sole thought was to outwit the oppressor. In the event, Fortune smiled – she refused to credit any higher deity – and they evaded capture. Somehow her aunt had passed word to one of her father's ex-comrades, now active in the Resistance, who was waiting with money and papers to take them to a flat where, for the next two years, Marta lived as Christina. It helped that she not only looked the part but spoke it. Her parents' rejection of their heritage meant that she had been brought up speaking Polish and lacked all trace of a Yiddish accent. Try as she might, she could not recollect how she had occupied the time, a regrettable lapse when telling the story, its tone subtly altered from horror to adventure, to the twins for whom boredom was a fate worse than death. Their string of questions as to what she ate, how she paid for it and whether she was searched, exposed further gaps to shake their faith in the narrative.

She never saw her parents or sister again. She knew that they were deported after the doomed uprising in the ghetto, although she didn't discover where until much later. She too was deported, along with most of the population of Warsaw, after the equally abortive nationalist revolt the following year. If nothing else, she was glad that her parents had been spared the knowledge of their Soviet allies abandoning the city to its fate. With their Polish papers and Aryan looks, she and her aunt were sent to a work camp in Germany. They arrived in the autumn and she spent most of the winter shovelling snow in the biting cold. In the spring, with the war turning against them, the Nazis put their prisoners on trains to the Ruhr, which were heavily bombed by the RAF. Several years later, she learnt that Edwin had been a navigator on the raids. While aware that it was futile – even dangerous – to do so, she could not help wondering whether his had been one of the planes that had shot at her as she scrambled out of the burning train and ran for shelter in the woods. Later still, in the adventure story she made of her life, this was the point when Mark would yell out, more excited than appalled, 'Daddy, you tried to kill Mummy!' It was also the point when, as she buried her head in the hotel pillow, her eyes filled with tears.

The next morning they hiked to a nearby farm and, claiming to be refugees from the fighting, offered to work in exchange for food. The farmer's wife, with a husband at the Front, could not afford to ask questions. She housed them in the barn and fed them on mealy porridge which, however unpalatable it might sound to her finicky children, was manna after the cabbage soup in the camp. They stayed there, milking cows and planting turnips, until the advent of the British troops. For the first time since their escape from the factory, Christina reverted to Marta. They were introduced to an intelligence officer, Squadron Leader Marks, who explained that he was on a mission to assist any surviving Jews. He pledged them his support and, with the help of an American refugee agency, set about finding them a home. This caused their greatest heartache since leaving the ghetto, for her aunt moved to Amsterdam to live with her one remaining cousin while agreeing with the Squadron Leader, soon to become Uncle Leon, that the best place for Marta to resume her education would be England.

Whenever she had told the tale to her children, she skimmed over the next three years since, impatient with their own schooldays let alone anyone else's, they had no interest in her long struggle at the age of sixteen to make up for the lost years of study and, moreover, to do so in a foreign language. They were anxious for her to forge ahead to Oxford and their father, so that the story could reach its climax in them. Pondering it in private, however, she could not dispose of it so fast and, despite her exhaustion, she was transported back to the Southampton villa where, in the company of children from all over Europe, she had been taught English by a Hungarian professor with a horror-film accent. They were not encouraged to talk about their former lives, either their means of escape or their families' annihilation. Most were grateful for this code of silence. They were still young enough to feel joy at being alive and eager to explore the new world in which they found themselves. The past was a closed book. It was only sixty years on that it had become her regular bedtime reading.

After she had been there several months, a middle-aged woman with plaits, wearing a felt suit and kid gloves – gloves which made a lasting impression on Marta – interviewed her about her future. Putting her respect for her dead father over her longing for independence, she expressed a wish to go to university. The woman promised to do all that she could to help. This turned out to be a mixed blessing when, to improve the mathematics that had been a weakness even in Warsaw, she had her placed in a class of eight-year-olds.

Lying in the pitch-black bedroom, Marta could feel the blush suffusing her cheeks as she recalled her unwitting response to a simple arithmetical problem. 'If one train leaves the station at 9.30 a.m. travelling at 60 miles an hour with 45 people on board, and another train leaves the station at 9.45 a.m. travelling at 80 miles an hour with 30 people on board, how many miles will the whole group have travelled by 10.15?' As her fellow pupils chewed their pencils, she struggled to choke back her tears. Her neighbour, a girl ten years her junior, tried to comfort her. 'It's not hard,' she said, 'I'll show you.' But the figures were far starker when the passengers she pictured were travelling in cattle trucks without food or water or sanitation, and the destination to which they were heading was death.

She matriculated at nineteen and gained a place at Oxford, where she confronted the full force of the English class system. As a foreigner, she had some measure of protection. People found her hard to pin down. With her exotic accent and murdered family, she might have been the granddaughter of the Tsar. She made no secret of being Jewish, but her friends made no mention of it either, any more than they would have done a harelip or a strawberry mark. She was invited to spend the weekend in country houses where grammar-school girls would never have been allowed through the door. She discovered the limits of toleration when talking to the grandmother of one of her friends.

'Since the War, life has become so distressing,' the old lady said.

'What is it that most upsets you?' she asked solicitously.

'Hearing about refugee children.'

'I agree. We must do everything in our power to find them homes.'

'No, dear, you've missed the point. It's not the children that upset me; it's hearing about them.'

Although her memories of Oxford were defined by love affairs and sherry parties, she had spent the majority of her time in the library. She was far too conscious of the quirk of fate that had saved her from the camps to neglect her work. She gained a reputation for brilliance to add to her aura of suffering, a combination which proved to be irresistible to everyone from beaglers at Christ Church and poets at Magdalen to socialists at Balliol and rugby blues at Teddy Hall. It was not until Edwin, however, that she met a man whose intellectual quest matched, while never mirroring, her own. His gentleness, his passion and his military record enhanced the attraction of his rangy body and piercing eyes. Behind the cricket and crumpets and choral evensong, there was a touch of the ancient woodland about him, a primal energy that she was eager to tap. The irony was that she found herself allied to a family who were just as clannish as any of her weekend hosts. Edwin was destined for the church, a career (they never thought of it as a vocation) his parents had considered eminently suitable for a younger son but which, to their fury, he had refused to renounce after his brother's ship was torpedoed in the North Sea.

They waited ten years to marry, during which Edwin served as a curate in Clapham, a vicar in Barnes and a chaplain at Oriel, while she travelled back and forth to the Hadza and wrote her first book, another bone of contention for her future parents-in-law, who held that the only acceptable work for women was motherhood for the upper classes, teaching for the middle, and domestic service for the lower. In age-old fashion, they mellowed once she gave birth to the twins, becoming the most doting of grandparents. With Edwin's blessing, she determined not to deceive the children as to her family's fate. Her pride in telling the story so as to honour the loss without dwelling on the horror faltered only when she woke one morning to find Susannah inking a number on her arm. 'I'm doing it for you,' she protested. 'We had a film at school and Julia said you weren't a real refugee because you didn't have a tattoo.'

The memory dispelled sleep still further and she lay back on the pillow, prey to morbid conjecture. The same inauthenticity that her nine-year-old daughter had identified in her life, others had identified in her work, maintaining that to locate Eden in a remote Stone Age tribe was a sign not of inspiration but of despair. Thrashing about in the heavy sheets, restless in mind and body, she feared that they might be right. Was her belief in childhood innocence the result of her early exposure to adult depravity? Had she misled generations of children, not least her own, by her insistence on human perfectibility, driving Mark to his death and leaving Clement and Shoshanna helpless against disease and indoctrination? Craving reassurance, she crept to the bathroom, but the splash of cold water failed to drown the accusatory voices in her head. So she slipped back into bed and, shrinking from Edwin's warmth for fear of waking him, turned on her side and tried to sleep.

3

Next morning, Edwin's headache was so severe that Marta suspected her 'better to be ill at home' should be amended to 'better to be admitted to the local hospital'. His complaints about the grey patches encroaching on his vision filled her with a new fear of his going blind. The hotel manager did all in his power to smooth their departure, even sending one of his porters to load their luggage on to the train. Much to her relief, Edward dozed through most of the journey, only to be roused outside Reading by a steward intent on serving him his complimentary coffee. They were met at Oxford by Mr Shepherd, who could barely conceal his distress at the changes four days had wrought on his employer. Edwin's silence in the face of his questions forced her to speak for him, although she insisted that he would be his old self as soon as they reached Beckley. 'Too much excitement,' she said, feigning a laugh at a phrase with disturbing intimations of second childhood. At least his splitting head gave her the perfect excuse to urge caution on a driver, whose reckless way with bumps and bends looked set to increase the agony.

Each familiar landmark brought further reassurance. They drove through the blazoned gateway, past a weather-worn trio of naiads, to the walled garden where Charlie Heapstone was battling with a serpentine creeper, a stray branch dangling over his brawny back. They drew up beside the ancient laburnum, decked with sun-flecked flowers, and shuffled into the hall, where Ajax leapt joyfully at them and Mrs Shepherd offered an equally warm, if more sedate, welcome. Pausing to greet them, she led Edwin upstairs and, after seeing him into bed, made her way down to the kitchen to brief her housekeeper. No sooner had she sat down than she was accosted by Karen who, according to Mrs Shepherd, had come up from her cottage in readiness for her return. With a self-obsession which could no longer be excused by youth, she made no mention of Edwin but flung herself on to a chair and declared that she wanted to die.

The cause, as soon became clear, was Frank, who had left her for the high priestess of a rival coven.

'I really miss him, Aunt Marta.'

'Of course you do, darling.'

'I really miss him looking after me.'

Grabbing some orange juice from the fridge, Marta escaped to check on Edwin. She made her way up the stairs, hiding the naked carton from the gimlet gaze of her mother-in-law, whose portrait hung ever-vigilant on the landing. She had reason to regret her impropriety when Edwin, determined to show that he was not incapable, insisted on opening the carton himself and pouring the juice into his glass.

'It won't come out properly,' he said.

'That's because you've opened the wrong end. You should have held it the other way up.' She watched aghast as he flipped it over, flooding the sheets with juice. 'It doesn't matter,' she assured him, contradicting herself by promptly bursting into tears.

The accident spurred her to action. Resolved to face up to her fears, she helped Edwin out of bed and, leaving him to dress, went down to her study to ring an old friend, the newly retired professor of cognitive neuroscience, Jacob Murr. While loath to offer a diagnosis over the phone, he listened as she listed Edwin's symptoms, before advising her to bypass their GP and head straight for the on-call neurologist in the Accident and Emergency unit of the Radcliffe. Returning upstairs to find Edwin grappling with his shoelace as though it were a knotty theological conundrum, she relayed Jacob's advice, expecting to encounter the usual resistance. His instant agreement filled her with both relief and dread.

Refusing to risk Mr Shepherd's driving, she called a minicab, spending the journey rubbing Edwin's cold hands and keeping up a constant flow of chatter in a bid to raise his spirits. As they turned into the hospital forecourt, she recalled her recent visit to a former colleague, Clive Gannon, in the urology ward. The elderly men were all sitting by their beds, their genitals laid out on their laps like hymn-books, with Clive at the centre, blithely unconcerned at exposing the object of pity that had once been an organ of delight.

She shrugged off the memory as they walked into the waiting room, where a host of hostile glances betrayed the fear that their age would grant them precedence. After installing Edwin in a chair and outlining his symptoms to the receptionist, she waited for his preliminary examination, while her neighbour, a ragged man with a grimy face and tombstone teeth, described how, having slipped in the street with a bottle in his pocket, he had stood up to find that his thigh was soaked. 'But thanks be to God,' he said in a thick brogue, 'it was blood, not whisky.' He cackled, emitting a stench, half-dungheap, half-brewery. Edwin sat, oblivious to the rankness, while she searched for a way to escape without destroying what remained of the man's self-esteem. She spotted a pair of empty chairs beside an elegantly dressed middle-aged woman but, just as she was plotting the move, the woman turned to the girl next to her. 'Excuse me, miss,' she shrieked. 'If you don't listen to me, I shall write to Interflora and have you arrested. I've written letters... I've lost my teeth and my eyes and my hair writing letters.' Marta pondered which was more painful, what the woman was saying or the fact that no one, not the receptionist nor the nurses nor the security guard nor a single patient, paid it the slightest heed.

After a ninety-minute wait in which she diagnosed Edwin with every disease known to science, he was summoned to see the neurologist. Her nerves were so frayed that she almost asked the drunk if she could take a nip from his bottle. The *Interflora* woman left without seeing a doctor. Marta imagined her returning to a frowsty flat crammed with china figurines and stray cats, a mainstay of her local church until the mania finally took hold and she started to polish the brasses in the nude or desecrate the altar. Edwin had had to arbitrate in more such cases than she cared to remember. No sooner had she brought him to mind than an Indian doctor came out and called her name. She wanted to tell her about Mark, as though his sacrifice on behalf of her country would ensure his father the preferential treatment they had hitherto refused. In the event, she sat beside Edwin in silence while the doctor explained that, after testing his eyes and reflexes, she had run an emergency CT scan which revealed an abnormality.

'Where?' Marta asked.

'The brain,' the doctor replied, as casually as if it were the elbow. 'We'll put you on an immediate course of steroids,' she told Edwin. 'They should reduce the headaches. Plus some anti-ulcer pills for the side effects. In the meantime, I'd like to admit you, ready for an MRI scan tomorrow.'

Edwin's look of horror led Marta to suggest the alternative of taking him home overnight and bringing him back first thing in the morning. His relief when the doctor agreed strengthened her resolve never to let anyone put administrative convenience before his comfort. She knew that there were a thousand questions she should be asking but she needed time to absorb the news, so she sat quietly holding Edwin's hand while the doctor wrote a letter to their GP. As she saw them out with a friendly but not ingratiating smile, Marta wondered if it were fears for Edwin's future or deference to his past that kept her from giving them the usual message of hope.

As soon as they returned home, Edwin went upstairs, rejecting her offer of help as though it were his last chance to demonstrate his independence before submitting to the medical machine. Marta went down to the kitchen and steamed open the doctor's letter. Although her respect for other peoples' privacy was such that Shoshanna had once accused her of showing an insulting indifference to the contents of her diary, the gravity of the case outweighed her scruples. The doctor wrote that he had a lesion on the corpus callosum, which a swift glance at the dictionary revealed to be the band of nerve fibres linking the two hemispheres of the brain. She was more exercised by *lesion*, a commonplace word that she now suspected of having a technical meaning. Looking it up, she found 'a region in an organ or tissue which has suffered damage through injury or disease such as a wound, ulcer, abscess or tumour'. Dismissing the ulcer, abscess and, especially, the tumour, she focused on the wound and, by bedtime, had managed to convince herself that what they had found was a superficial swelling caused by the shattered glass.

Her stratagem was exposed the following day when, an hour after Edwin's MRI scan, the consultant neurologist, a more conventional authority figure than his colleague, called them in to his office to explain that the scan had shown up the presence of a tumour.

'I'd thought I was going mad,' Edwin said, sounding almost relieved. 'But I'm not, you see!'

'Of course you're not, darling,' Marta said, struggling to stop the walls closing in. Her throat was parched and her palms and forehead broke out in sweat. To the dismay of her rational mind, she began to wonder if there might be such a thing as a benign tumour. With the consultant proposing to perform a cerebral biopsy the next morning, there was no alternative to Edwin's admission and she accompanied him to a small neurological ward, where his anxieties were heightened by a hearty anaesthetist who coaxed him into signing the consent form as though he were selling him a used car. He rallied when the man left and he was introduced to his fellow patients, who seemed strangely comforted by having a former bishop in their midst.

After seeing him settled, she returned home to be greeted by Karen. 'It's not good to sit and brood,' she said, 'so I've come to take you out of yourself.' Her well-meaning impulse misfired since, whether from a deliberate attempt to make light of anything medical or a nervous attraction to the very topic she wished to avoid, her conversation revolved around bogus surgeons who wormed their way into operating theatres and the extensive bric-a-brac a nurse in her coven had extracted from patients' bottoms in A & E.

The strain of Edwin's twenty-four hours in hospital was nothing to that of the week in which they waited for the results. Having urged him to hope for the best while preparing herself for the worst, she was doubly appalled when the consultant announced that the biopsy was inconclusive since they had succeeded only in taking tissue from the oedema and not from the actual tumour. Far from apologising for the failure, he made it sound as though it were a trial run for the second operation, scheduled for the following day. Edwin was readmitted to the ward to a cool reception from his former companions, whose faith in his talismanic presence had been shaken by his rapid return. The procedure would be much as before, except that the incision was to be made on the side of his skull, requiring a nurse to shave him. Marta upbraided herself for the mawkishness which, in the face of a mortal illness, led her to mourn the loss of his few remaining strands of hair.

Time was of the essence and the consultant promised to expedite the results, making an appointment to see them in two days. They arrived at the allotted hour, and Marta's heart sank when, no sooner had he ushered them into his office, than the consultant asked his secretary to make some tea, as ominous a sign as if he had called for a catalogue of coffins. Her suspicions were confirmed when, stroking his tie and staring at the photograph of his children, he announced that Edwin had a tumour the size of an orange in the centre of his brain and that it had spread to both lobes. Carefully positioning himself in the realm of science and out of range of messy emotions, he added that the tumour was a *Gliobastoma multiformae* Grade 4, and its location meant that there was no hope of surgery. With low-grade tumours, there might be a chance to 'debulk' them but, with one so virulent, the only available treatments were chemo and radiotherapy, which he urged them to try at once.

'So, how would you rate my prognosis?' Edwin's question smashed through the consolatory plural, showing that, no matter what support she gave him, in the final analysis he was alone.

'It's impossible, as I'm sure you'll appreciate, to give a precise answer but, on current form, I'd say three months if you do nothing and nine months to a year if you have treatment. Since there's no surgical option, this is the last time you'll see me. From now on you'll be under oncology.' With a broad smile, as though from relief that his part in the affair was over, he steered them out of the office.

Edwin suggested that, rather than going straight home, they take a stroll down the High. Scared of betraying her fears by acceding to his every whim, she made a show of checking that he was well wrapped up and extracted his promise to tell her the instant he was tired, before asking Mr Shepherd to drive them to All Souls. As they walked down the street that had formed the backdrop to their lives for over fifty years, she was racked by the thought that she would soon have to walk down it alone. Buildings now glowing with history would merely be greying with age. Seeming to read her mind or, more probably, sensing her quickening pulse, he assured her that he was neither shocked by the news nor frightened of death.

'All in all, I've had a decent innings, hit the odd six, been lucky not to get caught in the slips more than once.'

'Used far too many extended metaphors.'

'What do you expect? I spent a lifetime in the pulpit.'

She laughed and, for a moment, it was almost possible to believe that they were walking back from the Magdalen Commem Ball fifty-five years earlier. Whatever might have changed around them – and inside them (she tightened her grip on his hand) – their love had endured. Knowledge of that would help to sustain her through all the pain and indignity of the next few months. It would enable her to respect his wish to make light of his illness: to accept death as the simple fact of life it had been for both of them since their separate losses in the War and their joint loss of Mark.

'Three months,' he said.

'A year if you have treatment.'

'You're not going to give me the choice, are you?'

'Not on this one,' she replied, her eyes glistening.

'It can be a lifetime. Remember *The Mikado*, when Yum Yum and Nanki Poo expect to have only a month together before his execution, so they decide to call each second a minute, each minute an hour and each day a year?'

'I remember,' she replied with a grimace. Gilbert and Sullivan were the point at which her affection for her adopted country came to an end. She remembered too how, with no trace of self-mockery, he had tried to persuade her that Gilbert was not only a supreme wordsmith but a ground-breaking philosopher who, in Yum Yum and Nanki Poo's pledge, had anticipated Einstein's theory by twenty years. She laughed so loudly that, when Mr Shepherd came to pick them up, he assumed that Edwin had been given the all-clear. It broke her heart to disabuse him.

Pitting his desire for honesty against his horror of provoking pity, Edwin asked her to confine the news to the children. Hinting at enough to ensure their attendance but stopping short of actual disclosure, she invited them down for Sunday lunch. Aware of its being Clement and Shoshanna's first encounter since before the wedding, she trusted them to pull together for the sake of their father. Despite her championing of tribe over family, she felt threatened by any suggestion that they were at odds.

Shoshanna and Zvi arrived first. Marta kissed Shoshanna and smiled at Zvi, maintaining a distance that served to muddy the mother- and son-in-law relationship still further. It was plain from their private jokes and covert glances that the first three weeks of married life had treated them kindly. So she was confused to find that they had not only brought their own lunch but packed it in separate bags, issuing strict instructions that they were on no account to be mixed. Her confusion grew when she handed Shoshanna a cup of coffee for Zvi, which she deliberately ignored, leaving him to pick it up for himself. She waited until he went to the loo before asking if they were having problems.

'No, of course not,' Shoshanna said as if to a child. 'I'm deliriously happy. I'm just *niddah*.'

'What?'

'I've got my period, so we're forbidden to pass anything to each other.'

Zvi returned, commending a set of hunting prints whose only merit to Marta was age. Her relief at the arrival of Clement, Mike and Carla faded when Clement walked straight up to Shoshanna and asked if he were permitted to kiss her.

'Don't be ridiculous!' she replied, kissing him lightly on both cheeks.

'What about me?' Mike asked. 'Do I still have snogging privileges?' Shoshanna said nothing but, with a quick look at Zvi, gave Mike a perfunctory kiss. Marta breathed again as they cleared the first hurdle. She watched while Shoshanna and Carla hugged and then, after checking that everyone was settled, prompted Edwin to break the news.

'As you know, I've not been feeling myself of late. Blinding headaches... lapses of memory... loss of vision. I thought it was just tempus fugiting. But it wasn't. At least not entirely. I've spent much of the last few weeks in hospital – '

'What?' Clement said.

'Why didn't you say anything?' Shoshanna turned to Marta.

'We didn't want to worry you,' Edwin said. 'We wanted to be sure of the diagnosis.'

'Which is what?' Clement asked.

'A brain tumour.'

'That's not true!' Shoshanna yelled.

'It's in both lobes,' Edwin continued resolutely. 'There's no possibility of surgery.'

'There must be something,' Carla said. 'Some experimental... unorthodox treatment.'

'Nothing but chemo and radiotherapy,' Marta interjected. 'They might reduce the tumour for a while.'

'Quite,' Edwin said. 'There are some short-term expedients but nothing more lasting. I have to prepare myself – we all do – for the inevitable.'

Marta was moved by the children's response, the shocked silence interrupted by Shoshanna's sobs. She longed for Zvi to take her in his arms, to acknowledge that there were more important things in life than law, but he stood helplessly by her side, the clenched fists and swollen vein on his forehead attesting to his inner conflict.

'Don't cry, Shoshanna,' he pleaded. 'I can't bear it.'

With Zvi keeping his distance, it was left to Clement to reach out and hold his sister's hand. He himself said nothing, as though struggling to reconcile such malignancy with his faith in a benign universe. Mike and Carla sat grim-faced and even Zvi, who had known them for only a few months, seemed to share in the pervading grief.

'It's no tragedy,' Edwin insisted, with an acceptance too heartfelt to count as courage. 'I'm eighty-three years old. I've had more than my biblical span.'

'That must be the first time in years you've drawn comfort from the Bible,' Clement said, forcing even Shoshanna to smile.

They ate a surprisingly convivial lunch. Edwin regaled them with tales of the more bizarre figures he had encountered in the Lords, before reminding Clement of his fury when Mark invoked his ninety-minute seniority to sit in the Eldest Sons' Box at the State Opening of Parliament. She was struck by the irony that, with the steroids relieving the pressure on his brain, he was more relaxed and lucid than he had been for months. Her determination to enjoy the lull, however short-lived, faltered only when Shoshanna's question as to whether they should tell Helena set Clement wondering if their aunt had gone slightly senile.

'She seemed perfectly normal at... when I last saw her,' Shoshanna said.

'Then explain this. About three weeks ago, out of the blue, she sent me one of those actors' First Night cards. Some Shakespearian character on the front – '

'Hotspur,' Mike interjected.

'Hotspur, thanks. And the words *Break a leg* inside. Except that she'd drawn a neat line through *Break* and replaced it with *Mend*.'

'You know Helena,' Marta said uneasily, 'she's always been eccentric.'

'Runs in the family,' Mike said, and the three outsiders smiled.

The show of unity collapsed at the end of the meal, once Edwin, at Marta's insistence, had gone upstairs to rest.

'How can we be sure the doctors have got it right?' Shoshanna asked. 'Did you demand a second opinion?'

'Do you really think that's necessary?' Marta replied. 'Your father's changed so much these last few months. You mentioned yourself the way that he told the time. Mrs Shepherd noticed him counting the figures on his coins. And I've seen so many little things, or rather I've tried to blot them out. Suddenly they all make sense.'

'So what do we know about his consultant? And the department? You have the money to go privately.'

'It's not a question of money, darling, but of principles. And a principle's no less valid because it's under pressure.'

'You mean you'll let Pa die for the sake of a principle?' she asked.

'Nanna, that's a dreadful thing to say!' Clement interjected.

'It's Shoshanna, Shoshanna! Will you please stop treating me like a child?'

'I'm sorry. I wouldn't want to offend your principles.'

'Oh, ha ha! It's your fault this has happened.'

'Stop right there!' Marta said. 'I won't listen to another word.'

'When did Pa start going downhill? When he was hit by the glass!'

'Bullshit!' Mike said. 'Tumours aren't caused by trauma.'

'It might have bled into it and made it worse.'

'That's simply not true,' Marta said. 'There's no blame of any kind. End of story.'

She succeeded in halting the argument but, as she gazed at Clement, she was less convinced of having dispelled the guilt.

The next morning she took Edwin back to hospital for a preliminary meeting with the oncology and radiography teams, who outlined their plan to give him chemotherapy once a day for a week, followed by six weeks of radiotherapy. She listened in dismay while they explained, first, that they lacked clear evidence that the chemo was beneficial in such cases and, second, that it had to be given in particularly heavy doses to cross the blood-brain barrier. In spite of her resolve to view each new day as a bonus, she worried that it might be a treatment too far. Edwin felt no such misgivings, telling the doctors that he was 'putting myself in your hands', a statement confirmed all too literally in the afternoon, when he sat uncomplaining for four hours as they moulded a mask to his head. Two days later she brought him back to radiography, where he lay flat on his face all morning while they matched up the images from the MRI scan with the X-rays and drew an intricate web of guidelines on the mask.

The beginning of his treatment coincided with a further decline in his condition. The tumour took over their lives as relentlessly as a newborn child. Her initial gratitude on learning that he would be able to have the chemotherapy at home gave way to despair during two harrowing nights in which he gasped and shook and gulped and spewed, begging to be left to lie in his vomit rather than have to haul his aching body out of the sheets. Time no longer seemed such a worthwhile return for suffering, and she was relieved when the remaining four sessions were cancelled. After three days grace, they began the radiotherapy, for which they had to make a daily journey to the Radcliffe, where he was clipped into the mask and bombarded with rays. Her attempt to combine each trip with a treat, as though taking a child to the dentist, had to be abandoned when he grew progressively weaker. The steroids took a savage toll, his belly bloating while his legs and bottom wasted away. With his grey face, bull's hump, puffed cheeks and waxy skin, he no longer looked like himself but a man with cancer or, rather, a character with cancer in a TV soap.

For all their efforts at concealment, the news of his illness leaked out, exciting both genuine concern and morbid curiosity. Friends and colleagues made discreet enquiries, while journalists put more intrusive questions. The owner of their favourite Oxford restaurant sent a complete dinner for two – which was eaten by one, twice. A young man, fresh from publishing a history of royal pets, declared his intention of writing his biography and requested an interview 'before it's too late'. The children kept in regular contact; Shoshanna's commitments at work and home restricted her visits to Sundays, but Clement's empty diary left him free to come and go throughout the week. While grateful for his support, she was suspicious of his motives. After a lifetime of intellectual struggle, Edwin needed to conserve his strength for basic survival, yet, walking in on them one afternoon, she found them so locked in debate that they barely acknowledged her presence.

'With due respect to Descartes,' Edwin rasped, 'the soul isn't the breath in the machine, but the illusion that permits the machine to run in the face of imminent breakdown. So the question arises: at what point should the machine be scrapped?'

'I assure that you it arises for those of us who believe in the soul too.'

'What do we do when the machine serves no purpose: when it's clogged up and corroded but continues to guzzle fuel; worse, when its toxic waste contaminates its surroundings?'

'What a depressing conversation!' Marta interposed lightly.

'But a vital one,' Clement retorted.

'Yes, my dear,' Edwin added, 'I'm afraid it is. If only identity death could be as clearly determined as brain death. People see Granny living – for want of a better word – with Alzheimer's, gazing blankly at the wall, good for nothing but to open her bladder and bowels, and they think "Maybe she's happy in her own world? Maybe she's filling the wall with memories?" I very much doubt it, although I'm willing to grant the possibility. But what about someone who's terminally ill, with a pain that gnaws away at their whole being?'

'You won't have pain, my darling,' Marta said. 'Just say the word and they'll give you morphine.'

'But what will I do to the rest of you? The longer I live, the more life I'll suck out of you.'

'You give me life! You always have.'

'But that might change. Don't I deserve as much consideration as a sick dog you'd take to the vet?'

'You want us to help you die?' she asked in horror.

'When the time comes,' he said, looking at Clement. 'Who else can I trust? Not strangers. Not even myself. Only the people who love me, people who won't be offended by my decline so much as outraged by it, who'll leave me the dignity of being me.'

Clement's rapid agreement brought back memories of their conversation after Shoshanna's wedding. It was as if he were using his father's case as a dry run for his own. She herself was more guarded, insisting that her sole concern was for his comfort, but, as she witnessed his ever-increasing distress, she wondered if her true concern were to protect herself. The one thing she could promise him was that he would never be a burden. To be close to him even in his illness was a blessing. He slept a great deal, and she wanted nothing more than to watch over him, allowing her memory to range across more than four decades of married life. A bishop's wife had never been an easy role for her. She had been a gift to the headline writers: *Pot in the Palace*, when she admitted smoking hemp with the Hadza; *Wells Farrago*, when she opened the palace to striking miners. Edwin's wife, however, had been the role of a lifetime. A phrase from a letter he had written to her half a century ago came back as vividly as if she had read it that morning: 'Love means that I'd rather be with you than be myself.'

For the rest of his life, she was determined that he would be both.

4

On completing the radiotherapy, Edwin went back into hospital for a series of tests. Faced with the constant stream of doctors seeking to monitor his brain function, he joked that he had a formula ready to spout at the first sight of a white coat: 'My name is Edwin Granville. I was born in 1924. The prime minister's name is Gordon Brown.'

The joke fell flat when one of the white coats revealed that the radiotherapy had failed to shrink the tumour. Marta took Edwin home where, within days, he was showing a marked decline. He sat stock-still for hours and, when he did move, he invariably forgot the reason, causing himself much distress. He was given heavy doses of steroids which greatly increased his appetite. For all the satisfaction it afforded Mrs Shepherd, whose cooking hadn't met with such enthusiasm since Mark left home, the extra bulk made it harder for Marta to manage him. She cursed the irony that, whereas other cancers made people lose weight, his made him balloon. Confronted with tasks that would have daunted a younger, larger woman, she employed two nurses, Ruth and Linda, to bath and dress him. They gradually took over his care, until there was little for her to do but count out his pills, remembering which he should take on an empty stomach and which with food. She gave thanks that the regimen was so complex, conscious that the small mercy she was able to offer him amounted to a vital one for her.

She seized the moments when he was resting to work on her Royal Society lecture. She had been elected an honorary fellow and, as an additional accolade, invited to address her new associates on the afternoon of the admissions ceremony. It was so hard to focus on anything other than his illness that her first thought had been to decline, but Edwin refused to hear of it.

'Since when have you been a quitter?' he asked. 'Besides you don't have the right. It's a tribute not just to you but to anthropology. Have you forgotten how it used to infuriate you when diehards dismissed it as "sociology in tents"? Not to mention my mother who, no matter how often you explained, could never get a handle on it?'

'She thought I was a phrenologist.'

'Yes, and told all her friends you'd gone to Africa to measure the bumps on the natives' heads!'

Marta laughed and realised that she had no choice but to accept the invitation. As she typed up her notes on her trusty Remington, she relived the excitement of her initial encounter with the Hadza. People had thought it mad, and even indecent, for a young woman to be travelling alone through Africa. Edwin's had been a rare voice of encouragement. Her trip coincided with his curacy in Clapham. They joked that they would both be at the mercy of savages, a joke which in retrospect filled her with shame. Her reception in Kampala had been equally discouraging. The colonial government looked askance at anthropologists who, by living among the locals, fostered the subversive notion that whites were no different from blacks. She had to obtain permission to enter the savannah from the District Commissioner, who summoned her to a humid office where he sat sweatily swatting flies under a mildewed photograph of the Queen.

'I'd no idea you'd be so young,' he said in a manner at once avuncular and menacing.

'If you keep me waiting any longer,' she replied, 'I won't be.'

It was because she was young that she made light of the difficulties, both of the language and the terrain. It was hard enough to locate the tribe, entailing an arduous three-day drive through the Serengeti, but harder still to gain their trust. For once being short worked in her favour, since even the Hadza men were no more than five foot tall. In the end she won them round by a mixture of sympathy and blandishment, asserting that the Hadza had a history worthy of record. While neighbouring tribes disparaged them as thieves and murderers who had fled from settled communities to live as outlaws, her aim was to redress the balance and restore their good name.

She thought that the War had prepared her to survive anything but, whether because life in England had softened her or else conditions in the bush were tougher than those she had previously known, she found the first few months very wearing. No field report or guidebook had warned her of the long nights in rudimentary shelters and the incessant noise: the shrilling, shrieking and chirruping, and, most enervating of all, the cackling of the hyenas (many years later, taking the children to a Hollywood version of *King Solomon's Mines*, she scorned the entire film except for the soundtrack). She was similarly daunted by the lack of privacy. She came from a world in which it was easy to shut people out – indeed, one that was built on that premise – but, apart from going into the bush to have intercourse, the tribe remained constantly together. For all that there were no guards or walls, she might have been back in the ghetto, especially given the reeking bodies, the only difference lying in the undertone of wood smoke to the Hadza sweat.

She had to accept the fact, as wounding to her self-esteem as the District Commissioner's condescension, that she was as much an object of curiosity to them as they were to her. Even after the children had ascertained, with a complete lack of inhibition, that her hair was not grass, that she was white all over and that she was a real woman, their mothers expressed doubts as to whether she reproduced in the same way. Recalling their confusion, she amused herself by speculating on the impressions that a Hadza anthropologist would have gathered had she come to the West, returning to the tribe with the cautionary tale of *The Babylon People*.

Her lecture drafted, she left Edwin in the care of Clement and the nurses and went up to London to attend the New Fellows seminars at the Society. The thrill of being party to the latest scientific developments palled, as she listened to a young geneticist's account of implanting a growth chromosome from cows into pigs that caused them to triple in size with no decline in the quality of pork. The only defect was a weakness in the legs that required them to wear callipers. She baulked at his comparison of his butcher's hybrid (pow? cog?) with a nectarine, as if he were simply intervening at a different stage in the food chain. As he appealed for the audience's discretion to avoid inciting the animal rights lobby or, in his phrase, 'the flat earth brigade who refuse to accept that animals are subject to the same evolutionary forces as humans', she felt an unexpected sympathy for Noah's Ark.

She stayed in London overnight and, the following lunchtime, made her way back down a drizzly Pall Mall to the Society's headquarters, where she waited for her family to arrive. Carla was the first, wearing a bright batik dress that failed to conceal the tiredness in her eyes. 'Curtis sends his apologies,' she said, 'but his boss has just bought a large collection of 78s that he wants him to catalogue.'

'I quite understand,' Marta replied, unaware that she had invited him.

Minutes later, Clement and Mike came in with Edwin, whom they had driven down from Beckley that morning. As they led him slowly up the steps and into a hastily vacated chair where he sat with a blank look and a mild tremor, Marta felt the same thought running through all their heads: whether he would ever be well enough to make such a journey again.

Shoshanna was the last, blaming her delay on the sudden downpour and the dearth of taxis. Her sharp recoil from the porter who offered to take her sodden coat alerted Marta to her failure to allow for her daughter's diet. 'There must be something you can eat,' she said in dismay. 'What about salmon? That was safe for Zvi.'

For a moment Shoshanna looked pained, but a glance at her father put matters in perspective. 'Don't worry, Ma. I had a sandwich at my desk before I left. I'm happy to sit and chat while the rest of you eat. Truly!'

Deeply grateful for the fiction, Marta led the way to the lifts through a knot of smartly dressed new fellows and their families. Clement and Mike took

Edwin down in the first lift, leaving Shoshanna, Carla and herself to wait for the second. Just as its doors opened, two young men in morning coats ran up.

'Room for a couple of little ones?' the fleshier of the two asked.

'Of course,' Marta said.

'I'll take the stairs,' Shoshanna said.

'We can easily squeeze up, darling.'

'No, I could do with the exercise.'

As Shoshanna strode off, to the men's consternation, Marta realised that a squeeze was precisely what she wished to avoid.

After a subdued meal in the gloomy subterranean restaurant, Marta was glad to escape to the library for an official photograph. She returned downstairs for the ceremony, pausing only to smile at her family strategically grouped by the door, as she was escorted to the front of the hall. Sitting alongside the other new fellows, she studied the portrait of Charles II, the jovial features befitting the Merry Monarch sobriquet, until a steward, dwarfed by a huge silver mace, led in the formal procession. Following the president's speech of welcome, the four dozen new fellows were called up to the platform one by one, receiving their scrolls and resuming their seats by way of the archivist's table, where they added their names to those of the host of luminaries in the Charter Book. As the sole honorary fellow, she was left until last, hesitating only when the archivist handed her a quill which looked as venerable as the mace. She dipped it in the inkwell, signed her name and returned to her chair, relieved to have blotted neither her own copybook nor theirs.

She was less confident when, after a fraught family tea on the terrace during which a stubbornly independent Edwin tipped the milk jug over Carla's new dress, she returned to the packed hall to deliver her talk. Despite the catchpenny title, *Eden Revisited*, she intended it as a sober account of the lessons to be drawn from Hadza life in the first decade of a new millennium. Having thanked the Society for the double honour of the fellowship and the lecture, she took up the theme.

'Fifty-four years ago as a very young anthropologist, I made my first trip to what was then Tanganyika to study a little-known gathering-hunting society, the Hadza. It wasn't a popular line at a time when the emphasis – not to mention, the money – in academic circles was on examining social change. I was regarded as hopelessly old-fashioned for wanting to visit the tribe in its traditional setting rather than charting how such people had adapted to the growth of independence movements and urbanisation. For all that I disagreed, I could never have predicted the extraordinary impact that an account of the Hadza was to have on people across the globe. Wherever you went in the late sixties and seventies, be it a university campus or a peace rally, a pop concert or a protest march, you could be certain of finding at least one person wearing a T-shirt with the slogan *We are the Eden People*. To my mind, the reason for such identification is clear. The Hadza help us to answer a question that remains as urgent today as at any time in the past: 'How do we live an authentic life?' Some people seek answers in the Bible or the Quran, observing man-made laws that purport to be God's. They're so frightened of the conflicts of modernity that they cling to an ancient mythology. The Hadza, on the other hand, observe laws that go back much further and are rooted in the earth.

'From my very first encounter with the Hadza, I had a profound sense of coming home, an instinctive connection that went beyond that of family or nation to the deepest level of my psyche. I'm aware, especially in this august gathering, that it may not be best scientific practice but, having spoken to many other visitors, I've found the instinct to be widely shared: a feeling of kinship with our earliest ancestors.

'This isn't sentimentality. The human race is generally held to have descended from people who lived on the edge of the Central African savannah. Both external evidence and their own oral tradition suggest that, whereas other tribes moved on, the Hadza have stayed in the same place. In a very real sense they are our earliest ancestors, providing us with a family tree that stretches back two thousand generations. Is it any wonder then that the evolutionary psychologists, who make so much of an *ancestral environment* in which we developed our repertoire of *hard-wired responses*, have launched such a sustained and, if I may say so, intemperate attack on my work? For, in offering an account of this ancient people, who reject fixed gender roles and small family units, who exhibit neither elitism nor aggression, I've dared to challenge them on their own ground.

'My greatest challenge was – and is – to the field of biological determinism. At no time since the Calvinist heyday has the ideology of determinism held such sway as it does today. Not only our intellectual but our economic and political life are governed by the theory that human beings are mere mechanisms to ensure the survival of our genes. But it's important to remember that it is just a theory, and likewise to remember how previous dominant theories have been displaced. Plato believed in the Four Humours. Was he such an intellectual lightweight? Sir Isaac Newton, one of the most eminent former members of this Society, was a dedicated alchemist. So surely it's possible – I go no further – that current genetic theories will themselves one day be superseded? In the meantime, we should beware of building them into an overarching philosophy. From St Augustine's Original Sin through Hobbes's collective self-interest to Darwin's survival of the fittest, theologians, philosophers and scientists have focused on the vicious and competitive aspects of human nature. The same is true of today's biological determinists. Yet, when we visit the Hadza in their ancestral environment or, more pertinently, the *ancestral environment* of the Hadza, we find not greed, violence and constraint, but altruism and collaboration.

'Why so many intellectuals should be suspicious of altruism is a matter on which I can only speculate. We live in a system which depends on dissatisfaction, on our desiring more than we need and forever being enticed to desire more. By championing a tribe who desire little and have their needs totally fulfilled, I've shown how such a system is not preordained. Another reason to attack my work! Rather than engage with my arguments, my detractors have accused me of wanting to drag people back to the Stone Age. They've vilified me as a woman who, having strayed beyond the appropriate areas of female study, namely education and childbearing, misunderstood the political – i.e. the male – side of Hadza life. They assert – on what basis I've yet to discover – that the Hadza must have leaders, whom I failed to identify because I was kept away when the men conferred. Finally, shifting ground with breathtaking perversity, they allege that, in an egalitarian society, selflessness is in fact selfish, since, if to possess is to share, then it's more expedient to possess nothing.

'I speak as someone who, as a young girl in Nazi-occupied Poland, was exposed to the most brutal form of biological determinism. My critics have claimed, with as much sensitivity as they can muster, that, as an adult, I've sought to redress the balance, denying any form of determinism, insisting on the supremacy of cultural conditioning and distorting the evidence to fit my own agenda, all charges which I vehemently refute. There is, however, one analogy with my past that I would like to draw. Contrary to the widespread belief that Hitler wanted to wipe out every trace of the Jews from the face of the earth, the records show that he wanted to wipe out every Jew but to preserve the traces of our culture in a vast ethnological museum to be built in Prague. My greatest fear is that we're doing the same to the Hadza: turning a people who should be an example into a curio. The serpent in their Eden is us.

'The Hadza have been put under more pressure in the past thirty years than in the previous fifty thousand. Their harmonious existence has been threatened by a mixture of government policy, Christian mission-work and Western tourism. I myself have been hounded by the Tanzanian authorities, who saw *The Eden People* as a smear on the portrait of African life which they were at pains to promote. I was asked by one government minister why I didn't write an account of the Chagga farmers on Kilimanjaro who were growing coffee and making splendid progress. I was accused by another of trying to keep the Hadza primitive – their term, not mine – in order to continue studying them.

I've even been called a pornographer, who wanted the Hadza to remain naked so that white visitors could come and photograph them. For many years I was denied a visa to enter the country, leading my Hadza friends to fear that I'd abandoned them.

'The traditional Hadza values of gentleness, cooperation and sexual equality have been eroded as people are herded into villages, where Norwegian missionaries teach the women to plant maize. In economic terms the experiment has been a disappointment since most years the crop fails due to lack of rainfall, but in social terms it's been a catastrophe since, in good years, the planters refuse to share the grain, insisting on preserving what's theirs in anticipation of a bad harvest. Altruism, which was once their second nature, is being bred out of them and they're taught to put their own interest before that of the tribe. I'm loath to cite the Bible, especially when those who do so have done the Hadza such harm, but I'm reminded of the Genesis story in which Esau, the honest hunter, is tricked of his birthright by Jacob, the cunning farmer.

'Meanwhile, the missionaries collude with the military in forcing the children into schools where they're made to speak English. On my last visit five years ago, I was greeted for the first time in Swahili rather than Khoisan, the native click language. What's more, the girls, separated from their families, are regularly raped by men who've fallen for the myth of their sexual licence, with many being driven into prostitution. The Hadzaland has been damaged by ranchers, whose intensive cattle-breeding methods are a condition of Western aid. In a final insult, the government has banned the men from hunting game, as they have done for millennia, while turning their land into game reserves for trophy-hunting foreigners.

'To my lasting dismay, I myself have played an unwitting part in the Hadza decline. My books put the tribe on the tourist map and, as ever, the tourists are destroying the distinctive culture that first attracted them. In one camp, for instance, the Hadza have started to make loincloths out of skin, which visitors expect, rather than the bark they've used since time immemorial. They spend the tips they receive on alcohol, and a previously peaceable people has grown combative. We're exporting Western values of avarice, belligerence and commercialism, thereby enabling some commentators to rub their hands and assert that such values are universal. I'm past the age when I can survive in the bush; I must leave it to those who are younger and stronger to take up the cause. So many experiments in communal living have failed over the years, but the Hadza are far more than an experiment. We're in danger not only of destroying a unique and precious people but of losing a model of altruism that may be our last hope for the world.'

5

Despite his increasing frailty, Edwin begged Marta to take him into Oxford, rejecting her alternative suggestion of a stroll around the lake as indignantly as a child confined to the shallow end of a swimming pool. Having checked with the doctor, who assured her – rather too readily – that the journey could do him no harm, she asked the nurses to help him dress, their cheery condescension a double affront to a man more accustomed to the deference of his chaplain in the vestry. Desperate to assert himself, he insisted on buttoning his own coat, giving up in dismay after fumbling with every hole. When Linda, at her most powdery, exhorted him to 'leave the naughty buttons to us,' he let out such a plaintive wail that Marta would gladly have throttled her. Showing unsuspected restraint, she reminded them that her husband was eighty-three, not three, and led him down the stairs and out to the porch. With Karen's assistance, she helped him into the car, where, after making him a nest of pillows and sitting down beside him, she placed Mr Shepherd under such strict constraints that he drove most of the way in first gear.

On reaching town they tottered down the High, where their chance meetings with the Dean of Wadham (colitis) and the Bursar of Brasenose (gout) gave new meaning to the hoary joke about dons greeting one another with an organ recital. Shunning any further encounters, Marta led Edwin into the seclusion of New College Lane, where the ancient walls prompted Karen, whose enthusiasm for jewellery-making had waned since Frank's defection, to muse on the attractions of academe.

'Who's that?' she asked, pointing to a statue beside the main gateway.

'William of Wykeham,' Edwin exclaimed in a rare burst of lucidity. 'You remember, *Manners maketh man*.'

'Not any man I know,' Karen said with a sniff.

'The bishop who founded the college.'

'They should put a statue up to you,' Karen said, to which Edwin responded with a gurgle that mingled mockery, gratitude and incomprehension. 'Clement can design it. We'll start a subscription. Like Nelson's Column.' The gurgle grew louder and Marta felt a sharp tug on her arm as Edwin spun round and fell down in a fit.

She stared at the writhing body, aware of the need to act but unable even to feel. The perspective was all wrong. Instead of standing by her side, he was at her feet, his limbs jerking like Ajax's when he dozed by the fire. A trickle of foam formed at the corner of his mouth and the nightmare suddenly became real. She sank to her knees and clasped his hand, at which moment he fell still.

'He's dead!' Karen screamed.

'Nonsense! Do you have a phone?'

'I've got no more credit. I was going to ask. I've been ringing Frank – '

'Find mine and dial 999! Call an ambulance,' she added, no longer afraid to state the obvious. As Karen rummaged in her bag, she rubbed Edwin's hands and searched for words of comfort, but all that came to mind was a Polish lullaby her mother used to sing and which she feared would disorientate him further. So she whispered his name over and over in his ear, breaking off to confirm to Karen that they were at the front gate of New College and to reiterate the need for haste.

'Shall I take off my jumper?'

'What? What for?' she asked, as a disconcerting image flashed across her brain.

'To make a pillow.'

'Yes, of course. Good idea!' She continued to whisper his name, gazing up and down the deserted alleyway, regretting that they had ever strayed from the High. Although barely a minute had passed since their call, she was incensed by the ambulance's delay. She pondered asking Karen to phone Mr Shepherd but, given the urgency, sent her into the college for a porter. She sat, cradling Edwin's head, when a distraught middle-aged woman appeared at the end of the lane.

'Daddy!' she shouted, running towards them. 'Oh thank God!' she said, after peering at Edwin. 'I thought it was my father.' Marta stared at her in disbelief. 'Excuse me, but you haven't seen him, have you? Seventy-five. Bald. Alzheimer's. I turned my back and he'd vanished.'

'It's my husband,' Marta said, pain bleaching the outrage from her voice. 'Eighty-three. Bald. A brain tumour.'

'Yes, of course,' the woman said, lingering uneasily. 'I'm sorry... so sorry, but I must find my father.' Marta turned her attention back to Edwin and, by the time she looked up, the woman had gone. Moments later Karen arrived with the porter. Marta thanked him for coming, although his stock reassurance made her feel like a bystander.

To her intense relief Edwin soon recovered consciousness, although he showed no inclination to move. Indeed, he seemed so comfortable lying in the street that he started to sing. She made out only a few slurred words about 'arches', but the song was evidently known to the porter who, wearing his bulk lightly, squatted on the ground beside him and joined in. His rousing refrain of 'pavement is my pillow' not only struck her as the kindest of courtesies to Edwin but dispelled her fears that her husband had lost his mind.

The ambulance arrived in mid-chorus. While the men strapped Edwin to the stretcher, Karen argued that her assistance entitled her to next-of-kin status, even holding up her crumpled jersey as proof.

'It's out of the question,' Marta said. 'Mr Shepherd will drive you home. I'll ring when I have news.' Pecking Karen's cheek, she stepped into the van and took her place at Edwin's side.

On reaching the hospital, they were rushed through A & E and straight up to Oncology. 'Not to worry. We've been expecting the fits,' the consultant announced, as blithely as if he had been forecasting wintry weather.

'So why did no one warn me?'

'There was no point in alarming you unduly. But now they've occurred, I imagine they'll be fairly regular.'

'How regular's regular?'

'I don't think it's helpful to speculate, do you?' he asked, in a tone suggesting that there was something unsporting in her attempt to stay ahead of the game. 'We'll keep him in for a few days to monitor his condition. Check there are no nasty surprises.'

'Of course,' she said sourly. 'We wouldn't want any of those.'

'Given the risk – I'd almost say the certainty – that, with his immune system shot to pieces, your husband has shingles, I can't keep him among vulnerable patients in Oncology. So we'll send him to Infectious Diseases on the top floor.'

'What sort of infectious diseases?'

'E Coli... dengue fever. He'll be fine.'

After making sure that he was comfortable, she went back to Beckley where she found Ruth and Linda in the parlour, poring over the Travel section of the *Sunday Times*. She realised with a jolt that her horizons had grown so narrow in recent weeks that she had come to discard Travel as instinctively as Money and Sport. She gave them a brief account of Edwin's collapse and told them to take a few days off until his return. Then, overcome by fatigue, she broke her own rule and asked Mrs Shepherd to bring her a bowl of soup in bed.

Much refreshed the next morning, she returned to the Radcliffe where she spent most of the day with Edwin. She swiftly established a visiting routine, modified only by his growing derangement. Whether because of the tumour itself, the drugs or the claustrophobic room, he became convinced that he was in a cabin on a cruise ship.

'The children have sent me here because it's simpler. If I die, there won't have to be a funeral; they'll just tip me overboard and splash! Splash! Splash!'

'Darling, please!'

'When they offer you a ticket, make sure you refuse!'

'Think, darling, I'm here with you now. If you're on a ship, then so am I.'

'Please don't muddle me,' he said with a whimper. 'Am I going mad?'

'Not at all. They've put you on some extremely strong drugs to control the fits. As soon as they've reduced the dose, you'll be fine.'

'I'd be better off dead.'

'We all lose track of things as we get older.'

'Then we'd all be better off dead.'

Notwithstanding his despair, she remained hopeful that the one virtue of his regression to childhood might be the recovery of his faith. She knew the comfort it had once brought him and longed for it to do so again. That hope was dashed during a visit from the chaplain, who strode into the room in the regulation mask and gown like an army padre in desert fatigues. Goaded into action, Edwin showed that, although lying flat, he was far from supine.

'Did no one ever tell you not to hit a man when he's down?' he croaked. 'I got shingles because my defences were shattered; I'm not going to get God.' He gave a dry laugh, which turned first into a wheeze and then into a prolonged fit of coughing. The chaplain fled, but Edwin's victory proved to be hollow, sapping what little lucidity he had left and plunging him into torpor. When a junior doctor examined him two hours later, with the usual request for the name of the Prime Minister, she gave up hope of 'Gordon Brown', expecting to be dragged back to the Wilson or even the Macmillan era. In the event he said nothing, simply flashing a drugged smile which, try as she might, she could not pretend was serene.

'Then who's that?' the consultant asked, pointing to Marta.

'If you say your mother, I'll kill you,' she said lightly.

'Good,' he said. She stared at him aghast. 'Good,' he repeated. 'I'd like that.'

The visiting restrictions in the closed ward strengthened her resolve to confine the news of Edwin's readmission to the children. During painful phone calls in which Shoshanna hit at her irresponsibility in taking Edwin into Oxford and Clement at God's in keeping him alive, they both promised to visit the following day, Clement arriving by train at nine in the morning and Shoshanna driving up with Carla after lunch. Their responses to their father's new ward were very different, with Clement suspecting a conspiracy behind his transfer to Infectious Diseases and Shoshanna reassured that it was effectively a private room. Far from taking comfort from the presence of his family, Edwin was unsettled by the four masked figures huddled around his bed. So Marta sent Clement back to Beckley, only to find herself similarly dispatched half an hour later when Shoshanna offered to keep vigil while she and Carla went out for tea. Though the two files poking out of her bag threatened to limit Shoshanna's vigilance, Marta seized on the temporary respite, choosing to go to the Randolph, its old-world opulence as far removed from the brutalism of the hospital as the pot of Earl Grey was from the vending-machine tea.

They sat quietly in a secluded corner of the lounge beside a large urn of arum lilies. 'Shall I be mother?' Marta asked, reaching for the teapot. 'Oh I'm so sorry...' The cosy English idiom had never sounded so cruel.

'Not to worry,' Carla said, smiling bravely. 'I can live without pouring.'

'Tell me about yourself, your work, how everything's going with Curtis!' Marta said hurriedly.

'All at once? Wow! Work's great. I've accepted a commission to design – design, mind – and make a window for the Beatrix Potter museum in Windermere.'

'That's wonderful!'

'I hope so. I haven't told Clem yet. I know nursery animals aren't exactly his thing, and I'm sure they were looking for a woman. But with his current block...'

'He's not blocked! As I understand it, a block is something you can't control.' Edwin's illness had left her increasingly impatient with Clement's frittering of his talents. 'He's simply depressed.'

'Life on the Curtis front is less rosy.' Carla's abrupt change of tack felt like a rebuke. 'I wish he'd been able to come to your Royal Society lecture.'

'Really? Why?'

'To shake up his ideas. He's the ultimate determinist. In his view, we're not just doomed to repeat the mistakes of past generations but our own past lives. If I'd known the full story when we met, I'd have run a mile. He seemed so quirky... intriguing. Now I'm not sure he isn't a little mad. If I challenge something he says or suggest we might have a problem, he'll relate it to a time when we were Lollards in the fourteenth-century Marches or a mercenary captain and his mistress in eighteenth-century France. From as far back as he can remember – or, rather, as far back as he's regressed – we've been doomed to destroy one another.'

'Mightn't it perhaps be time to walk away and break the cycle?' Marta asked gently.

'Yes, it might. Yes, it is. Except for one thing: I'm hooked. There's something about him that touches me more deeply than anyone since Mark. He's so lost, so vulnerable. I start to wonder if it's just that I want to mother him; then we make love and I realise that it's so much more. I know how hard it is for you to comprehend; we're all in awe of your relationship with Edwin. But in some unfathomable way I need Curtis.'

'And yet he makes you unhappy.'

'Wretched. I tell him and he says it's all part of the pattern. I think he feels he's being honest.'

'At least you have your faith.'

While she had long found the Christian view of suffering as ordained by God and superseded by Christ to be both inconsistent and disempowering, Marta had some sympathy with the Buddhist view that it was the pathway to a spiritual life. The distinction broke down when they returned to the ward to find Edwin insensible with pain. Shoshanna sat by his side, a strange, almost beatific, expression on her face. The reason became clear when she announced that she had something to tell them.

'I wasn't going to say anything – that is not to anyone but Zvi – for another few weeks.' Marta's heart skipped a beat. 'But I think we could all do with some good news, don't you?'

'Say what, darling? Don't keep us in suspense!'

'I'm pregnant, Ma! It's two months.'

Marta felt dizzy with delight, almost tripping over Edwin's drip in her rush to kiss her.

'I'm so happy, my darling.'

'Thank you, Ma. I'd virtually given up hope. I know you don't believe in miracles.'

'No, but I believe in gifts, and this is the best I could ever have wished for.' Moreover, with her daughter only four months married, she would never have dared to wish for it so soon.

'Really?'

'For you. For us. For us all.'

'Yes, it's wonderful,' Carla said, as she crossed the room to hug Shoshanna, veiling the pain of frustrated motherhood in the joy of becoming an aunt.

'Truly wonderful,' Marta echoed. Neither Carla's bittersweet tears nor the poignancy of learning of new life in a ward of deadly infection could dampen her euphoria. This was the news for which she had waited so long: the prospect of a grandchild who would legitimise her love for future generations. She had spelt out her priorities as a young woman, when she refused to marry Edwin until she had finished her thesis or to start a family until three fieldtrips later, but, while there was no point in regrets, let alone recantations, she was ever more aware that all the honours and awards on her shelves failed to conceal the lack of grandchildren's drawings. She dreaded the invitation to another ruby wedding or seventieth birthday party where they were handed canapés by the hosts' doe-eyed granddaughter or listened to an oboe recital by their precocious grandson. Shoshanna's announcement opened up a world of possibilities where, in swift succession, she pictured herself gazing at the dinosaur in the Natural History Museum, shouting 'Behind you!' at the pantomime, and refurbishing the doll's house in the nursery, her moist palm a token not only of her own excitement but of the hot little hand soon to be clutching hers.

She turned her attention to Edwin, whose vacant features were thrown into relief by the flurry of emotion around him. Pulling up a chair, she sat down and clasped his hand. 'Did you hear, my darling? You're going to be a grandfather.' She broke off on realising how little chance there was that he would survive for seven months. 'He smiled, did you see?' She appealed to the younger women, both too caught up in their own fantasies to collude in hers.

'I saw nothing, Ma,' Shoshanna said sadly. 'Not even a twinge.'

'It's the drugs he's on to stop the fits. They wipe him out.'

'But he has to take them for the rest of his life,' Shoshanna said, her quavering voice suggesting that the phrase had been given new meaning by the life she was bringing into the world.

'Now I don't want you worrying about your father. He has the very best doctors and, as soon as they give us the go-ahead, we'll take him back to Beckley, which is sure to cheer him up. The only thing you must think about – the only thing he'd want you to think about – is yourself.'

'Can I be hearing right?' Shoshanna teased. 'Marta Gorski telling me to look after number one!'

'But it's not just number one, is it?' Carla said. 'Not any more.'

Marta promised Shoshanna to tell no one, not even Mrs Shepherd, at least until the end of the first trimester, but she secured a special dispensation for Clement, whose response when she broke the news at dinner, was further evidence of his depression.

'Of course I'm pleased for Nanna, but it won't make any difference to me. I can't see Zvi letting a child of his spend time with wicked Uncle Clement, the one we don't speak about, that is not until he's old and toothless and it's a question of wills.'

Marta lost patience with Clement who, in voicing his fear of rejection, had revived hers. She was determined that nothing should threaten her relationship with her grandchild and ready to go to any lengths, short of shaving her head, to show that she would not be an obstacle to a Lubavitch upbringing. Lying in bed that night, she was seized with regret that Shoshanna and Zvi were not Moonies or members of some other extreme cult, so that any responsible judge would award custody of the child to her. Having dismissed the thought as nocturnal whimsy, she found it returning over breakfast, on the drive to the Radcliffe and, most distressingly, as she sat watching Edwin take his day-long nap.

It felt somehow treacherous to be musing on her future grandchild while Edwin lay in front of her, as helpless as a babe in arms. For two days his whimpering as he wet himself was his sole sign of life. Then, as she sat by his bed struggling with the crossword, he began to speak.

'Marta?'

'Yes, my darling!' She rubbed his hands, hopeful that the restored speech might herald a fuller recovery.

'Do you love me? Did you ever love me?'

'How can you even ask?'

'Then help me to die.' Her hopes fell as fast as they had risen.

'You'll feel better soon, I promise.'

'I'm not a child!'

'I know you're not. You're my brave, wise, honourable, wonderful man.'

'Then why won't you treat me like one? I can't bear it. The noises in my head... are they in my head or in the room? The people... the questions... the pills. No more pills!'

'We'll soon have you home. There'll be no more noises.'

'You stupid, stupid woman!'

'Eddy, darling!'

'I have nothing.'

'You have me,' she said softly.

'And what do you have? A decrepit old man. Dragging you down. Down and down... down and down... down and down... down and down...' The phrase revolved like a stuck record. 'Sick and useless. Dragging you down.'

'Never! How could you? You're my life.'

'Then prove it. Take that pillow. Smother me. Smother me. Smother me. Smother me. Smother me.'

With tears streaming down her cheeks, Marta moved to the window and stared at the unrelieved view of the car park. She wiped her eyes on her hand and her nose on a tissue, before returning to Edwin's bedside to find him asleep.

Gazing at his bloated face, she wondered why she should object so strongly to what, in view of his condition, was a perfectly rational request. She had no faith in any God who might be offended by his words, while her faith in medical progress stopped short of miracle cures. It was as though she were turning her personal tenacity into a general precept. Even at the blackest moment of the War, she had refused to consider the possibility of defeat. But she had been young, with everything to live for. Edwin's one hope was to be blind to his own decline, losing the very reason which she held to be humanity's raison d'être.

Three days later, when he was satisfied that they had the fits under control, the consultant called Marta and Clement into his office and told them that they could take the patient home, promising that, when the strain of caring for him grew too great, he would refer them to a hospice. Marta baulked at a word which conjured up her last visit to Uncle Leon, stuck in a ward full of sad, shrivelled people, looking like balloons left up at the end of a party. She was grateful for Clement's vehemence as he dismissed the idea out of hand.

'Never! My father isn't going to die among strangers. My father is going to die at home.'

Her suspicion that his resolve cloaked a darker purpose was confirmed over dinner.

'I was speaking to Pa this afternoon.'

'He's so out of it,' she said quickly. 'It's impossible to know what he's saying.'

'This was crystal clear. He asked me to help him die.'

'He said something of the sort to me. I took no notice. It was the pain speaking.'

'No, it was Pa. The doctor came in, and he begged him to stop his treatment... give the bed to someone who still had hope.'

'He's back in his own bed now, so the question won't arise.'

'"You mustn't give up," the doctor said in his greetings-card voice. "Your son's here. Think of him." "I am, Doctor," Pa said and looked at me plaintively. He was thinking of me so much that he couldn't ask me again. He couldn't put me through the pain of relieving his pain. He should have had more faith. All my life he's been here for me. Now I shall be here for him.'

'You talk as though you were sending him off on a holiday!'

'Aren't I?'

'Be real!'

'I can appreciate that it's hard for you. Anything to do with euthanasia must smack of the Nazis.'

'Trust me, that's the first time I've made the connection. My concerns are far more basic: to be one hundred per cent certain that, were we to take any steps to... to do what your father asks, we'd be freeing him from his misery not ours.'

'His misery is ours. There's no distinction.'

'We can't be sure what's going on in his head.'

'"Help me to die" is a pretty fair guide.'

'But that's only part of the time. Even your Aunt Helena opposed capital punishment because of the risk of hanging an innocent man. Who's to say we wouldn't be making the same mistake?'

'Don't pretend, Ma. You know as well as I do what he wants. You heard the doctor this morning say that he couldn't guarantee he wouldn't live for another few months. Live! When the only sign of life is that he's pissed himself – bleating like a baby with a shitty nappy!'

'You still haven't explained how you can square your belief in a loving God with taking away the life He gave.'

'The same way I can square it with my belief in abortion.' She winced at the shrewdly chosen analogy. 'God wants us to show how we can assert our humanity. And I maintain, with every ounce of my being, that humanity is a more precious gift than life. Euthanasia may be illegal, but Christ taught his disciples to put love before the law, and so should we.'

Marta escaped further debate by claiming exhaustion. Once again, she envied the Hadza their simple accommodation with death. At first sight it had been deeply disturbing. No dish of roast locusts or unwashed body had posed a greater threat to her professional detachment than the moment a sick old woman announced that she would not be travelling with the tribe when they set off for the next camp. Neither the woman's family nor the elders sought to dissuade her. They merely ensured that she had a sufficient supply of food and water and then left with the minimum of fuss. Six months later they returned to discover her bones, stripped clean by predators and scorched white by the sun. No one displayed the least shock or grief. The woman remained with the tribe but at a different level of consciousness, one of the living dead whose spirits survived through the stories that were told of them, rather than the dead who vanished from memory.

6

Illness imposed an inexorable rhythm on the house. With Edwin no longer able to climb the stairs, they converted the morning room into a bedroom. The makeshift arrangement filled Marta with foreboding, which was compounded by Clement's reminder that it was where they had placed his grandmother's coffin. He himself had taken up permanent residence at Beckley, his mournful presence adding to the prevalent gloom, although, when she suggested that he might be happier spending a few days at home, he was so offended that she never raised the subject again.

At least she managed to dissuade Shoshanna from travelling back and forth, on the promise of regular – albeit heavily censored – bulletins on her father's state. She relished their nightly conversations and the link to a world in which health was a given not a gift. Although *godsend* was not a word that came easily to her, no other began to convey the marvel of Shoshanna's pregnancy. It was only the thought of the new life growing inside her daughter that saved her from despair at the malignancy growing inside Edwin. She mulled over every change in Shoshanna's condition, offering advice when asked, calming fears when needed, rejoicing at how the imminent birth had brought them closer.

One evening, however, their conversation took a different turn. From the start she could tell that Shoshanna was worried, the suspicion that she was holding something back increasing when, without a word of explanation, she announced that she would not be going into the office the following day. The more she denied that there was anything wrong, the more Marta felt the need to see for herself. Having reflected on it overnight, she decided to take the train up to London after breakfast, waiting only to tell Clement, who showed as little interest as if she were setting off for the shops.

Her resolution held firm until she reached the house and recalled Shoshanna's lifelong dislike of surprises. Even as a child, she had filled her letters to Father Christmas with strict instructions on models and sizes. The memory unnerved her and she hurried up the drive before she had a chance to turn back. Zvi answered the door, seeming to confirm her worst fears, until he explained that both he and Shoshanna were at home for Yom Kippur. Without a pause, she told him that she had come to be with her daughter on the holy day. Ignoring the distrust in his eyes, she followed him through the house and into the garden, where Shoshanna, inadequately dressed for the blustery October weather, stood next to a sturdy man with a matted beard, wearing a butcher's apron and clenching a knife. As she recoiled in alarm, the cluck of a hen at his feet made her feel both foolish and ashamed.

'Ma, what on earth are you doing here?' Shoshanna asked, brushing her cheeks with cold lips.

'She's come to keep Yom Kippur with us,' Zvi said.

'Nonsense! She's never kept Yom Kippur in her life.'

'But what are you doing, darling?' Marta asked rapidly. 'It's freezing out here. Why the chicken?'

'It's *kaparot*,' Shoshanna said. 'Part of the ritual. And I can't stop to chat. Rabbi Silberman has a busy day.' Marta apologised silently to the rabbi for her mistake. 'Are you sure you want to watch, Ma? You must be tired after the journey. Go indoors. I won't be long.'

She insisted on staying, choking back her revulsion as Shoshanna took the white hen in her right hand and, under the rabbi's guidance, swung it above her head. Seeing her daughter's distress as the bird shuddered and squawked, its feathers flying, she longed for Zvi to intervene, but he stood impervious, bobbing back and forth as he read aloud from the Bible.

After Shoshanna had swung the bird three times while muttering a prayer in broken Hebrew, the rabbi grabbed it from her and crossed to a pile of sawdust, where he cut off its head in a neat stroke, carefully holding the twitching body so that its blood spilt on to the wood. He then spoke a blessing and covered up every drop of blood.

'Are you all right, darling?' Marta asked anxiously, as her daughter began to retch.

'I'm more than all right; I'm blessed,' she replied. 'That's the point of the ritual. By rights I should die for my sins, but by God's mercy a hen has taken my place.'

'I think you'll find your ancestors in Poland did *kaparot* for hundreds of years,' Zvi said.

'But Shoshanna's pregnant,' Marta said, blotting out the image of her tender-hearted grandmother brandishing a headless chicken. 'Couldn't she be granted an exemption?'

'On the contrary,' Shoshanna said defiantly, 'it's because I'm pregnant, I have to do it twice.' She nodded as the rabbi pulled a rooster from its cage. 'The hen stands for me and a girl baby. The rooster's for if it's a boy.'

Marta's resolve to respect her daughter's beliefs was sorely tested as she watched her repeat the ritual with an even more recalcitrant fowl. She waited while the rabbi once again drained its blood over the sawdust before curiosity got the better of her. 'How many sins can an unborn child commit?'

'It's in case the mother eats – inadvertently in this instance, I'm sure – a proscribed food,' the rabbi replied. 'That would become part of her flesh and therefore of the foetus.' He picked up the still pulsating rooster and put it in a basket along with the hen. As though reading Marta's mind, he explained that they would be given to the old peoples' home.

'Two birds with one stone!' she exclaimed.

Sighing heavily, Shoshanna accompanied Zvi and the rabbi inside before returning to the garden. Marta feared that she had driven Zvi away, until Shoshanna revealed that he had left to go to the Chabad House.

'He's to be flogged. Largely symbolically,' she said in an unsought reassurance. 'The men all take it in turns.' She led the way into the house and Marta was once again saddened by how little of the furniture she recognised from the Notting Hill flat.

'I can offer you something to drink, but no food. We're fasting.'

'That's fine. So am I,' Marta said, with a blush. 'But is there no exemption from that either?'

'Sure, but I don't need it. I'm fine.' As if to belie her words, she clutched her stomach. 'It's nothing. Just wind. How's Pa?' Then a second wave of pain shattered the facade and she turned to her mother for support.

'What is it, darling? Tell me,' Marta asked, uneasily stroking Shoshanna's wig.

'I've been bleeding,' she said, sounding like a frightened child.

Marta let out a silent scream. This was one horror from which she would never recover. For the first time she envied Edwin his incomprehension. 'How much?'

'It won't make you squeamish?'

'I'm your mother!'

'There were reddish-brown stains on my pants. Not plain red; then there would have been no confusion. Something else. So Zvi took them to the Rabbi.'

'What? Why?'

'I was too embarrassed to go myself.'

'No, I don't mean why Zvi and not you! Why show them to the Rabbi at all?'

'I had to make certain that I wasn't *niddah*, that Zvi and I could still touch.'

'You need a doctor, not a rabbi,' Marta said, biting back her rage. 'You must have a scan. I'm sure – absolutely sure – that everything's fine. But just to relieve any doubts.'

'I saw the doctor. She said it's nothing. There's no sign that it's coming from the uterus. She thinks there must be a scratch on my cervix and that the internal examinations I've been giving myself have made it worse.' Marta struggled to maintain her composure. To comply with the modesty laws, Shoshanna was putting her baby at risk.

'I'm due for my eleven-week scan at the end of the week. I might be able to ask them to bring it forward.'

'Would you like me to ring my friend Jan Walters? She's head of obstetrics at King's.'

'They can't do anything invasive. Zvi wouldn't allow it and I would never go behind his back.'

It was clear that Shoshanna's deference to Zvi went way beyond the decor. Marta felt the blow to her lifelong principles as her daughter walked meekly into her cage and handed her husband the key. Nevertheless she held her tongue for the sake of the child.

'I promise Jan will respect your wishes. It's south London: they deal with every creed and culture under the sun. She's sure to give you the all-clear and we'll feel complete fools for having made a fuss. Too bad! You need to set your mind at rest.'

Shoshanna's swift compliance betrayed the extent of her fears. She steeled herself for disappointment by insisting that a top consultant would never be free at such short notice, but Jan proved her wrong, as Marta had predicted, by agreeing to see them that afternoon. She quickly rang Clement to warn him of her late return. He assured her that he had nothing to report, since Edwin had spent the morning asleep, and sent his love to Shoshanna.

Despite her mother's appeals, Shoshanna refused to eat so much as a piece of matza. 'You must have something,' Marta urged. 'You're in danger of stunting the baby – or worse!'

'This isn't cheating at Champney's, Ma,' Shoshanna said with a wounded expression, 'it's deceiving God.'

Moreover, she insisted on driving to the hospital, leaving Marta uncertain whether her irascibility owed more to hunger or the busy road. On arrival, they took their seats in the crowded waiting room, the only two skirts in the array of saris, niqabs and shalwar kameez. After ten minutes Jan came to fetch them, full of apologies for the wait. Marta felt awkward that her first phone call in months had been to ask for a favour, but Jan made it plain that their friendship, which stretched back more than three decades to an anti-apartheid rally in Trafalgar Square, transcended such niceties. They had time to exchange only the most basic news, Marta congratulating Jan on her girlfriend's taking silk, Jan condoling with Marta on Edwin's illness, before Jan ushered Shoshanna into the consulting room. Marta remained in the outer office, studiously ignoring a secretary who did little to hide her disapproval of the special treatment.

After twenty minutes, Jan came out to explain that Shoshanna had gone for an ultrasound and wanted her mother to join her. Although at any other time she would have relished the request, her one concern now was with what the scan might reveal. Assuming an air of confidence, she strolled into the room and introduced herself to the radiographer, who asked her to take a seat while she gently rubbed gel on Shoshanna's stomach. She gripped her daughter's hand as the radiographer switched on the machine. At a stroke, all her fears were dispelled by the flicker of life on the screen.

'It's alive,' Shoshanna said, her voice a mixture of awe and relief as she gazed at the tadpole-like body and pounding heart.

'It most certainly is,' the radiographer said. 'Listen, you can hear the heartbeat. Perfectly regular.'

'That's my baby, Ma.'

'I know, darling. What did I tell you? He... she's beautiful.'

As the radiographer took measurements, clicking buttons that sent dotted lines across the grainy, ghostly image, Marta stared at the giant head which, however much other organs might challenge it in the future, was asserting a primal precedence. She felt a deep surge of love for Shoshanna, who barely registered the radiographer's commentary as she contemplated the living, breathing being in her womb.

At the end of the scan they returned to the waiting room while Jan assessed the results, a procedure Marta had come to regard as a formality. As Shoshanna sat in a daze, she worked on a smile that would penetrate her neighbour's niqab. After half an hour, Jan called them into the consulting room, where she explained with a bluntness more suited to her clash with a policeman outside South Africa House that, given Shoshanna's age and symptoms, they had done a test to measure the Nuchal Fold Thickness: in laywoman's terms, the thickness of the skin at the back of a baby's neck. 'I've found an abnormality which might – and I stress *might* – be indicative of Down's syndrome.'

As she strove to take in the news, Marta longed to tear away the euphemism and be left with the savagery of *Mongol*, to create a world where the ugliness of language matched the bleakness of reality. For the first time since receiving the call about Mark, she found herself wishing that there were a God so that she could justify her despair. She wanted to comfort Shoshanna, who sat motionless beside her, but she was afraid to look her in the face. So she squeezed her hand while fixing her eyes on the pens in Jan's pocket.

'You're lucky to be at one of the few centres in the country where the test is routinely carried out,' Jan said, stripping the words of their meaning. 'You've got two choices. The first is to wait another four or five weeks for an amniocentesis.'

'No!' Shoshanna cried, sounding more alarmed by the procedure than by its possible result. 'My husband would never allow it. Nor would I. It's against our beliefs.'

'Which leaves the second choice.' To Marta's relief, Jan made no comment on the marital veto. 'A Chorionic Villus Sampling, which you can have at eleven weeks. In fact, I'd strongly recommend you have one this afternoon. We pass a tube through the vagina and cervix into the womb. It sucks off a small amount of foetal tissue in the placenta. There are no needles. It's no more invasive than a smear test.'

'I don't know. I need... I really need to talk it over with Zvi, my husband. But I can't call him. Not now.'

'Of course not. It isn't something you can discuss on the phone,' Marta said, worried that Zvi would object.

'No, what I meant is that his will be off. He's spending the day at the Chabad House.'

'It has to be your decision,' Jan said. 'But my advice is to take the test for your own peace of mind. If it makes you any easier, I've personally carried it out on several Orthodox Jews.'

'You have?'

'Several.'

'And did you find any... any Down's?'

'In some cases. By no means all.'

'And what did they do? No, I don't want to know!'

'Everyone's different. But I don't have to tell you that. What I can say is that, whatever they decided, they were in possession of the full facts. They could weigh up their options without being rushed.'

'So when would I get the results? Later this afternoon?'

'It takes a few days, I'm afraid. But I promise I'll do everything in my power to push things along.'

For all her scruples, Shoshanna agreed to take the test. Jan led her into the consulting room while Marta waited in the office, where the secretary's newfound solicitude heightened her fears. Dismissing the statutory cup of tea, she sat in silence, alert to every echo, until Shoshanna emerged, her face drained of emotion. Sensing her eagerness to return home, Marta said a quick goodbye to Jan before heading back to the car, where her hesitant inquiry as to Shoshanna's fitness to drive met with a resounding 'yes', which was refuted as soon as they took to the road. After a fraught encounter with the rush-hour traffic, they reached Paddington, where Shoshanna thanked her for coming as if she were a distant cousin at a funeral. She made her way on to the train, downing two large whiskies and blaming herself for having chosen to visit, let alone suggested the consultation.

She arrived home, anxious to confide in Clement, only to find herself called on to comfort him when, the moment she stepped through the door, he launched into a graphic account of his father's latest lapse. 'He pissed himself in his chair. Right in front of me.'

'He's done it before.'

'But this time it was my fault! I have to struggle to work out every word he's saying. Half an hour earlier I thought he was asking to go to the loo, so I heaved him out of the chair. He's such a dead weight, I didn't think I'd manage.'

'You should have called Ruth or Linda.'

'And listen while "we" are asked if we want to do a "wee-wee"? No thanks! I finally got him to the commode, but nothing. I even put his hand on his cock... I'm sorry; I can't bear it! He just stared at me like it was the ultimate humiliation. But it wasn't. Because half an hour later, he began to make exactly the same noises and I ignored them. I sat oblivious as the piss trickled down his legs.'

'You mustn't blame yourself. I'd have done the same. I can only make out one word in ten.' She stroked his hair, which felt more effective than stroking Shoshanna's, while thinking of Edwin, trapped in a hall of mirrors, his scream distorted into a smile. 'Where is he now?'

'In bed. I think he's asleep, although it's hard to tell. Ruth cleaned "our messy boy" up... It's clear we've maligned her. The only way she can deal with the horror – the only way either of them can – is to treat him like a child incapable of reason, rather than an adult who's lost his mind.'

'I must go in and see him.'

'No, wait!' His desperation unnerved her. 'How much longer will you let this go on?'

'It's not up to me.'

'If I'd realised what it'd be like, I'd have insisted we put him on a plane to Switzerland when the tumour was first diagnosed.'

'Please!' The image of the ultrasound flashed through her brain.

'In any civilised society, he'd be allowed to die now, while he still has some vestige of dignity.'

'Dignity, dignity! What's so special about dignity? Did the prisoners in a concentration camp have dignity? Do women who are raped have dignity? Should we show our compassion by killing them too?'

'Why are you being so melodramatic?'

'It's a reasonable question, given that dignity seems to be your sole concern.'

'But they have, or had, the chance to get their dignity back. Pa just faces the prospect of watching it disappear, a little more every day.'

'No, Clement. He's almost blind and his mind is clouded. It's you who can't bear to see your father like this. And I suspect it's not just him you're thinking about. If you're frightened of what might happen to you – '

'I'm not!'

'Then it would be perfectly natural. But you can't kill people because they offend your sense of propriety. You believe in God. That should be enough. Don't try to play God too.'

'What became of my look-life-straight-in-the-eye mother? Since when did you allow reason to be muddied by sentiment?'

'Not muddied: informed!'

'Don't get me wrong! I'm not trying to imply you can't see what Pa's going through. I know how hard it must be for you.'

'This isn't about your father. Why don't you ask me about my afternoon – why I stayed on longer in London?'

'I thought you were having a good time with Susannah.'

'I took her to the hospital.'

'Why? Is something the matter with her?'

'No, not with her. Although it's a moot point.'

'What?'

'Or perhaps I should say an ontological question?'

'You're making no sense!'

'I'm sorry.' Endeavouring to put her impressions in some sort of order, she described events at the hospital. 'It's my fault. If I hadn't suggested seeing Jan, she might never have known anything was wrong.'

'Thank goodness you did! At least now she can have an early abortion.'

Marta shrank from a word which had once been as neutral as *appendectomy*. 'She might decide not to have one.'

'Come on! You know as well as I do, Susannah's not the person to look after a Down's syndrome child.'

'Shoshanna!' she shouted. 'Shoshanna,' she repeated more quietly. 'You're so keen to give everyone their dignity; give her hers! And that's just the trouble. It's not as easy for Shoshanna as for Susannah. Her faith won't allow it.'

'But why? I went through the Bible with a fine toothcomb for my Modern Nativity series, and the references to abortion are even more inconclusive than the references to gays.'

'You'd know more about that than me. Although the doctrine that all human life is sacred because it comes from God seems plain enough. But, since they don't permit amniocentesis, it's academic. Whatever happens is God's will. *Que sera sera.*'

'That's fine if you're living in a Doris Day movie!'

'The question for the rest of us – even those who fought for the right to abortion – isn't when life begins but when it begins to be human. And that's been determined in different ways at different times.'

'Precisely! It's all about social control. It isn't God's will, but the bishops' or the rabbis' or the imams'.'

'Try another scenario,' she said, taken aback by his passion. 'What if it were a gay gene they'd tested for?'

'There isn't one. At most there might be a cluster.'

'All right then: the gay cluster. Sooner or later, scientists will identify it and enable parents to abort gay children. How will you feel then?'

'Being gay isn't a disability.'

'Not to you, maybe. But it is to some people.'

'Fortunately, they're the very people who are so rabidly anti-abortion that they won't be able to have one, or, if they do, they'll put themselves through the same hell they wish on us.'

'Revenge isn't a valid philosophical position.'

'I can't believe we're having this discussion. Whatever happened to a woman's right to choose?'

'It's as strong as ever. But it isn't an absolute – any more than any other right. Choice always comes with constraints.'

'Ma, you're seventy-seven. I want you to live forever; I really do. But, unless those scientists who inspire you with such hope come up with something fast, it's not going to happen. You'll have the grandchild you've always wanted – and I'm sorry, truly, that I couldn't give him to you – but you'll have him for how long? Ten, twelve years at best? Shoshanna (are you happy now?) will have him for the rest of her life, when he isn't a four year-old ten year-old, but a four year-old forty year-old. How will she cope with that?'

Marta drew a deep breath and asked him to accompany her to her bedroom. Refusing to let his questions weaken her resolve, she moved to the dressing table and unlocked a drawer, itself a rare event in a household that prided itself on its lack of secrets. She pulled out a photograph which, despite its artful restoration, bore the indelible marks of its three-year concealment beneath her vest. She handed it to him without a word, following his glance as he studied an image as familiar to her as any in the room: the bashful woman in an embroidered blouse, with a basket in one hand and a cloth in the other; the darkly handsome man in shirt sleeves clutching a book; the pair of identical twins, aged three or four, dressed in pale skirts and shoes so polished that they reflected the light. Their only distinguishing features were that one wore a bow which had slipped towards her ear, while the other had a blotch on her cheek which, if it were a smut and not the result of the picture's travels, might account for the cloth. They were holding hands, but their pose was more formal than that of their parents and it was unclear whether their intimacy were genuine or assumed for the camera. At their feet – a detail that never failed to hearten her – lay a single doll.

'Is this your family?' Clement asked.

'Yes.'

'But you always said that you had no photographs of them.'

'I lied.'

'Why?'

It was a question she had often asked herself, coming up with so many answers that she had avoided the need to address a single one. At times she felt that she wanted to preserve a part of her that was Polish from assimilation into her English life; at others that she wanted to protect the past from the intrusive gaze of the present. At times she felt that she wanted to keep the rounded individuals of her memory from becoming the standard victims of newsreels; at others that she was reluctant to entrust her sole remaining relic to less reverential hands. One emotion, however, never left her, causing her to lock the picture away, and that was guilt, not just the familiar guilt of the survivor, but her specific guilt towards Agata. It was that which had made it impossible to show the picture to any of her children, especially the twins.

'You and your sister look so similar, it's uncanny.'

'Is it?'

'You've always said you were older.'

'So I was. Just as Mark was older than you.'

'You were twins?'

'Give me back the picture, Clement, please!' She was gripped by panic until he handed her the photograph, which she clasped to her breast.

'Which is you?'

'Who knows? I've always assumed I'm the one on the left because of the livelier expression, but I can't be sure.'

'I'd no idea you were a twin.'

'Nor did my mother. That's what went wrong.'

'What?'

'I'm sorry, I'm nervous. Let me try to explain. Poland, seventy-odd years ago; it was a different world. No clinics, no scans, just a doctor and his forceps. Especially the forceps. Mine was a difficult birth, a twenty-six hour labour. My mother never spoke of it; I only found out the truth much later from my aunt. It wasn't until I was safely delivered that the doctor realised there was another baby. My mother was exhausted, far too exhausted to push, so the doctor pulled Agata out with his forceps, but he applied too much pressure, causing permanent damage to her brain.'

'Why did you never say?'

'Oh darling, how I used to love all your *whys*! Now they simply weary me. We were brought up together till we were four. Which is how I can date the photograph. Then some time before her fifth birthday – our fifth birthday – Agata was taken away.'

'You were split up?'

'I said it was a different world. Such things – much worse things – happened then. She was put in a home. I was taken to visit her a few times. She looked very happy playing with the other children. They had a small farm. I even remember feeling jealous... but I might just be trying to make myself feel bad.'

'You must have been bereft!'

'I expect so. She was my sister.'

'She was your twin!'

'Then again, soon afterwards I was bereft of so much more that who knows if the lesser loss wasn't simply subsumed? She came home on special occasions, but my parents were afraid that if she stayed she'd hold me back. I was the normal one... the clever one, who was to be given all the opportunities.'

'So they sacrificed her for you?'

'Until the Nazis came and she returned to us for good. The home closed, sending as many children as possible back to their families. I don't think we need spend too long speculating on what happened to the rest. I was ten years old when she joined us in the ghetto. All my resentment of the Nazis, of the pain and privations of my life, were focused on her. I resented the fact that she could look so like me yet be so different. I resented the hours my parents devoted to trying to make sense of her prattle. I resented our having to share a mattress in an already packed room and, worse, that she thought it was a game when she wet it. I resented the fact that my father – my dear, kind father – hit me for the first and only time when I stole some of Agata's rations and said they were wasted on her. You know the best thing about leaving the ghetto? It wasn't the extra food or the space or the cleaner air; it was breaking free of her. It was becoming myself again without the permanent shadow hanging over me. But of course it has; it's hung over me ever since. I'm living the life she was denied, first by nature and then by the Nazis. In a way I suppose I'm still trying to make it up to her. I've always thought it was something we had in common, you and I.'

'I'm not sure Mark would appreciate it,' Clement said ruefully. 'He never even liked my work.'

'He was so very proud of you. And I was proud of you both. You've no idea how excited I was to hear I was having twins, both excited and terrified at the same time. But once I knew all was well... that I had two perfect little boys, I felt as if I could wipe out all the horrors of the past.'

'But you never told us.'

'No. It seemed unfair to burden you with my expectations. And you were so happy together. Such strong individuals and such a devoted pair. I didn't want to show you a world where twins were less compatible... where identity was more brutal. So my twin became my younger sister.'

'A matter of minutes.'

'In one sense. And years in another.'

'Did Pa know?'

'Your father knows everything about me.'

'And he agreed you should keep it from us?'

'He trusted me to do what I thought was best.'

'And now, after all these years, you've changed your mind?' Clement gently prised the photograph from her hand and stared at it again.

'Not to try to reconcile you to Shoshanna's decision – and remember it is her decision, not yours or mine – but to show you that whatever she decides comes at a price. Would I have been happier if Agata had never been born? Or if she'd escaped and I'd been left to take care of her ever since? Was it just the law of nature that the stronger, fitter, brighter one survived?'

'Not in the case of Mark and me.'

'Mark's death was an accident, a tragic accident; Agata's was part of a systematic plan.'

Clement seemed stunned by her revelations and, after returning the photograph to the drawer, which she pointedly left unlocked, she led him downstairs. They entered the morning room to find Edwin sitting as impassively as a waxwork. The impression was sustained as she kissed his sallow cheek, prompting Linda to remark that 'we' were spending an hour out of bed, as if she had carried him from cot to playpen. Marta defied her disapproval to perch on the arm of his chair.

'How are you, my darling? Have you had a good day?' She checked Linda's attempt to answer for him with a brittle smile. He gazed at her with a vacancy that she prayed was confined to his eyes. 'Are you in pain?' She might have taken his silence for a negative had Clement not intervened.

'He knows. You can see that he knows. Isn't that pain enough?'

'We can't increase the steroids,' Linda said. 'It might be dangerous.'

'Oh sure,' Clement replied. 'He might have to postpone the round of golf he had planned for the morning.'

'You take a break, Nurse,' Marta said, 'we'll sit with him now.'

'Well, I have been on my feet since lunchtime.'

'That's settled then.'

She watched as Clement knelt at Edwin's side, rubbing his hand. 'How do you feel, Pa?'

Edwin turned his face towards him before slowly articulating the syllable 'Ark!'

'No, it's Clement, Pa. Clement!'

Clement was so distressed by a confusion that struck at the very core of his being that she longed to share her suspicion that, in invoking Mark, it was not that his father had failed to recognise him but rather that, at the end of his life, he was reliving its greatest loss. Fearing, however, that the disclosure would hurt him still more, she kept silent.

The next four days passed in a haze of sickness and anxiety. Marta pondered the irony that her worries about Shoshanna should keep her from dwelling on the full horror of Edwin's condition. She rang her every evening, red pencil in hand, sticking to the key markers of Edwin's decline such as the insertion of a catheter and the switch to a morphine pump, rather than expounding on the day-to-day degradations. Then, on the fifth day, Shoshanna pre-empted her call with the news that she had had the result of the Chorionic Villus Sampling.

'Oh yes?' Marta said breezily, as if she could influence the outcome by her tone.

'It's bad, Ma. It's the worst. My baby has Down's.'

The days of anticipation did nothing to temper the shock. Marta grabbed hold of a chair to keep from falling.

'Oh darling, I'm so sorry.'

'There are different degrees of Down's, of course. Jan made that very clear.'

'Then there's hope?'

'But it's Down's. Down's! The good news is that, now the bleeding's stopped, I should carry for my full term.'

'And how are you feeling?' Marta asked, despising herself for the inanity of a question which avoided the more dangerous one of 'What are you going to do?'

'Right now I feel numb. Dazed. Dead. Zvi says it's a test. Like Abraham sacrificing Isaac.' Marta wanted to slap him. 'Except that, in our case, we have to let the child live.'

To her dismay, Shoshanna misconstrued her failure to mention abortion. No matter that she had already resolved to refuse one, she was offended by her mother's withholding the solution she proposed so readily for everyone else. It was as though they were living in a soap opera where, even when behaving out of character, people remained true to type.

She reminded herself that the decision on keeping the baby rested with Shoshanna and Zvi. Set against their dilemma, her own feelings were an irrelevance. She agonised nonetheless and, after a sleepless night in which the various options hammered at her brain, she went down to the morning room where she wearily told Ruth that she would give Edwin his breakfast. No sooner had she lifted the spoonful of apple puree to his mouth than he clamped his teeth on it. At first she presumed that he was playing games and felt a rush of anger as at a wayward child. Then she caught sight of his eyes and was appalled by their desolation. Either he was unable to open his mouth or he could no longer make the link between spoon and tongue and food. Whichever it was, she knew at once that she must ask Shoshanna to come to Beckley. Faced with this vision of her future, she would defy the zealots and take the necessary steps.

She voiced her request with such urgency that Shoshanna drove down the next morning. Marta had expected her to look pale, but she was not prepared for the haggard figure waiting for her in the drawing room, her eyes raw from weeping and her skin as lustreless as her wig.

'Before you say anything,' Shoshanna said at once, 'we're definitely keeping it. "Thou shalt not kill" is one of God's commandments.'

'God lets a lot of babies die,' Marta said gently.

'That's His choice. We don't have one. I'm not prepared to discuss it. Not with you. And certainly not with Clement.'

Marta said nothing, trusting that the sight of Edwin would put her case more eloquently than any argument. She led her into the morning room where Clement and Linda were sitting on either side of the bed, the nurse examining charts and Clement gazing at the recumbent figure like a pilgrim at a shrine. Shoshanna and Clement exchanged a cursory kiss, while Linda, with rare sensitivity, withdrew to the parlour. Shoshanna took over the vacated seat and held her father's hand, visibly shocked by his deterioration. The effect was heightened since Marta had persuaded Linda to reduce the morning's morphine, insisting that her husband would wish to be at his most lucid for his daughter's visit. She felt no qualms since she knew that Edwin – the old Edwin, the true Edwin – would consider it a small price to pay for the chance to concentrate his daughter's mind.

'It's Shoshanna, Pa... Nanna,' she added as a concession. 'Doesn't he know me?' she asked when neither name elicited a response.

'The only thing he knows now is pain,' Clement said.

'You mustn't give up, Pa. I'm going to have a baby. Don't you want to see your grandchild?'

'See?' Clement interjected. 'Even if his eyes haven't totally gone by then, his mind will have.'

'It's God's will,' Shoshanna said routinely. 'Blessed be the Lord of the Universe.'

'What is?' Clement asked. 'His condition or yours?'

'I don't have to justify myself to you. I came to see Pa.'

'Clement's right, darling,' Marta said. 'I was too caught up in my own concerns to see.'

'Clement's always right! Well, this has nothing to do with him. It's my body,' she said tauntingly. 'My right to choose.'

'I know how you feel, Nanna,' Clement said, as Marta braced herself for the outburst that never came. 'You think God is punishing you for your past mistakes... your relationship with Chris.'

'You know nothing about me. You never did.' Her involuntary flinch suggested that he knew more than she cared to admit.

'Illness... impairment isn't a punishment, I know.'

'You wish!'

Edwin's groan cut them short and Clement moved forward to check on his catheter. Finding that the bag was full, he called Linda, who brought a welcome air of detachment to the room. Shoshanna stood up to give her space, but she insisted that there was no need, emptying the bag as casually as if it were a vase. Marta watched as Shoshanna's desire to prove herself as resilient as her mother and brother prevailed over her newfound modesty code and lifelong squeamishness. Seizing the moment, she proposed that Edwin be given a bedpan. Linda, eager to avoid 'mishaps', agreed, attaching him to the pulley above the bed and winching him up eighteen inches where, for several harrowing seconds, he was left dangling before she laboriously lowered him. When Shoshanna, horrified by Linda's intimate discussion of her father's bowels, fled from the room with a cry of 'This is intolerable!', Marta trusted that Edwin would forgive her this latest humiliation. Rubbing his unresponsive hand, she was convinced that, if ever his suffering were to serve a purpose, it would be now.

Having glimpsed Shoshanna striding off into the woods, she was relieved when she returned in time for lunch. The relief quickly faded as she watched her unpack her Tupperware, her resistance to Mrs Shepherd's game pie showing that she was in no mood to compromise.

'How much more of this can he take?' Shoshanna asked, gazing at the empty chair at the head of the table.

'This is just the beginning,' Clement replied.

'I thought the consultant said that, if he had no treatment or the treatment failed, he had a maximum of three months.'

'Everyone's different,' Marta said. 'Your father may be eighty-three but he has the constitution of an ox.'

'You told me you were thinking of stopping any active treatment,' she said, choosing her words with care.

'We've moved far beyond that,' Marta said. 'He's off all medication except for steroids. They could reduce those and increase the morphine, but it would simply prolong the agony. The consultant explained that taking patients off steroids makes them slip into a coma and you think the end is at hand. But, since they're given no water, the swelling in the brain goes down and they come round. So paradoxically they can last longer.'

'Are you sure he's having enough morphine?'

'To do what?' Clement asked.

'To stop him suffering! What do you think?'

'We could give him too much morphine and stop him suffering forever.'

'I didn't hear that,' Shoshanna said, loudly chewing her sandwich.

'Shall I repeat it?'

'Not now, Clement,' Marta said, to no avail.

'It's for God alone to take life.'

'We wouldn't be taking his life but shortening the process of his death.'

'And you accuse me of self-deception!'

'What he is now isn't just a travesty of what he was, but an affront to his deepest beliefs.'

'What does he believe? I've lost track.'

'He believes in humanity and we're failing him. I believe in God and He'll welcome him.'

'"Thou shalt not kill!" How does that fit with your belief in God?'

'Very easily. For a start, in some translations, it's "Thou shalt not commit murder."'

'How convenient!'

'No, accurate. Some killings aren't murders: a terminally ill man; a defective foetus.' Marta blenched as he articulated the link that had been implicit from the start of the discussion, although, to her surprise, Shoshanna made no attempt to respond. 'Besides,' Clement added, 'if you're so keen on the Commandments, what about "Honour thy Father and thy Mother"? How better than by honouring his wishes? You were with us in the hospital when he said he wanted to die.'

'That was weeks ago. He isn't saying it now.'

'He can't say anything now! It's too late. But look at his eyes; they say it all.'

'That's enough, Clement,' Marta said. 'Shoshanna's upset. She's not as used to him as we are.'

'Then she should bow to our better judgement. I can't bear to see him like this a moment more.'

'Exactly!' Shoshanna said. 'You can't bear it! You, you!'

'That's just where you're wrong. I could walk away today, go abroad for the winter and never have to see him again. Where can he go? He can't even get out of bed!'

'That's true, darling,' Marta said.

'You, of all people, Ma, should remember who were the greatest enthusiasts for euthanasia,' Shoshanna said defiantly.

'I remember more than you think,' Marta replied, the faces in the photograph blotting out those in the room. 'But your father's case is different. His isn't an "inferior life" but a mockery of one. It's no longer a life at all, but an existence. His every function is impaired.'

'It's easy to accept God's will when it suits us. We have to learn to accept it when it doesn't.'

'Your father no longer believes in God.'

'Who knows? The Lord may be using this to restore his faith. You've no right to deny him that chance.'

'How can he have a faith when he doesn't have a mind?' Clement asked.

'I wanted him to see his grandchild,' Shoshanna said, turning to Marta. 'That may not be possible. But one thing I can guarantee: if you do anything – anything at all – to harm Pa, you won't be seeing him either.'

Shoshanna left the table and returned to the morning room, assuring Marta and Clement, when they came to join her, that Edwin's blinks were signs of recognition and his involuntary lip-movements smiles. She sat by his side for half an hour and then, after a strained goodbye to her mother and brother and a promise to her father to visit him at the weekend, drove home, leaving them to lapse into the familiar routine. The difference lay in the burning question hanging in the air, which Marta forced herself to address at dinner.

'I can't, Clement,' she said, refusing to elaborate. 'Whatever we may have agreed before, I can't do it. Your sister would never forgive me.'

'She need never know.'

'No? She'll pick up on the slightest change in his condition. And I can't lie. Not to Shoshanna.'

'So she'll let Pa suffer to salve her conscience?'

'It won't be long now, please God!'

'How long is long? Every minute is a lifetime for him.'

She made no answer, acutely aware that, for all her pledges to stand by Edwin, she had failed him at the critical moment. She trusted he would understand, having understood her so well for fifty years, that she had to look to the future: not just to her own need for the child but to the child's need for her, as it struggled to find a place in a world that worshipped perfection.

'I'll take care of everything, Ma. All I want from you is your blessing. If what's holding you back is a fear of antagonising Shoshanna, don't worry! There's no reason for her ever to find out. Why not take a break? Stay with a friend for a few days? You're wiped out. No one would blame you.'

'Except myself! How can I abandon your father now, when he needs me more than ever?'

'No. What he needs is what you won't give him.'

'You say that, but how can you be sure?'

'Ma please! Must we go through all this again?'

'Yes!' she said, startled by her own vehemence. 'And again and again and again. This isn't some old sofa we're throwing out. It's your father. My husband. My life.'

'And his life, Ma? Doesn't that count for anything?'

'I should be with him. If we do it, I should be here to hold his hand.'

'That's fine by me, but what about Shoshanna?'

'We could keep it from her for a day or two. I could stay with him – with you – and then leave... Oh, I can't believe we're sitting here, discussing it in such a cold-blooded way!'

'It won't work, Ma. What about Linda and Ruth and Mr and Mrs Shepherd? Are they all to be sworn to secrecy? Then there's the death certificate...'

'Please! I can't think straight.'

'Then let someone else do the thinking for a change. I know how much it hurts, but what difference can one night make after fifty odd years?'

'More than you'll ever know.'

'Besides how would he recognise you? He's buried somewhere deep inside himself.'

His heartfelt conviction swayed her. He was right about Edwin's wishes. She had no ethical objections to them, only gut fears. Whatever the pain of deserting his deathbed, it was nothing to that of letting him linger on in misery. Dying was not always as clear-cut as it was on a certificate. For weeks she had been a widow in all but name.

'You're right, darling, thank you. Thank you for your clarity and for your patience. I know I've only made things harder with all my niggling, selfish doubts. You have my blessing – of course you do – along with my gratitude. I'll go away. Yes, I shall invite myself to stay with Valerie Sinclair. She's been begging me to go down for too long.'

For all their sakes, they agreed that the visit should take place right away. So, quitting the warmth of the hearthrug, she went to her study to phone Valerie, whose panic at the lack of notice threatened to wreck the entire plan. A gentle reminder of their scratch suppers in the Serengeti reassured her, and Marta arranged to take the train to Lewes the following day. Determined to spend the final night with Edwin, she pulled up a chair beside his bed, leant back on a mound of pillows, and peered into his empty eyes.

Contemplating a face that was a palimpsest of her past half century, she found herself transported back to an Oxford lecture hall where they sat side by side for a talk on comparative – or, as it was then, *primitive* – religion. Gathering up his notes at the end, he pocketed her fountain pen: unwittingly it had seemed at the time, but, weighing up her memories, she wondered whether to credit him with more guile. Eager to atone, he invited her, first, to tea in his rooms and, then, to a punt on the Cherwell. All his diffidence disappeared the moment he picked up the pole. It was evident that he had done his homework when he apologised for reading theology.

'Why?' she asked.

'Didn't the rabbis at Auschwitz put God on trial for crimes against humanity?'

'I'm not a rabbi,' she said, prompting him to head for the bank, where they exchanged their first kiss. Thirty years later, when he lost his faith in God but elected to stay in the Church, he equated it with the Auschwitz rabbis who, having found God guilty as charged, gazed at the gathering clouds and prepared for evening prayer.

While never renouncing the humanist creed of her childhood, she had been grateful for his religious belief and, more specifically, his Anglicanism. Like his Englishness, it stood for the triumph of insularity over experience, a sign that he had remained untainted by the forces that had ravaged her world. Which was why she had been hit so hard by his apostasy. Now she had to take heart from the conviction both that their current goodbye would be final and that releasing him was the ultimate act of love.

After a night which, although sleepless, was strangely restful, she packed a small case and gave instructions to the nurses. At ten thirty, with Mr Shepherd waiting outside, she took a last leave of Edwin. Hoping against hope that he would somehow acknowledge the magnitude of their parting, she was doubly dismayed by his blank expression. She kissed his swollen lips and walked slowly from the room. Meeting Clement in the hall, she drew him aside and, despite her best intentions, demanded further assurances that he knew the optimum dose of morphine to deliver. His melancholy nod dispelled any doubt and she clasped him as tightly as if he were the one about to die. Then, with a quick farewell to Ajax, whose reproachful stare threatened to shatter her resolve, she hurried down the steps and into the car.

4

CLEMENT

1

'Blessed are the merciful: for they shall obtain mercy' echoed through Clement's head in counterpoint to his sister's Old Testament injunctions. The more she spoke, the more assured he grew of his position. She denounced him as irreligious, when it was precisely his faith in the afterlife that had allayed any lingering doubts about helping his father. It would be far harder were he dispatching him into a void.

Confident of God's blessing, he was now concerned to obtain his mother's. Swift action was essential, but her distress at Shoshanna's departure forced him to postpone the discussion until dinner. As a declaration of intent, he put on a shirt and tie, finding to his surprise when he entered the drawing room that she had made a similar effort, exchanging her blouse and slacks for a turquoise kaftan. Cheered by the concurrence, he went down to the cellar in search of a good bottle of claret, before grabbing the first that came to hand when the dusty racks brought his father's death chillingly close.

Either from the excellence of the wine or a determined attempt to blot out the horror on the other side of the wall, they joked their way through the first two courses, but the pudding made them pause.

'Trifle,' his mother said. 'It's your father's favourite.'

'Was,' he corrected gently.

'I can't, Clement,' she said, in a sudden change of tack. 'Whatever we may have agreed before, I can't do it. Your sister would never forgive me.'

'She need never know.'

'No? She'll pick up on the slightest change in his condition. And I can't lie. Not to Shoshanna.'

'So she'll let Pa suffer to salve her conscience?' He struggled to excise any note of bitterness from his voice.

'It won't be long now, please God!'

'How long is long? Every minute is a lifetime for him.'

He waited for a reply, but she concentrated on her food. It was outrageous that she should submit to Shoshanna's blackmail. He knew how much she longed for a grandchild, but he refused to believe that she would put her own desires before his father's needs. Torn between tenderness and exasperation, he explained how he would see to everything while she took a well-earned break, ensuring that any suspicions Shoshanna might have would fall on him alone.

He felt his mother's anguish, as she agonised over both the plan and its consequences before finally giving her assent. With neither of them wishing to dally at table, they returned to the drawing room to find Mrs Shepherd laying a fire. 'I thought you needed warming. It's October,' she added to avoid confusion. After a few glum words about 'the Bishop', whose title she invoked more reverently than ever, she poured their coffee and went out.

'Now you've made up your mind, you should go at once,' he said, returning to the subject of the visit. 'Too much anticipation diminishes pleasure.' What he meant and she knew that he meant and he knew that she knew that he meant – a sequence which could extend as long as a childhood dare – was that it was Thursday night and he needed to attend to everything before Shoshanna's Sunday visit. She went out to phone Valerie Sinclair, a Somerville colleague who had accompanied her on one of her later fieldtrips to the Hadza. Valerie, a birdlike woman, whose fondness for white ankle socks had baffled Mark even before he heard her described as a bluestocking, had been vanquished in some faculty dispute and retired in high dudgeon to Sussex, from where she fired off long missives to her friends as if she were back in the bush. As predicted, she was delighted to welcome his mother, who confirmed that she would leave the next morning and, in a rare sign of dependency, asked him to look up the times of the trains. That settled, she announced that she would spend the final night at his father's bedside, insisting that she had slept in tougher conditions than a wingback chair.

Having made sure that she was as comfortable as could be – his only practical contribution being a stack of pillows – he went upstairs to ring home. A momentary panic on reaching the answer-machine was dispelled when Mike cut in to say that he had leapt straight out of the bath. 'Tell me about your day,' Clement charged, eager to hold on to the tantalising image for as long as possible. Mike obliged with a wry account of teaching the history of slavery to an ethnically diverse class of fourteen-year-olds, who regarded him as one of the oppressors.

Mike then asked about his father and he explained that he was going ahead with the plan. 'Would you like me to come down?' Mike asked. 'Given the way the Head's pussyfooting around me, I suspect he'd allow me the day off to floss my teeth!'

'No, I'd rather be on my own. If anything should go wrong – '

'You said it was foolproof!'

'So it is. But there's always an *if* and I don't want you to be implicated... involved.'

'I hate to think of you having to manage on your own.'

'I won't be. You'll say I'm imagining it, but I feel – I can't ever remember feeling it so strongly – Mark's presence all around.'

'My eternal rival,' Mike said enigmatically.

'He would have done it. No question.'

'You do know exactly what to do?'

'You sound like my mama,' Clement replied, finding that even that failed to silence him. So he described how he had consulted their GP friend, Jimmy Naismith, who had outlined an infallible procedure. A slight twist of the dial on his father's morphine pump would turn a palliative into a lethal dose.

'I'm proud of you, Clem,' Mike said, leaving him tempted to change his mind and ask him down, less for moral than for emotional support. He yearned for the warmth of his mouth, the touch of his skin, the vigour of his flesh thrusting into him. He had kept him at bay for too long, blaming the effect of the drugs on his libido, when the truth lay in the effect of the virus on his psyche. Fearing, however, that Mike's presence would be a distraction, he resolved to stand firm. So, after telling him he loved him with no 'You could never love me as much as I love you,' to protect himself, Clement put down the phone. He washed, changed and slipped into bed, trying to blank out the image of the last vigil in the room below. Then, remembering his pills, he jumped up and dashed to the basin.

The next morning he ate an early breakfast and went for a walk in the woods, in part, as he told Mrs Shepherd, to clear his head, but in the main to avoid his mother. Refreshed, he stole back into the house by the kitchen stairs, venturing down to the hall only when his regular checks at the bathroom window showed that Mr Shepherd had driven round to the front. He was relieved to see, from her coat and case, that his mother had not lost heart and, from her relaxed expression, that she had managed to sleep.

'No, not a wink,' she replied when he asked her. 'I remembered, which was far more restful.' Then, moving so close to him that their cheeks brushed, she whispered tentatively: 'You're quite sure of the dose?'

Her question offended him. Rather than risk an answer, he made do with a slight nod. When he looked up, he found that his eyes had filled with tears.

He carried her case down the steps, waiting while she said goodbye to Mrs Shepherd and Ruth and stroked Ajax's muzzle. As they in turn watched him kiss her, he entreated her loudly to have a complete rest. 'Promise me you won't worry about Pa. We'll look after him.' Then abandoning all restraint, he added: 'He'll still be here when you get back,' at which she pulled away and climbed into the car, saying something to Mr Shepherd which sent them speeding down the drive.

He returned indoors, following Ruth into the morning room where she was preparing to give his father a bed-bath. 'Poor man,' she said, gazing down at the living effigy. 'All this must be specially hard for someone like him. The other day Linda and I were changing him and he looked at me and went "Shi...." Well, we thought it was *number twos*; you know how they speak their minds when they get to this stage.' Clement grimaced. 'So we winched him up, but he wouldn't do anything. "Naughty boy!" I said, only joking you understand. It wasn't until we winched him down, that Linda noticed my brooch. It was a sheep.'

Had Clement felt any qualms about his plan, they would have been banished by Ruth's story. Rather than skulk about the house, he strolled into the village, where the general concern about his father's health and the occasional wary inquiry about his own led him to beat a rapid retreat. He walked back via the cottages and, on impulse, called on Karen, whom he found threading beads in a kitchen that reeked of camphor. She announced that she and her coven were 'delivering charges for Uncle Edwin's recovery'. He felt a twinge of unease and, refusing a mug of nettle tea, returned home. Suddenly shy of sitting in rooms so redolent of his father, he went upstairs until dinner, after which he told Ruth that, like his mother, he would spend the night in the morning room.

'Any more of this and you'll be docking my wages!'

'I wouldn't think of it!'

'I was having you on. Besides, I'm on contract,' she said, as though anything less would demean her.

After Ruth's departure, he sat studying his father's face, making a conscious effort to memorise features he would never forget, when he was seized by a profound urge to sketch him. He went up to his room and, for the first time in over a year, took out a pad and pencils. The Roxborough disaster had sapped both his confidence and his will. On his way to the studio the following week he had thrown up in the corridor, assuring an anxious neighbour that it was caused by the lingering fumes of resin. Subsequent visits confirmed his revulsion. He had aimed to assist devotion and to provoke debate, not to put one man in hospital and another behind bars. Yet he refused to compromise by settling for mere technical facility. If the truth were so dangerous, the only honest course was silence.

Immediately, all his uncertainty and self-disgust dissolved. It was as though the decision to act had reached to his very core and reignited his creativity. He returned to the morning room, determined to preserve his father's features on paper even as he was releasing him from the world. Despite his lack of practice, the line flowed freely and he was filled with a deep sense of peace. He knew then that it was time, and he leant forward to whisper his intentions in his father's ear, triggering a slight shift in his breathing, which he took for a sigh of approval, and a gentle moistening of his eyes. At a stroke, his father shed fifty years, his hair turned raven and his skin olive, and he found himself staring at Rafik. He shrank back in horror before realising that it was another sign. At long last he had taken control.

With infinite care, as though adjusting the needle in his father's arm rather than the dial on his pump, he increased the flow of morphine, flooding his body with life-giving death. The long-case clock in the hall struck twelve, as if to signal the approach of sleep. He sat back to keep vigil but, once again, the artist in him prevailed and he picked up his pad and pencil, determined to capture his father's final hours. Never before had he felt so sure of himself: that the rightness of his actions was untainted even by the desire to see himself in the right. Honouring his father in the way he knew best, he focused intently on the tranquil face, until grief threatened to turn the drawing into an aquarelle.

It was a token of his father's great spirit that it should leave his body with so little fuss. There was no death rattle, not even a rasp, just a slow withdrawal until what had been passive became inert. The transition was at once imperceptible and pronounced. Gazing at the unchanged features, Clement recognised that the one irreversible change had taken place. He kept hold of his father's hand, refusing to let it go even to check the pulse. He resolved against waking the household, not to arrogate the moment to himself but to allow his father to rest in peace. Besides, it felt more fitting to inform people at the start of a new day. So for three hours he sat by the bed, barely stirring, until he heard the clock strike seven. Recalling his father's insistence on winding it himself, he was gripped by a searing sense of loss. Hot tears streamed down his cheeks and he laid his head on the hollow chest, howling into the blanket. Then, drying his eyes, he stood up with a cramp and hobbled to the door, before remembering to reset the pump.

His first stop was the kitchen where Mrs Shepherd was frying bacon for her husband's breakfast. He was startled by her extreme response to news that she must have long expected. As she clung to a chair, body slumped and face drenched with tears, he was seized by the notion that her relationship with his father might have been more than it seemed. He steeled himself for a lachrymose confession, complete with pleas for the family's forgiveness, only to despair of his soap-opera sensibilities when she paid tribute to 'the finest gentleman anyone could ever hope to meet'. So fierce was her sorrow that she made no acknowledgement of his, a glancing reference to 'your poor mother' being her sole recognition of those higher up the hierarchy of loss. She sat, wrapped in her memories, until, passing over the apostasy that had caused her so much pain, she comforted herself with the assertion that he had 'gone to a better place'.

Leaving her to break the news to her husband, he went up to the parlour to intercept Linda before she began her shift. He was glad that it was her rather than Ruth, since the laxness that had irritated him in the past made her less likely to notice any anomalies in the drip. Far from being suspicious, she wasn't even surprised. 'I could see it was his time to go. What a blessing you were with him! Too often it's only one of us.'

'I'm sure you do all you can.'

'Oh don't get me wrong. I count it a privilege. A true privilege. When people ask me how I bear it, I tell them I wouldn't swap places with any midwife. Did you notice a change in the air? A sort of fluttering?'

'I must have nodded off,' he replied and hurried upstairs to ring his mother. His bystander's account, a safeguard against eavesdroppers, added to the sense of unreality. His mother showed no such concern, replying with a muted 'Thank you,' that fed his paranoia.

'That's "Thank you for ringing me," Valerie, if you're listening. "Thank you for being with him," Mrs Shepherd, if you've picked up the phone.'

'Hush darling! Don't upset yourself. There's no one on the line but us.'

Recovering, he assured her that the end had been peaceful: a gentle susurration as his father's spirit returned to God.

'There can be no more miracles,' she said, giving no clue as to whether she was speaking personally or in general. After thanking him for being there, so formally that she seemed to be trying to convince herself, she said that she would take the first train home. As soon as she put down the phone, he rang Mike, catching him on his way to school. Imperturbable as ever, he promised to turn straight round and drive to Beckley, collecting Carla en route. Clement was grateful to have one less person to tell, afraid that, even if he succeeded in sticking to the story, repetition would make it glib.

His mother made no mention of Shoshanna. Suspecting that she would have no time to call her in the flurry of leaving and that nothing would fuel his sister's resentment more than being excluded, he reluctantly picked up the phone. His fears proved to be justified when, no sooner had she absorbed the news, than she demanded to know the exact time of death.

'I'm afraid I can't say,' he replied. 'Somewhere in the early hours.'

'Be sure to ask the nurses. It's important,' she said, so vehemently that he presumed it had some religious significance.

'Neither of them was there. Only me.'

She made no comment, asking instead after their mother. For all that her absence had been central to the plan, he decided not to allude to it, at least for the present. 'She's very calm. I don't know whether it's sunk in yet. She's been expecting it for months, and now it's finally happened. I suppose it's the difference between an inevitability and a fact.' Her silence left him in little doubt of her disdain for such distinctions. Then, instructing him to arrange nothing without her, she hung up to ring Zvi.

Having survived the conversation with his sister, he felt strong enough to call his aunt, whose demand to be told that 'he didn't suffer. I can't bear to think of him suffering,' betrayed her true priorities even in grief. Her insistence that the funeral should not be 'some hole-in-the-corner affair' reminded him that, like it or not, his father had been a public figure and there would be widespread interest in his death. Loath to deal with it himself, not least after his recent mauling by the press, he rang Lucy, his father's part-time secretary, who promised to drive over from Oxford after lunch.

He returned to the morning room, where Linda had been joined by Ruth. They had removed his father's pills, smoothed his bedding and detached the syringe-driver from his arm, as though any remaining connection to the world would detract from the mystery of death. He accepted Ruth's offer to call the doctor but, the moment she left the room, Linda resumed her homespun metaphysics, prompting him to plead exhaustion and flee upstairs. He hurried past the gilded array of ancestors, or 'rogues gallery' as his father had put it, but, catching the eyes of Squire Hubert Granville and his great-grandson, General Mark, he felt that their glazed expressions had grown more forgiving; he may have failed in his duty as an heir but he had fulfilled it as a son.

He lay on his bed, trying to adjust to a world without his father, when he was roused by the scrunch of tyres on gravel. Moving to the window, he was relieved to see that it was Mike and Carla. He ran down the stairs, narrowly missing Ruth, who frowned at behaviour unbecoming to his years, let alone his loss. Taking a moment to collect himself, he walked out to greet Mike, relishing the reassurance of his steady heartbeat and cool breath. Mike's emphatic 'I'm so very sorry' signalled that he had said nothing to Carla who, after discreetly hanging back, came forward and threw her arms around his neck. He led them straight into the morning room to pay their respects, marvelling as his inveterately dry-eyed lover wiped away a tear. They then adjourned to the drawing room and sat in companionable silence.

Half an hour later, the doctor arrived to sign the death certificate. After submitting to the statutory condolences, along with a pointed effusion of gratitude for his father's patronage of the local youth band, Clement showed him out and returned to the drawing room, where he found Mrs Shepherd serving coffee and biscuits and expounding her baking schedule in anticipation of a houseful of guests.

'I'm best when I'm busy,' she said, dismissing his suggestion that she ring up Waitrose. 'Mr Shepherd too. He heard the news and then went straight out to clear the Well Walk. But he sent young Charlie Heapstone home.'

'Pity!' Mike said.

'The Bishop was very fond of him,' she said sharply. 'He'd have wanted it.' Then, with a glare as stern as if he had insulted her cooking, she left the room.

Mike flushed, as Clement and Carla burst out laughing.

'She thinks you're a ruthless plutocrat trampling on the poor working man,' Clement said. 'Serves you right for being such a lech!'

Mrs Shepherd's confusion lifted their spirits and they regaled each other with anecdotes about his father, laughing loudly and, in Clement's case, uncontrollably, until Shoshanna and Zvi's arrival cast an instant pall over the room. As they stood at the door, wreathed in disapproval, Clement felt as if they had caught him dancing in the family vault. Taking hold of himself, he moved first to his sister, who kissed him perfunctorily, and then to Zvi, whose 'I wish you long life' as they shook hands, was so patently formulaic that it threatened to spark another fit of giggles.

'Where's Mother?' Shoshanna asked. 'Upstairs?'

'She's not here,' he replied, 'she went to stay with Valerie Sinclair.'

'Valerie Sinclair?' she asked incredulously.

'She's on her way back.'

'Since when?'

'Yesterday morning. She was looking wiped out, so I insisted.'

'You insisted?' It was as though grief had drained her of any speech but echoes.

'I thought it for the best and so it's proved. At least she's been spared all of this.'

'Let's get this clear. You told her to go?'

'Suggested. Advised.'

'No one said anything to me. I was here two days ago.'

'So was I. I've been here for weeks.'

'Pa's condition was stable. You were worried he would linger on.'

'Don't upset yourself, Shoshanna,' Zvi said.

'Or else that he could go at any time,' Clement said. 'Fortunately, it was the latter.'

'Fortunately for who?'

'For him. Who do you think?'

'You said on the phone you were alone with him,' she said slowly. 'No nurses.'

'Yes, it was a stroke of luck. I like to think that on some level he knew it was me. Of course he gave no sign.'

'Yet only two days ago you were worried he'd linger on for weeks.'

'We've just been through all that. It was impossible to predict. He gave up; he'd finally had enough.'

'Who'd had enough? Him or you?'

'I don't follow,' he replied.

'Come on, guys,' Mike said, 'give us all a break. Your father's just died.'

'Am I right?' Shoshanna asked Clement. 'There's no point trying to act the innocent. It won't wash, not with me. You got rid of Ma. There were no nurses around. So you took matters into your own hands, in spite of everything we talked about – everything we agreed – only two days ago.'

'Susannah, you're crazy,' Mike said.

'It's Shoshanna! Oh, what's the use?' she asked. 'If your boyfriend's prepared to kill his father, why should you remember my name?'

'No one's killed anyone!' he replied. 'That's libel.'

'So sue me.'

'Let's all take a deep breath,' Carla said. 'We're in shock.'

'Are we?' Shoshanna asked. 'I think some of us are unnaturally calm.'

'Would you rather we were all as hysterical as you?' Mike asked.

'You should try showing some respect,' Zvi said, 'Shoshanna's just lost her father. As well as some consideration for her condition.'

Clement stared at Shoshanna's stomach and wondered if her response would have been different had her baby been healthy.

'I just want an honest answer, Clement. After all, you claim to set such store by your integrity! Did you or did you not kill Pa?'

'Not kill,' he said wearily. 'Release, if you like.'

'No!' Shoshanna cried, sinking her head first in her hands and then on Zvi's chest when he moved to comfort her.

'Don't say any more, Clem,' Mike said. 'You're not thinking straight. You've been up all night.'

'Don't worry,' Clement replied. 'I know what Shoshanna believes... that is I know what her religion tells her to believe. But I also know what she feels. She's my sister.'

'Stop talking about me as if I'm not in the room!'

'I don't understand,' Carla said. 'Are you saying that Clement helped Edwin to die?'

'Killed, Carla,' Shoshanna said. 'Let's call a spade a spade.'

'And let's call a mercy a mercy. I'm glad you know the truth, Nanna,' Clement said, avoiding both her adult names. 'I aimed to keep it from you, but now I want you to see what I did for Pa... how far I was prepared to go in order to help him.' He choked back his tears, scornful of cheap sentiment. 'Do you think it was easy for me? Well let me tell you it wasn't! But I can promise you one thing; it was easy for him. He felt nothing, just slipping into a deeper and deeper sleep.'

'So how did you do it? Pills? Or did you smother him with a pillow?'

'Of course not.' He shuddered. 'It was the morphine. I simply upped the dose.'

'That's enough, Clem,' Mike warned.

'It's a little late to protect him now,' Shoshanna said.

'Clement acted out of love. Whereas you were willing to let your father suffer for your own selfish ends.'

'It's God's law,' Zvi said.

'Says who?' Mike asked.

'The Torah.'

'Oh I see. All other laws, in Britain at least, are discussed and debated. We're to believe that this one – the law of laws – fell clunk clunk out of the sky!'

'But it's against the law of the land too,' Shoshanna said, 'the law you uphold, the one that's discussed and debated. You'd do well to remember that the next time you sneer at us. Now may we go in and see him, or have you disposed of the evidence? Buried him before we arrived?'

'He's in the morning room,' Clement said flatly.

Shoshanna and Zvi went out, leaving an atmosphere of despondency. Clement tried to explain himself to Carla, who replied that she had 'learnt very young that love meant letting go'. The exchange was interrupted by Mrs Shepherd, who was worried about lunch 'what with two koshers and one picky eater.' Clement, ignoring the jibe at Mike, whom she had yet to forgive for his heartlessness, suggested that she make something vegetarian, since Shoshanna and Zvi were sure to spurn anything from their kitchen. The surmise was confirmed when, venturing no further than the doorway, Shoshanna announced that they were driving into Oxford to buy food.

They were gone two hours, arriving back minutes before his mother and Valerie. While appreciating her kindness in escorting her bereaved friend home, Clement was dismayed by Valerie's presence, with its hint of a world beyond the family circle, especially since Shoshanna barely allowed their mother to take off her coat before interrogating her.

'Did you know about this?'

'For Heaven's sake,' Mike interjected. 'Edwin's only just died.'

'Somehow I don't think that comes as any surprise. How could you, Ma? After everything we said... everything we agreed. It's murder!'

'Susannah dear,' Valerie said, 'you're upset. Take care you don't say something you'll regret.'

'You don't know the half of it!'

'What is it you want of me, darling?' his mother asked gently.

'Tell me you knew nothing of what Clement planned to do. Look me in the eye and tell me.'

'What?' Valerie asked. 'What did Clement do?'

'Ma had no idea,' Clement said. 'That's why I got her out of the way. Yes, it's true, everyone; I murdered my father. I hacked him down in the prime of life!'

'Clement, you're overwrought!' his mother said.

'Would anyone mind if I poured myself a drink?' Valerie asked weakly.

'Well, I won't let you get away with it,' Shoshanna said to Clement. 'He was my father too. My wishes... my beliefs should have been respected. Come on, Zvi, we're leaving. There's no place for us here.'

'Darling, don't be like this. Now's the time when family needs to stick together.'

'You have your family, Ma. He's there. I thought you wanted me... These last few weeks I thought we'd grown even closer. But all you wanted was the child. Sad isn't it how we always want what we can't have?'

'You're my daughter!'

'And Clement's your son. And we both know which counts for more.'

Clement watched as Shoshanna and Zvi walked out, leaving the others with information that they had no wish to digest but no chance to deny.

'Oh Hell! Was the door open the whole time?' Mike asked. 'Does anyone know if the nurses have gone home?'

'No one will listen to Shoshanna,' Carla said. 'She feels hurt... bereft, so she's lashing out at whoever's nearest to hand.'

'Hormones!' Valerie said. 'If any of you are in doubt about the havoc pregnancy can wreak on the emotions, take a look at my comparative study of the Bari women in Colombia and the Canela in Brazil.'

Clement turned to his mother, who sat in silence, as though weighed down by her double loss. 'Do you want to see him, Ma?'

'I want to see him walk into the room as he was six months ago. I want to see him cycle down the High as he did fifty years ago... Yes, darling, I want to see him. But we're neither of us going anywhere. There's time.'

At half-past two, Mrs Shepherd summoned them for a meal which was unexpectedly jolly and, when she handed Mike a minuscule bowl of vichyssoise made from 'leeks that Charlie Heapstone planted', downright bizarre. At quarter to three Lucy arrived and, with her trademark efficiency, contacted church and college authorities before fielding the barrage of calls they received after Harry, determined that his brother-in-law should be given his due, informed the *Telegraph* and *The Times*. The vicar of Beckley arrived, 'touting for business' according to Mike, who remained hopeful that Edwin's well-publicised loss of faith would ensure that he was buried without religious trappings.

'Sorry old chum,' Clement replied, 'the trappings were the one thing in which he believed.'

The vicar left after paying a tribute to his father which Clement, fighting back tears, would have preferred him to save for the pulpit. He was succeeded by Karen, whose histrionic display spoke less of her sorrow than of her insecurity. Clement forgave her for the sake of his mother, who sat tenderly stroking her hair, assuring her that 'Uncle Edwin' had loved her very much. Her promise that she could stay the night at the hall left Valerie, scenting a rival, looking piqued.

The next two days were given up to paperwork. It was as if the petty bureaucracy surrounding death served the deeper purpose of diverting grief. The newspapers treated his father generously, both in space and spirit, honouring his achievements as well as retracing his controversies, with every single broadsheet citing Mrs Thatcher's condemnation of 'this turbulent priest'. Letters of condolence arrived by the sackful, including one from the village postman. Among the heartfelt testaments from people whose lives he had touched were several vicious attacks from fundamentalists, claiming that 'Bishop Judas' would now be repenting his evil ways. To his surprise, Clement found that his anger was defused by their naivety. They condemned no one to hell but themselves.

His chief concern was his mother, who was handling her husband's death far better than her daughter's disaffection. He longed to stop her humiliating herself: to stem the stream of contrite messages on Shoshanna's answering-machine; but he was afraid that it would seem like asking her to play favourites. Apart from one quick call to Carla, demanding to be kept informed of the funeral arrangements, Shoshanna had not made contact with any of them since she stormed out of the house. She had not, however, been idle, as became clear when, halfway through planning the order of service with the vicar, Clement was rung by the undertaker with news of a likely delay caused by the police request for a post-mortem.

'But why?' Clement asked. 'My father had a brain tumour. His death had been expected for weeks.'

'I'm only the humble Mercury, Mr Granville,' the undertaker replied. 'Experience has taught me never to question the ways of Her Majesty's constabulary.'

Cloaking his apprehension in a show of outrage, Clement rang the station where, after confronting a surly subordinate, he was put through to an inspector who disclosed that there were 'suspicious circumstances'.

'What circumstances?' Clement demanded. 'My father was eighty-three with an inoperable brain tumour.'

'I'm sorry, sir, that's as much as I can say at this moment in time. We'll be back in touch shortly.'

Clement put down the phone, reporting the setback to the vicar, whose wan smile betrayed his embarrassment. Following his hasty departure, Clement explained the position to Mike and Carla. 'It doesn't make sense,' he said. 'What can have got into them?'

'Your sister,' Mike replied without a pause.

'No, that's not possible.'

'I'll bet you any money you like! You heard her the other day. She thinks you're the anti-Christ... well, obviously... you know what I mean. She's totally under the thumb of those maniacs.'

The more Clement pondered, the more he knew that Mike was right. Nevertheless, as they sat in the drawing room with his mother, Carla and Valerie later that afternoon, he asked Carla to ring Shoshanna for confirmation. It came when, after a long silence, she slammed down the receiver with a cry of 'You must be insane!'

His mother tried to find excuses for Shoshanna's behaviour. 'It's so out of character. She's done many foolish things in her life, but never something like this.'

'Hormones,' Valerie said, with dry certitude. 'Take it from me. I spent thirty-five years in a women's college.'

'It's pure spite,' Mike said. 'She didn't get her own way, so she's making you pay for it.'

'No,' Clement said quietly, 'you're not being fair to her.'

'Fair? Do you have any idea what this could mean?'

'It's too easy – for me at any rate – to see her as the irritating kid sister running to Nanny whenever Mark and I ganged up on her.'

'You were always so good with her,' his mother said. 'Both of you.'

'But this is far more than telling tales. Shoshanna was right. I haven't taken her seriously. I pictured the Lubavitch as her latest fad... something she was promoting, like a pop star or a brand of jeans. It's finally hit home that her faith is as real to her as mine is to me.'

'Even so she can still see reason,' his mother said. 'We did at least teach her that. I propose we head straight down to London and offer her whatever she wants, as long as she withdraws the charge.'

'I'm afraid it's not that simple,' Mike said. 'You don't spend twenty years in a north London comprehensive without becoming something of an expert on the law. The matter's out of Susannah's hands. Now that the allegation's been made, the police have a duty to investigate. All Clem can do is speak to his solicitor.'

'No way,' he replied. 'That would give the accusation legitimacy. I'm not going to play by their rules.'

'What nonsense!' his mother said. 'If you don't call Gillian Wrenshaw, I will.'

'It's all so ridiculous! Who do they suppose would benefit from Pa's death?'

'You,' Mike said quietly. 'You're now a very rich man.'

Chastened, Clement went to ring Gillian, whom only that morning he had consulted as the co-executor of his father's will. Having outlined his position in the broadest terms, he was taken aback by the urgency with which she insisted on making him an appointment for the following afternoon. So, with the funeral indefinitely postponed and both Mike and Carla anxious to return to work, he agreed to drive back to London after tea. He worried about leaving his mother, despite her assurances that she would be well looked after by Valerie.

'The only person you must think about now is yourself,' she said. 'Not that there'll be any problem as long as you keep a clear head. Explain that it's simply your sister's fantasy. We'll all back you up.'

'Thank you, Ma.'

'Of course I shall instantly admit to my own involvement if there's the remotest chance of you being charged.'

'There isn't,' Clement said, assuming an air of confidence. 'The police will see straightaway that there's nothing to be gained from proceeding with the case.'

'Promise me that, like it or not, you'll take Gillian's advice. You know how headstrong you can be.'

'Headstrong? Me?' he asked with a smile. 'Don't worry, I promise I'll be as good as gold.'

'Make sure he sticks to it,' she said to Mike, as she stood on the steps seeing them off. Touched by her concern, Clement gave her an especially warm hug and climbed into the car, waving furiously until her receding figure was blurred by tears.

To his surprise, his sense of loss grew sharper the further they drove from Beckley until, by the time they arrived home, it had completely overwhelmed him. Unable to stop shaking, he agreed to go straight to bed, grateful for Mike's solicitude as he brought up soup, fruit, hot whisky, and finally himself, slipping beneath the sheets to make first soothing, then passionate love. Fully recovered the next morning, he felt an irresistible urge to clear out the attic, greeting Mike on his return with three large piles, labelled Friends, Oxfam and Dump.

After lunch they drove to Cheapside, where they were shown straight into

Gillian's office which, in its oak-panelled sobriety, brought back memories of his housemaster's study at school. Gillian, a huge woman who avoided all exertion, beckoned them to chairs beside her desk. After reiterating her condolences and saluting the historic association of the Granvilles and the Wrenshaws, she explained that she had spoken to the police but learnt little of note. The coroner would hold an inquest, which he would immediately adjourn pending the outcome of the criminal investigation. There was no requirement on any of the family to attend.

'Then will they release my father's body?'

'Maybe, maybe not. It depends on the extent of their inquiries.'

'How extensive can they be?' Mike asked. 'Clement was the only witness.'

'I'm afraid they'll cast their net wider,' she said, munching through the plate of fig rolls that her secretary had brought in with the tea. 'The nurses. Doctors. Housekeeper. Marta. Susannah. Carla. That friend of Marta's who's staying.'

'Valerie Sinclair? She's loopy,' Mike said. 'No one could take her seriously.'

'Let's hope not, since I gather she was there when Clement made some form of confession.'

'And will do again,' Clement said.

'Clem!'

'As your lawyer, I firmly advise you against it.'

'Don't worry,' Mike said. 'He's given us his solemn oath. Discretion and valour and all that.'

Clement nodded but, away from Beckley and his mother's anxieties, he felt a compelling need to speak out. His efforts at secrecy were not merely futile but wrong. Having fulfilled his pledge to his dying father, he had a duty to proclaim what he had done for the sake of others in a similar predicament.

For all his brave words he knew that he could be punished for breaking the law, but he took heart from the long line of rebels and visionaries who had defied unjust laws, stretching back to Magna Carta. Besides, once the full facts of his father's condition were known and a succession of doctors and nurses had testified to his desire to die, any prosecution would be quietly dropped. His father had spent his life fighting against the forces of unreason. What a golden opportunity to carry on the fight after his death! He closed his eyes and pictured the columns of newsprint, far friendlier than those for the *Pier Palace Christ* or *The Second Adam*, in which experts and pundits would acknowledge the justice of his stance. He anticipated the opinion polls: *In a recent survey, ninety-eight per cent of those questioned endorsed Clement Granville's actions...* until a painful recollection of the Deedes and Zvi tendencies caused him to reduce the percentage to *eighty-nine*. Even if, through a gross misuse of resources, the case came to trial, no jury would ever convict him. Given five minutes in the dock, he would persuade them of his fervent belief that love was more sacred than law.

His chance to speak out came sooner than expected. The following morning, after Mike had left for school and while he was trying to decide whether he felt ready to return to the studio, he received a visit from two policemen investigating his father's death.

'Come in,' he said. 'I'll be happy to talk to you. You may be surprised at what I have to say.' After leading them into the sitting room, he described in detail how he had helped his father to die, grateful to be in London rather than Beckley as the officers probed his motives.

'What you seem to be suggesting,' one said, 'is that a person's value depends on his mental or physical health. But everyone is equal in the eyes of the law.'

'And in the eyes of God which, I might add, are a good deal sharper. But, if we're to respect every human being, then we must respect my father's wish to end his life.'

'Except that he wasn't the one who ended it. You were.'

'He'd made his feelings abundantly clear to anyone who listened. My mother. The nurses. Even my sister.'

'Have you never made a decision and then changed your mind at the last minute?'

'My father no longer had a mind to change. Believe me, I appreciate the need for safeguards as much as the next man. But we're not talking about a totalitarian state eliminating a dissident or even an overzealous doctor assisting a patient. This was a highly intelligent man making a judgement about his impending lack of judgement. He wasn't a burden. He didn't fear that he was a burden, except to himself. He'd become an affront to his own faith in humanity. You might say he was no longer in a position to be affronted. That was his point.'

'But we can't get away from the fact that you killed him.'

'Freed him. I see it as the equivalent of helping a blind man across the road.'

2

Having made his statement, Clement heard nothing more from the police. After four days he rang Gillian, who explained that they were still gathering evidence. He was amazed that they could find enough people to question, his father's world having shrunk so dramatically towards the end. They had spoken to his mother, Mike and Carla, all of whom claimed to have been astounded by his confession, his mother's silence secured by the fear of incriminating him. They had spoken to the Shepherds, Karen and Valerie. It was a fair guess that they had also spoken to Ruth and Linda, Shoshanna and Zvi. Meanwhile he took heart from Gillian's assurance that, in a case of such media interest, the police would consult both the CPS and an expert barrister before deciding to prosecute and, until then, he should carry on as normal.

That proved to be surprisingly easy. Inspired by the van Eyck altarpiece in Ghent, he decided to paint a series of panels for his father's coffin. With his mother's encouragement, he commissioned Robin Barford, a neighbour in the studios, to carve an oak frame to display them. He chose six key episodes from his father's life: singing in the choir at Winchester; sitting in the cockpit of a Spitfire; leading a rent strike in Clapham; processing past the West Front of Wells; defending *Spirit of the Age* at Synod; attended by an angel on his deathbed. It would be an opportunity not only to honour his father's memory but to work unconstrained by any thought of criticism. The coffin would be on show at the funeral and then locked away in the family vault, to be glimpsed through the grille, a rare note of colour amid the dusty greys and browns that had struck such a chill in him as a child.

He was engrossed in the Wells panel, enjoying the challenge of depicting a façade that amounted to a who's who of medieval Christianity on a panel twenty-eight inches by twelve, when he was distracted by the entryphone. Convinced that no cold callers, whether fresh fish salesmen, Jehovah's Witnesses or the Greens, would be so insistent, he answered it with a grumpy 'Yes! What?' only to modify his tone on learning that it was the police. Two officers, one familiar from his previous visit and the other a Sikh, came up to the studio.

'Clement Granville?' the Sikh officer asked, with disturbing formality.

'Yes.'

'I'm arresting you on suspicion of the murder of Edwin Granville. You do not have to say anything, but it may harm your defence if you do not mention when questioned something which you later rely on in court. Anything you say may be given in evidence.'

Clement's first thought was for the painting, as he gazed at the cathedral's solitary tower and longed for an hour's grace to add the second. Recognising that he was in shock, he asked simply for a few moments to clean his brushes. At a nod from his colleague, the Sikh agreed. While Clement picked up a rag, the policemen stood by the door, showing as little interest in the room as if they had tracked him down to a warehouse. It was as though they were afraid of lighting on an image that would require them to treat him with respect.

They led him outside and, to both his relief and dismay, none of his neighbours was passing. The only witness was a young mother with two howling children, on whom the police car acted as a timely deterrent. He sat in the back with the Sikh, who resisted all attempts at conversation, refusing even to reveal where they were heading, as though he were a schoolboy to relish the surprise. Prompted as ever by memories of *Morse*, he claimed the right to make a phone call, which was denied. Twenty minutes later they arrived at Albany Street station, where he was bustled into a small room, reeking of stale tobacco, and officially charged. After handing over his belt, keys and valuables, which were sealed in a plastic bag as at a mortuary, he was at last allowed to ring Mike, only to be diverted to voice mail. Loath to leave a message, he called Carla and, ignoring her audible panic, told her to contact his mother and Mike and to ask Gillian Wrenshaw to come to the station at once.

The cell officer escorted him downstairs. Unlike his colleagues, he turned out to be both affable and chatty. He locked him up and returned with the offer of a cup of tea, which Clement refused, regretting it moments later, when he sat in stony silence on a bottom-numbing bench and stared at the unrelieved expanse of off-white wall, his only stimulated sense that of smell. Gagging on the residual stench of Vim, vomit, and sweat from the recent occupant, he gave way to despair. His certainty that his release was a mere matter of time was threatened by the removal of his watch. He envied Carla, who could use the lack of distractions to help her meditate, whereas he had never felt more earthbound.

He was roused by the return of the cell officer with a florid young man wearing a houndstooth suit, correspondent shoes and an extravagant button-hole, who introduced himself as Dunstan Livesey, solicitor.

'Where's Gillian?' Clement asked, terrified that she might have abandoned him.

'In bed at home after an op to fit a gastric band. She'll be back at her desk next week. I'm holding the fort till then. Fear not, I've been well briefed.'

'So perhaps you can tell me why I've been charged with murder?' Clement asked, offended by Dunstan's brashness. 'Gillian was adamant that, at the very worst, it would be aiding and abetting a suicide.'

'Yes, that's what we hoped,' Dunstan said smoothly, 'but the fact that they've rejected it suggests they mistrust your motives.'

'That's preposterous! Under my father's will, I stand to inherit a large estate and a great deal of money. He had a few months at most to live. Why should I jeopardise it all by murdering him?'

'It's not for me to speculate. My job is to ensure that you have the best possible defence. Though I should warn you there's been a slight hiccup. The police have refused to grant bail; they want to take you before the magistrates in the morning.'

'Why? Do they suppose I'm going to rush to the nearest old peoples' home and bump off the residents?'

'It might be better not to make a fuss,' Dunstan replied, with the air of a man who would send back a bottle of house red if it were insufficiently *chambré*. 'We'll have you out first thing in the morning. In the meantime, is there anything else I can do for you?'

'No, thank you, you've been very helpful,' Clement said, conscious of his urge to escape and reluctant to detain him. 'Oh yes, of course, my pills! It's vital I have my pills.'

'You're on medication?'

'I have HIV,' he replied, wondering where Dunstan had been last autumn.

'The police can be very suspicious of pills.'

'I'm not Hermann Göring! Would you please ring my boyfriend and ask him to bring in my combination therapy as soon as he can?'

The need for the pills gave an edge to his anxieties, and he tortured himself with the consequences of a single missed dose. Finally the duty officer came in and, disproving Dunstan's predictions, handed him a small box. As he gazed at the six life-saving tablets, he felt faint, not just from relief but from the connection to Mike. Picturing him counting them out with supreme care, his eyes began to mist. The Atazanavir was meant to be taken with food but, for once, he would have to compromise, his momentary regret at rejecting the glutinous cottage pie checked by a glance at the seatless lavatory and encrusted rim.

Sometime in what he took to be the early hours, but the duty officer assured him was half-past ten, the light in his cell was dimmed and he lay down on a bench as narrow and hard as a luggage rack, pulling the threadbare blanket over his chest and resting his head on a pillow that felt like the remnant of a dormitory fight. No matter how he arranged his limbs, he was unable to relax. A raucous lullaby echoed from the next-door cell and he reconciled himself to a sleepless night, only to find himself jolted awake the next morning when the cell officer brought in a transport café breakfast. Hunger banished all qualms and he attacked it so greedily that he buckled the blade on his plastic knife. Despite the glaze of grease on everything from the toast to the tomatoes, it tasted surprisingly good. He had just finished eating when the officer returned to take him to the washroom, producing a sponge bag, razor and change of shirt, which were further evidence of Mike's concern. He was then loaded into a van alongside a rancid man with a briary beard, whom he took to be his neighbour of the previous night. Far from bursting into song, he communicated solely by a series of snarls and growls, responding to their escort's curt commands with garbled curses.

At the courts, he was led straight down to a cell which was older, colder and dingier than the one at the station. He studied the graffiti on the walls and bench, wondering first at its provenance, given how carefully he himself had been searched for knives, and then at the ubiquity of *woz*, a word no shorter or easier to scratch than *was*. After a lengthy and unexplained delay, he was taken up to the courtroom and into a glass-enclosed dock where, overcome by fatigue, he was scarcely able to drag his feet the last few steps. Clinging to the back of a chair, a gesture that he suspected would be misinterpreted, he gazed into the public gallery to find his mother, Mike, Carla, and, to his surprise, Jimmy Naismith. Swiftly turning away, for fear that his mother's airborne kiss would unnerve him, he fixed his attention on the dais where a single judge on a swivel chair confounded expectations of a bench of magistrates. The clerk read out the charge, which sounded more sinister than it had at the station, and he entered a resolute plea of *Not Guilty*. After the extensive preliminaries, the proceedings were blessedly brief. Dunstan applied for bail, which the judge granted, stipulating merely that Clement should report to the Albany Street station once a week.

The security officer led him back to the cells, where Dunstan joined him to wait for the paperwork, after which he was released, taking the lift to the concourse to meet his family and friends. Walking past the overcrowded benches, he detected the same air of resignation and misery as at the Immigration Tribunal, albeit with a broader ethnic mix. He stood listlessly, while his usually unruffled mother hugged him as though he had spent three weeks trapped down a coalmine rather than a single night in a cell. Then, recollecting her own incarceration, he berated himself for his coldness and returned the embrace. Jimmy rushed off to his surgery with the promise that he was with him 'all the way'. Dunstan went back to his office after claiming that they had taken the first step on the road to victory. Mike drove the rest of them home, where he produced a large tray of Danish pastries, which Clement, already repenting the excesses of breakfast, felt obliged to eat.

After he had given them a blow-by-blow account of the arrest, regretting for the sake of his story and Mike's politics that the blows were metaphorical, his mother announced that she had been to see Shoshanna.

'You rang her?' he asked, with a sense of betrayal.

'She rang me. She wanted me to understand why she did it. She talked about truth and justice and how the very first commandment was honouring God.'

'Yes,' Mike said. 'And the very first crime was killing a brother!'

'Not now, please,' Clement said, anxious to protect his mother.

'She said that they couldn't live with the thought that they were covering up the crime.'

'How unspeakably selfish!' Carla said.

'It seems selfish to us, but for them to see a breach of the Law and ignore it is like... I don't know... it's like seeing an accident and leaving the victims to lie bleeding in the road.'

'Bullshit!' Mike said. 'I'm sorry, Marta. I know she's your daughter, but anyone can see that she was out for revenge.'

Despite Mike's scepticism, Clement found his mother's explanation all too plausible. Shoshanna had pledged herself to a sect for whom the Law was an absolute good. To his surprise, he found his bitterness towards her tinged with pity.

Three days later he returned to court. This time he was represented by Gillian, who, having recovered from her operation, described how the band controlled the volume of food that reached her stomach, which, given the mountain of flesh beneath her smock, struck him as the surgical equivalent of the Mont Blanc Tunnel. After the rigours of the waiting room, the call into court came as a relief. Apart from entering freely with Gillian, Clement noted little difference from his previous appearance. The same air of confusion reigned on the legal benches, where four young women solicitors pored over vast stacks of papers pertaining to clients whom they had barely met. The clerk consulted the usher and various nondescript officials, while the judge, in nominal charge of proceedings, waited patiently for guidance. His ruling, when it came, was short and to the point, as he gave the order to send the case to trial in the Crown Court, directing Clement to attend the preliminary hearing the following week. 'If you fail to report promptly when required, you will be guilty of an offence and either be fined or imprisoned or both.'

'I hadn't expected it would be so soon,' Clement said to Gillian over coffee. 'The police have finally released my father's body and we need to fix a date for the funeral. But how can we, if I'm in the middle of a trial?'

'Don't worry. The Preliminary Hearing is just a formality. The judge will ask the Prosecution to complete the service of its case within forty-two days and set a date for the Plea and Directions hearing in about two months' time.'

'I'd no idea the law was so labyrinthine,' he said.

'Oh, this is nothing,' she replied, spooning in the sugar.

As Gillian had predicted, the Plea and Directions hearing was set for the fifth of March, although both she and his newly-briefed barrister, Lloyd Jessop, warned of a possible postponement, should the Prosecution request more time to gather medical evidence. Meanwhile the funeral was set for the fifteenth of January, which would allow Clement to oversee arrangements during the holidays at Beckley. While dreading the prospect of his first father-less Christmas, he was determined to keep up a front for the sake of his mother, only to discover that she was doing the same for him. Despite the absence of both her husband and her daughter, she insisted on its being festivity as usual. So Mr Shepherd and Charlie Heapstone set up the giant fir tree in the hall, which Clement decorated with Mike, finding to his surprise that he missed the annual regression to childhood when he and Shoshanna bickered over who should have the crowning glory of placing the star. Mrs Shepherd draped the drawing room with boughs of holly and sprigs of mistletoe, the latter permitting Karen to claim the festival as her own. That done, she kept her distance, joining them briefly on Christmas Day for presents and Boxing Day for punch.

'She's got a new man,' Mrs Shepherd confided, 'he busks.'

Carla came for Christmas, before leaving to spend New Year with her parents. Her pain at being a 'middle-aged singleton', ill concealed by the self-deprecating phrase, was increased by her split with Curtis. Sitting in Clement's bedroom, where twenty years before, on her first visit to Beckley, she had shyly confessed her attraction to Mark, she revealed what she had kept from him during the weeks of the investigation, namely that Curtis had turned violent.

He took her in his arms, appalled to picture what lay beneath her new-found taste in long sleeves. 'Tell me it's none of my business, but would it help you to talk about what he did?'

'Not really. What do most men do when they're violent? Hit. Punch. Slap. The usual. The next day, of course, he couldn't have been more contrite, begging me to forgive him. When I asked why he did it, he said it wasn't really him... that is he claimed to be helpless to break the pattern, blaming the eight-eenth-century mercenary like a determining gene.'

'Oh for God's sake!'

'Then he promised that, if he hurt me in this life, he'd make it up to me in the next.'

'Before hurting you again, presumably?'

'I didn't ask. I should have ended it then and there, I know. But it was as if he was two or three different personalities and I was still fighting to keep hold of the one I loved... yes, I really did use the 'l' word! Finally, when he shook me so hard I thought I'd pass out, I grabbed my statue of the Buddha – you know, the jade one Mark gave me all those years ago – bashed him on the head with it and ran. I was scared stiff that I'd killed him but, when I went back to the house the next morning with Rachel from next door, he'd disappeared, leaving only a smear of blood on the floor to show that I hadn't imagined it. I've changed the locks and put in a new alarm system, but I've not heard a sound from him since.'

Clement returned to London on the second of January, heading straight to the studio to repaint the final panel of his polyptych after Mike asked him whether the angel was supposed to be a self-portrait. Satisfied that any resemblance to artists living or dead was entirely coincidental, he gave the finished work to Robin, who assembled it and delivered it to the undertakers in Oxford. The next time he saw it was on the eve of his father's funeral, when the coffin was laid out in the Beckley dining room, ready for the relatives to pay their last respects. His fears that his family would object to his presence – let alone, prominence – among the mourners were assuaged when with one voice they expressed outrage at the charge. Even Aunt Helena pledged her support. 'You have the whole Petersham Women's Institute behind you,' she said. 'I've told everyone that, whatever else, you've always been a model son. I only hope that, when I'm gaga, someone will do as much for me.'

On the morning of the funeral he hid in his room, partly to reflect on his father but mainly to avoid a painful confrontation with Shoshanna and Zvi, who were driving down from London. At half-past one, conscious that he could put it off no longer, he made his way into the dining room where he found his sister and brother-in-law alone, examining the painted panels. Catching sight of Shoshanna, he was immediately struck by how huge she looked, blurting it out before he could stop himself.

'That's because you haven't seen me for three months,' she said, startled.

'Whose fault is that?' he asked.

'Yours, Clement,' Zvi said softly. 'You were the one who...'

'Killed my father? If that's what you think, why not say so?'

'That's not what we think, Clem,' Shoshanna said. 'At least it's not that simple.'

'Really? Then why turn me in to the police?'

'Maybe we did think so at the time. I'm not saying we were wrong – '

'I should hope not! Stick to the Good Book and you can never go wrong.'

'But I was hurt. Everything I believe... everything I am: you just trampled underfoot. This is my faith, Clem. I used to envy your faith so much. Don't hate me now I've found one of my own.'

'You do realise I could land up in jail?'

'Surely it won't come to that?' she asked anxiously. 'Ma said you'd hired a top QC.'

'Lloyd Jessop. The man who got the Arsenal footballers off last year.'

'And it was blindingly obvious they were guilty.'

'Thanks! That makes me feel a whole lot better.'

'Say something, Zvi,' Shoshanna said wretchedly.

'Like what?' he asked. 'Like why did your brother come clean to the police? If he'd kept silent, none of this would have happened.'

'Oh I see, it's all my fault! Nothing must be allowed to soil your lily-white consciences, but poor godforsaken Clement is already so far gone, what does it matter if he's saddled with another lie?'

Shoshanna started to cry. Zvi leant over and held her so gently that, despite himself, Clement was moved. They were interrupted by Karen, who had supplemented her usual black clothes with a home-made black beret, black nail-polish and deep purple lipstick. She gazed at brother and sister, at once embarrassed and intrigued.

'Aunt Marta said to tell you that the undertakers are here.'

'Then we'd better put on our coats. Are you two ready?' Clement asked, as Zvi wiped away Shoshanna's tears.

'I am,' Shoshanna said. 'Zvi isn't coming.'

'He's not?'

'I intend to stay here and pray for the righteous of all nations. I shan't go to the service.'

'It's hard when you remember what the Church has done to Jews,' Shoshanna explained.

'It's hard when you remember what the Church has done to Christians,' Clement replied, raising an unexpected smile. He felt a flicker of their former intimacy. 'You haven't told me what you think of the coffin.'

'It's beautiful,' Shoshanna said. 'Truly beautiful. Pa would have been so proud.'

Clement watched as the six pallbearers entered and lifted the lead-lined coffin on to their shoulders and into the hearse, before taking his place with his mother and sister in the first car of the cortège. On arrival at the church, they were greeted by a crowd of onlookers, reporters and cameramen, all heavily muffled against the cold. He acknowledged ruefully that his notoriety had now eclipsed his father's and wished that, rather than training their lenses on him, the photographers would focus on the coffin. His mother clasped his arm 'for support' but, as she led him resolutely down the path, he wondered whether she meant his support for her or hers for him. He walked beside her down the nave and into the front pew, where he sat for the vicar's words of welcome, rose for the opening hymn and knelt for the prayers. He resumed his seat as Roderick Britten, his father's oldest friend and closest ecclesiastical ally, read from the first chapter of the Second Book of Samuel, in which the Amalekite tells David how he stabbed the dying Saul at his own request.

Clement sensed the unease emanating from the rows behind at his choice of such a passage in place of the traditional psalm or verses from St John. After a spirited rendition of *Dear Lord and Father of mankind*, in which he felt the congregation's relief at being back on home ground, he prepared for further controversy when John Remington, his father's former chaplain, now Bishop of Stroud, entered the pulpit to give the address.

'No one at this service today can fail to be aware of the circumstances surrounding it. Indeed,' he said, staring at an unlikely group of mourners in the Lady Chapel, 'I fear that there are some people here precisely because of the circumstances surrounding it. The usual sadness of death has been compounded by the question mark over the manner in which Edwin Granville died. Edwin expressly asked that there should be no eulogy at his funeral, a request with which I'm happy to comply, not least because no words of mine could begin to do justice to this great and good man. Instead, I'd like to take the opportunity to explore the predicament in which we all – none more so than Edwin's son, Clement – now find ourselves. I don't intend to discuss the specifics of a case which is currently the subject of legal proceedings or, for that matter, the state of the law, except to note that, like Edwin himself on an earlier occasion, I broke ranks with my fellow bishops when they opposed a recent bill to legalise a limited form of euthanasia. Rather, I wish to examine the broader issue of the authority on which we as people of faith – the Christian faith in particular, but I trust that my remarks will apply to all people of good faith – base our lives.

'We heard a passage from the Second Book of Samuel, the only one in the entire Bible to feature what we now know as euthanasia. In it, Saul asks the Amalekite to end his suffering and the young man – and, in my view, his youth is significant – agrees because, in the words of the Authorised Version, "I was sure that he could not live after that he was fallen." This account differs substantially from that in the last chapter of the First Book of Samuel which immediately precedes it – a difference, incidentally, that you might suppose would give pause to all those who uphold the Bible as a flawless document in which every word comes straight from God – when, after the man, described as the king's armour-bearer, refuses his request, Saul falls on his own sword, thereby breaking another taboo, that of suicide. In the version we read, however, the Amalekite takes the news of Saul's death, along with his crown and bracelet, to David who, displaying the ruthlessness to which he is all too prone, has him killed, not – and this is the nub – because he has broken Mosaic Law, but because he has "slain the Lord's Anointed".

'David's concern with the status of the victim rather than the justice of the act is a clear case of pragmatism, and one which the Bible writer nowhere condemns. On the contrary, then, as now, rulers were expected to behave pragmatically. We feel uneasy when politicians launch any kind of moral crusade, if only because human nature is such that it invariably backfires. Bishops and priests, on the other hand, are expected to preach moral absolutism, even – I might almost say, especially – by people who never set foot inside a church. I would argue, however, that we too should embrace pragmatism, not in the popular sense of time-serving and compromise but in the original sense of judging actions by their consequences, spiritual and ethical as well as social and economic. Absolute truth, like absolute virtue, is to be found only in God.'

Clement heard a rustle in the nave and longed to know if the congregation was affirming the bishop's message or seeking to distance itself from it. Conscious, however, that on this of all days he must observe the proprieties, he fixed his gaze on the pulpit.

'We live in a world that is, and will always be, imperfect. It defies logic to uphold an unchanging law when change is the law of the universe. Rather than imposing a set of antiquated penalty clauses, we should weigh up the consequences of peoples' conduct. But there are those who prefer to live "by the book". If they're Christians, that book is the Bible, although, as we know full well, other faiths make equal claims for their scriptures. There are obvious attractions in declaring one book to be the fount of all truth, in obeying its laws and eliminating doubt, just as there are in retreating to a mock Georgian house in a gated community, safe from the threats and confusions of the modern world. But, in each case, it's a false security; in each case it's to cut ourselves off from the richness of life. Which is the true sin against the Holy Ghost. God gave us a universe of infinite variety, and the cost – as well as the joy – of that is moral complexity. The Bible exists to help us to make up our minds, not to close them. It's a guide not a rulebook. It was written by men about God, not by God for men. We must interpret it according to our own hearts, and the human heart has always been closer to God than the human hand.

'The greatest of all Biblical interpreters was Christ. He took Moses' Ten Commandments and simplified them to two: *Thou shalt love the Lord thy God* and *Thou shalt love thy neighbour as thyself*, the latter of which remains the best basis for a practical morality that I know. It demands both love and empathy, the *Judge not that ye be not judged* which Christ extolled in the Sermon on the Mount. Far from being a recipe for anarchy (or for throwing the lawyers among you out of work), it's an acknowledgement that the only sound basis for judgement lies, not in laying down a set of hard-and-fast rules, but in putting oneself in another's shoes. To take an obvious example, St Thomas Aquinas, who can be nobody's idea of a heretic, overrode the Eighth Commandment, insisting that the poor had a right to appropriate the necessities of survival from the rich, an act he deemed to be "not strictly theft", in terms very similar to those of his legendary contemporary, Robin Hood. In the same way, surely we can see that for a son to have the courage – the moral courage – to end the suffering of his terminally ill father is an act that is "not strictly" murder?

'I would like to conclude by relating the concepts both of empathy and euthanasia to God. For what is the Incarnation but the greatest act of empathy in the history of the world? God so loved his people that he took on human form. And what is the Crucifixion but the greatest act of euthanasia? For it was God's infinite mercy that he gave up His Son to be killed, to free humanity from its suffering and sin.'

Clement wiped his eyes. He had been expecting the bishop's theme but not such a ringing endorsement. While the choir sang Stanford's *Justorum Animae*, he cast a sidelong glance at Shoshanna, but her face remained a mask. He sat in silence as the vicar enjoined the mourners to remember his father in their own ways, which, to his surprise, meant that his mind was filled not with brightly coloured images but a pellucid white light. He stood to sing *To Be a Pilgrim*, a hymn which summed up his father's mission and valour without betraying his beliefs. He then bowed his head as the pallbearers approached the coffin, raised it on to their shoulders and carried it down to the family vault.

Taking his mother's arm, he walked behind, fearing for the slightest slip as the pallbearers negotiated the narrow transept doorway and bore the leaden coffin almost vertically down the vertiginous steps. He sensed their relief as they laid it on the catafalque, hugging the walls of the cramped chamber while the clergy and close family squeezed into place. The vicar rehallowed the vault, to the muffled strains of Elgar's *Nimrod*, which filtered down from the nave where the rest of the congregation had stayed seated. Clement stared at the rows of coffins which had once been the stuff of nightmare but now seemed no more daunting than an attic full of trunks. His gaze lingered on Mark's, distinguished by its brighter varnish, and his thoughts turned to the brother, whose ninety-minute seniority had been multiplied by many years in death. He wondered how long it would be till his own flesh rotted and they were identical once again.

He broke off as the solemn words his father had spoken over so many coffins were now spoken over his. As earth joined to earth, ashes to ashes and dust to dust, he followed his mother in scattering soil on the lid. No matter that his father was to be laid to rest on a ledge and not in the ground, the symbolism remained constant. He held out the trowel to Shoshanna, who surprised him by shaking her head, moving instead to the grille where she placed a small stone. So he handed it to his aunt who, after tipping out the soil as daintily as if she were potting a plant, passed it to his uncle and cousins until, by a dismayingly roundabout route, it reached Carla and Mike. At a nod from the vicar, the pallbearers stepped forward, lifted the coffin and edged it into the vault. Clement watched as the undertaker formally locked the gate, leaving only the tip of a choir stall and wing of a Spitfire to rescue his father from the drabness of death. Then he took his mother's arm, which felt unusually heavy, and led her back up the steps.

He felt the rush of air even before he heard the thud when Shoshanna, two steps below him, stumbled and fell. Everything seemed to be happening both at once and in slow motion, as his mother tore herself from his arm and leant over Shoshanna, trying with the aid of his cousin Alice to pick her up. 'No,' Shoshanna screamed, clutching her stomach and doubling over, the darkening patch on her skirt a stark reminder of the baby she was powerless to protect. Meanwhile, the congestion on the steps had caused panic in the crypt.

'Ring for an ambulance!'

'Someone call a doctor!'

'Give us some air!' Aunt Helena cried, stifled by the fusty presence of her ancestors.

While the bishop produced a phone from his cassock, Clement ran into the nave and, seeking to drown both the echoes of Roxborough and the thunder of the organ, appealed for a doctor, at which three, the local GP, his father's oncologist, and his mother's friend, Jacob Murr, leapt up to offer their services. He watched helplessly as the two elderly specialists deferred to their junior colleague who, after the briefest examination, insisted on taking Shoshanna straight to hospital, without waiting the twenty or more minutes for an ambulance to arrive from Oxford. Calling on the oncologist's help, he lifted her up the steps, where Clement absorbed the full horror of her agonised face and bloodstained skirt. As her body went rigid and Jacob vetoed any notion of squashing her into a car, he heard himself suggest that they take her in the hearse. He expected to be shouted down, but the only protest came from his mother and was quickly overruled by Jacob. The two doctors carried Shoshanna through the church, where the bemused mourners looked aghast at the trail of blood. Clement stood stupefied, while the rest of his family hurried up from the crypt, leaving Mike to pull him back to the present and out to the porch.

He watched as Shoshanna was laid out on the bier and Marta, brooking no objections, crouched by her side. Carla and the GP joined the undertaker in the front, and the vehicle sped off like a getaway van. Clement returned to the house, where he broke the news to Zvi, whose impassive reaction chilled him.

'I must go to her. The Radcliffe hospital, you say?'

'It's in Headington.'

'I'll find it.'

'Would you like me to come with you?' Clement asked tentatively.

'No...! No, thank you. I'll be fine,' Zvi replied, striding out to his car.

Clement walked into the dining room and contemplated the table laden with food for three hundred people. In the event there were seventeen. Mrs Shepherd, reluctant as ever to blur boundaries, put on an apron and chivvied the waiters who, ignorant of the reason for the over-catering, thrust trays of sandwiches at the handful of intrepid guests. The only taker was Bill Mullins, home from a tour of duty in Iraq and looking self-conscious in a suit.

By seven o'clock, when his mother and Carla returned, all the guests had left, his aunt carrying bagfuls of food that he had earmarked for the caterers.

'Your sister's had a miscarriage,' his mother said, although her face had anticipated the announcement.

'I'm sorry,' Clement said lamely.

'They're keeping her in overnight. Zvi's with her. He looked so lost.'

'What about her?'

'I don't know. I asked how she felt – such a stupid, stupid question – expecting her to say *empty*, but all she said was "I don't feel; I don't think I'll ever feel anything again."'

Clement, desperate to blot out the phrase *blessing in disguise*, asked if she would still be able to have children.

'I don't know that either,' his mother replied. 'It may be too soon to say.'

'Or too cruel,' Carla added.

'It's so strange that it should happen then... that it should happen there,' Clement said. 'It's as if there were some outside force, some pull from beyond the grave.'

'Don't go there!' Mike said. 'It was pure coincidence.'

'Tell that to Shoshanna and Zvi! In their world there's no such thing. All that happens is the will of God.'

3

Clement listened while Lloyd urged him to plead guilty to the secondary charge of attempted murder, as casually as Gil might press him to accept a reduced fee for a prestigious commission. Standing firm, he asked him why, having taken on the case, he was now so eager to be rid of it.

'Not at all. Believe me, I'm happy to go the full twelve rounds, but my job is to serve your best interests. Think of the Law as like your dear old nanny, utterly sound and on the whole very wise, but not at her best when dealing with anything morally ambiguous or complex, which the Granville case undoubtedly is.' Clement wondered whether to be more disturbed by the metaphor or the abstraction. 'If we go with murder, there are only two possible defences: diminished responsibility and provocation. Diminished responsibility doesn't automatically mean that you're potty. It may be a temporary state brought about by specific circumstances, say witnessing your father's suffering. But the psychiatric reports don't give us much help on that score. In fact you appear to be alarmingly sane.' Clement smiled politely. 'As for provocation, the strict definition... Let's go to *Archbold*... Bear with me a moment. Yes, here we are: *Some act, or series of acts, done or words spoken by the dead man to the accused which would cause in any reasonable person...* blah blah blah... *a sudden and temporary loss of self-control...* blah blah blah... *as to make him or her for the moment not master of his mind.* Another no-go area, I'm afraid.'

'So I'm sunk?'

'Not necessarily. We've now received most of the prosecution evidence. The key point at issue is the precise cause of death. And I'd say we'd hit on our defence here, where the pathologist states that, although he found an excessive amount of morphine in your father's blood, it's impossible to determine that he died of that rather than the natural disease process.'

'So why not stick with "Not guilty" to murder?'

'There's the small matter of your confession.'

'Can't we claim it was extracted under duress?'

'And several public statements to similar effect.' Clement felt his hopes sink as rapidly as they had risen. 'But I've had a quiet chat with my opposite number, who's hinted that the Crown may be willing to accept the lesser charge.'

'Which means what exactly?'

'Well, the irony is that attempted murder involves a greater degree of intent – the intent to kill – than murder, which may only involve the intent to commit GBH. But there's no mandatory life sentence and the judge can exercise his discretion.'

'I was hoping to give the jury a chance to exercise its humanity.'

'Humanity comes in all shapes and sizes. Not just the happy-clappy fruit-cake, but the retired nurse, the librarian who gave up her job to care for her bedridden mother, the cab driver working nights to support his autistic son. It's one hell of a gamble!'

Clement promised to consider his options over the weekend and give Lloyd an answer on Monday. He spent hours on the phone canvassing opinion but, even when he downplayed the pathologist's report, his friends all said the same. So first thing on Monday morning, he rang Lloyd to authorise the negotiations. The barrister expressed relief but, as if to obtain full credit for his strategy, insisted that a successful outcome was by no means certain. Three days later, he phoned with the news that the Crown had agreed to the compromise. To Clement's surprise, the trial would go ahead as planned, but there would be no jury, no calling of witnesses and no testing of evidence.

Clement spent the next few weeks putting his affairs in order, even though Mike, whose motto might have been *Be Prepared* were it not for the precedent, counselled against defeatism. On the tenth of March, accompanied by Mike, his mother and Carla, he arrived at the Old Bailey, protecting himself from the massed ranks of reporters and photographers by picturing a red-carpet premiere. The anomalous nature of the case meant that his family, who would have been confined to the public gallery as relatives of the accused, were admitted to the whole building as relatives of the victim. So they entered by the main door to be met by Gillian, who escorted them through the security gates and up a short flight of stairs to the lobby. There they found Lloyd studying the Court Lists.

'Just checking there are no last-minute changes. We're in Court One,' he said, as proudly as if it were the Centre Court at Wimbledon. 'Before the Honourable Mr Justice Wellingsley. He's the senior judge sitting so – and this will interest you, Mrs Granville – he has the right to the Old Bailey sword above his chair.' Clement watched as his mother, whose only concern was the safe release of her son, thanked him for that nugget of tribal lore. Lloyd then directed his junior, Alex, to take them to the canteen, while he went to consult the prosecution counsel in the Bar Mess.

'It's like the two front benches hobnobbing in the Commons tea-room before trading insults in the Chamber,' Mike said, as they went up in the lift.

'Maybe that's why so many MPs are lawyers,' Clement replied.

Walking into the busy canteen, he spotted a section partitioned by a grille. 'Is that where defendants have to sit?'

'No way,' Alex said, with a grin. 'That's for the staff.'

Mike and Alex ordered coffee, while Clement grabbed one of the drab Formica tables. He sat between Carla and his mother, who took hold of his hand without speaking.

'Don't worry, Ma. Everything'll turn out fine.'

'Your father would be devastated. He'd have put up with any amount of suffering rather than see you go through this.'

'I'm sure the judge will understand,' Carla said. 'He'll let Clement off with a caution.'

'I should have done it. My life's over. I'm an old woman.'

'Rubbish, Ma. I wish I had half your stamina.'

'It's gone, darling. First your father, then Shoshanna, now this.'

Clement looked at her lined face and liver-spotted hands as if for the first time, and shivered.

Mike and Alex returned with the coffee and they whiled away the wait with a game of Spot the Journalist, scoring double for distinguishing between tabloid and broadsheet, until they were silenced by a request on the tannoy: 'All the parties in Granville please proceed to Court One.'

Clement was unsettled by the general exodus. Leaving the others to take the lift, he and Mike walked down the stairs, enjoying a rare moment of calm.

'I know you don't want to think about it,' Clement said, 'but I may be sent to jail.'

'You must try to be confident.'

'But not naive. You won't – I may be paranoid but I need to say it – you won't find someone else?'

'Oh Clem,' Mike said, oblivious to the throng as he stopped to give him a kiss.

'I won't mind... that is, I'll understand if you want to relax the "three strikes and you're out" rule or bring somebody home.'

'Never. No matter how lonely it gets.'

'I'm afraid I'll have the opposite problem. Enforced intimacy.' He baulked, as dimly remembered scenes from a French porn film filled him with foreboding.

'You're a strong man, Clement, whatever you may think. And if the worst should happen – not that I'm saying it will, of course – then you'll learn just how strong. It may be a different kind of strength to the other guys, but they'll recognise and respect it, I swear.'

Clement squeezed his hand, fearful that words would betray him, as they entered the Italianate splendour of the Grand Hall. Clusters of lawyers sat around tables and stood beside pillars, while a gang of journalists gathered at the courtroom door. Lloyd, bewigged and gowned, directed them to a bench, where Clement perched between his mother and Gillian and studied the overhead fresco. Glimpsing the legend *Moses Gave Unto The People The Laws of God*, he stood up and moved away.

'Is something wrong?' Gillian asked.

'Not at all. I'm just tense,' he replied, finding a more congenial canopy in *Poise The Cause in Justice's Equal Scales*.

An usher opened the courtroom door and Lloyd escorted Clement to the dock, where a security guard led him down a small flight of stairs and subjected him to a rigorous body search.

'Again? I was searched twice on the way in.'

'We don't want you throwing stuff at the judge now, do we?'

'Like what? Bread rolls from the canteen?' Clement asked, eliciting no response. He stood uncomfortably close to the thickset man with round-the-clock shadow, listening to the muffled sounds of the court filling up above.

'Shouldn't I take my place?'

'Not till after the judge's entered. He bows to the court, see, and he wouldn't want to bow to you now, would he?'

Clement shrank from the graphic illustration of his inferior status, hidden from view until the usher's booming 'All rise!' and the ensuing rumble confirmed that it was safe for the guard to lead him up. He entered the vast dock and surveyed the scene. The judge sat in front of him, gazing inscrutably at a pile of papers, beneath the sword which, in a perverse way, honoured them both. The clerk sat directly below, with the lawyers in the well of the court: Lloyd and his opposite number on the front bench; their juniors on the second; Gillian, Dunstan and two Crown solicitors on the third. His family, partially obscured, sat behind them, while, in the public gallery, confounding fears of a crowd of latter-day *tricoteuses*, he spotted several friends: Robin Barford and three neighbours from the studios; Douglas, a fellow volunteer from the immigration helpline; Jimmy Naismith and his wife, Julia; Anita, playing truant from school; and, particularly welcome, Christine from the Welsh retreat, who had been out of touch for over a year.

He stiffened his resolve by twisting round to inspect the press pack, hungry for blood. Only the jury benches remained empty, apart from a solitary artist who picked up her pad the moment he appeared. He was both comforted and confused by her presence, wondering whether she knew and even admired his work and, more urgently, whether her sketch might be the one thing in the court to do him justice.

He stood to confirm his name and enter a plea of guilty, before sitting on one of the green leather chairs with backs so cracked and seats so warped that he presumed they must have been preserved for their historic associations. The prosecution counsel opened the proceedings, outlining the case for attempted murder, based on the evidence that would have been presented had there been a full trial. Instead of the word-spinning that would have followed a 'not guilty' plea, he soberly set out all the mitigating circumstances, including testimonies to the victim's wish to die and various medical statements, regularly referring the judge to the copies in front of him. After little more than an hour, he sat down and Lloyd rose to offer further grounds for mitigation, notably Clement's close relationship to his father, his unstable health and its effect on his state of mind. To Clement's chagrin, he had ruled out the prospect of calling him, claiming that it would raise the emotional temperature without advancing his cause.

The judge ordered a brief adjournment, and Clement joined his family and lawyers in the poky conference room that Lloyd had booked to evade the attentions of the press. Carla and Alex fetched food, which his mother and Mike urged on him with the clear subtext of 'who knows when you'll get your next decent meal?', but he was unable even to eat the sandwich he had taken to appease them.

'It's odd,' he said, 'when I was young, during the panic over Section Twenty-Eight, it seemed quite possible that, as a gay man, I'd end up in jail. Then, in the early days of AIDS, there was all the scaremongering about HIV positive people being sent to camps. The one thing I never bargained on was this.' Having plunged them into gloom, he sought to lift them out with a series of comic reflections on the judge, prosecution counsel and security guard, which fell so flat that, despite the uncertain outcome, the summons back to court came as a relief.

The judge resumed proceedings with a short statement. 'This is a sad, indeed a tragic, case. There's no doubt in my mind that we're dealing with a genuine mercy killing, prompted by exceptional circumstances. But, just as we cannot be allowed to take justice into our own hands, neither can we take mercy. The defendant is a man of honour and integrity. There's no risk of his re-offending, nor does he pose any threat to the community. On the contrary, the community will be diminished by his exclusion. It is plain that no purpose will be served by keeping him behind bars for any undue length of time.' The elation Clement felt at the beginning of the speech evaporated. 'I have it in mind to recommend his release at the earliest juncture consistent with the need to discourage the public from assisting a suicide.' He addressed Clement directly. 'I therefore sentence you to a period of three years imprisonment.'

As the Court rose, Clement's one thought was to keep his knees from buckling until he was out of sight of his family and friends. He fixed his eyes on the ground for fear of encouraging the gallery's cries of 'Shame!' Three years of his life had been obliterated in seconds. He needed time to adjust, but it was already being snatched away, as the guard grabbed his shoulder and marched him out. He felt intensely cold, not sick or shocked or scared or any other expected sensation, but physically frozen. His teeth chattered; his arms shook; his whole body quaked. He longed to ask for a blanket, but he was afraid of being rebuffed. From the moment he descended the stairs, he felt his treatment change. He was led to a desk in a low-ceilinged hall where a reception officer brusquely asked his name, before ordering him to empty his pockets and take off his belt and tie. As on the night of his arrest, he was most distressed by the confiscation of his watch.

'Aren't we allowed watches in prison?' he asked, trying at once to steady his voice and conceal his ignorance.

'Is it gold?'

'I think so.'

'Then it's worth more than £50.'

'But its value to me is sentimental. It was my brother's... He died,' he said, hating himself for the plea.

'No prisoner's permitted a watch worth more than £50. It's been booked and you'll get it back when you're released.'

He signed the inventory and was taken to a cramped holding cell, which was empty apart from a bench. Despite a fear of being sick, he was grateful for the lack of a lavatory. He sat alone, trying to adjust to the sudden transformation, daunted by the dank silence and the feeling of eyes staring at him through the peephole. Moments later, an officer announced that his 'legals' were there to see him. Lloyd came in, but Gillian stayed in the corridor, grinning and raising her thumb, which deeply offended him until Lloyd whispered that she was claustrophobic.

'Believe me, you got the best possible deal. It was clear that the judge wanted to be lenient, while at the same time sending a strong message to society that it's not on to kill your parents.'

'Let's hope society'll thank him.'

'Besides, as I'm sure you're aware, three years is actually only eighteen months.' Clement wondered if this new method of calculating were another reason for depriving him of his watch. 'Or less... fifteen, since, if you keep your nose clean, you'll be eligible for tagging.'

'No time at all, really!'

'That's the spirit! The important thing is not to let yourself brood. You're an artist; think of it as a learning process.' Deciding that the first lesson was to avoid vapid conversations, Clement turned to the wall, leaving Lloyd floundering. 'Well, good luck. If there's anything you need, you know where to find me.'

'Likewise,' Clement said, as the barrister hurried out. Then, realising that he didn't have the least idea where he was being sent, he called the officer, who was surprisingly forthcoming.

'Brixton.'

'How much longer's it going to be?'

'How long's a piece of string? First, the clerk has to prepare your warrant. Then we have to wait till there's enough of you to fill up a van.'

'Will my mother and my... friend be allowed to say goodbye?'

'Where do you think you are? Gatwick airport? You'll be given a Visiting Order to send out from the nick.'

The officer's departure left Clement with nothing to curb his increasing obsession with time. The man who had been happy to spend an entire morning rapt in contemplation of a patch of red or blue was determined to keep track of every minute, as though it were the only way to survive the loss of liberty. Despite his fear of alienating the staff, he asked for updates at intervals which he swore were at least half an hour and they insisted were only five minutes, until he no longer knew if they were baiting him or he were going mad. Finally, with the clock in the hall reading half-past four, he was handcuffed to an officer and led out to a van, where the cuffs were removed and he was locked in one of eight small cubicles. Feeling totally cut off, he leapt up and pressed his face to the frosted glass, desperate to catch every last glimpse of freedom.

On arrival at Brixton, he was instantly aware of a change in the quality of light, which he prayed was due to nothing more sinister than the massive walls. He was once again handcuffed and escorted to a holding cell, where he sat on a scuffed bench with six companions who, to his relief, paid him no attention. His first interview was with a doctor, who chewed his pencil and questioned him about his health.

'Touch wood, it's fine,' he replied, 'I'm asymptomatic. My T-cells hover around the 600 mark and my viral load's undetectable. But it's imperative I have my pills. I'm on an easy combination. Ritonavir-boosted Atazanavir, Tenofovir and 3TC, which I only have to take once a day, but it makes missing a single dose even more dangerous.'

'I'll order some up from the pharmacy. Then tomorrow I'll get one of the nurses to speak to your clinic doctor.'

'Will you have them here?' Clement asked doubtfully. 'They're expensive drugs.'

'Do you suppose you're the only man in Brixton with HIV? You'd be surprised.'

Returning to the holding cell, he was directed to a hatch which he took to be some kind of checkpoint, only to be offered a cup of tea by a prisoner, whose affability stood in sharp contrast to the notice that *Each prisoner is entitled to the following: 1 Sachett of Sugar; 1 Sachett of Milk; 1 Teabag. Do Not Ask For Extras. The Cleaners have their Orders.* Not even the misspelling could hide the fact that he had moved to a world where even the smallest indulgence was rationed.

He was summoned to an office and asked to confirm his name, date of birth and sentence. Questioned about distinguishing marks, he was about to cite his appendix scar when he caught sight of the officer's heavily tattooed wrist. His last jot of dignity vanished with the blunt order to strip naked. While his unwashed clothes were placed in a box to be kept for his release, he stood with his hand held casually in front of his genitals, afraid that any more marked concern for modesty would expose him to ridicule. He waited tremulously to be told to touch his toes as an officer shone a torch up his anus and inquired about '*maladies honteuses*', but the language in which the fear was couched alerted him to its inauthenticity. Instead, he was provided with a flimsy gown and sent to line up at a second hatch, where he was given the regulation uniform of blue tracksuit with red flashing, maroon T-shirt, grey socks and underwear, black shoes for workshops and brown slippers for the cell. Kitted out and handed a first night pack of razor, soap, toothbrush and toothpaste, he was sent back to the holding cell, where the reception officer gave him his prison number, which he promptly forgot.

With one officer in front and another to the rear, the seven new arrivals were escorted on to a wing packed with prisoners, several of whom ran up to greet old friends with playful punches and bear hugs, until the leading officer genially told them to 'save the snogging for later'. While four of his companions stayed behind, Clement and two others were taken up to the hospital wing. Having presumed that it was on account of the HIV, he was deeply shocked first to learn that he was deemed to be a suicide risk, and then to be locked in a stark metallic cell that would be enough to drive anyone to thoughts of suicide, let alone a man so alive to colour.

Just as misery threatened to overwhelm him, he was visited by the prison psychologist. For all his qualms, he was grateful for the show of sympathy. The mere use of his Christian name was enough to make him lower his guard. The psychologist asked about his family and whether anyone knew that he had been sentenced, before reminding himself with a laugh that the trial had featured on the six o'clock news.

'Have you been abused or interfered with?'

'I've only just arrived!'

'I don't mean in here! By an uncle or teacher or friend when you were a child.'

'Sorry to disappoint you. Only self-abuse, or doesn't that count?' Clement's relish of his retort faded as, watching his interrogator make a note, he suspected that he would now be classed throughout the prison system as a chronic masturbator.

The doctor's remark about HIV encouraged him to ask if he might share a cell with another *positive* prisoner. He assured the psychologist, whose stock assumptions would have been comic in any other context, that he was prompted not by a desire for sex or even a fear of intimidation but by the hope of companionship. The psychologist left with a sceptical smile and a promise to do what he could. A few minutes later, although with the current concertinaing of time it was impossible to be precise, an officer brought him a meal of stew and sponge, which he rejected, and his pills, which he devoured as hungrily as if he were an addict rather than a survivor.

'Did you go to a public school?' he asked so abruptly that Clement steeled himself for a stream of invective.

'Yes,' he replied apologetically.

'Good. We find it helps.'

Then leaving him with the unexpected freedom to switch off his own light, the officer went out. Clement closed his eyes, but the prospect of sleep slipped away when, at regular intervals, the peephole was thrust open and a torch shone on to his face. After five or six such intrusions, he wondered whether they were checking that he were still alive or confirming the psychologist's report of his onanism. Eventually, exhaustion prevailed, and the alternating light and darkness formed the pattern of his dreams.

The next day was one of introductions. After a visit from the governor, who expressed a concern that he might think he was better than everyone else and a hope that he would soon be transferred somewhere more suitable, he was led up three floors of the five-storey building and down a clanging metal walkway to his cell. As he walked through the door, an acrid stench foreshadowed the announcement that he was to be 'twoed up'. The officer beat a hasty retreat and he surveyed his new home. Sanitation having assumed more prominence in his mind than he would ever have thought possible, he gazed in dismay at the stainless steel unit with its basin, lavatory and cracked mirror tile. He turned away, first to the noticeboard, where the only comfort to be drawn from the graphic display of collagened lips, siliconed breasts and shaved vaginas was that his cell-mate was not a racist, and then to the bunks, which brought back memories of Wells and his fights with Mark over who should be on top. Here there was no contest. Not only was the upper bunk occupied, but a glance at the weights on the windowsill made the cell's pecking-order clear.

The officer came back and took him to join a line of prisoners at a supply hatch, where he was handed his bedding, plastic plate, bowl and cutlery, and a hot-water flask for the urn. On returning to the cell, he found two forms slid under the door, the first offering a choice of weekly menus and the second of education, training or work. Clement, for whom official forms held no terrors, found himself as baffled as a pensioner applying for benefits. He could no more decide between the kitchens and workshops than between the chicken curry and macaroni cheese. The former decision at least was spared him when the residential governor, claiming to be doing him a favour, allocated him a job as a cleaner.

Convinced that he was wreaking revenge on someone whom he presumed had never made a bed, let alone mopped a floor, Clement trudged back to his cell where he found a slight, balding man lying in wait. 'Barry Jenkins, a Listener,' he said, holding out a curiously delicate hand. 'Anything you want to get off your chest, any gripes or hassles, I'm your man. We're trained by the Samaritans, so mum's the word!'

'Pleased to meet you,' Clement said. 'You've come at just the right time. I do have a problem... a big one. I was asked to choose a job. Then, before I had the chance, they've given me one as a cleaner.'

'What? You're a jammy bastard, you are!' Barry said. 'Some blokes'd give their right arms for a cleaning job.'

'Seriously?'

'Course you must turn it down.'

'Why, if it's such a plum job?'

'Because you'll be marked down as a nark, see! There's not enough work to go round. Half the blokes here are stuck in their cells all day. And the ones who aren't are doing muppet jobs in the workshops. The best jobs are in the kitchens – extra grub, see – and cleaning, when you get to spend time outside your pad.'

'But why should anyone think I'm an inform... a nark? I've only just arrived. I don't know anything.'

'Let me give you a word of advice. No offence like?'

'Of course not.'

'Watch your back! Ninety-nine per cent of the cons on A-wing are animals waiting for their next kill.'

'I don't expect I'll be here for long,' Clement said, shrinking from the image. 'I saw the governor this morning and asked for a transfer to Bulling-don, a prison near Oxford.'

'A day's too long in this shit-heap. They'll break you just for the crack of it. I've two tips for surviving in the nick – and, trust me, I've been in a few. First, keep your brain busy: read books; watch TV; exercise; sleep. The second: never look at the door. You're OK with the window. Most of us don't feel like jumping out of a third-floor window – though I wouldn't put it past some of the psychos in here – but the door's different. You can go mad waiting for it to open. It's the door that keeps you trapped, see!'

He left with an exhortation to 'keep smiling', which Clement had never felt less like heeding. His spirits were further lowered by a visit from the chaplain, who exuded the fresh-faced fervour of a man who refused to let experience sap conviction. Clasping Clement's right hand in both of his, he placed himself squarely in front of the noticeboard, leaving it unclear which of them he was trying to shield.

'I know you by reputation, of course.'

'Which one?' Clement asked.

'What? Oh that's good!' he said, forcing a laugh. 'I'm proud to call myself a Bible-based Christian, but that doesn't mean I'm here to judge you.'

'Thank you.'

'Prison can be particularly hard for someone like you. For most of the men it's in their blood.'

'You are joking?'

'Spend a few days here and you'll see that *criminal class* is no hyperbole. So please, don't be shy! If you need to talk, my door's always open.'

'That may be a problem since mine appears to be permanently locked.'

'What? Oh yes.' The chaplain repeated his laugh. 'Put your name down for tonight's service. It won't be what you're used to, but it may be a revelation. God bless.'

The chaplain went on his way, leaving Clement alone with thoughts that threatened to pervade the cell. Sometime in mid-afternoon he was joined by his cell-mate, a huge West Indian with dreadlocks and thigh-thick arms. Clement stood up to introduce himself.

'You don't have to get up for me, man. I ain't royalty.' He gave a throaty chortle, revealing a silver front tooth. Ignoring Clement, he moved straight to the chest of drawers and took out a tube of cream, which he spread liberally on his hands. 'I have to pay for this from my canteen. That's wrong, man. It should be provided. You need asbestos fingers to pull steaming T-shirts off rollers.'

'You work in the laundry?'

'Hey man, you're good. You should be on *Mastermind*. I'm Dwayne.'

'Clement.'

'*Clem*ent... Cle*ment*. What kind of a name is that then? I never met a Clement before.'

'My parents called me after their favourite prime minister.'

'No shit, man. I reckon I'm lucky my dad didn't call me Margaret. He used to say "She's one sexy lady!"' Dwayne turned to the noticeboard as if for confirmation. 'So what are your deps then?'

'I beg your pardon?'

'Your deps, man? Your depositions? Your sentence?'

'Oh, three years for attempted murder.' For the first time Clement made light of the charge.

'Hey, you the fellow that was on TV last night?'

'I don't know. I didn't watch.'

'You're famous, man!' Dwayne's face clouded. 'Hey, you're not a batty boy?'

'No, I'm not,' Clement said, intent on making a distinction that would be vital for his sanity and their relationship. 'I'm a gay man.'

'What's the difference?'

'The same as the one between nigger and black.' Dwayne drew himself very close and Clement braced himself for a blow, but all that hit him was a gust of sour breath.

'You can call me nigger if you like. I'm cool. I'll knife you in the ribs, but I'm cool.' Then, flashing him a broad smile in which the silver tooth glinted like the threatened blade, he tapped Clement on the cheek and, wiping his feet on his counterpane, hauled himself up to the top bunk. He remained there absorbed in his magazines – either the women's breasts in *Men Only* or the men's pectorals in *Men's Health* – until, at five o'clock, they were let out to fetch their supper and breakfast trays, and evening medication.

'This is gross, man,' Dwayne said, toying with a spam fritter. 'I wouldn't feed it to my dog.'

'Oh, do you have a dog?' Clement asked eagerly.

'No-oo. You deaf or something? If I gave him this, he'd be dead.'

Clement ate his meal, grateful that the shock of incarceration seemed to have dulled his sense of taste. As Dwayne turned back to his magazines which, to judge by the trembling of the bunks, were of the *Men Only* variety, he resigned himself to an evening of introspection, resolving that first thing the next morning he would ask to visit the library. A shout of 'Chapel' reminded him that he had put his name down to go and, unsure of the protocol, he consulted Dwayne, who told him to 'ring for room service,' only for the officer who answered the bell to announce that he was too low down the list.

'But the chaplain invited me specially,' he said, with a rush of alarm.

'Tough! We don't have enough escorts. So you'll just have to pray on your own. I'm sure Dwayne here'll help you.' Dwayne made no comment. 'I said I'm sure Dwayne will help you.'

'Yes, sir,' Dwayne replied, with a rancour that spoke volumes. 'Cunt,' he spat at the officer's back.

'I'd no idea that there would be such an enthusiastic congregation.'

'It's so's they can get out of their pads. Talk to their mates off the other wings. Buy and sell gear. I mean, man, where you been all your life?'

In cloud-cuckoo-land, Clement thought, stretching out on a bed which convinced him that prisoners would be better served by an osteopath than a psychologist. At ten o'clock he surreptitiously took his pills, only to discover that his discretion had been unnecessary when, half an hour later, Dwayne stood at the basin struggling to swallow his own dose.

'Hey man, what you staring at?'

'Nothing. I'm sorry... this cell is so small.'

'Don't you go getting no wrong ideas. Just because I take these pills I ain't no batty boy... oh excuse me, *gay man*!' He chuckled. 'No sir. This here,' he said rubbing his crotch, 'is top quality *Kitekat*. Specially designed for pussies!'

Clement was obliged to revise his opinion of the authorities. The accommodation was neither arbitrary nor cruel. But, while he was no longer afraid of being vilified or harmed on account of the virus, he gave up any hope that his cell-mate would be a soul mate. Glancing furtively at Dwayne rolling a table tennis ball along his biceps, he had never felt so alone.

Having finally managed to close his eyes and blot out his surroundings, he was jolted by a loud blast of reggae music. As Dwayne played his 'sounds' with no concern for him or, to judge by the shouts from the neighbouring cells, anyone else, despair as much as cowardice kept him from complaining. He pressed his pillow over his ears, but it was no more use as a muffler than a support. The nightmare grew worse when he looked up to see Dwayne's face leering at him.

'Hey, Mr Prime Minister, this one's for you,' he said. Listening to the hate-filled lyrics, Clement feared that his relief had been premature. Four tracks later, he was grateful for the noise, which offered some distraction from Dwayne's unrestrained bowel movements... although nothing could drive away the smell. Returning to his bunk, Dwayne switched off the light as abruptly as he had switched on the music. Then, after playing two more songs, he plunged the cell into a blessed silence.

Clement's reprieve proved to be short-lived, as he adjusted to as strange and disturbing a nocturnal soundtrack as any in his mother's African stories.

From the yard came the din of barking dogs and booming exchanges between blocks. Across the landing a man screamed that, unless he were let out, he would hang himself, sparking cries of 'Schizo' and 'Nutter', with even the duty officer telling him to 'Shut the fuck up and get some rope!' Meanwhile, the constant clanging on the pipes attested to either dangerously defective plumbing or sinister codes.

Lying back with his senses numb and brain pounding, he wondered if sleep deprivation were to be a part of his sentence. He felt as though he were being sucked into a vast hole and refused to close his eyes for fear of becoming permanently trapped. He must have dozed off in the early hours, because he was roused by a sustained drumming on the pipes. Stealing a hurried glance at Dwayne's watch, he saw that it was only a quarter to five. He used the loo and instinctively flushed it, inciting Dwayne to a torrent of abuse. 'What's up with you, man? You sick or something? Don't you never think of anyone else?'

'I'm sorry. I was startled. The pipes.'

'It's the Muslims. The righteous ones. The holy brothers. They have to pray, man. And I have to sleep. Right?'

Dwayne fell asleep, compounding the cacophony, but Clement remained wide awake. At breakfast, he felt as if he had spent the whole night crying, although his cheeks were bone dry. With a fluttering in his stomach that went beyond panic, he sat on the edge of his bunk unable to move until even Dwayne noticed and, glancing up from the cornflakes and UHT milk that had replaced the proverbial porridge, told him to ask the doctor for tranquillizers. 'There ain't no shame, man. Half the nick's on tablets. Whatever gets you through the day.'

'Thanks, I'll be fine,' Clement replied, afraid that taking them would sanction thoughts of suicide, 'I just need some air.' Recklessly encroaching on Dwayne's territory, he moved to the window. 'I just need some air,' he repeated, hauling himself up to one of the three inch panes that made bars superfluous and peering out at the desolate vista. He felt strangely heartened by the sight of an officer playing with a dog, albeit an Alsatian, but, when he tried to convey his pleasure, all Dwayne replied was 'If the screws here had their ways, man, they'd change the dogs with lions.'

Mid-morning Exercise gave him a chance to go down to the yard, but his relief at being outside was tempered by the dismal surroundings. Every wall and walkway was profligately covered in rolls of razor wire and the entire area wrapped in acres of meshing. The fitter men were working out, racing around the perimeter as if in training for an escape, kicking a ball in a roisterous free-for-all and practising martial arts. Only the parallel bars remained untouched, like the climbing frame on a sink estate. Meanwhile the indolent majority loitered aimlessly, their sole exertion being to stamp their feet in a bid to keep out the cold. As he tried to blend into the background, afraid of provoking an assault by an inadvertent glance or gesture, he found himself approached by a stream of baleful men. But, far from the crazed killers of his imagination, they were dealers offering supplies of drugs, tobacco and phone cards. Having declined the offers with enough grace to retain their goodwill, he was even more alarmed to be accosted by a man so intricately tattooed that he resembled a piece of William Morris wallpaper.

As he stared in dismay at the sinuous pattern of swastikas, the man announced that he was the drummer for the Aryan band, Ploughshare. 'You have a problem with that?'

'No,' he replied faintly.

'All the bleeding hearts bang on about saving pandas and polar bears and what have you, but the white race is the most endangered species on the planet and nobody gives a fuck.' Clement wondered if he were trying to recruit him. 'Word is you're a wicked artist. I want you to draw my picture to send to my tart. Make sure she won't forget me. I'll pay.'

'Oh, you don't need to do that,' Clement replied.

'Course I do. You should never do nothing for nothing in here, mate. You ask for nothing, they think you're nothing. I'll give you some burn.'

'Burn?'

'Baccy.'

'I don't smoke.'

'No problem. You can give it me back then,' he said, with a broad grin and a half-friendly poke in the kidneys.

Clement's success with the portrait led to other commissions on similar terms and he spent several Association periods in a corner of the landing, softening the lines of hardened faces in front of an appreciative crowd. Finally, even Dwayne took notice, asking him to draw him a woman.

'Anyone in particular?'

'A sexy woman, man. I want to see her tits and pussy. I want to rub my face in her cunt juice. You understand?'

'I understand.' It was a fitting irony that, with his artistic dreams in tatters, he should have ended up as a prison pornographer. The success of his new role did nothing to alleviate his depression. Each morning he woke up exhausted, as though he had spent ten hours in the studio. He suffered from permanent nausea and his gut felt as constricted as if it had been fitted with one of Gillian's bands. He lived on his nerves. Death seemed to lurk around every corner. The need for constant vigilance was compounded by being cooped up day and night with Dwayne. Passing wet sheets through the presses put a severe strain on his cell-mate's back. Claiming to be feeling 'well ill', he made an appointment to see the doctor, whose standard diagnosis was *malingering* and whose sole expression of sympathy came on the disclosure of his own slipped disc.

'He said I'm the most healthy person he's seen this week.' Dwayne said. 'I asked him: "Where you been working, man? The morgue?"'

The doctor passed him fit, but the works manager demurred, insisting that Dwayne take time off to recuperate from an injury whose seriousness was made clear to Clement when he demanded to swap bunks, a true loss of face for someone with a deep compulsion to be on top.

Clement's days were now as fraught as his nights, with the morning and afternoon naps which had been his one solace destroyed alternately by Dwayne's music and his taunts. Everything he did seemed to irritate his cell-mate, whether it was reading: 'You just get all them library books to show you're better than me; you can't tell me you really enjoy them'; or opening mail: 'What's that? Four letters today. It seems like the whole world's your friend, man. I ain't had four in the last ten months.' Clement's retort that correspondence was a two-way process backfired when Dwayne asked him to check the spelling of a note he'd written to his girlfriend, an effusion of sexual violence he described as 'nice', for no other reason than that the word *nice* occurred in every second line.

Nothing incensed Dwayne more than to be asked the time. Nonetheless Clement braved his anger three times on the afternoon of Mike's first visit, even after his warning that 'If you bug me once more, you won't be off to no visiting room but the hospital.' Meanwhile, he tortured himself by picturing everything that could go wrong, from a crisis at the school through a tailback on Brixton Hill to a riot on another wing which left him without an escort. Just when he was convinced that, even allowing for Dwayne's malice, visiting hour must be over, he was hauled out of the cell, searched, made to put on an orange tabard, and ushered into a crowded hall. He walked up to the dais where an officer took his name and number and pointed to a table, at which, for the first time in three weeks, he saw a face that wasn't a threat. Guards patrolled the hall and balcony, routinely ordering people to display their hands, but Mike's hug was more precious than any contraband, imbuing him with hope.

'Great gear,' Mike said. 'Orange has to be your colour.'

'I'll bear it in mind.'

'I've been worried about you. On the phone you sounded so distant. But, seeing you in the flesh, you look terrific.'

'You've never been a convincing liar.'

'A little thinner, perhaps.'

'It's not the Ritz! We're locked up with our dirty plates from five at night till eight in the morning, so half the tea – that is dinner – ends up out of the window. Is it any wonder the place is infested with rats?'

'But you're surviving?'

'I've learnt to keep my head down. Prison's like the rest of the world writ large... packed with people ready to hurt you, betray you and drag you down in order to feel better about themselves.'

'You've not been bullied or got at in any way or...?'

'Don't worry. Granted my cell-mate's an acquired taste. Dwayne. He's put in a request for a new mattress on the grounds that the old one's giving him nightmares. I kid you not! We do have one thing in common.'

'What?'

'Guess?'

'Come on, Clem...'

'Humour me. Think of your three least favourite letters.'

'Ah!'

'You see? Although "in common" is putting it too strong. As he never ceases to remind me, Dwayne is a red-blooded male. But I'm bored with me! I want to hear all the gossip from home.'

Mike duly obliged, conveying the love and support of so many friends that Clement wondered if he had simply memorised his address book. 'I talk to your mum regularly. I asked if she'd like to come today, but she said "next time". I think she was afraid she'd be intruding.'

'Sounds like Ma.' The thought of her selfless love was almost too much to bear.

'Carla's up in the Lake District putting the finishing touches to her window. Not that I see the appeal of all those smug little animals myself.'

'That's because you never knew Nanny Goddard.'

'But she's done a splendid job.'

'Tell her to send me a photo. Poster-size. I'll stick it up on the wall.' He smiled at the thought of Dwayne's bemusement.

'I went to visit Newsom in the Mildmay.'

'I've written to him but I've yet to receive a reply,' Clement said, troubled by Mike's change of tone.

'I shouldn't expect one. Not for a while. But he's being brilliantly looked after. And he says that if anything'll help him pull through, it's the thought of being around when you're released.'

'I don't suppose you've heard anything from Shoshanna?'

'You don't suppose right.'

'She's written to me twice.'

'I hope you chucked the letters straight in the bin.'

'Not on your life! Even an estate agent's circular would be welcome in here.'

'What? Advising you they have a prospective buyer for your bijou south London cell?' Mike asked, triggering Clement's laughter. 'Sorry, that was tasteless.'

'Yes, it was, and all the better for it... Shoshanna asked if there were anything she could do for me.'

'Certainly. How about an apology and a divorce?'

'Come on, it's never going to happen. I think the letters themselves are a kind of apology. I asked her to go and see Ma as often as she can and carry on writing to me.'

'You're a good man, Clem. I've always known it, but never as surely as I do in here.'

Despite the constraints of the setting, they chatted so freely that Clement felt almost human. When the time came for Mike to leave, he sank into such despair that, for the first time, he understood those prisoners who preferred not to send Visiting Orders than to be reminded of 'life on the out'. His misery increased when he returned to the cell to find Dwayne locked in a heated dispute with an officer about the pair of speakers he had ordered from Argos.

'Them are sitting there at reception. Reception say it's not their job to bring them and Canteen say it's not their job to fetch them. I've been waiting two weeks. I've paid £3.95 delivery. That's thieving, man.'

'So what am I meant to do about it?'

'Go get them for me. This is the Prison Service, man! Why they call it a service makes no sense to me.'

'Because we devote our lives to looking after scum like you! Don't you think that wog-box of yours causes enough aggravation already? Now if you're a good lad and keep your nose clean, your Uncle Gordon may think about going to collect them in a week or so.'

Dwayne's reaction was so predictable that Clement suspected the officer of engineering it. Venting months of frustration, he flung a chair at the wall before springing on his tormentor. Clement flattened himself against the bunks as the officer blew his whistle and was joined within seconds by four colleagues who fell on Dwayne, pinning him to the ground and frogmarching him off for a spell in solitary, while he shrieked that 'The bastards are twisting me up!' Left alone, Clement cleared up the mess and made some tea, recycling his two o'clock teabag, whipping it out to ensure that there was enough left for one more cup. Then he lay back on his bunk to contemplate his own spell in solitary, made all the more attractive by the discovery that Dwayne had not been wearing his watch.

4

Clement was given only three hours to prepare for the move to Bullingdon. At nine o'clock the principal officer told him that he was to be transferred and, at noon, he was led out to a cross between a refrigeration van and a Portaloo, much like the one in which he had been brought from the Old Bailey. Despite the discomfort, he savoured the brief return to the outside world, grateful even for the M40 lane closure which extended the journey by an hour. On arrival, he was taken through the same reception procedure as at Brixton but, whether because he had grown stronger or simply tougher, he felt no humiliation. Standing stark naked in front of the officers, he knew that pride was not the same as dignity. They could strip him of his clothes, but not of his self-respect.

Kitted out in a burgundy tracksuit, he was taken to an interview room where he had a bruising encounter with Senior Officer Willis, a gaunt man with a pencil moustache, clipped white hair and chipped teeth, who displayed an alarming hostility towards him, as well as an unexpected familiarity with his case. 'This is a Category B prison. You should be in Category A. Strings have been pulled and I don't like it. I don't like it one little bit. I have my eye on you, lad. Step out of line just the once and I'll be down on you like a ton of bricks. Understood?' Clement nodded. 'Good.'

He escorted Clement down the landing to a cell which was cleaner, brighter and, above all, fresher than the one in Brixton. An elderly man sat on the bottom bunk, carving something out of cardboard. He jumped to attention as the officer walked in.

'Your new pad-mate, Parker. You'll show him the ropes.'

'Yes, boss.'

'A word to the wise, Parker. Never use the wrong toothbrush. And make sure you sleep on your back!'

Willis went out, leaving Clement with his cell-mate, an owl-like man with a few strands of hair ineffectually combed over his bald spot who, unless prison had prematurely aged him, had to be in his seventies. Since the prisoners' code ruled out a direct question, Clement speculated on his crime, picturing tax evasion, benefit fraud and identity theft, before fixing on a refusal to pay his Council Tax in protest at cuts in local amenities. Although perturbed by his greater sympathy with white-collar crime, he was grateful that the physical threat ever present with Dwayne had been reduced.

'Am I on top?' he asked. Parker grunted his assent before jumping up and dividing the cell into two 'halves', which were so blatantly unequal that Clement assumed he was either myopic or trying his luck. Resolving not to object but to reclaim his rights by stealth, he clambered on to his bunk from where he surveyed the room. It was the familiar hotchpotch, with the welcome addition of a rickety TV on the chest of drawers and the even more welcome absence of pin-ups, the only female presence being a matronly face in a frame on the windowsill.

'Your wife?' Clement asked.

'What's that?' Parker spun round, gripping his Stanley knife like a cornered schoolboy.

'This photograph. Is it your wife?'

'That's right.'

'She has a kind smile.'

'Oh yes.'

'Does she live nearby?'

'What?'

'For visits?'

'She's dead.'

'I'm sorry.'

'It's not your fault.'

Parker worked in silence until tea when, after responding tersely to Clement's questions on Bullingdon life, he grew more voluble on the subject of his modelling and the many Golden Hinds and Cutty Sarks he had bottled for sale by a prison officers' charity. Eager to make the most of his short time with the knife, he returned to his ship for another hour, before asking if Clement minded his watching TV. Clement was so disarmed by the courtesy that he put up with a programme in which a group of minor celebrities was submerged in a submarine. After a battle royal between a daytime newscaster and a footballer's ex-wife over the benefits of Botox, Parker switched it off. Rummaging under his bunk, he produced a bottle of cloudy liquid and offered Clement a drink. 'It's cider,' he said, in response to his dubious expression. 'First, I leave the apples to rot. Then I ferment them in sugared water. The kangas allow me the bottles for my ships.' Clement downed a mug with enthusiasm, which he paid for in the early hours when he was struck by agonising cramps and chronic flatulence. His one consolation was that Parker slept through it all, waking up to dismiss his mild reproaches with the claim that a trip in the 'meat-wagon' would upset anyone's stomach.

Clement soon settled into the new routine, learning the basic hierarchies among both prisoners and staff. Time, as ever, hung heavily on his hands, although at least it could now be measured on a cheap *Star Wars* watch, which not even Willis could overvalue. Parker went to work every morning, filling bags with polished stones for sale in design shops, a task that would have defeated one of Carla's Zen masters. Left alone in the cell, Clement had the perfect opportunity to plug the gaps in his reading but, despite an appeal to the governor, he was refused permission to bring in any books. While resigned to the constant flow of drugs, the authorities were intent on blocking the entrance of *Madame Bovary* and *Buddenbrooks*. Their only advice was that he ask a friend to present them to the library in the hope that he be allowed to borrow them first.

One afternoon, as he lay on his bunk, grappling with a formulaic thriller, he was summoned to see the Head of Learning and Skills. The fear that he would be offered a choice between basic plumbing and GCSE maths faded when she asked if he would be willing to teach art.

'Don't you have anyone on the staff?'

'We did. He was sacked for selling prisoners' underwear to America.'

'I'd have thought it was cheaper there.'

'Soiled underwear.'

'Oh! I see.' He shuddered.

'It's one of the most popular courses and we can't find anyone suitable. We'd pay you £2.35 an hour and give you enhanced status.'

'Would that mean my own cell?'

'As soon as one becomes available.'

For all his doubts about his abilities as a teacher, he accepted. He was amazed at how rapidly the news of the course spread and, at Association that evening, he was waylaid by several prisoners keen to take it. He realised with dismay that the twelve places would be grossly oversubscribed, earning him more enemies than friends. He explained that it was not in his gift; although he was determined to earmark a place for Stick, a hyperactive man in his early twenties, with permanently tousled hair and track marks on his arms. He still felt guilty for his misapprehension when, after trailing him round the exercise yard, Stick had sidled up and introduced himself.

'They call me Thick,' he lisped. 'Do you know why?'

'Take no notice. They're the ones who are ignorant.'

'Go on, guess!'

'Because you've not had the right educational opportunities?' he proposed hesitantly.

'No, because I'm thin as a thick insect.'

Clement's relief that Stick had failed to catch his drift vanished when a group of onlookers pointed it out, in the hope of provoking a fight. Far from satisfying them, Stick seemed to see Clement as a brother in confusion, further warranting his sobriquet by clinging to him like a burr. Assured that he felt nothing more for him than for a stray dog, Clement resolved to take him in tow.

'You like reading then?' Stick asked, spotting the luridly covered thriller.

'Most things.'

'Me too! Last week I read a book about the Gulf War that was one and a half inches thick. Before that I read one about Rommel that was two inches thick. That only took me nine days.' As he talked, Stick's tic grew worse and he cast repeated glances over his shoulder. 'Can I lend a phone card? Ring my kid?'

'Of course,' Clement said, shocked at the thought of such a callow father.

'You what?'

'Of course you can borrow it.' He held it out to Stick, whose hands seemed to be operating independently as one reached out to take it while the other pushed it away.

'You didn't ought to do that! It's wrong!' He sounded affronted. 'See, you wouldn't just be giving it to me but taking it away from your own family. I know God says, if someone asks you for something, you got to give it to them but I bet you He understands.' Clement was as bemused by his point of reference as by his change of heart. 'Do you want to hear my joke?'

'If you like.'

'Who's the biggest liars in the world?'

'I don't know. Who are the biggest liars in the world?'

'Chemists, cos they keep making things up.'

Scarcely had he delivered the punchline when he was felled by an actual punch. As Stick clutched his jaw, Clement stared at the three men who had crept up behind them.

'Beg pardon, your honour,' one said with a mocking bow, 'but this little tart has some business with us. It's pay-up time.'

'Tomorrow,' Stick squealed.

'You can't add up, Sunshine. The day after yesterday equals today.'

Stick's terror galvanised Clement. Feeling that nothing the men could do to him would be as painful as the knowledge of his cowardice, he pressed forward. 'Leave him be!' he ordered, thankful that his voice at least had not betrayed him. The men gazed at him dumbfounded. 'I can see that he owes you – '

'You're fucking right he does. Big time!'

'But I'm sure there's some way it can be settled.'

'You're right there too. Mr Phillips is waiting for him in his cell.'

Stick whimpered.

'He's just a boy.'

'He's a tart. A little tart,' one of them said, signalling his disgust with his foot. Clement searched for the officers but they were both deep in conversation, no doubt with the trio's associates. He tried to pull Stick away, only for one of the men to grab his arm and hiss in his face: 'I won't tell you again. Keep your nose out of places where it don't belong. Else you'll be next on the list.'

Refusing to back down, Clement pushed the man off and leant over to help Stick up. He felt a wrench on his shoulder and steeled himself for a blow when the command to 'Give it up!' made his attacker freeze. Clement assumed that the clash had been spotted by one of the officers, but a quick glance showed that they remained occupied at the far end of the hall. His rescuer turned out to be a mountainous bodybuilder, reputedly the strongest man on the block, a claim that might soon be put to the test.

'Lay one finger on him and you'll be pissing out of plaster trousers.'

'Leave it out, Des!' said one.

'This has nothing to do with you,' said another.

'I say different. Now get the fuck out!'

Clement watched amazed as the three men yielded to Des's quiet authority. Muttering curses and with a final face-saving kick at Stick, they slipped away. Stick jumped up and immediately began punching the air. 'I could take them. They came at me from behind. Two minutes more and I'd have had them.'

'Piss off, freak!' Des said.

'I tell you I could have – '

'I said "Piss off!"' As Stick slunk away with an injured expression, Clement gazed at Des, wondering at his change of mood. 'You should steer well clear of that little bastard. He's anyone's for a Twix.'

'Do you know what it was all about?'

'Drugs. More dealers here than King's Cross. But don't worry. They won't bother you again. Not if they know what's good for them.'

'Why?'

'I've been watching you.'

'You have?'

'I've been watching out for you.'

'Who are you?' Clement asked nervously.

'Desmond Connelly.' Clement shook his head. 'Rafik's friend.' Clement's heart missed a beat. 'I was sent down eighteen months ago.'

'I remember.' Clement's gratitude for his rescue was soured by rancour towards the man he blamed for Rafik's deportation.

'Since then I've done a lot of thinking. Well I've had the time, haven't I? I know I was a total arsehole. But Jesus forgives me.'

'Jesus Christ?'

'He found me here in this nick. I went to a prayer group run by one of the screws. He brought me the good news of Jesus' love.' The mention of Christ turned Clement's thoughts back to Rafik. For all his offer of protection, he remained unsure how much Desmond knew of their friendship and how far his jealousy had been cured.

'I wonder...' he asked tentatively. 'Have you had any news from him... Rafik?'

The cloud that swept over Desmond's face anticipated his answer. 'Not from Rafik, no. I wrote to the only address I had in Algeria. To him. To his father. Not a word!'

'Me neither! I went down the Embassy route, but it was hopeless.'

'Then, after a year – no, more like a year and a half – of silence, I got a letter six weeks ago. The landlady of our place in Willesden, she forwarded it. Somehow she registered it was important.'

'Maybe the stamp?'

'Maybe,' Desmond said, as though the thought had just struck him.

'And...?' Clement asked anxiously.

'It was from one of his friends... a teacher. The one Rafik used to say had taught him everything.'

'Really?' Clement was determined to give nothing away.

'He wrote that Rafik was dead.'

Clement steadied himself as the floor began to shake and the room drained of colour. The news to which he had thought himself inured began to seep through his body. He pictured the lustrous olive skin and limpid brown eyes that he had made such vain attempts to capture. Turning back to Desmond, he felt a renewed resentment of the man who had known the comfort of Rafik's flesh rather than the struggle for its depiction. His Christ was dead, and the journey that had brought him here was complete.

'Did he say what happened?' he asked, both needing and dreading the details.

'Near enough. He'd been in prison and released in some sort of government amnesty. That didn't please his friends, the mullahs, who sent him death threats. Then, when he went into hiding, they kidnapped two of his brothers and swore to kill them if he didn't give himself up.'

'But his brothers' threats to kill him were what led him to run away!'

'Tell me about it! They'd treated him so badly... they'd made him feel so bad about himself that, when it came to the crunch, he didn't believe he deserved to live.'

Clement was tormented by the image of the man whom he had painted as Christ taking on the role for real, sacrificing his life to save his persecutors. Moreover, he could not dispel the feeling, however fanciful, that Rafik's hand lay behind his encounter with Desmond. Intrigued by Desmond's transformation from murderer to knight errant, he wondered whether it could all be ascribed to his conversion and, if so, how he justified his sexuality. In a bid to find out more, he accepted Desmond's invitation to the prayer group the following Friday, finding his worst fears confirmed the moment he entered the room.

'Officer Willis!' he said.

'It's Jim in here. Isn't that right, Jim?' one of the group said.

'That's right, lad. No worldly distinctions inside this room. We're all of us sinners in the eyes of God.'

'You said it, Jim,' the man replied, relishing his temporary licence.

The room filled with so many unlikely converts that Clement wondered whether, as in the Brixton chapel, the main attraction was an excuse to escape their cells. Desmond took a seat at the far side of the circle, nodding to him briefly before picking up his Bible. Stick grabbed the chair beside him, nudging it so close that their thighs brushed, giving him a momentary sense of satisfaction and a lingering one of unease. With everyone gathered, Officer Willis (Clement remained suspicious of the *Jim*) announced a period of silent prayer which, as soon became clear, was as nominal as every other silence in prison. Voices were raised from all points of the circle: 'I want to thank you Lord for the blessing of this nick where I can get near to you with no distractions,' from his left; 'I feel your Holy Spirit, Lord, like a golden crown on my head,' from his right. Meanwhile, 'I thank you Lord Jesus for giving me the greatest fix ever,' came from the seat next to him, prompting a couple of guffaws and several groans. After a peremptory Amen, which cut through all pretence of equality, Willis called on a young Scotsman to read the Gospel. No sooner had he provided chapter and verse for the familiar story of the woman taken in adultery than the entire group opened their Bibles, although Clement noted in bewilderment that Stick turned to Acts.

He sat silently while Willis encouraged them to analyse the text. After three variations on the theme that we were all miserable sinners unworthy of salvation unless we obeyed the Word of the Lord, Stick put up his hand.

'Sir, sir, please, Jim sir!' he said, bobbing up and down like a four-year-old. 'Can I tell my joke, sir?' His request met with a chorus of 'No's. 'It's about the story, sir. Honest!'

'But is it clean, lad?' Willis said. 'Can you put your hand on heart and tell me it's fit for your mother?'

'He's not fit to have a mother!'

'Shut it, lad!'

'Cross my heart and hope to die, sir... Jim sir!'

'Very well then,' Willis said stoically. 'Keep it clean, mind.'

'There's the Lord Jesus. He's walking through the desert one day and he sees all these people picking on this prossie... sorry, Jim sir, tart. And he says, "Let anyone who hasn't ever sinned chuck the first stone at her." And he looks at them, happy cos he knows that they're evil and wicked sinners like us. And then he hears this stone whizzing past his ear. And he turns round to see who's disobeyed him. And there's the Holy Virgin Mary standing there with a great pile of stones. "Mam," he says, all hurt – I mean hurt cos she's shown him up, not cos the stone hit him – "Mam," he says, "I thought I told you to stay at home!"'

Stick gazed around, hungry for approval, to be met with sighs, groans and grimaces.

'Any repetition of that, lad, and you'll be barred,' Willis said. 'Understand?'

'But it's the same story,' Stick pleaded.

'Understand!'

'Yes, sir,' Stick replied sullenly.

While Willis took exception to Stick, Clement was far more disturbed by Joe, a young Nigerian, who claimed that the moral was 'Even when the Muslims mock you and persecute you, you mustn't fight back but leave them to the angels who'll throw rocks at them once they're dead.' With Willis letting the remark pass, Clement put forward the alternative view that the story exemplified God's all-forgiving love and that they shouldn't be misled by the final 'Go, and sin no more', which scholars had shown to be an interpolation.

'What scholars?' Willis asked.

'I'm afraid I don't have their names to hand.'

'Surprise surprise! Not a scrap of evidence.'

'But it wouldn't be hard to get hold of them. I did a lot of research for a painting called the *Two Marys*.'

'We know all about your paintings,' Willis said. 'Filth!' Clement's hope that Desmond, whose dead lover was implicated in that filth, would once again ride to his rescue was dashed by his silence. 'Whatever Mr Hippy-hair here thinks, we're not stupid, are we lads? We know how books are made. We know how words go missing over time. But this isn't your Jeffrey Archer or even your Shakespeare. It's God's book: the Holy Bible. A book like a great wall that keeps the Devil out and the righteous in the ways of the Lord. Remove a single brick and the wall will crumble. Where will we be then?'

'In Satan's hands?' one of the men asked.

'Right! Locked up in Hell for ever.'

'With respect,' Clement said with blatant insincerity, 'that's not faith but fire insurance. If you read the Gospels – and I'm sure everyone here has – ' His voice faltered as he found himself staring at Stick – 'you'll know that Christ makes very little mention of sin.'

'Remember, lads, the Devil quotes scripture for his own ends.'

'His overwhelming concern is with God's redeeming love. We must all hold on to that. Be proud that God created us in His image. Be proud that Christ took on our flesh.'

'And what have we done with that flesh?' Willis asked. 'Defiled it. Debased it. Made it a cesspit of foul lusts and diseases, as you should know better than anyone.' Clement wondered if Desmond's offer of protection would hold good against partisan officers. 'What do any of these men have to be proud of? They've destroyed their families. Left wives without husbands... children without fathers. It's shame they should be feeling, not pride.'

Clement detected a rumble of discontent at Willis's shift from *we* to *they*. He recalled Mike's denunciation of shame and longed to free his fellow prisoners from an emotion that sentenced them twice. 'None of us here needs to feel ashamed,' he said, emphasising the pronoun. 'Why should you make these men feel worse about themselves than they already do?'

'To bring them to God. To ensure that, even though they're the lowest of the low in this world, they'll be God's chosen ones in the next.'

A burst of Amens and Hallelujahs left Clement convinced that his own words had fallen on deaf ears. Seizing his advantage, Willis ordered the group to bow their heads in prayer before bringing the meeting to a close. While the men broke up the circle and replaced the chairs in rows, Willis confronted Clement. 'Don't think I don't know your game,' he said. 'It's not enough for you to defy the Bible on your own account. You want to bring these men down with you. Well, I won't let you. That lad,' he pointed to Stick, who for no discernible reason was balancing a chair on his head, 'was giving himself to every man on the block for a packet of smokes until he found the Lord. That man – ' he pointed to a stocky man with a goitre – 'was cutting his wrists as regularly as the rest of us – ' he scowled at the sight of Clement – 'most of us – cut our hair. Are you telling me they're no better off?'

'I admit they've found something, but I'd dispute the fact that it's Christ.'

'Are you doubting the love of God?'

'Not at all. Just your interpretation of it.'

'Get back to your cell. One more word and I'll have you on report.'

'Yes, Jim,' Clement replied deliberately.

'Yes, sir,' Willis thundered, to Clement's delight. He walked back with a restored sense of purpose. Echoing the prisoner who thanked God for enabling him to approach Him without distractions, he thanked Him for locking him up in order to show him new ways to be free.

The next morning Clement was called to see the deputy governor, a rumpled middle-aged man with exceptionally large hands, which he wrung repeatedly during their conversation. 'I hope you've settled in all right,' he asked, like a headmaster greeting a junior member of staff whose function eluded him.

'I'm not climbing the walls, if that's what you're getting at. My cell-mate seems a decent enough chap.'

'Yes, I wanted you placed with a lifer. Experience has shown that they make the most placid prisoners. It's the men serving five years or less who have something to prove.'

'All Parker's out to prove is his skill at model-making. Except, of course, his devotion to his dead wife.'

'He might have thought of that before he killed her,' the deputy governor said tersely, leaving Clement open-mouthed. 'But I must confess to having a further motive for summoning you. We have an honourable tradition of prison literature in this country. Think of Malory, Bunyan and Daniel Defoe. And, of course – ' he added, as if in deference to Clement – 'Oscar Wilde. Sadly, we don't have a comparable tradition of prison art. That may of course mean that we're locking up the wrong people.' He laughed mirthlessly. 'Either way, we'd like to redress the balance. I've been authorised by the Chief, who's something of a fan of yours, to ask if you'd paint a piece for the prison chapel.'

'Really? I'm flattered... although I can't say I feel inspired. Quite the reverse.'

'Isn't that the artist's fate? One per cent inspiration and ninety-nine per cent perspiration?'

'It certainly would be in here. To tell the truth I've taken a long break – over a year, in fact – from painting. I'd only just picked up my brush again before my arrest and that was... that was a one-off.'

'Surely that will make it even more of a challenge?'

'I must admit I'm tempted. If anything's going to keep me sane, it's work. But I need time to think. May I let you know in a day or two? I'll have to get a sense of the space.'

'That's easily done. I'll ask one of the officers to take you there right now.'

'No, there's no point when it's empty. I have to see it in use.'

The first opportunity came the following Sunday, when he joined the line of prisoners braving the taunts of 'God Squad' as they waited for the officers to escort them across the yard.

'They jeer at us for being Christians,' Desmond said, 'but they're quick enough to ask us to say a prayer for them when they're up in court.'

Stick ran out at the last minute. 'Will you walk with us?'

'Sure,' Clement said, to Desmond's visible annoyance.

'D'you want to hear my joke?'

'No!' Desmond roared.

'Go on,' Stick pleaded, 'it's religious.'

'So long as it's short,' Clement said, offering a compromise.

'There were three lads in this playground... no, this café... no, playground... well, it don't matter.' Desmond moved away in disgust. 'There were three lads anyway. The first one, he says, "My dad's a teacher; he makes me clever for nothing." The second one, he says, "My dad's a doctor; he makes me well for nothing." The third one, he says, "My dad's a vicar; he makes me good for nothing."'

'Excellent,' Clement said, his smile under increasing strain as Stick dissected the pun.

They entered the chapel, a sombre room painted a municipal beige, with a vase of peonies on the altar, a wooden crucifix suspended from the ceiling and the Stations of the Cross hanging like cheap pennants on the wall. Feeling as depressed by the confused churchmanship as by the tawdry furnishings, Clement made his way to the seats where, true to his Anglican training, he kept a respectful distance from his neighbour until one of the officers ordered him to 'fill up the gap'. Stick needed no encouragement, sitting so close that Clement yearned for a cloud of incense. After the opening hymn, *Holy Holy Holy*, in which, despite sharing his hymn book, Stick muddled not only the tune but the words, the chaplain called up a prisoner to read the lesson: Christ's account of the Last Judgement in Matthew 25. Although the halting delivery marred even the crude cadences of the *Good News Bible* and Stick's schoolboy giggle on 'naked and you clothed me' was a profound irritation, Clement found the references to prison-visiting strangely moving. He was less convinced when, in a generous, if laboured, attempt to reach out to his congregation, the chaplain preached on the need to let Christ into their lives.

'Don't keep Jesus standing on the front step. He doesn't have a search warrant. He won't break the door down like the police. He's waiting for you to invite him in. Would you rather leave it till you're up in the dock on Judgement Day? "Who's this?" God will ask. "Never seen him before, m'Lud!" Jesus will reply. And you'll be sent down not just for life but for eternity.'

After leading the prayers of intercession, with only those for families and friends receiving any response, the chaplain drew the service to a close. He stood at the chapel door, greeting the men as if they were going home for their

Sunday roast. Holding Clement back, he asked if he might have a quick word and led him up to a tiny office.

'I must apologise for the mess,' he said, dumping a pile of service sheets on the floor. 'I share it with my Free Church, Catholic and Sikh colleagues.'

'Practical ecumenism?' Clement asked.

'We're never here at the same time.'

Shifting in his seat, like an actor unable even to play himself authentically, the chaplain asked if he would agree that there were many different paths to God.

'Of course.'

'Then I urge you not to dismiss Officer Willis's. He's complained about your disrupting his prayer group. He claims that you put your own will above the Good Book.'

'Not my will. My mind, my spirit. I can't sit there like a statue while he demeans God's love.'

'To you, God may be love. To someone else, He may be self-restraint. You're living among men who need *don'ts*, who can't – who've patently shown that they can't – exercise the same freedom of choice as people outside. It would be cruel – no, downright wicked – to deny them the chance.'

'So there are the sheep and the goats and then the in-betweens: the goats in sheep's clothing whose bleating gets them through the gates?'

The chaplain's response was to call an officer to escort him back to his cell, where the tedium of prison life took on its distinctive Sunday timbre. Clement spent the afternoon reading a dog-eared biography of Bobby Charlton, while Parker watched a Western, unable to decide whether he had seen it before. At five o'clock they collected their tea and breakfast trays, to which Parker added his modelling tools and glue. Eager not to betray himself by an anxious glance at the Stanley knife, Clement watched a programme about loft conversions while Parker worked on a scale model of the *Titanic* until, with unwonted clumsiness, he cut through the hull. Setting it aside, he joined Clement in playing Monopoly with the men in the next-door cell. Their neighbours held the board, threw the dice and moved the pieces for all four players, with everything proceeding smoothly until one of them claimed that a double three had landed Parker's old boot on his Bow Street hotel. Clement, with a total recall of the board dating from boyhood, insisted that the correct position was Marylebone Station, refusing to back down even after Parker's conciliatory offer to pay. The game collapsed in bitter recriminations, with Clement taking full advantage of the dividing wall to hurl around charges of chicanery, demanding to know 'Whatever happened to honour among thieves?'

Over the following weeks he grew fully attuned to the Bullingdon rhythm.

He learnt how to supplement his food and eke out his canteen, renouncing regular shampoo and deodorant, along with the assumptions behind them, for the sake of extra chocolate and tea. He created a niche for himself by drawing portraits of the prisoners and their families. One man who had brought him a snapshot of his daughter, a lantern-jawed pub singer, the self-styled Newham Nightingale, was so thrilled with the result that he planned to use it on a poster advertising her availability for 'weddings, christenings and acquittals'. Everyone valued his unique take on likenesses which, by any objective standard, were better captured in photographs or, in some cases, mugshots. The wonder was that, after the cynicism of the art world, he should encounter such enthusiasm in jail.

He was unsure if it were his example or the supposed soft option that had generated so much interest in his class. They met in a fusty art room, whose small barred windows let in insufficient light and whose cracked cream walls were inimical to a vibrant use of colour. He gazed dolefully at the rudimentary materials that Officer Braden had laid out on the table: six boxes of cheap powder paint, one between two, which were certain to lead to conflict; twelve brushes, either caked with ancient paint or balding; thirty sheets of sugar paper. His intention to range the desks in a circle around the walls was thwarted by the officer, who insisted on their all pointing towards the front. When everyone was finally settled and introduced to the alien concept of sharing, he smiled awkwardly at the twelve expectant faces and outlined both how he proposed to proceed and what he hoped that they would achieve.

Given how the class had been oversubscribed, he had looked for a degree of indulgence from the chosen few, but his admission that this was his first taste of teaching fostered the suspicion that they were being short-changed. He began by asking what sort of artists they wanted to be, prompting a near unanimous cry of 'piss artist', which they immediately set about demonstrating, until Officer Braden weighed in with the warning that anyone who failed to produce at least three decent pictures by the end of the week would be thrown out. Although he baulked at imposing the standards of the workshop, Clement was grateful for the officer's ability to concentrate the men's minds.

'What I suggest is that, for the first few lessons, we should all tackle the same subjects,' he said, 'the view from the window, a still life and a model... I'm hoping Officer Braden will oblige.'

'I'm not taking my clothes off!'

'Don't worry,' Clement said, struggling to make himself heard above the catcalls. 'I'm sure we'd all rather you were fully dressed... The point of the exercise is to show that, while we each have a singular vision, the world remains recognisably the same.'

The principle came under increasing threat when the staff houses were transformed into playschool blocks and lunar landscapes, the vase of chrysanthemums into an octopus and a triffid, and the officer's pitted face into a bowl of liver and an armoured tank.

He soon gave up hope of discovering a prodigy. The closest he came was Joe, the young Nigerian from Willis's prayer group. The classes created a bond between them, which they consolidated during intimate chats at Association. Joe confided that he had come to the country to study law, but his funding had run out and he had been drawn into an elaborate infection racket, whereby healthy Africans faked symptoms at HIV clinics and then sent genuine patients to give blood in their place. When their positive diagnoses were confirmed, they became eligible for income support, preferential housing and a raft of benefits. Joe claimed to have harboured misgivings, not least about reinforcing the view that Third World immigrants were crippling the NHS, but he had justified himself by invoking both the racism of hospitals in which black faces were interchangeable and the evil of Britain's colonial past. Everything had proceeded according to plan until the ringleaders grew greedy, insisting that Joe take a second test in his own right to prove that he was HIV negative and then sue the hospital for misdiagnosis and emotional distress. The subsequent police investigation brought the scam to light.

'It is a very good thing that I'm here,' Joe said. 'In three years I study and take my exams to become a lawyer. My heart is light.'

When Joe failed to turn up for either the class or Association, Clement sought out Desmond. 'You haven't seen Joe by any chance? He's not been around all day. Have you heard if he's ill?'

'No, he's gone to the VP unit.'

'You mean he's a sex offender?' Clement asked, choking back nausea.

'Did I say that? No, he's running scared of the Muslims. They're harassing him day and night.'

'In what way?'

'Asking why he doesn't grow his beard... why he won't pray to Allah... threatening him with deep shit if he won't convert.'

'He never mentioned anything to me.'

'So he had no choice, poor bugger! He goes up to the VPU and gets banged up with the nonces or he stays here and gets jugged.'

'What?'

'Jugged! Burnt with boiling sugar.'

'Good God! They do that in the name of religion?'

'They blow people up in the name of religion, don't they? You think I'm biased because of Rafik. But that's what opened my eyes.'

'Why Joe? Why have they singled him out?'

'Because he's black, in case you haven't noticed! White blokes don't even figure on their radar. Half the Muslim Brotherhood were sentenced for selling drugs, which is against their religion. But, so long as they don't sell them to other Muslims, their imams tell them it doesn't count.'

'Come on! I can't believe that.'

'Ask anyone here... Nixon!' He called to a safe-cracker with a pronounced resemblance to the former president.

'No, don't bother! Really,' Clement said, embarrassed. 'I'll take your word for it.'

'And so you should,' Desmond said, 'since it's you and me and all the wimps in power who are letting them get away with it. Take this nick. We all have the right to freedom of conscience, right? Even though half the cons in here don't know what a conscience is. So the Muslims have to be let out of their pads five times a day to wash and pray. That's the law. And they have to be allowed a minister. Only they don't have a proper one, like us and the Left-footers, and even the Sikhs. So the Governor lets them use a con. You must have seen him, swaggering about in his little white cap and beads like he's something special?'

'Not so as I've noticed.'

'He's special all right. Specially evil. He's fighting to stop the government sending him to America on account of a bomb he planted at their embassy in Sudan. And every day – not once a day, but five times – he gathers them all to pray, spouting at them in Arabic. So what do you think he's telling them? I get the feeling it isn't *Love thy neighbour.*'

'Now you're being paranoid. They'll have to have an officer present, just like us.'

'Sure they do, but they're talking Arabic. Arabic! How many of these fuckwit screws do you think speak Arabic? The only GCSE they've got is in key-rattling! I'm stuck in here for another eight years so I'm safe, but I'm telling you I wouldn't want to be going back on the out as quick as you.'

Clement returned to his cell with a heavy heart. He trusted that Joe at any rate was secure in a unit where no self-respecting prisoner ever ventured. In his absence, the class's talent level plummeted. Even so, and in spite of demarcation disputes more suited to a playgroup, Clement enjoyed teaching, not least on account of the link with Mike. He felt doubly excited to be greeting him on his first visit to Bullingdon and longed to compare notes but, sensing that Mike was more sceptical than charmed, he asked him instead for a report of Newsom's funeral. Having been forced to mourn his former lover alone, he was eager for a full account of an event from which he had felt cruelly excluded. Mike duly obliged, describing a ceremony which had bordered on the surreal, from the moment when, as one of only two mourners to be wearing a tie, he had been mistaken for a priest by the crematorium attendant and directed to the robing room. While grateful for the touches of black humour, Clement refused to believe that Mike was not embellishing his picture of the coffin being carried by a chapter of Dykes on Bikes and of the culture clash when the 3.30 mourners in T-shirts, jeans and radical drag collided with the 4.00 mourners in heavy suits, sashes and bowler hats from the south London lodge of the Orange Order.

'Newsom chose the music himself. There was a sticky moment when the coffin came in to the sound of Ella Fitzgerald singing *The Way You Look Tonight*.'

'I hope you kept a straight face.'

'Just about. Though I totally lost it during his yoga teacher's eulogy, when she praised the way he practised right to the end. "Even when his buttocks lost their grip, his thighs remained supple."'

'You're making it up!'

'I swear to God!'

Their laughter drew hostile glances and, gazing round apologetically, Clement caught sight of Stick talking to an older woman with a baby.

'That's odd.'

'What?'

'Stick. The young chap with the hair three tables away. I knew he had a son but not a baby.'

'Why should you? Does he tell you everything?'

'Pretty much, or so I thought.'

'Should I be worried?'

'About Stick? Good lord, no! Not at all. He's modelling for my Crucifix-ion. I told you about the governor's commission?'

'You said he'd asked, yes.'

'I was... I am petrified. But it's too good an opportunity to miss. A chance to shape the image specifically to my fellow prisoners. I have an idea, which I'm not telling anyone – '

'Not even me?'

'Not even Stick and he's the model! If it works, it'll make waves. Prison's left its mark on me. I'd like to repay the compliment.'

'And that guy's your Christ?'

'Among other things.'

'He couldn't be more different from Rafik.'

'But if you shared my beliefs – which, unless you drove here via Damascus, I know you don't – you'd see that as a plus. He's a sweet man, though he can be something of a handful. He's been in and out of institutions since he was twelve. He told me the other day that I didn't understand what it was like to be sent away from home so young. "Oh, don't I?" I said. "I was sent away at the age of eight." "What you done then?" he asked with a wide-eyed respect, as if I were one of the Kray brothers. I hadn't the heart to tell him that my only crime was to have been born into a fee-paying family.'

'Two cultures.'

'I'm afraid it's more like one and a half. But he really wants to pick himself up and do his best for his son – and I suppose for his baby. He showed me a letter he'd written to his wife who, I must admit, I'd pictured as somewhat younger. He asked me to check the spelling, which was a joke. He prayed for his son "to be kept safe mentally and fiscaly". There was only one *l*, but I was amazed that he knew the word at all.'

'Are you sure it wasn't *physically*?'

'What? Oh shit!'

'Don't worry. You may be right. We'd all like to protect our loved ones from the long reach of the Revenue.'

'I'm so stupid. Not his bad spelling but my twisted values.'

For all Mike's attempts to cheer him, Clement's self-reproach cast a chill on the rest of the visit. He vowed to make up for his error when Stick modelled for him the next day, but his resolve was sorely tested when he walked down the landing to find him cowering from a small crowd which stood hooting at his newly bald head. His initial shock at seeing how the boyish face had been hardened turned to fury at Stick's lack of consideration for the painting. Before he had a chance to remonstrate, Stick ran up and grabbed his T-shirt.

'Sir, sir,' he appealed, to Clement's dismay and the crowd's derision. 'You'll say you told me to do it for the picture! Promise us you will, please!'

'But I didn't. Quite the opposite. Whatever were you thinking?'

'He thinks with his arse!'

'Makes a change from what he usually does with it.'

Stick's cell-mate explained that he was in trouble with the authorities since, having shaved his head without permission, he no longer matched his photograph on the prison computer. His anger melting, Clement offered to do what he could, although he held out little hope given that many of the officers were opposed to the painting itself. Stick took heart, displaying a touching faith in the power of an Oxford accent, and started to sneer at the 'losers' who were off to the workshops while he earned a higher rate for standing still.

'I'm gonna be famous. Have my picture in all the papers.'

'Yeah. Under the headline *Vicious Thug*.'

'No. *Reward For Lost Pet*.'

'Reward for putting him down, more like.'

'You painting him bare-arsed then? Full brooch and earrings?'

'Certainly not.' His decision that the crucified figures would be wearing prison uniform had been taken long before the governor's red-faced request that "perhaps there shouldn't be any nudity?"'

'Thank Christ for that!'

'No point anyway. Not with Stick. Nothing there.'

'What about my kid? How do you make him out then, Clever Clogs?'

'Don't push it, son!'

'You have two children,' Clement interjected rapidly. 'I saw you with a baby in the visiting room.'

'That ain't his.'

'Tis too!'

'It ain't his baby, it's his stash.'

'Say hello to Charlie.'

'Charlie seemed very well-behaved,' Clement said, baffled by the burst of mocking laughter.

'You should have seen what was in his nappy. Gets right up your nose, don't it, Stick?'

'Leave it out!'

'Smell all that lovely white shit.'

'Oh I see!' Clement finally picked up the insinuation, understanding the reason for both Stick's agitation and his haircut. He was awestruck at his ingenuity in finding the one hiding place that even the most zealous officer wouldn't search. As they were led down to the art room, he thought of ways to incorporate Stick's new image into his central figure, the nicks and cuts on his scalp becoming the scars from a latter-day crown of thorns.

He entered the room, setting up the easel while Officer Kirkbride unlocked the supply cupboard and Stick stared vacantly out of the window, finding even the vista of matchbox houses preferable to work. The officer went out, leaving Clement to study the canvas on which the broad outline of three crucified figures was taking shape. The responsibility was daunting. In the cheerless prison chapel, the picture would be the unique focus of attention. By embodying the link between the two thieves and Christ, he would give hope to all the thieves – and thugs, frauds, rapists and murderers – in the congregation. He was taking a risk in using Stick, not least in view of his congenital inability to keep still. Nevertheless, after twenty years of choosing models, he had learnt to trust his instincts. So, after dragging him away from the window and reinstating him in the correct pose, he started to paint. He quickly found, however, that the music he had put on to keep him occupied was too distracting. Exasperated by the snapping fingers and tapping feet, he switched it off, diverting Stick's complaints by inviting him to tell him about his son.

'I don't even know his name.'

'Melvyn,' Stick said proudly. 'Me and Kath wanted to give him a start in life.' He laughed. 'He's a case. The other day we was talking. He said to me, "Shake the phone, Dad. Are you shaking the phone?" "Yes," I said, shit-scared my card was gonna run out. "Me too," he said, "it's like we're shaking hands." An he's only six.' His face clouded. 'I remember the first ever time I picked him out of his cot. I swore I'd always be there for him. Now look at me! What good am I to him in here?'

'You won't be inside for ever.'

'Seven years. Seven poxy years. An he'll be...'

'Thirteen,' Clement said, kicking himself for his impatience. 'Just when he needs you most.'

'I got nothing off of him on Father's Day. That's the hardest day of the year in here.'

'It wasn't easy for me either.'

'Do you have kids then? I thought you was bent.'

'No, I don't,' Clement said wincing, 'but I had a father.'

'Yeah, but you topped him cos he had Old Timers.'

'I suppose that's one way of putting it.'

'What if they turn Melvyn against me – Kath's mum and dad – and he won't let me go to his wedding, or take him down the pub when he gets his driving test?'

'Why expect the worst? What about your faith? Doesn't that help?'

'Course. I give my problems to God to solve them and He does. Trouble is I'm always grabbing them back again. What a useless piece of shit!'

'Wait till the painting's finished. You'll see yourself in a new light.'

'Yeah, as a frigging thief!'

'Not only.'

'What d'you mean?'

'You'll see later. Don't move! Hold that pose!'

'Why can't I see it now?'

'Because that's how I work. I'm superstitious. Besides we agreed.'

'But it's my face you're using!'

'Trust me, there's nothing to get worked up about.'

'Officer Willis said I had to watch out, that you painted a picture for Westminster Abbey and gave the Lord Jesus a hard-on.'

'That's a filthy lie!'

'He said it was a filthy picture... It's my face; I have a right to see what you're doing!' Too fast for Clement to stop him, Stick strode over and stared at the painting. 'Fucking hell, it's me three times!'

'Christ and the two thieves, yes.'

'Why? Couldn't you get no other mug to stand here then?'

'Quite the opposite; you've seen how jealous the others are of you. I've painted it like this because it's what I want to say. Not just that Christ is in us, but that we are all Christ.'

'You mean, like lots of gods like?'

'No, like lots of bits of the same God. We aren't separate from Him. How can we be when He created us out of Himself? Think about it: what else was there?'

'The Garden of Eden?'

'Long before that. Long before space, long even before nothingness. There was no blank canvas, no paint, just God. We are all of us – and now I am speaking literally – made of God's love.'

'What about the geezers in the nick?'

'Love – God's love – can't be divided. It's in us all.'

'What about the nonces on the rule?'

'Them too.'

'No, they're sick bastards who are gonna burn in Hell!'

'There is no Hell. Can't you see that it's just being held up to frighten you? Like locking little kids in the coal shed, except that now they're locked in there forever and the coals are burning hot.'

'Officer Willis said you'd try to mess with my head.'

'He's a fine one to talk...! No, I tell a lie – '

'Yeah, at last you admit it!'

'There is a Hell. Of course there is. But, in His eternal torment on the Cross, Christ is the only one in it.'

'Shut it, can't you? What are you trying to do to me?' Clement despaired of his ineptitude in the face of Stick's distress. 'You said I was gonna be one of the thieves. I wanted to be the good one. I thought... I hoped that, like that, like, I could get into Heaven, even though I'd done wrong.'

'And you will!'

'You never said I'd be both of them.'

'I was afraid you might be confused.'

'I am bloody confused!'

'That's because the painting isn't finished. If we can only get back to work, you'll see.'

'And you never said anything about how I'd be the Lord Jesus.'

'You didn't ask.'

'I never thought anyone could be so thick... When I was at nursery school, we did a Christmas play. I was going to be a shepherd but I did summet wrong and the teacher changed me into one of Herod's soldiers.'

'That was twenty years ago.'

'I've done much, much worse since then. If I wasn't fit to be a shepherd, I'm certainly not fit to be the Lord Jesus!'

'Of course you are. That's what I've been trying to explain. Christ took your flesh, like he took mine, to show once and for all that we are fit.'

'You're doing my head in!' Stick grabbed the brush jar, slammed it against the table, broke it and brandished a shard. Clement watched aghast at the way Stick's natural volatility had been heightened by the cocaine. Nothing in his life, not even the Roxborough protest, had prepared him for such unprovoked violence.

'Come on, Stick. This isn't you,' he said, trying to calm him.

'What do you know about me? Nothing. Think you know everything, you do!'

'Not at all,' Clement said, as the blood coursed through his veins. 'I want to know more. Much more. Tell me about Melvyn.' He aimed to keep Stick talking until his anger burnt itself out.

'Fuck off! I'm not telling you nothing. You'll just use it against me.'

As Stick waved the glass in the air, it was clear that he was excited, even aroused, by his own potency. Clement feared that it would take too long to bring him down. His best hope was to make a quick dash for the door. All other concerns vanished, however, when Stick moved dangerously close to the painting.

'Take care!' he shouted.

'What?'

'The picture. You'll damage the picture!'

Heedless of his own safety, Clement thrust forward, ready to grapple with Stick to protect the painting.

'Come on then if you think you can take me!' Stick taunted. 'You think you're hard, do you?' he asked, wielding the glass wildly. Clement grabbed his arm, but Stick was too fast for him and slashed his face. Clement felt a searing pain and a gush of warmth on his cheek. He heard a scream, but found to his surprise that it wasn't his. He looked up and saw, first, that Stick had slit his wrist and, then, that the blood had splattered the canvas. Aghast at the confusion of suffering, he ran to the door and jammed his hand on the bell.

5

Six months into his sentence, with his face newly stitched and bandaged, Clement was moved to the Vulnerable Prisoners Unit. The governor insisted that it was for his own protection, admitting when pressed that he couldn't risk further injury to someone with such a high public profile. Dismissing Clement's protests, he explained that the VPU not only housed sex-offenders but drug dealers and their defaulting clients, former policemen and informers, travellers and victims of intimidation. 'That makes me feel much better, sir,' Clement said, with an irony the governor ignored. Yet, for all the horror of his position, Clement refused to be cast down; there was a reason for his suffering this latest ignominy, which in time would become clear.

With keys rattling more ominously than ever, Officer Henshaw unlocked the doors, first of the VPU and then of Clement's cell which, from the feral smell, seemed to have been harbouring a pack of wild cats. Learning that his cell-mate was on a 'PIG course', Clement seized the opportunity to explore. A cursory glance at the photographs, prayer shawl and stack of Hebrew books showed that this cell-mate was not only the first Jew he had encountered in prison but a scholar. Hoping for a lively exchange of views, he was taken aback when the door opened on a heavily built, heavily bearded man with a Chassid's fringes poking out of his tracksuit top. With a pang of guilt, as much for his alarm as for his prying, he held out a hand and introduced himself.

'Clement Granville.'

'The painter?'

'You know my work?'

'I know your story: how a prisoner stabbed you when you forced him to take up an obscene pose.'

'That's nonsense!'

'It's no concern of mine. You Gentiles fight it out amongst yourselves! I have no interest in your religion or your art.'

Clement felt deflated. 'You haven't told me your name.'

'No. I remember the way it used to sound. Shlomo Marcus. There, that's the last time you'll hear it. At least from me.'

Shlomo set about dividing the space. Unlike Clement's previous cell-mates, he was scrupulously fair, resolving any imbalance in Clement's favour and even offering to vacate the top bunk. Watching him settle down to study, Clement speculated on both his crime and the cause of his segregation, convinced that he was no sex offender, but either a racketeering landlord who had found himself locked up among his former tenants, or else the victim of militant Muslims.

The sight of Shlomo put him in mind of his sister who, despite being the one member of his immediate family yet to visit him, had been a diligent correspondent, her letters an odd mixture of media gossip and the humdrum details of Lubavitch life. Her last had described how she and Zvi had spent a week living in a homemade hut in the garden for the festival of Sukkot. It had drizzled non-stop through the makeshift roof, but she claimed not to have cared since it was a link with the exiled Jews in the desert. Although he detected an element of bravado in her account, he had no doubts of its sincerity. He had finally accepted that Susannah would never be coming back and Shoshanna was here to stay. Her letters were a way both to remind him of it and to show that she wanted him to remain part of her life.

It suddenly struck him that this might be the reason for which he had been searching. Had God placed him with Shlomo in order to deepen his understanding of his sister's faith? He would have to tread carefully, since it was evident that his cell-mate would not invite intimacy. So, instead of engaging him in conversation, he picked up his newspaper, but his throbbing cheek made reading impossible and he gazed wistfully at the TV, weighing his need for distraction against Shlomo's for quiet. When the boredom grew too intense, he switched on the set, promising to keep the sound down. 'No need,' Shlomo said coldly, 'after five years at a yeshiva, I'm impervious to noise.' Flicking through a treasure hunt, horse racing and children's cartoons, Clement opted for a chat show hosted by a former model, whose hourglass figure was running rapidly out of time. Appalled at her fatuousness, he seized on the chance to escape for tea. His hope that Shlomo would introduce him to the Unit was dashed when, barely looking up from his book, he announced that his food would be sent up later. So he made his own way to the hatch where a queue had already formed.

To his delight, he spotted Joe and walked over to him but, instead of a hug or even a welcoming smile, he gave him a curt nod and stared at his tray. Chastened, he took his place at the end of the line. Watching Joe pick up his food and return to his cell without a single backward glance, he struggled to account for his transformation, wondering if he had been so traumatised by life on the Unit that he believed any friendship, and above all one with a gay man, must be tainted, or else if he had become so mistrustful that he saw every new arrival as a threat.

Mourning the loss of a kindred spirit, he was doubly grateful for the cordial greeting of a plump West Indian, who appeared to have spent his entire canteen allowance on peroxide. 'I'm Dusty,' he said, 'as in Springfield.'

'Pleased to meet you. I'm Clement.' As he held out his hand, he was intercepted by a pug-nosed Scotsman with LOVE and HAT inked on his knuckles.

'Take care! Yer don't want to mix with that nonce!'

'Oh fuck off, Ron, you cripple!' Dusty pranced around, twiddling his little finger in mockery of Ron's missing one, before shaking his box of breakfast cereal in his face. 'Mm, paedo pops,' he said, with a defiance which in ordinary circumstances might have earned Clement's respect but here made him feel sick.

He collected his food and hurried back to the cell but was unable to bring himself to eat. Ten minutes later, Shlomo went out and returned with two plastic cartons.

'It's sent in from a kosher supplier in Oxford,' he said. 'For three weeks the governor refused to allow it. So I ate nothing, even in the infirmary. They asked if I was on hunger strike. "Yes," I said, "for clean food".'

Next morning Shlomo went off to his course, leaving the cell to Clement. Just as he was making out a request to go to the library, Officer Henshaw brought a package from the governor, containing the first three of Trollope's *Barchester Chronicles*. Clement appreciated the gesture more than the novels which, however sympathetically chosen, were redolent of Roxborough and Major Deedes. He nevertheless turned to *The Warden*, losing himself so completely in the intrigues of the cathedral town that he almost forgot to fetch his lunch and, still more remarkably, two hours later to prepare for a visit from his mother and Mike.

He had considered putting them off until the wound healed, but he had been afraid that that would alarm them more. So he sauntered jauntily into the hall in a bid to defuse the shock and spent much of the first half hour trying to put a brave face on the bandaged one. He promised that he would be safe on the Unit, listing the former policemen, informers and gypsies among his fellows. His mother was reassured, especially by the policemen, whom she seemed to regard as there for his personal protection, but Mike's grim features showed that he had identified the chief omission.

'The thing that upsets me most is the painting,' Clement said.

'Did he attack that too?' his mother asked.

'No, but he might as well have done. I conceived it around him. I can't just slot in someone else.'

'He looked so harmless with that baby on his knee!' Mike said.

'It was my fault as much as his. I should have known that for someone like Stick an idea can be as painful as a fist.'

'You're dealing with it admirably, darling,' his mother said. 'I'm so proud of you.'

'Well he'd better keep out of my way,' Mike said darkly.

'Now, I want to hear all the gossip,' Clement said, anxious to lift the mood.

'I've racked my brains to think of some,' Mike said, 'but I've been up to my eyes, what with the beginning of term and the extra admin. On top of that I spend every spare minute with Brian and Blossom filling in grant applications for next year's retreat.'

'Wales again?'

'Devon. A converted rectory, no less. My next job is to stop Blossom booking a signer before we know if we're taking anyone deaf.'

'It's good to see some things don't change,' Clement said. 'How about you, Ma?'

'Oh, not much has changed here either. Still trying to adjust to life without your father. You expect the nights to be hard, but they're nothing compared to the mornings. You've turned back the clock... you've returned to the people you loved, then you wake up to a world of loss.' Clement tightened his grip on her hand. 'But I must be mad! You don't want to hear all this.'

'Of course I do.'

'Well I don't want you to. And I'm not on my own, so you needn't worry. My friends have all been wonderful. Though if I'm invited to any more kitchen suppers where "It'll be so much cosier, just the three of us," I swear I shall scream. After a lifetime of making my own rules, I refuse to be turned into a social solecism.'

'You could never be that,' Clement said tenderly.

'Shoshanna's been very attentive. The Sabbath makes weekends difficult, but she drives down every other Sunday.'

'What about Karen? Still the wild girl in the woods?'

'Believe it or not, she's turned up trumps. Nothing's ever too much trouble for her. It's a joy to see how she's finally growing up. I give much of the credit to her new boyfriend.'

'The busker?' Clement asked, horrified by the hint of Aunt Helena creeping into his voice.

'He's a very mature young man. Battling to save the planet. Especially the dolphins. He recently organised a die-in at Tesco.'

'A what?'

'I'm not quite sure what it entailed, apart from Karen, dressed as a tuna, chaining herself to the fresh-fish counter.'

Returning to his cell in the straggling line of VPU prisoners, Clement received a graphic illustration of his new status in the hisses, curses and shouts of 'Beasties!', 'Wankers!' and 'Nonces!' that reached him from the other wings. The basic human need for someone to love, as manifest in Wells and Beckley, had been replaced by an equivalent one for someone to loathe. Their righteous indignation might have carried more weight had it not been coupled with threats of 'I'm gonna fuck your missus up the arse' and 'I'm getting out next week to rape your mother'. He wanted to break ranks and assure the hecklers that his presence there was an anomaly, that he was an Ordinary Decent Criminal just like them, but he knew that, if his faith were to be anything more than a *Barchester* convention, he had to stick with the group and accept their stigma as his own.

The isolation of the Unit meant that time passed even more slowly than elsewhere in the prison. Like most of his fellows, Shlomo spent the day on various rehabilitation courses, leaving Clement in the company of the Proudies, the Pallisers, Lord Peter Wimsey and other handpicked characters from the governor's shelves. Although he was loath to admit it, the 'paedo pops' incident had discouraged him from fraternising. Nevertheless, when Shlomo's evening prayers, albeit quieter than Dwayne's 'sounds' and less sinister than Parker's Stanley knife, became oppressive, he escaped to Association. He was immediately accosted by George, the taciturn traveller who shared Joe's cell.

'Joe's tried to top himself!'

'What?'

'He's shit-scared of the Muslims.'

'But not in here! I thought he was safe.'

'You're safe nowhere. The priest thingummy... you know, the bomber?'

'The imam.'

'That's your man. He put a fatima on him.'

'A what?'

'A fatima. So all the other Muslims would bump him off on account of how he snitched to the governor.'

'But there aren't any Muslims on the Unit.'

'There is now. That new man, Mehmet. Twoed up with Dusty.'

'I haven't met him.'

'You don't want to, mate. Beast!' George spat. 'All last night Joe yacked on about how he'd been put here, special, to do the job. Then, this dinner, when I come back from my Assertiveness Course, I found him on the floor, bleeding. Cut both his wrists.'

'So is he all right? Where is he?'

'In the hospital. But they won't keep him long. He'd be better off ghosted.'

'Dead?'

'No, mate! Sent to another nick. Course news travels quick. My cousin – '

'I'm sorry, I have to go. Thanks for letting me know.'

'Remember what I say; you're safe nowhere. I'm telling you this because you're a gentleman and not a beast.'

Shrinking from the compliment, Clement returned to the cell where, with less regard for Shlomo's reading than for his prayers, he relayed the conversation, meeting with a marked lack of sympathy.

'I already heard. It's just attention-seeking. He slit across his veins when, as everyone knows, if you're serious, you slice down.'

'Really?' Clement asked, instantly disproving Shlomo's claim.

'Not that I blame him. How else can he escape from all those maniacs?'

'There are fanatics in every religion,' Clement said pointedly. 'People who take the letter for the law.'

'I hear what you're saying. But there's one big difference that you and all your six-of-one-and-half-a-dozen-of-the-other friends seem intent on ignoring... one very big difference. Torah permits a Jew to stone anyone who stops him from practising his faith. The Quran instructs the Muslims to make war on the infidels who live around them. Even if they're decent, honourable, fair-playing infidels like you. And no matter how hard you try to dissuade them, there'll always be Muslims ready to obey.'

As Shlomo went back to his books, Clement switched on the news which, with its consecutive reports of atrocities in Iraq, Afghanistan and the West Bank, made the religious conflicts appear more intractable than ever. Convinced that the only hope lay in dialogue, he resolved to make a start in his own cell.

'May I ask what you did?'

'What?' Shlomo asked sharply.

'Your job? Before you came here.'

'Oh, I see. I was a *shochet*, a ritual slaughterer. No doubt you think that's barbaric.'

'I'll admit I'm a typical Englishman when it comes to a love of animals.'

'Yes, of course. The English speak of butchery as if it means violence or clumsiness. You just have to read the crime reports. "He butchered her," in great big letters. To a Jew that would mean he killed her with the utmost delicacy, with a blade that was razor sharp and brought instant death.'

'It's a fine distinction.'

'It's far more than that. It shows respect both to the animal and to God. Torah says: "Be holy people to me and don't eat *treif*."'

'What?'

'Anything that's not kosher. I'm proud of the part I've played in upholding that commandment.'

Shlomo climbed off his bunk and used the lavatory, which Clement might have taken as a diversionary tactic had not the sounds emerging from behind the curtain betrayed a genuine need. He was keen to resume the conversation but Shlomo, as determined to protect himself from forbidden thoughts as from forbidden foods, rebuffed his attempts both for the rest of the evening and over subsequent weeks.

October passed into November, and the chill in the cell intensified. With Shlomo remaining aloof, although the frequency of his prayers showed him to be in regular contact with God, Clement sought to make sense of his many inconsistencies: from his aversion to taking a shower, which seemed particularly perverse given Shoshanna's account of Zvi's daily attendance at the mikvah, to the lack of any letters or visits from members of his tight-knit community. The suspicions about the nature of his crime, which had been aroused on learning that the PIG course he attended each day stood for the Price of Instant Gratification, were confirmed when, one Association, Ron handed him a newspaper report of his trial for abusing his ten-year-old son.

Clement read it with growing revulsion, feeling as if the words were crawling over his skin. He crumpled the paper into a ball and flung it into a corner; then, still alert to its noxious effect, he picked it up, tore it into strips and flushed them down the lavatory, where they stuck to the bottom of the bowl. Although the offence remained the same whether it were his own son or somebody else's, the betrayal of trust was far worse. Two contrasting images flashed through Clement's mind. The first was of his father patiently teaching Mark and himself to fish one summer at Beckley. The second was of Shlomo, hefty, saturnine Shlomo, bearing down on a quaking ten-year-old boy... He rushed to the basin, sure that he was about to vomit, but all that emerged was a string of phlegm. He returned to his bunk and, lying very still, tried to summon up some sympathy for Shlomo's plight: that of a learned man laid low, less by something within himself than by the exigencies of his culture; a man of powerful sexual needs who, forbidden to make love to his wife during the extended period of her menstruation, turned instead to his son, a boy who, in a very real sense, belonged to him, who was as much his flesh as his own penis and, arguably, not subject to as strong a taboo.

After all, the Torah, in which his faith was absolute, commanded a man with a stubborn and a rebellious son to take him to the elders of the city to be stoned to death: a passage from Deuteronomy which even the most literal-minded chose to gloss over. Like an abusive priest he had not only relied on fear to buy silence but believed he was acting on the authority invested in him by God.

Clement's abhorrence of paedophilia – he struggled to substitute sin for sinner – had been coloured by Newsom's account of his stepfather, who had married his mother in order to gain access to him. Even so, he refused to subscribe to a tabloid agenda. He could not dispel the suspicion that paedophiles were paying the price for the newfound acceptance of gay men. The language used by the judge who had sentenced Oscar Wilde was little different from that of a *Daily Mail* editorial on 'the evils of internet grooming'. While he knew full well that the one was consensual and the other coercive, he was less sure that the general public, let alone their moral guardians, had drawn such a clear distinction. They needed an outlet for their outrage, which, as ever, was compounded by guilt. The demonisation of paedophiles was an admission, however tacit, of the way that society at large was abusing children, with many parents, either from lack of time and energy or from simple disinclination, dumping them in front of television and computer screens, where they were exposed to unsuitable material or, worse, targeted by unscrupulous men.

Exhausted by the strain of reserving judgement, Clement left the cell one evening for Association. Standing in line at the pay phone behind a bullion-robber whose appearance on *Crimewatch* had made him a local celebrity, he found himself invited to join a poker game. 'Thanks but no thanks,' he said, aware that his emotions were too transparent even for bridge.

'Suit yourself,' said a man who was rumoured to have used his daughter as a stake.

Clement waited his turn, squirming as he listened to the robber's marital endearments. Perplexed by his wish to broadcast them to the entire landing, he decided that it was a deliberate attempt to assert his normality, an impulse he recognised in himself. The revelation of Shlomo's crime had plunged him into despair. He had almost half his sentence still to serve and was no longer sure that he could endure it. He was desperate to talk to Mike, and no sooner had the man put down the phone than he rushed to grab it. The sound of the familiar voice reassured him although, conscious of the crowd of eavesdroppers, he could only hint at his pain.

After talking to Mike, he felt less inclined than ever to chat to his fellow prisoners, so he sat flipping idly through a boat-building magazine as if in a doctor's waiting room. He looked up to see Dusty, who had returned to the Unit in a neck-brace after a violent clash with Ron on the Anger Management Course.

'So it was nothing serious?' he asked.

'Don't you believe it! If you had open-heart surgery here, they'd have you back in your pad the next day. All the doc asked was was I allergic to anything. "Yes," I said, "fists".' Dusty giggled, then grimaced at the pain. 'Here,' he said, 'a sweet for a sweetie.' As Clement held out his hand to accept, he pictured Dusty offering the bag to a child.

'Better not. Bad for my teeth.'

'Pity.' He placed one in his mouth and sucked lubriciously. 'Any time you change your mind, just knock on my door.'

Seething with resentment that, through no fault of his own, he had been snatched away from the ODCs on his former wing and thrown into this snake pit, Clement asked for a transfer. Although he was confident that he faced no threat either from Stick, whose psychosis had been fuelled by the drugs, or from anyone else, the governor remained obdurate, informing him five days before Christmas that his request had been turned down.

'But I reiterate my hope that you'll go back to the painting.'

'I appreciate that, sir,' Clement replied, 'but it's quite impossible without my original model. To start again with somebody else wouldn't just pose practical problems, it would undermine everything I'm trying to say. I'd be upholding the distinction both between the penitent and impenitent thieves and between them and Christ.'

'Yes, yes,' the governor said irritably, 'let's not get bogged down in metaphysics. In view of your refusal – somewhat precious to my mind – to accept a substitute, I've canvassed the officers and drug counsellors, all of whom have spoken of Dawson's progress. On their recommendation, I'm prepared to let you resume work with him.'

Clement wondered whether, having refused the transfer, the governor felt the need to make a concession or whether his change of heart were a direct result of the pressure that Mike had promised to bring to bear. He smiled at the thought of the governor's office submerged in sacks of protest letters.

'I knew you'd be pleased,' the governor said, catching him unawares.

'And Stick... Dawson, has he agreed to come back?' Clement asked, finding to his surprise that he was almost as anxious to be reconciled with his model as to return to his painting.

'So I'm given to understand. No doubt pecuniary considerations have played their part. My one stipulation is that there should be an officer in the room with you at all times.'

Clement had not anticipated that the first of these would be Willis, who appeared to have volunteered in a bid to cause them all, himself included, maximum discomfort. After a jibe about Clement's being more at home 'on the rule', he sat beneath the window, leaving Clement to face Stick, who was standing by the wall.

'You've grown your hair,' he said.

'Not really. It grew itself. I see you got a scar.'

'Yes, it's faded, but I don't expect it'll ever completely disappear.'

'It was me as did that to you!'

'My boyfriend thinks it's fetching. After all, lines are supposed to give a face character.'

Stick chuckled. 'Half the time I can't make out what you're saying. But I know it's clever. Honest!'

'You're very kind.'

'Don't make me laugh! It's cos of me that you're in with them beasties.'

'No one's a beast, Stick. They're men like you and I.'

'I'm real sorry. I've prayed and prayed to say sorry, haven't I, sir?'

'I'm reading, lad,' Willis said unconvincingly.

'I'm such a worthless piece of shit.'

'If you say that again, I won't begin work on the painting.'

'Did somebody mention *work*?' Willis asked, looking up. 'Surprise surprise! I thought I'd dozed off and woken up at a meeting of the Mothers' Union.'

Refusing to be provoked, Clement studied the canvas while Stick kept resolutely to the far side of the easel. He had banished any scruples about posing as Christ, relishing the prospect of the triple portrait: 'Like when you have your photo taken in a machine!' He quickly grew bored with the delay. 'Same as when you left it, is it?'

'I'm afraid so. You may even have done me a favour by enabling me to get some distance.'

'Do you want us to stand farther off?'

'What? No, not a step. I should have known what to expect. Look at Titian.'

'You what?'

'One of the greatest painters of all time. The story goes that he was totally happy with a finished picture, only to look at it six months later and find, in his own phrase, that it might have been painted by his worst enemy.'

'Who was that then?'

'What?' A glance at the eager face was enough to erase all suspicion of mockery. 'Himself.'

After struggling to place Stick in his former pose, he tentatively set to work.

'You aren't seriously planning to paint him like that?' Willis asked.

'Is there a problem?' Clement replied, puzzled.

'Our Lord in prison uniform!'

'That's right, boss,' Stick broke in. 'It's like saying being in the nick is like being crucified.' Willis shook his head in disbelief.

'Or even,' Clement added gently, 'that being in prison is still being with Christ.'

'I warned the governor it would be blasphemous.'

'I'm sure he appreciated your input, sir.'

'Pardon?'

'But there's another way you can help. I've decided to include a fourth figure of the Centurion,' he said disingenuously. 'I'd like to model him on an officer.'

'You use me or any other member of staff in any way, shape or form, laddie, and your picture will be firewood – and you'll be toast!'

Clement had barely recovered his stride when he was forced to break off for Christmas. The holiday was particularly poignant in prison, where the cooked breakfast and the goody bag and the taped carols blasting out from the canteen felt more like parodies than gestures of goodwill. Faced with the muted festivities, Clement was glad to be sharing a cell with someone for whom it was just another Thursday. He went to chapel, ate his turkey twizzlers and watched seasonal specials on TV, but declined to put up even a handful of his stack of cards. While telling himself that it was a courtesy to Shlomo, he recognised that it was the best defence against despair. There was nothing more calculated to expose the pretence of normality than the newspaper chain across his neighbour's door.

His first visit of the New Year was also his first from Shoshanna. In a recent letter, she had expressed the desire to see him along with concern about her reception. Having assured her of its warmth, he found himself shaking all the way to the hall and was grateful for the conciliatory presence of Carla, who greeted him at the table with her usual broad smile.

'Great scar,' she said, tracing it with her finger. 'Super sexy.'

'What do you think?' he asked Shoshanna who stood up, making no move or comment. 'Any advance on *sexy*?'

'You look well,' she said, kissing him rapidly. 'I was afraid that... you know, the stress and the diet would damage your cells.'

'Quite the reverse. I had a test at the end of November. Curiously, it seems that all my counts have gone up, while my viral load is still undetectable. Of course we can't discount the idea that the authorities are trying to lure me into a state of dangerous complacency.'

'Of course we can,' Carla said. 'You look better than I've seen you in years.'

'How's Zvi?' he asked Shoshanna.

'He's well... wonderful. Frantically busy at work and in the community. He's away this weekend with our youth group.'

'He said to send you his best, didn't he?' Carla nudged her.

'Yes, of course.'

'My cell-mate's one of your lot,' he said, uncertain if he wanted to establish the link or punish the lie.

'A Jew?'

'A Lubavitch.'

'Is that an accusation?'

'Not at all. If it were, I'd tell you what he did.'

'I know what he did.'

'You do?'

'He's the son-in-law of a friend, who owned the house where I studied the Kabbalah.'

'Small world!'

'But that's not why I know the story. The reason is that it's so rare... so rare and so shocking. How many Christian child molesters are there in here?' she asked, in a voice so shrill that she might have been addressing the entire hall.

Squirming in his seat, Clement gave thanks for Carla's intervention.

'Listen, both of you, I have news!'

'A man?' he asked.

'I wish! No, I've booked to go in May on a purification practice to India and Nepal.'

'Brilliant,' he said, muffling his disappointment. 'You deserve a holiday.'

'It'll be far more than that. We visit several of our holiest sites, including Bodh Gaya and the Deer Park of Sarnath.'

'I'll rephrase that: you deserve a pilgrimage.'

'Mike's promised to look after Pearl Bailey.'

'That's great.' For all his boyfriend's unfulfilled love of cats, Clement wondered if he would have offered so freely if Carla had been travelling to Santiago de Compostela.

'Since we're swapping news, here's mine,' Shoshanna said. 'I'm selling the agency.'

'You're not?' Clement asked. 'To do what? Stay at home and keep house for Zvi?'

'And his child. I'm pregnant.'

Clement gazed at her and, for the first time since his sentence, his eyes filled with tears. 'That's fantastic. Truly! I'm so happy for you, Nanna. How long?'

'Three months.'

'Then the baby's due in June? The same month as my release. We'll have a double celebration... That's if you want.'

'That's why I'm here. Never in a million years did I mean this to happen. I still believe what you did was very wrong. But I know that you had your reasons.'

'Thank you... It's strange. I always imagined prison life would be utterly alien but, in many respects, it's no different from how it is "on the out", except that you see things from an oblique angle. I sometimes wonder if I'll ever be able to look at them squarely again.'

'Of course you will,' Shoshanna said. 'You said yourself you'll be released in a few months. Think June.'

'Right now it's hard enough to think January. Next Tuesday will be a year since Pa's funeral.'

Shoshanna's hand instinctively reached to her stomach. 'I know. I went down to the crypt with Ma when I was in Beckley last weekend. She was so thrilled to see the colours on Pa's coffin. You're a wonderful painter, Clem. You have a very special gift.'

'Well I'm back at work on my Crucifixion. They're letting me use my old model.'

'The madman who gave you that scar?'

'The same.'

'You never give up, do you?'

'I hope not. Learn, yes; change, yes; give up, no.'

The glow of the visit faded when Clement returned to a freezing cell. Shlomo explained that the duty officer had forgotten the code for the Unit heating.

'Can't he ask someone?'

'I suspect that he wanted to forget.'

'That's outrageous!'

'It'll pass. Last winter it happened several times. I had to wear socks on my hands and, look, I still have all my fingers.'

'We should speak to our lawyers.'

'It'd only make things worse. Turn on your television. Tell me about your visit.'

'You want to talk?'

'If it helps take our minds off the cold. Was it your mother and your... friend?' Shlomo spoke the word as if he had a strong urge to clear his throat.

'No, my sister and my sister-in-law. My sister's a Lubavitch.'

'I know.'

'How?'

'You told me.'

'No, I didn't.'

'Then somebody else did. What does it matter?'

'It's because of my sister I'm here,' Clement said swiftly. 'She told the police I'd committed murder. Doubtless you share her belief that we should take the Bible literally?'

'How else should we take the Word of God? Torah was given to Moses on Mount Sinai.'

'Says who? Moses?'

'Are you an anti-Semite?'

'With a Jewish mother? I think not!'

'Then why are you so hostile?'

'Because I believe with all my heart that to place so much trust in a book – any book – is as dangerous as burning it. Books should stimulate debate, not stifle it. Think of the Muslims destroying the library of Alexandria – surely the greatest loss in the history of civilisation – because it held books that denied the truth of the Quran.'

'The mistake you make is to suppose that there's only one kind of truth. Torah has four: literal; subtextual; metaphoric; and kabbalistic. Not that that's any help to you since, with no knowledge of the language, you can't even hope to understand the first.'

'I don't dispute that, as a Hebrew speaker, you appreciate the nuances of the text better than me. But the Bible is far more than nuances. Won't you admit in turn that large parts of it have been superseded by science?'

'Such as?'

'Such as... almost everything.' Clement strove to curb his exasperation. 'But let's stick with the biggie. Genesis Chapter One.'

'You say that Torah is disproved by science. I say it starts from the opposite standpoint. Torah is concerned with cause and science with effect. Torah describes the purpose of the universe; science explains its nature. Torah's story of Creation begins in the infinite consciousness of God; Darwin's theory of evolution develops in the finite mind of man.'

'That's very elegantly put.' Clement mimed applause. 'But you can't get away from the crucial fact. Genesis speaks of the world being created in seven days. Now that may have a subtextual truth, and it may have a metaphoric one, and for all I know it may have a kabbalistic one, but it sure as hell doesn't have a literal one.'

'You forget two things. First, when Adam and Eve ate the apple, the whole nature of reality changed, so the seven days of Creation aren't the same as seven days now. Second (and here I'm happy to invoke science), time, as Einstein showed, is relative to the speed at which we move and the physical conditions around us. Although the variations in the speed at which men move remain small, those between God and man are boundless. So a day to God is very different from a day to us.'

As Shlomo returned to the Hebrew commentaries that were his constant study, Clement reflected on his arguments. It was heartening to hear him echo his own distinction between human and divine timescales, even if they disagreed on the cause. Whereas Shlomo located the split in the Garden of Eden, he located it at the moment of Creation, when God sacrificed a measure of His freedom to give us ours. It was not that mankind forfeited perfection by disobedience, but that God acknowledged that imperfection was the price of human existence. This had consequences way beyond biblical exegesis. Whatever bishops or rabbis or imams might say, moral relativism was not an indulgence or a sin, but a recognition that absolute truth was to be found only in God and that it was both futile and dangerous to demand perfection in a world which would always be at one remove from the infinite from which it derived.

Keen to honour his belief, he had a sudden urge to make a sketch of Shlomo. He stepped off the bunk, picked up his pad and pencil, and leant against the chest of drawers, from which slightly cramped position his cellmate's face emerged, literally and figuratively, out of the shadows.

'What are you doing?' Shlomo asked, both suspicious and shy.

'Drawing you. Do you mind? I'm thinking of making a picture of Lot and his daughters.'

'Wicked girls, who got their father drunk and then seduced him.'

'I see it rather differently. He was a tyrannical patriarch who refused to treat his children as autonomous beings. He even proposed to prostitute them to his fellow townsmen. So they took their revenge by leaving him with an unbearable burden of guilt.' He stopped short and gazed at Shlomo, who was struggling to interpret this new biblical subtext.

'So you know about me,' he said, after a long pause.

'Yes.'

'It's all lies, put about by my wife... my enemies.'

'Would you like to talk about it?'

'No.'

'I'm a stranger to you but not to grief.'

Shlomo stared at him in confusion. 'My son, my Daniel,' he said haltingly, 'was in an accident at school. Nothing serious – Blessed be the Lord God of the Universe! – but they took him to hospital. When they examined him, the doctors found other bruising. They questioned him. They had no right to do that without my consent! He didn't know what he was saying. There's so much filth around. Children pick it up.'

'I thought you were a closed community.'

'Not closed enough,' he said grimly. 'The doctors twisted his words to make it sound like he was accusing me. I would never hurt him. He's my son. I love him more than life.'

'Does he know that?'

'Of course he does.'

'But he never visits. You never ring.'

'It's better that he thinks I'm dead. It's better that they all think I'm dead.'

'All?'

'Leib and Malkie, my daughters.' Clement was struck by the incongruously small family. 'It's Daniel's birthday next week,' Shlomo said with a gulp. 'He'll be twelve. What sort of a man will he become with no father to guide him? How will the girls be safe without me to protect them?'

'Then speak to them. Speak to him.'

'And say what? How... No!'

'You might start by buying him a birthday present.'

'What do you suggest I find in here? Drugs?'

'Can't you ask a friend to buy something on your behalf?'

'You, you kill your father and have friends who write to you every day! I'm the victim of a smear campaign and all my friends vanish.'

'I could draw something.'

'What?'

'Do you have a photo of him?'

'Why?' Shlomo shrank, as from the threat of voodoo.

'I could make a sketch of him. Or better still his namesake! How about a comic strip version of the story of Daniel? I'm a dab hand at lions!'

'Why?' Shlomo asked in amazement. 'I can't pay you.'

'I thought Jews believed in *mitzvahs*.'

'So?'

'It's a chance for me to do one for you.'

After re-reading the Book of Daniel, Clement settled on a sequence of ten frames, focusing on the early episodes of Nebuchadnezzar's dream, the burning fiery furnace and Belshazzar's feast. He toyed with including Susanna and the Elders but decided that false charges of adultery were uninteresting to the average twelve-year-old and inappropriate to one who had been abused. He worked in pen-and-ink, which was not only best suited to his format but allowed him to avoid a tiresome trek to the office each time that his pencil needed sharpening. For all that Parker had been permitted his Stanley knife, the officers in the Unit were determined to maintain the blanket ban on blades.

Weeks passed and, to his surprise, he grew quite content. At first he worried that he might be becoming institutionalised, but he realised that, on the contrary, he had been given the means to escape. As he worked on the painting by day and the drawings by night, he found himself living increasingly inside his head. The prison bars were no more intrusive than the locks on the studio window. He relished the paradox of his double sentence. Just as a deadly virus had inspired him to produce his most vital pieces, so a spell in jail had taught him to be truly free.

He finished the comic strip at the end of March and handed it to Shlomo, who had resolutely refused to take an interest, as though preparing himself for the inevitable moment when Clement perceived that the drawings had value and kept them for himself.

'Are you showing them to me or giving them to me?'

'Giving, of course. I've said so all along.'

'Why?'

'I've told you, it's for your son. I only wish I could have made it in time for his birthday. See, his name on the cover. In the bubble from the lion's mouth. *To Daniel from Daddy.*'

'He calls me *Tateh.*'

'Oh hell! I can ink it out.'

'No don't. You might spoil it.' He studied each drawing in detail. 'This is too good for him.'

'He's your son!'

'I mean he won't realise what it's worth.'

'Its worth is what he gives it. No more, no less.'

Shlomo burst into tears, great heaving tears as emphatic as his snores. Clement hovered at the edge of the bunk, embarrassed by the older man's vulnerability. 'Careful, you don't smudge the ink!' he said, in a vain attempt at humour.

'I'm sorry. It's not fair. I shouldn't...'

'Of course you should.'

'Please don't pity me. I've no right to anyone's pity after what I did.'

'Except your own?'

Shlomo made no reply or, if he did, it was choked by weeping, but later, when they'd switched off the light, he seemed eager to build on their new-found rapport. 'May I ask you a personal question?'

'Whatever you like.'

'Were you never attracted to women?'

'As the man said, I experimented with heterosexuality when I was younger but it ended when they went back to their wives.'

'You seduced married men?'

'That was a joke!'

'But you have a faith?'

'Yes.'

'So how can you be what you are and be true to God?'

'I'd turn the question round and ask how anyone with a genuine understanding of God could find it a problem. We're wrong to think of body and spirit as separate. God gave us the flesh, and the flesh is a route to God. You believe in Genesis. Forgive me if I misquote, but there's a line in the Creation story: "And God breathed into man the breath of life and man became a living soul." What does that say to you? To me, it's very clear: that body and spirit are the same and both come from God. And, for once, science and religion are singing from the same hymn sheet. Just as Einstein showed that energy and matter are one, indeed that matter is simply superconcentrated energy, so Genesis shows that spirit and body are one, that body is simply superconcentrated spirit.'

'Then you think all sexuality is equally valid?'

'No, not all,' he said, with a pressing need to dissociate his sexuality from Shlomo's, 'but any that's truly loving: between people who enter into it freely: which is in no way exploitative or forced.'

'You mentioned that you have a friend.'

'I have a boyfriend, yes.'

'And you consider it to be the same as a marriage?'

'I do, yes. Though Mike would disagree. He says that our sexuality defines our general attitudes; I say that there are basic attitudes common to us all. You can compare it to the debate between isolationist and assimilationist Jews,' he said, too pleased with the analogy to worry whether it might cause offence.

'My wife and I have been married for twenty-five years. You wouldn't think it'd be possible to live with someone that long and still feel a stranger. I told myself that it was the difference between men and women. But it was the difference between me and her.'

'Every relationship involves some kind of compromise.'

'But not a lie... I married too young. I didn't know any women apart from my mother and my aunts and one sister, who was so much older that she might as well have been an aunt. I had six brothers. I was the last but one. Fine boys. Powerful men.' Clement felt his own pain bleeding into Shlomo's. 'Three of us slept in the same room. Almost on top of each other. But we were clean. You must believe me.'

'Of course! Please don't upset yourself.'

'I never touched one of them. I never even touched myself. First thing every morning when he came to wake us for *schul*, my father brought us a bowl of water to wash our hands, in case they'd accidentally touched somewhere shameful overnight. I can't speak for my brothers, but for me it would have had to have been by accident. Never by design.'

'All boys experiment.'

'All but one. Not with myself or with them. Though sometimes I might have wanted... You're the first person I've ever told, but what does it matter? In a world of shame, every confession is shameful.'

'Some might say the exact opposite.'

'We'd go to the mikvah together. They called us dirty Jews. But tell me, who else in Stamford Hill bathed every day? In my case, though, they were right. A clean skin but a putrid soul.' Shlomo's self-loathing threw light on his refusal to shower. 'I thought that, when I married, my feelings would change. My wife was a good and a beautiful woman. But, to me, she was like seaweed clinging to my legs... No! I tried to love her. But the more I tried, the harder it felt. One day I went to a newsagent's in Bethnal Green and bought a magazine... one with pictures... pictures of men. The shopkeeper was Bangladeshi. He gave me a look of such scorn. I wanted to shout: "If that's how you feel, don't sell it!" Then I realised it was me he was scorning, standing so conspicuous in my suit and *tallis*. I hurried back to the car with the magazine hot in my hand. I drove to Epping Forest where I sat in a lay-by, leafing through the pages, terrified that each flashing headlight was a police car sent to arrest me – '

'It's not illegal.'

'It was to me... Even so, I felt I was where I belonged. The only other time I've been so certain was when I stepped off the plane for the first time at Tel Aviv.'

'So what did you do?'

'Nothing. For years I did nothing. And then one day... one day I saw my son, my pure undefiled son...'

'Yes?' Clement said gently.

'No! No more. Nothing more. I should be dead.' Clement felt the bunks sway as Shlomo ground his head into the pillow. 'I don't expect you believe in the Devil.'

'How can I when I believe in God?'

'Then I'm truly doomed. You say that body and spirit are one. And I know you're trying to help me. But my one hope was that they were separate: that I could escape from my body and all it had done.'

'That's not to escape from sin but to plunge into it. I can't speak for Judaism, but there's a classic Christian distinction between Sin with a capital *s* and sins with a small one. Sin is a refusal to accept God's grace. For some of us that can be a refusal to accept the bodies into which God breathed His soul. After all, Christians believe that one man's body redeemed the world.'

'Do you?'

'As usual, I twist it round a little. Redeemed, no. Revitalised, yes. And I

wouldn't be so exclusive. Everyone's body has something of the same potential. Not to change the world, perhaps, but to change another person's life.
Suppose you make love to someone and give them a new sense of purpose or
of possibility, let alone fresh hope to someone who's in despair, wouldn't it be
uniquely restorative? Come to think of it, wouldn't it be a sort of redemption?'

'So you think making love can make you a better person?'

'I think that's what the words mean.' Clement waited for Shlomo to reply,
wondering if his silence indicated assent. Then, with a feeling of dread, he
watched as a hand slid down from the upper bunk. He slowly reached for it,
fighting his revulsion at the moistness of the palm, the hot, heavy flesh of a
man who had committed such a heinous crime.

'You did a *mitzvah* for me before.'

'Yes.'

'Do you think that you might do another now?'

Clement shuddered. All his instincts yelled 'no'. It was hard enough just
to hold his hand, the same hand that had pressed down on the helpless and
terrified boy. Nevertheless, to reject him would be to renounce his most precious beliefs: that Christ was to be found in us all and, aesthetic considerations aside, he might have modelled his Crucifixion on Shlomo.

'Do you?' Shlomo asked more urgently.

'Yes,' Clement said blenching, and he knew that he had never uttered a
more costly yet critical 'yes' in his life. He had no choice but to agree, being
bound by an obligation far greater than that of Mike's communal rota. It was
his chance to show Shlomo a sexuality that was neither brutal nor furtive; for
the first time he understood the concept of temple prostitutes. He explained
that the virus limited his freedom of action but, as Shlomo lumbered down
from the bunk, it was clear that his prime wish was to be held. Clement was
overpowered, initially by Shlomo's smell, then by his bulk, and finally by
his need. He felt that his own body was simply a terrain to be charted and
conquered. Shlomo's idea of masculine intimacy owed more to the wrestling
ring than to the fireside, with each plea to 'Relax!' or 'Go slower!' serving to
inflame him, giving Clement a painful insight into Daniel's bruises. He felt
Shlomo's slick belly slapping against his own as he thrust ever harder between
his thighs, until he came with such a frenzy of yelps and grunts that Clement
jammed his hand over his mouth for fear that he should attract an officer.

His passion spent, Shlomo gave way to tears. 'Don't worry,' he said, 'I'm
happy. Or at least I'm not sad.'

'Try to sleep now,' Clement said, discovering to his dismay that, rather than
returning to his own bed, Shlomo took it as an invitation to squeeze in beside
him.

'Thank you so much.'

'My pleasure.'

'But you didn't...'

'Don't worry. You did enough for us both. Just promise me one thing: You won't feel ashamed.'

'I won't. I don't.'

Waking the next morning with a numb left leg and a nagging backache to find himself face to face with a beaming Shlomo, Clement struggled to see his devotion as endearing. Fortunately, Shlomo was so struck with his new sense of himself that he failed to detect the edge with which he urged him to be back in his bunk before Unlock. After submitting to a deep kiss that felt far more intrusive in daylight, he massaged his leg while Shlomo used the lavatory.

'You told me you believed in *mitzvahs*; now I believe in miracles,' Shlomo said, as he strutted around the room in his underpants, giving Clement a full view of the pale, pendulous chest with its tufts of hair so thick that they looked like plumage.

'The miracle's in you,' Clement replied.

'You've no idea how much this means to me. You're talking to a man who wouldn't let his children play in the paddling pool on the Sabbath in case their splashing caused a blade of grass to grow. I want to call the Rabbi and tell him what's happened.'

'Would that be wise?'

'He prayed I'd find my way back to righteousness, and I have.'

'Perhaps you should call your wife first? Ask her to come and visit. See if you can reach some understanding.'

'She hates me, and she has every reason to. But I never gave her AIDS. There are men in the community... whatever the Rabbi says, they visit prostitutes when their wives are *niddah*. But they don't use condoms because it's against the Law. There are women walking around with putrid guts and no one says anything. At least I didn't do that to her.'

'May I make one more suggestion?'

'As many as you want.'

'Take a shower. Then you'll feel as clean outside as in.' Noting Shlomo's reluctance and fearing that he might have betrayed himself, he added quickly, 'Think of it as a mikvah.'

'A mikvah has to have rainwater flowing in.'

'Given the state of the plumbing round here, I doubt that'll be a problem.'

'Will you come with me?'

'I'm not sure it would be a good idea,' he replied, determined to quash any hint of dependence. 'We don't want to excite gossip.'

Shlomo agreed and, at the beginning of evening Association, he gathered his towel, shampoo and soap and made his way down the landing. His departure provoked a couple of jeers, which Clement dismissed as he stood at the basin and studied himself in the tarnished mirror, wondering how such vigorous lovemaking could have left so little trace on his skin. He poured himself a cup of coffee from his flask and was settling down with *Kipps* when Dusty burst into the cell. Clement's surprise at the breach of etiquette turned to anger when he asked if it were true that Shlomo was taking a shower.

'So what? Have the men on this Unit nothing better to think about? What next? That he's flossing his teeth?'

'You don't get it, do you? Why do you think he's not had a shower in eighteen months?' Clement maintained his silence and his cell-mate's confidence. Whatever his past suspicions, he now realised that Shlomo was frightened of being aroused by the naked men. 'Shall I tell you? It's because that sick bastard, Ron Castle, and some of the others threatened to kill him.'

'What? Why?'

'Why do you think?'

'But on this wing there're so many of you.'

'Thanks for that. Yes, but he's the only Jew. He keeps apart like he thinks he's better than the rest of us. Something about that got on their tits.'

'So why the showers?'

'That's where it all happens in this nick. The gym showers for a fuck. The wing showers for a lynching.'

'Do they know he's there?'

'If they didn't before, you can bet they do now.'

'So why didn't he tell me? Why did he agree to go?'

'Maybe he felt strong? Maybe he had enough of hiding or stinking or... who knows? I'm not a fucking trick cyclist! But he's there.'

'I must get down there.' Grabbing his towel as a cover, Clement made for the door.

'Who do you think you are: John Wayne? What can you do?'

'Reason with them.'

'This is Bullingdon nick, not Oxford and Cambridge!'

Clement pushed past Dusty and ran down the landing, to be stopped by Officer Henshaw.

'Where are you going, Granville?'

'Taking a shower, sir.'

'Why are you running?'

'I was afraid there'd be no more hot water.'

'In that case, you'll just have to have a cold one, won't you?'

'Yes sir.'

'Now run along – slowly! Else I'll personally stick you under the cold tap for half an hour.'

'Thank you, sir.'

Clement walked on as briskly as possible, conscious of the officer's eyes on his back. He arrived at the shower room to find his entrance barred by Brian Heald, a burly ex-policeman.

'No one's allowed in there.'

'I've come for a shower.'

'They're all occupied.'

'I don't mind sharing.'

'I bet you don't,' Heald said with a sneer. 'Just go back to your pad like a good little bender.'

'You've no right to stop me!'

'Oh haven't I?' Heald said, with the confidence of one long used to equating his right with the law. Clement grabbed Heald's arm and prepared for a scuffle, when he was stopped in his tracks by a stifled scream.

6

Clement stood with three men from the Unit in a locked yard outside the chapel. He watched while prisoners from the other wings were led past, their wordless hiss the only concession to the setting. Among the crowd he spotted Desmond, who as ever turned away from the scar that he saw as a personal reproach, and Stick, who saluted him with a whoop and a wave that earned their own hoot of derision. When everyone else was safely inside, the officers unlocked a side door and led his three fellows to the back row and Clement himself up to the front where, by special dispensation, he was to sit with his mother, Mike and Carla. He scarcely had time to greet them before the governor stepped forward to thank 'so many distinguished visitors for gracing the proceedings' and welcome the Bishop of Buckingham, whose 'longstanding interest in prison reform makes him uniquely qualified to perform the dedication'. Clement marvelled at the deftness of a man who had made no secret of his hope of securing the Bishop of Oxford or his fury at having to substitute the suffragan.

The governor resumed his seat and the chaplain announced the first hymn. While the rest of the congregation worshipped the King all glorious above, Clement struggled to keep from staring at the carefully veiled painting over the altar with its echoes of Roxborough. At the end of the second hymn, the bishop crossed to a wobbly lectern to give the address. He began by extolling the redemptive power of art, citing a dried-grass elephant he had been sent from Kenya and a Crazy Gang cabaret he had recently attended in an old peoples' home, before commending Clement as 'a man who might well have responded to his incarceration with bitterness and despair but, instead, has taken the opportunity to use his talents for the benefit of his fellow prisoners and the greater glory of God.'

While grateful for the compliment, Clement was dismayed to find his life repackaged as a Victorian tract. It was a relief when the bishop turned his attention to the painting, albeit a surprise to hear his generous tribute to a 'Crucifixion for our times' which, to Clement's certain knowledge, he had yet to see. He sat with bated breath as the bishop crossed to the altar and, after fumbling with the rope to the unconcealed mirth of several prisoners, finally drew back the curtain. A cry of 'Bloody hell, it's Stick!' broke the tension, while a second one of 'There's three of him!' conveyed the general state of shock. Clement felt both the excitement of the congregation as they grappled with the image and the disappointment of the invited journalists, who had hoped that his Calvary would be a place of scandal as much as pain. He smiled at the thought that the governor might come to regret his prudishness, when he found that nonconformity was less newsworthy than flesh. For his own part, he gave thanks that, although limited resources had required him to work on a smaller canvas than he would have chosen, the three stark figures were clearly visible to every seat in the chapel.

'Congratulations, darling!' his mother whispered. 'It's brilliant.'

'I second that,' Mike said. 'What's more, it's a new twist on twins.'

With a start, Clement acknowledged a link to which he had been blind throughout the months at his easel. He could transcend everything but the circumstance of his birth. No only child or younger brother or even fraternal twin would have hit on such an image. The identical yet distinct men, with the shorn one in the middle embracing the fate that his dishevelled companions were straining every muscle to escape, were the embodiment both of his deepest beliefs and of the bond between himself and Mark, the second self who had encouraged him to reach out to all the other selves, making the brotherhood of man an actual as well as a poetic truth.

With a sense of having come full circle, Clement threw himself into the final hymn, his mother's surprise at his revivalist fervour offering a timely reminder that he was soon to return to a world where decibels would be sacrificed to decorum. Before pronouncing the blessing, the chaplain invited the guests to join the prisoners and staff for light refreshments at the end of the service, adding shyly that they had been prepared by his wife. The officers watched in impotent fury when, barely waiting for an Amen, the prisoners broke ranks and headed for the food. Clement led his family through the throng, delighted that they were the first to break down the social barriers. Pressed by the chaplain's wife, he took a rock cake, putting it down in relief when the governor summoned him to meet the bishop.

'Felicitations on a splendid painting!' the bishop said, gripping his hand like an arm-wrestler. 'I feel discomposed... unsettled. Its aesthetic qualities demand respect, even if one questions its theology. I'm sure it will make the prisoners think.'

'And maybe even think better of themselves?' Clement said. 'It's really important for the men in here to accept the Christ within... to see themselves as saviours as well as sinners.' He felt a pang at the thought of his doomed attempt to save Shlomo.

'I suppose you learnt that from your father?'

'In one way. But in another way from my mother.'

'Of course. A most remarkable woman. I must go and greet her. We share an interest in battered wives.' Clement led him to his mother, who was chatting to Desmond, their physical disparity so marked that they seemed to have stepped out of a cartoon. While the bishop and his mother talked, Clement took the first opportunity after nine months segregation to assure Desmond that Stick's attack had been no reflection on his vigilance. Just as his words appeared to be having some effect, the governor dragged him off to meet the journalists. For all his horror at being paraded like a performing seal, he regretted the governor's departure, which licensed the group to throw off all semblance of artistic concern and quiz him on his relationship with Stick, the origin of his scar and life among the paedophiles. Finally, relying on her youth and gender to mitigate the offence, one of them asked outright if he had been buggered.

'Not lately,' he replied. 'Why? Have you?'

Feeling as sullied as by Dusty's advances, he hurried away to rescue Carla from a mild-mannered bigamist, seizing the chance to ask about her trip to the East. 'Thanks so much for all the postcards. I especially liked the one where the rocks were shaped like snakes.'

'Oh yes, that's Yangleshö, where Guru Rinpoche battled with wrathful spirits and demons.'

'I feel as if I've been doing a fair amount of that myself.'

'He won.'

'Ah, that's another matter! But it obviously agreed with you. You look so rested.'

'So would you after a retreat in a Himalayan *gompa*. Five blissful days of meditation and prayer and flower and light offerings.'

'Did you find what you were looking for?'

'I discovered what I was looking for.'

He registered the distinction. 'Will you go back?'

'Who knows? On the coach I read the *White Lotus Sutra*. The title alone is supposed to invoke Enlightenment.'

Before he could reply, his mother walked up with Mike. 'We've been taking a closer look at the painting,' she said, linking arms. 'It really is remarkable, darling. Dangerous and true and full of love.'

'That's what worries me,' Mike said.

'Love of humanity,' she added quickly.

Stick sauntered up to them, his tracksuit weighed down with rock cakes. 'This your old lady, then, boss?'

'That's right.'

'And this your mate?'

'Yes, this is Mike. And my sister-in-law, Carla. This is Stick.'

'It's me... I'm the one in the painting,' Stick said, a claim Clement trusted was superfluous.

'You did very well,' his mother said. 'I've sat for Clement myself, so I know how hard a taskmaster he can be.'

'Handsomest geezer in the nick! That's why he chose me. That, and of course cos I'm cheap,' he said with a laugh. 'I mean for a model, like.'

'We understand,' Mike said with a smile.

'Here, I've got a joke for you.'

'Not now, Stick,' Clement said.

'Don't worry, it's religious. There's this geezer, see. He spills bleach on a priest. What do you suppose happens?'

'I don't know. What does happen?' Carla asked.

'He gets done for bleach of the priest. Hang about! I think I should have said he's Chinese.'

'It still made me laugh,' Carla said.

'I'm not worried any more,' Mike whispered to Clement.

Their conversation was interrupted by the bishop, who came up to take his leave. 'This must be your model,' he said, holding out his hand which Stick took innocently.

'That's right,' he replied, wincing, 'handsomest geezer in the nick.'

'He's certainly done you proud.'

'Would you sign my Bible then?' Stick asked. 'I wasn't sure I wanted you to and then I thought to myself, Stick old son, how many times do you get to meet a bishop?'

Clement exchanged a glance with his mother.

'I'd be honoured,' the bishop said.

'Make sure you put Bishop and not just your name, won't you? Or how will anyone know?'

'Who should I make the greeting to?'

'Me of course! Oh I see...' He laughed. 'Nigel,' he said, gazing around defensively. 'Our mum would never forgive us if you wrote Stick.'

Looking as proud as if it had been signed by St Paul, Stick rushed off to show the inscription to Willis. 'Now I really must make a move,' the bishop said. 'I've a fête to open in Faringdon. Such a pity your father couldn't have been with us today.'

'For so many reasons,' Clement replied.

'When we were both ordained, he and I, we took it on ourselves to stand in the person of Christ. Christ raised Lazarus from the dead. I like to think that, in other circumstances, He would have put him gently to sleep.'

He clasped Clement's hand with a force that anticipation failed to temper, and followed the governor out. The officers swiftly rounded up their charges, allowing Clement to say a brief farewell to his family before taking him back to his cell.

His final days in prison passed without incident. Freedom was such a momentous prospect that he preferred to concentrate on the practicalities: requesting the laundering of his clothes prior to his release; using up his remaining canteen allowance to buy chocolates and sweets to dispense on the Unit; lobbying for a chance to say goodbye to Stick. After being summarily turned down by the principal and senior officers, he appealed to the chaplain, who arranged for them to meet in the art room.

'Do I get my £2.60 for coming?' Stick asked anxiously, as their escorts converged.

'I'm afraid not. You'll just have to tell yourself that the best things in life are free.'

'You're a laugh, you are.'

'But I did wonder if you might like my watch. Something to remember me by.'

'You serious?'

'I'm almost embarrassed to mention it. It's nothing special.'

'Course it is. It's Darth Vader! Cool!'

'And I know you'll be fine. You're on top of things now.'

'Course I am. Well not quite on the straight and narrow,' he said, with a grin. 'Sometimes I need stuff so bad I do things. There's this geezer on the wing. He's almost as posh as you. I see him right in here and he's going to fix me up with a flat on the out.' Clement bit his lip. 'But I'm going to chapel regular. So when I think I might do summet wrong, I'll look at myself in the picture and see what I can be.'

They talked stiffly for several minutes, until the chaplain moved away from the window and warned them that it was time for the officers to take them back to their cells.

'Good luck then,' Clement said, giving Stick a clumsy hug.

'Leave it out!' Stick said, affronted. 'I ain't bent!' Then, poking Clement gently in the ribs, he asked: 'Do you want to hear my joke?'

'Why not?' he said flatly.

'There are three kinds of people in the world: them that can count and them that can't. Good ain't it?'

'Yes, Stick, I think that that one really is.'

Clement spent his last day in prison gripped by a sense of foreboding. He was haunted by thoughts of Wilfred Owen dying a week before the Armistice. His fears seemed to be borne out when, at five o'clock, Dusty knocked on his door and entered his cell.

'Only one more night to go then?'

'Fingers crossed.'

'Come down to my pad. I got something fabulous to show you.'

'Not now, I'm sorry. I'm busy.'

'Busy doing nothing more like!'

'I'm sorting things out in my head.' All Clement's instincts told him to stay put.

'Think you're too good for us, do you?'

'No, of course not.'

'Now you're getting out, it's so long and fuck off to all your old friends!'

'Not at all,' Clement said, taken aback by Dusty's presumption.

'Come with me then. I don't charge.'

Afraid of appearing aloof, Clement walked slowly out on to the landing, where he was seized by a gang of four or five men (panic made precision impossible) and half-dragged, half-propelled down the corridor. He put up a spirited fight, grabbing hold of a doorpost and lashing out with his feet, until his fingers were prised away, his arms twisted behind his back, and he was frogmarched to the showers. A terror of meeting the same fate as Shlomo gripped him after they passed an officer who, far from intervening, waved them on with a smirk. He wanted to shout that they had made a mistake: he was an ODC sent to the Unit for his own protection; but there was an arm choking his windpipe. Besides, unable to see his assailants' faces, he had no way of knowing whether his protestations would carry weight.

He lost his bearings, conscious only that he had been flung on to a tiled floor beneath a shower. Expecting a jet of either scalding water or boiling sugar, he was doubly disorientated by the icy torrent streaming over him. The friendly faces and gales of laughter confirmed that, rather than taking a last chance to settle imaginary scores, they were giving him a traditional send-off. He felt a rush of relief, followed by anxiety about his soaking clothes and, finally, a sense of schoolboy abandon as he fought back, drenching his attackers, who ran from the room in mock horror. He staggered to his feet, wringing the worst of the water from his tracksuit, and made his way, dripping and squelching, to his cell, only to find that it had been invaded in his absence, with his furniture turned upside down and 'Good Luck!' and three smiley faces scrawled in shaving foam on the wall.

At seven thirty the next morning, he was led down to reception where he changed into his own clothes, retrieved his property and filled in a questionnaire on his treatment in prison. Having affirmed that he had no complaints, he received his meagre discharge grant and was taken to the main gate, where he shook hands with the escorting officer, who suddenly seemed no more intimidating than a hotel porter. He stepped outside and, ignoring both the fluttering in his stomach and the cluster of waiting photographers, made straight for Mike. After a welcoming kiss, to the accompaniment of clicking shutters, Mike drove him the few miles to Beckley, where he insisted on walking over to the church before lunch. With Mike and his mother on either arm, they took the path through the woods, the variegated colours a joyful corrective to the ubiquitous prison grey. On arrival, Mike waited in the yard and his mother in the nave while he went down into the crypt alone. Adjusting his eyes to the gloom, he drew up a prie-dieu beside the grille and sat to commune with his father.

'Well, it's over! To be honest, there were a few rough patches in prison, when I started to wonder if it had been worth losing fifteen months of my life to spare you two or three. But, now that I'm out, I realise it was worth every minute. I did what we both knew was right. And besides, what's fifteen months? A nanosecond in the face of eternity! So you see, Pa, I haven't lost anything. Not even time.'

He knelt in prayer, until the memory of his companions brought him up short. Promising his father to return soon, he made his way up to the nave.

'Sorry I've kept you.'

'Not me, darling,' his mother said. 'But I worry about Mrs Shepherd. She's pulling out all the stops.'

'Then we'd better go back via the cottages,' Clement said. 'It'll be quickest. Even if we pop in on Karen.'

'Must we?' Mike asked. 'Today of all days.'

'No, of course not... not if you don't want to.'

'In any case she won't be there,' his mother said. 'She spends most of her time in Headington. She's besotted with Darren.'

'The busk... the boyfriend?' Clement asked.

'That's right. I wouldn't be surprised if they got engaged. The other day she told me, apropos of I don't know what, that "That which is solitary is barren." I thought it was code for "I'm pregnant," but, apparently, it's in the Wicca creed.'

They walked home, with no diversions or encounters. 'I can't believe how quiet it is after prison,' Clement said. 'One thing you never get used to is the noise... incessant, insufferable noise!'

'Then why not stay here for a while, darling?' his mother asked, making the appeal he dreaded. 'You'll find London equally noisy. And, besides, Mike will be out all day at school. Don't you agree, Mike?' she asked eagerly. 'Clement should recuperate here where it's peaceful and we can all look after him.'

'Whatever he wants. It's up to him.'

'No, it's not,' Clement said, giving him a dark look. Although the last thing he wanted was to offend his mother, after fifteen months away, he was determined to sleep in his own bed. Moreover he had the perfect excuse. 'Don't forget this,' he said, lifting his left trouser leg to reveal the electronic tag. 'I have to be home every night at seven.'

'Oh, darling!' his mother said. 'How barbaric! Does it chafe your skin?'

'Not at all, I promise. They only put it on me this morning and, already, I hardly notice it.'

It's inhumane... inhuman.'

'It's only for ninety days. And then I'll be as free as air.'

'They'll be fitting you with a microchip next!'

Clement gazed uneasily at Mike, wondering what it was in his mother's past that made her find a tag so repugnant. To his relief, she let the matter drop, and they returned indoors for a celebratory lunch, which he would have relished even if it hadn't been his first decent meal in fifteen months. Mrs Shepherd had excelled herself; nevertheless, as she pressed him to extra slices of pâté and duck and spoonfuls of apple charlotte, he was forced to ask for a doggy bag to avoid either upsetting his stomach or wounding her pride.

Two hours later, armed with enough soups, casseroles, pies and cakes to feed an entire Bullingdon wing, he said goodbye to his mother and drove up to London with Mike. The sluggish traffic gave him time to consider his position. It wasn't just the tag on his ankle that kept him tied to prison. The better part of his imagination was locked up with Dwayne and Parker and Dusty and Stick.

'A penny for them,' Mike said.

'I'm sorry. It's all so bewildering. To be a name again instead of a number. To be able to look ahead without worrying who might be creeping up behind. And the air's so pure.'

'It's ninety-nine per cent diesel!

'Trust me, it's a tonic after Bullingdon. I'm sorry. Take no notice. I'll be fine as soon as I'm home.'

Having braced himself for a seismic surge of emotion on reaching the house, he was distressed when, far from the soaring chords of the *Ode To Joy*, he didn't even hear the theme tune to *The Archers*. His impassivity made him fear for his future both as a man and an artist. It didn't help that his homecoming was so low-key. For all his insistence that there should be no fuss and veto of an early-release party, he hadn't expected Mike to take him so literally that he had failed to buy a single flower. Curbing his disappointment, he made a desultory stab at opening his mail while Mike prepared dinner. His spirits rose when they sat down to eat, the candlelight supplying the romance that the lima bean casserole lacked. The mood was marred only by his fit of sneezing, which Mike attributed to stray hairs left by Carla's cat.

'She wasn't allowed in the bedroom, I promise.'

'Is that a hint?'

'How about an offer?'

'In which case it's the best I've had in fifteen months.'

He was suddenly overcome by exhaustion, leading Mike, who was convinced that it was a ploy, to suggest that they abandon the pudding and head upstairs. The instant he slipped into bed, he was hit by all the emotion to which he had thought himself dead. The fresh sheets, warm duvet and soft pillow moved him deeply, even before he slid into arms which assured him that nothing was different while allowing him to acknowledge what had changed. Savouring Mike's kiss, at once protective and arousing, he felt his body regain its integrity. He switched off the light, swearing that he had not grown shy but, rather, that after fifteen months of nothing but seeing and hearing (he refrained from adding smelling) he wanted to trust to taste and touch. He explored Mike's flesh with his fingers, tongue and penis. He giggled and sighed and groaned before breaking down in sobs, which Mike comforted with his caresses. Then he lay back, while Mike rekindled his passion so effortlessly that he blushed. Moments of tenderness gave way to moments of delirium, after which they stretched out, limbs intertwined and trunks united in a newly germinated tree of life.

The next morning, after Mike left for work, Clement stayed in bed, balancing the urge to visit the studio against others to stroll through the park and simply loll around the house, before realising that what he wanted was not to choose so much as to enjoy the luxury of choice. Struck by a craving for anchovies and pineapple that would have been perverse even in pregnancy, he went down to the kitchen. He had just filled his plate when, by a coincidence at once sublime and disconcerting, his mother rang to tell him that Shoshanna had given birth.

'He's perfect. A boy. Five pounds seven ounces. No, I mean seven pounds five ounces! Shoshanna's fine. Even the labour was straightforward. Zvi was there.'

'I'm very happy, Ma. For Shoshanna. For you. Even for Zvi.'

'He wasn't due until next week. I'd planned to come down to help out.'

'You can come now... whenever. There's always a room for you here.'

'Really? I don't want to intrude. Especially not now.'

'You know you could never intrude.'

'Thank you, darling. Then I'll come this afternoon. Meanwhile will you go to the hospital?'

'Do you think they'll want to see me?'

'I'm sure of it.'

It wasn't until he put down the phone that he realised he had forgotten to ask which hospital it was but, on ringing back, he found that she was already engaged. After a forty-minute wait, which for once was bearable, he learnt that Shoshanna was just across the park, in the Wellington. Two hours later, furnished with the finest bunch of lilies that St John's Wood had to offer, he made his way into the foyer and up to the obstetrics ward. He stopped outside Shoshanna's room and gazed through the open door to where she lay, cradling her baby, with Zvi in a chair by her side, their whole beings focused on the child. Anxious not to disturb them, he was about to slip away when Shoshanna looked up. 'Clem!' she called in a voice midway between pleasure and shock. He blenched to see her instinctually pull the baby closer but was reassured when, after exchanging greetings and comparing notes on their respective deliveries, she asked if he wanted to hold him.

He gathered him up with a sense of trepidation that was quickly replaced by awe. He gazed at the fluttering eyelids and the tiny hands with nails as small as a doll's, choosing to concentrate on the peripherals rather than trying to fathom the mystery of the whole. He wondered if he should remark on some family resemblance, but for now he looked like nothing other than his sleepy, solemn self. So, instead, he asked whether they had picked a name for him.

'Zalman,' Zvi said.

'Zalman,' Clement experimented. 'That's great. Simple… strong.'

'Wise,' Zvi added.

'Of course.'

Eager not to outstay his welcome, he returned home to wait for his mother, whose hunger to see her new grandson left her barely a moment to draw breath before asking him to accompany her to the hospital. They arrived to find Carla strolling up and down with the mewling baby, while Shoshanna and Zvi looked on, their evident longing to be alone surrendered to a wish that everyone should share in their happiness. As Carla gazed dotingly on the bundle in her arms, Clement wondered if she were nursing her own maternal ambitions or if the journey East had taught her the wisdom of acceptance. Recalling his earlier glimpse of Shoshanna, Zvi and Zalman, he found himself picturing another trio of Carla, himself and the baby she had asked him to father. Mike had been right to dissuade him, although his arguments had been too clinical. He would be true to Mark, not by living his life, but by living his own to the full.

He watched as, with Shoshanna's blessing, Carla handed Zalman to his mother. Seeing her hold the grandchild for whom she had yearned so long, he prayed that nothing would threaten her relationship with Shoshanna. He wondered whether he too might play a role in his nephew's upbringing, or whether the religious imperative would preclude it. While excited by the prospect of helping, in however small a way, to shape the boy's future, he knew that what counted weren't his feelings, or even Shoshanna's and Zvi's, but Zalman's. Indeed, were he to be given three wishes to pronounce over his cot, they would all amount to the same: that he should have a wealth of opportunities from which to choose; the wisdom to make the right choice; and the courage to stand by it.

Two days later, he received further proof of Shoshanna's and Zvi's change of heart when they invited him to Zalman's *B'rit*. Moreover, the invitation extended to Mike who, mindful of how much it had cost them, accepted, despite his horror of what he saw as 'symbolic castration'.

The following week, they drove up to Hendon for the ceremony. Having relied on his parents' descriptions of the engagement party and wedding, Clement was fascinated to see the Lubavitch world for himself. His mother was more circumspect, extracting a promise of good behaviour as if he were twelve years old on a visit to Aunt Helena. Urging her to relax, he left her in the hall and walked with Mike into the sitting room, where, if any of the two dozen guests harboured reservations about the notorious parricide and unashamed sodomites in their midst, they kept them to themselves, switching languages in order to welcome them.

'I feel as if I'm at a Buckingham Palace garden party,' Mike whispered, after replying to the third successive question about the best route from Regent's Park to Hendon.

'They're making the effort,' Clement replied, 'which is all we can ask.'

They were interrupted, first by Zvi's announcement that the *mohel* had been held up, and then by an elderly man with sad eyes, who came over to introduce himself. 'My name is Reuben Levine. It was at my house that Zvi and Shoshanna met. They've asked me to be one of Zalman's godfathers.'

'Congratulations,' Clement said quietly.

'We have another connection. My daughter.'

'Really? What's her name?'

'You don't know her. This is very hard for me. But if you have a moment to spare, she'd like to meet you.'

Intrigued by the mystery and eager to escape an oppressively masculine atmosphere reminiscent of Bullingdon, Clement suggested that they take advantage of the delay to seek her out. He followed Reuben to the dining room where, spying his mother and Carla among the women, he wondered whether they also felt out of place or were united by an act of baby worship. Reuben waited at the door, finally catching the eye of a young girl, who fetched his daughter, a tall, beaky woman in an ill-fitting wig.

'This is Sorah.'

'Clement Granville,' he said, holding out his hand, which Reuben gently deflected.

'I know,' she replied. He was taken aback, until he recalled how conspicuous he and Mike must look with their light suits, smooth chins and bare heads. 'I'm Shlomo's wife,' she said, causing her father to sigh.

'Oh my goodness!'

'I'm very pleased to meet you.'

'You are?'

'May we talk in the garden?'

'Yes, of course,' Clement replied, before realising that she had addressed the question to her father, who gave a brief nod, as though aching to shrug off the connection. Clement followed Sorah through the kitchen into the garden, which was as well kept and impersonal as a bowling green. She paced up and down the patio, finding it so difficult to speak that he wondered whether to prompt her.

'I went to see him last weekend,' she said eventually.

'Where?'

'The hospital wing in Albany. His face is a mass of bandages. The hot sugar they... they poured over him has burnt through several layers of skin. He'll have to have reconstructive surgery. Even so, the doctors warned me he'll be permanently disfigured. What's it to do with me? Why should I care?'

'But you do.'

'Yes.'

'Albany on the Isle of Wight?'

'Yes.'

'It's a long way.'

'The entire prison is for... for men like him. I think he feels happier there.'

'What about you?'

'I'm not the one who was hurt; at least...' Clement watched as her expression clouded. 'But I'm glad I went. I felt we reached a kind of understanding. Not that it changes anything. Not remotely. It isn't just that he's no longer the man I married. I find it hard to think of him as a man at all.'

'What is he then?'

'I won't use words that will make you laugh at me.'

'I wouldn't dream of it.'

'Not to my face, no... He was so calm in court. So calm and cold and cruel. He put his lies before Daniel's truth. Which made it doubly unforgivable. He betrayed him a second time. But seeing him in the hospital, I felt he'd finally got what he deserved. Now he'll be scarred for life just like Daniel. Strange that it should have been sugar! He always had a sweet tooth.'

'I'm so sorry.'

'I told him I'd be coming here today,' she said, composing herself. 'Your sister's been a good friend to me. He made me promise to thank you.'

'Me? Whatever for? If I hadn't insisted he take that shower... if I'd been more sensitive to tensions on the Unit...'

'He said that the things you'd talked about with him – the things you'd done for him – had changed his life.'

'Really?' Clement asked apprehensively.

'He also wanted me to tell you how important it is that Zalman's *B'rit* is taking place on the eighth day.'

'To fulfil the Torah?'

'Of course. But, according to Shlomo, doctors have discovered it's the day a baby's blood-clotting abilities are at their highest. He said it proved once again how Torah anticipates science.'

'I'm sorry to interrupt!' Clement spun round to see Reuben. 'But you must come back inside. The *mohel* has arrived.'

As they walked through the kitchen, Clement gave him an encouraging smile, receiving in return a nod of thanks. Sorah joined the crowd of women assembled at the sitting room door while the men went in. A chubby, bespectacled boy moved towards Reuben. Clement recognised him even before they were introduced.

'This is my grandson. My Daniel,' Reuben said. 'This is Mr Granville, who drew those pictures for you.'

'Oh!' Daniel said, shifting his feet.

'It was your father's idea,' Clement said, wondering if he were allowed to mention him.

'Did you meet him in Israel?' Daniel asked.

'No, in...'

'Don't tell me,' Daniel said quickly. '*Tateh's* on a top-secret mission for Mossad. That's why he's changed his identity. That's why he can't come home, in case he puts us all in danger. Do you understand?'

'I understand,' Clement said softly.

'It's for our own good!'

Daniel broke away and, avoiding a trio of teenage boys, stood alone by a silver cabinet. Clement moved to Mike, who looked fraught.

'Where were you?' Mike hissed.

'Somewhere quite unexpected but rather cheering,' he replied, grateful that the start of the ceremony removed any need to elaborate. He watched the sea of men parting before a plump, middle-aged woman who entered with Zalman, whom she handed to a red-haired man, who handed him to Zvi, who

anded him in turn to a third man, whose luxuriant beard and richly embroidered prayer shawl exuded authority.

'It's like pass the parcel,' Mike whispered, within earshot of Reuben who, far from taking offence, began to explain.

'That's the *mohel*, who'll perform the cut.'

Clement was both amused by Mike's discomfiture and reassured by the rare sign of weakness. 'Why is he putting Zalman on that chair?' he asked.

'It's Elijah's chair. To show that he's mystically present. A kind of guardian angel.'

'Like pouring him a cup of wine at Passover?'

'Not exactly. When Elijah was escaping from Ahab and Jezebel, he casti-gated his fellow Jews for breaking the Covenant. He himself was rebuked by God, who declared that, from then on, he had to be present every time the Covenant was sealed. In other words every *B'rit*.'

'So it's a sort of punishment?' Mike asked, betraying his continuing unease.

'If so, it's a very pleasant one, since it's a sign that the Jews are keeping faith with God... Oh, now it's my turn.' With the *mohel's* blessing concluded, Reuben sat down in the second chair, arranging the folds of his prayer shawl, while the *mohel* picked up Zalman and laid him in his lap.

Clement found himself with an unimpeded view, as the *mohel* severed the baby's foreskin before making a second incision, sucking up the blood through a small pipette. Zalman let out a howl, more of outrage than of pain, which intensified as first the *mohel* and then Zvi spoke a prayer. The Rabbi blessed a cup of wine and passed it to the *mohel*, who put a teaspoonful on Zalman's lips, to no discernible effect. He bandaged the baby's wound and handed him to Zvi, who cradled him proudly in the crook of his arm, while his friends clapped and cheered and chanted to welcome the latest member of their com-munity. Suddenly, three young men linked arms and gyrated through the crowd. Clement watched in amazement as the sedate sitting room turned into a heaving dance floor. Seizing his chance, he grabbed Mike and pulled him into the throng.

'This is to make up for the engagement dance they banned us from two years ago,' he whispered. 'This is to make up for every dance they've banned us from for thousands of years.'

With his arm draped casually around Mike's waist, he kept just the right side of discretion. As he gazed towards the women huddled in the doorway, he spotted his mother, Carla and Shoshanna at the front. He gave them a sweeping bow, to be rewarded by a wave from his mother, a thumbs up from Carla and a cryptic smile from Shoshanna, which he resolved to see as a sign of acceptance. Whatever differences they might have had in the past, whatever differences they might have in the future, this was a day of celebration. Zalman Edwin Latsky, starting out on a glorious adventure, had entered into a covenant with his God.

Acknowledgements

The Arts Council England provided me with generous financial assistance towards the writing of the novel and the Hawthornden Trust with an idyllic setting in which to start work.

I am deeply indebted to the following individuals and institutions for their help with my research: Anna Arthur, Rev Peter Baker, Mark Borkowski, the Governor and staff of Brixton prison, Beverley Bryon, Martin Carr and the Royal Society, Mark Cazalet, Phil Chapman, William Coley, Rev Tom Devonshire-Jones, Glen Donovan, Susie Dowdall, Julia Dunn, Katy Gardner, Patrick Gibb QC, Nicholas Granger-Taylor, Wesley Gryk, Naomi Gryn, Professor J F La Fontaine, Charles Leigh, The London Library Trust, Dr Tali Lowenthal, Reva Mann, Dr Edward Norman, Dr Tudor Parfitt, Professor John Peel, Ruth Posner, Gary Richards, Rabbi Mark Solomon, Dr Penny Thexton, Catherine Walston, Dr David Watt.

Rupert Christiansen, Marika Cobbold, Emmanuel Cooper, Harriet Cobbold Hielte, Liz Jensen, Julia Pascal, Ann Pennington, Mark Simpson and Timberlake Wertenbaker offered judicious advice on early drafts of the novel and Hilary Sage saved me from my most egregious solecisms.